STELLA CAMERON
LORETTA CHASE
LINDA LAEL MILLER
JOAN HO

In a season of joy and magic, celebrate love with enchanting tales of Yuletide romance by four of your favorite authors—a delightful and heart-stirring collection of stories that captures the warmth and wonder of Christmas . . . and the rapture of love everlasting.

And for more
Christmastime enchantment—

CHRISTMAS ROMANCE

Christmas Love Stories

For More Christmas Love
from Your Favorite Romantic Authors
Don't Miss

AVON BOOKS PRESENTS: CHRISTMAS LOVE STORIES
AVON BOOKS PRESENTS: CHRISTMAS ROMANCE

Avon Books Presents:

A CHRISTMAS COLLECTION

STELLA CAMERON • LORETTA CHASE
JOAN HOHL • LINDA LAEL MILLER

AVON BOOKS NEW YORK

AVON BOOKS
A division of
The Hearst Corporation
1350 Avenue of the Americas
New York, New York 10019

Published by arrangement with the authors
Library of Congress Catalog Card Number: 92-90555
ISBN: 0-380-76833-X

First Avon Books Printing: November 1992

Printed in the U.S.A.

RA 10 9 8 7 6 5 4 3 2 1

Contents

Stella Cameron
THE GREATEST GIFT
1

Loretta Chase
FALLING STARS
111

Linda Lael Miller
THE SCENT OF SNOW
199

Joan Hohl
FOOTSTEPS IN THE SNOW
291

Avon Books Presents:

A CHRISTMAS COLLECTION

The Greatest Gift

Stella Cameron

For my mother, Selina Lloyd-Worth.
At Christmas we were children together.
Rest in God's greatest gift.

1

Cornwall, 1818

CHRISTMAS, CHRISTMAS, CHRISTMAS! GAD, BUT he hated Christmas!

"Do not become overly excited, John," Sir William Granville heard himself tell his son. "There are almost two weeks yet to go and two weeks of fussing is hardly a good thing in a six-year-old boy."

"I was not fussing, Papa," John said from his place before the nursery windows. "All I said was that I hope we do not get snow before Uncle Edward and Aunt Lindsay get to Tregonitha for Christmas."

That word again. "Tea is late," William said, scowling. "And snow at Christmas so close to the Cornish coast is by no means a certainty."

"Tea is *not* late, Master William," Nanny Thomas said with asperity. The old lady who had once been nanny to William and his younger sister, Lindsay, rocked her chair by the fire with vigor. "And I told John we'll be seeing snow shortly. I feel it in my bones. There's many would say that's as good a sign as you'll be getting."

Nanny Thomas's legendary bones were no part of the reason for Sir William's presence at nursery tea . . . today or on any day during the previous ten. Not one afternoon visit had he missed in that time. He flipped his watch into a palm and frowned. "Definitely late," he muttered. His being here was undoubtedly foolishness. The girl would come, deposit her tea tray, and leave. He would ensure that his glance was most casual. Her eyes would not meet his at all.

All exactly as should occur between a knight of the realm and a servant.

Foolishness, damn it!

What shy, unworldly young girl would be other than repelled by him, anyway? And what man of his mature years and experience would allow an awareness of such an unsuitable innocent to linger in his mind . . . and other sensitive regions?

Bloody hell!

"See how frost paints the windows, Papa?"

Ten days previous, chance had brought him to the nursery at tea time. Chance had brought him here in time to all but collide with the chit in the doorway. Startled, she had looked at him on that occasion. Light green eyes the color of a tropical sea at sunset. That she wore spectacles had been a fact he noted only after she had turned from him. She had turned quickly, but without showing sign of shock or disgust. Perhaps her poor sight had veiled the full extent of his disfigurement.

"Papa, the frost—"

"Yes, yes, John." William had stood too long without moving. His old leg injury ached. He limped to join his red-haired son and peered through spines of ice on leaded panes. "Frost paints the whole world today," he said of the glittering white landscape surrounding Tregonitha. "The estate is in disguise. This morning, when I rode to visit tenants, there was ice on the pond near Calvin's cottage and Granny Whalen boasted as to the number of icicles her roof had *grown,* as she put it."

"I shall go out and—"

"You'll do no such thing, Master John," Nanny said tartly. "By the time you finish your tea, it'll be dark. Soon enough for more of that foolishness tomorrow."

"If Nanny's snow has not arrived by morning we'll—"

A tap at the door interrupted William.

The girl entered, carrying her heavy tray, a tray made to seem even heavier than it might be in light of its bearer's small stature.

William clasped his hands behind his back and remained in the shadow of velvet draperies. She had yet to say an audible word in his presence. He didn't even know her name.

"Good afternoon," Nanny Thomas said, a smile wrinkling her thin cheeks. "How are matters in the kitchen today? No doubt Cook's in a rare flame and putting everyone through their paces."

A murmured response was spoken too softly for William to hear. With an inclination of the head, and a bobbing curtsey, the girl set the silver tray on a satinwood tea table in the center of the room.

"Esmie, isn't it?" Nanny said, with unusual animation.

"Yes, ma'am," the diminutive girl whispered. Her movements were rapid and economical.

Esmie? Yes, it suited her well. A small, energetic creature, her dark, almost black hair escaped a simple white cap to curl in shiny clusters about her heart-shaped face. Her skin was very white—almost too pale—her nose pert and her mouth sweetly bowed.

But it was her eyes that intrigued him, and he was determined to see them clearly once more. "Perhaps you would dispense the tea for us, Esmie." Her name felt unusual, and altogether pleasing on his lips. "Nanny Thomas's rheumatism gives her pain on these cold days."

She bobbed again, but made no attempt to look at him.

William glanced at Nanny and found her regarding him speculatively. Her raised brows made words unnecessary: she was thinking that she didn't recall discussing her rheumatism with him. Now that he thought of it, William was not at all sure the old lady *had* rheumatism.

He moved a little closer to the girl. "Why should your duties in the kitchen be more arduous than usual?"

Without raising her face, she handed him a cup and saucer.

"Christmas," Nanny said before Esmie could answer. "Cook's all of a twitter with baking and pickling and what not. She's determined to show up the Hawkeslys' cook."

"I didn't know Cook had met any members of my sister's and her husband's staff."

"She hasn't. But your nephew always makes a rare nuisance of himself in the kitchen when he comes. Our cook lets me do this, says Master James. And our cook makes that. And why don't you do this or that the way our cook does?"

William chuckled. "James is like his mother," he said of the four-year-old. "I'm sure you recall that Lindsay was a precocious child who could at times, be unwittingly annoying."

Esmie took a cup of milky tea to John, and as she approached the boy, William saw her smile unreservedly for the first time. She spoke to his too-serious son in low tones, and the boy grinned. When he was happy, he reminded William—almost painfully—of Maria.

William barely restrained an impulse to ask what the two found so amusing. "How does your family fare, Esmie?" He was at pains now not to show that he saw Nanny's narrow scrutiny.

Esmie, in the act of arranging currant cakes and little fruit tarts on plates, looked at him fully. Muscles in his back stiffened. Behind round, wire-rimmed spectacles, her eyes reminded him of those belonging to a particularly beautiful cat—one possessed of deep and gentle intelligence. She passed her tongue over full, soft lips.

"Sir William won't bite you, girl," Nanny said comfortably and took a noisy swallow of tea.

William saw no sign that his scars disturbed Esmie. Encouraged, he nodded whilst the stiff sensation in his back marched on to his stomach and clenched as though he had been struck a blow. The creature wasn't a beauty, surely, and yet she stole his breath. He found himself mentally removing the spectacles, loosening hair he knew would tumble about her shoulders and breasts in a riotous black cloud—smoothing hidden white skin that, given her shy nature, had undoubtedly never been touched by a man in a moment of passion.

He tensed his thighs, marshaled his errant thoughts, and said kindly, "Where is your family lodged?" With the exception of Nanny Thomas and Cook, all the household staff at Tregonitha returned to their own homes in the nearby village or in the fishing town of Fowey each weekend. William believed families should waste no opportunity to be together—besides, and more importantly, he valued periods of complete privacy and peace. "Are you Polrithen people?" he asked.

Her throat moved convulsively. "I live in Fowey, Sir William," she said clearly. "Close to the harbor."

Oh, clearly indeed. William managed to contain his surprise. That voice, with its suggestion of a break that might resemble laughter were her countenance not so reserved, held nothing of a working class mode of speech. And it held nothing of the Cornish burr common to the area and to all his servants who were—at his insistence—local people.

"Near the quay?" he persisted. No, he had never seen her in Fowey. Had he done so, the event would have been remembered.

"Yes, Sir William," she said and he couldn't fail to note the rapid rise and fall of her breast beneath a plain gray dress and white apron.

She would wonder at his persistence but no matter. "In sight of The Ship Inn?"

"That inn is close by, Sir William." With a start, she looked to the cakes and continued placing them on plates.

Her hands were small, but long-fingered—long-fingered, smooth, and white. The fair Esmie of the lovely face and cultured voice had hands that would disgrace no lady.

He was becoming fanciful. It was obviously considerably past time for a visit to a certain discontented married lady in London—a lady who would long since be wondering if he would ever seek her company again.

William attempted to conjure the image of the obliging Mrs. Sutton, and failed. Even before this pointless interest in a serving girl, he'd been aware of a growing disinterest in, even an abhorrence for, such women.

Esmie took a plate to Nanny Thomas, and a second to John, who grinned again. Another almost conspiratorial glance passed between the two.

What, William wondered, was that about?

Then she was before him once more, holding out a plate, looking at him steadily this time.

"Which do you think I would prefer?" he said. "The currant cake? Or one of the tarts?"

She frowned slightly and regarded the choices. "I think," she said slowly and with evident serious consideration, "that all of them would benefit you, Sir William."

He laughed aloud. "And what, pray, does that mean, my girl?"

Esmie didn't laugh aloud but mirth shone in her eyes—a delightful sight. "I mean that a slim gentleman such as yourself could do worse than to partake liberally of his cook's wholesome baking. That lady is practicing for the Christmas festivities, and I'm sure she would appreciate your opinion of some of the fare she intends to offer." Her chin was raised and she held her bottom lip in straight, strong, little teeth.

The break in her voice had been warm this time, and the speech delivered with a genteel assurance no girl of her station should be able to assume.

This girl had not been born into the serving class.

She was not what she appeared to be.

How had she gained employment in his house? The answer was all too obvious: through falsely representing herself.

Silently, William took the plate. His bow was brief, dismissive, before he returned to a contemplation of Tregonitha's winter ensemble.

Within seconds, the door opened and closed softly.

William took a few moments to compose himself, then looked to John who sat on the window seat holding his teacup, the plate on the velvet cushion beside him. The boy was too thin, too pale. He was also too solemn—although the mysterious Esmie seemed to have a way with the child's grin.

"What amusement is it that you and the servant share?" William asked.

John's cup rattled in its saucer. "N-none, Papa."

Deceit bred deceit. At what bitter cost had William learned the evil self-serving dishonesty could spawn! "As you say, John." No doubt whatever small intrigue existed was of no consequence, but, if necessary, his son must be reminded that trust was the greatest gift and that trust must be earned and treasured.

"Papa," John said tentatively. "Before . . . before, you were going to say something about tomorrow."

"We'll wait and see what tomorrow brings." He should spend more time with John, and he'd been about to suggest that they ride out together on some estate business. "How are your lessons?"

"His lessons are well enough," Nanny said, so sharply as to surprise William. "You need to be attending to yourself, Master William."

He chose to ignore the comment. "I expect you are anxious to see your cousin James."

John drew his thin shoulders up to his ears. "I suppose."

"And what does that mean?" William sat on the window seat and eased his leg. Winter's cold invariably aggravated the site where, some years before, knife wounds had been left too long untended. He leaned toward John. "Come now. A short while since, you were all agog about the coming season. Now you are subdued."

"James will bring his new brother," John said in a small voice.

"The infant, Simon?" He cast a glance to Nanny Thomas who shook her head. "Your new cousin will be brought by his parents, your uncle and aunt. I had thought you would be looking forward to that."

Another shrug was William's reward.

"You do not like babies?"

"I don't know any," John said with a near pout. "And James will be boasting again because he has one and I don't."

"I see," William said, and he feared he did indeed see, all too clearly. Lindsay had remarked, on far too many occasions, that John was too solitary and that he needed companions. *"Marry again,"* she had instructed William, with her usual directness. *"You are a passionate man and you need a wife—and children. And John needs brothers and sisters."* Well, he and John must make the best of things as they were. There could be no question of risking a repeat of the horror that had already touched their lives.

"John," Nanny said. "Run along down to the kitchens, there's a good boy. Ask Cook for some more tarts."

"But we've still got—"

"I know that," Nanny said briskly. "But we'll make her happy if she thinks we've eaten them all."

"But—"

"Do as Nanny asks," William said. "And later, you shall join me in the study and help me go over some accounts."

The boy's face brightened. "Very well, Papa." He sped from the room, slamming the door behind him.

"John needs brothers and sisters," Nanny announced.

"We'll not speak of that."

"A six-year-old lad shouldn't think of looking at dusty figures as a treat, Master William." She put aside her cup and saucer. "He'll do anything just to be with you. We both know as much. But that's not enough—for either of you."

"John does well enough."

"Even if he did, the same can't be said about you." She settled her shawl more closely about her. "Esmie's a pretty little thing, wouldn't you say?"

He set his teeth.

"Yes, I think you *would* say." Nanny sounded smug. "I saw the way you looked at her."

"Enough," he told the old woman, a warning in his voice.

"Don't think I haven't noticed how you've suddenly taken a liking for nursery tea every afternoon. That didn't happen before the day you ran into the girl up here. And you don't take your eyes off her, either."

"I'd best be on my way."

"Sit where you are." Nanny's tone brooked no argument. "And give me the respect of my years. I know you almost as well as you know yourself, my boy. Perhaps better. It was I who became a mother to you after your own dear mama died and your father married that flibbertigibbet, Belle. And it was I who nursed you when you returned from the sea battle that brought you a knighthood—and almost cost you your life. I know you, William. The girl Esmie has caught your eye."

True enough. "She isn't local." And even were his interest appropriate, he would have no part of anyone who deliberately concealed truth.

"You don't know that," Nanny said. "She said her people are from Fowey."

She said. "Do you know her last name?"

"Bennett, I think. Esmie Bennett."

"How long has she been employed here?"

Nanny frowned. "Robins said she engaged the girl a fortnight ago."

Robins was his housekeeper, a canny woman not given to making hasty decisions. "What else do you know of her?"

"Nothing that I remember. Except Robins mentioned that she's capable and willing."

"Where was her previous position?"

Nanny made an irritated sound. "I'm sure I don't know these things. You'll have to ask Robins. Or better yet, the girl herself."

"She's not what she'd have us believe her to be," William said. "No serving girl speaks as does Esmie Bennett. And no serving girl carries herself as does Miss Bennett."

"She affects you."

William set down his cup so hard the china clattered. "Don't presume to tell me my feelings." He got up and began to pace.

"I'm right." Nanny rolled her lips in. "Good. Give yourself a chance to know someone who touches your heart."

"We're talking about a so-called servant," William said, more loudly than he intended. "A chit of a maid, for God's sake."

"Don't you ever take the Lord's name in vain, my boy."

"Boy?" he thundered. "I'm thirty-five, for *God's* sake. And I have no interest in a deceitful female who is no more than a child."

"Four and twenty."

"What?" William stopped his awkward pacing.

"Esmie Bennett is four and twenty, and she's as honest as the day is long. I feel it in my bones and my bones—"

"*Don't* extol your bones to me again."

"John needs a mother."

"He had one. She cannot be replaced."

Nanny drew herself up in her chair. "*You* need a wife. There's no question of replacing, William, only starting afresh. You've mourned Maria long enough. If Esmie's not what she seems, there's a reason. Give her a chance. It's Christmas, the time for great things. Great blessings. Be open to receiving a blessing for yourself and John."

William opened his mouth to argue once more, but closed it again and collected his composure. "This is ridiculous. I've no interest in the girl. And God knows, she could have no interest in me."

"No, of course not." Nanny lifted the lid of her sewing box and removed a needle. "I expect you'll be suggesting to Robins that Esmie should be dismissed."

"No! I mean, certainly not."

"And why not if you're so convinced she's devious?"

"I . . . Well, as long as she works well and causes no problems with the other servants . . . Well, then . . ." He gestured vaguely.

"Quite right," Nanny agreed. "Very fair. But you always were a fair lad, Master William. And with all the preparations under way for Lord Hawkesly and Lindsay's visit we'll be needing every bit of help we can get."

"Exactly so." He nodded and drew himself up. "Soon enough to ascertain about previous employment after the holiday celebrations."

Youthful cries from outside brought him back to the nursery windows, which overlooked the kitchen gardens. William looked out in time to see John running along the path between the frost-covered remnants of vegetable rows gone to seed. His red hair shone like a beacon, and he wound his arms like windmill blades.

Behind him hurried a small figure swathed in a dark cloak. " . . . cap!" was the only word William caught, but he knew it was Esmie Bennett who rushed in John's wake. As she went, more of her black hair slipped free to fly behind.

John had smiled at her, relaxed with her, and appeared the child he so rarely appeared at other times.

And, regardless of her doubtful background, she intrigued William.

Perhaps she was the daughter of some genteel family in financial embarrassment. She could have been forced by such circumstances to seek a position beneath her station.

"Indeed, yes," he murmured. "After the holiday celebration will be soon enough to enquire further about Esmie Bennett."

Nanny Thomas made a noise that might have been a chuckle, only it immediately proved a quite violent fit of coughing.

2

"YOU'LL CATCH IT IF ROBINS EVER SEES YOU."

Esmie jumped and whirled to see Fennel, another of Tregonitha's housemaids, watching her with malicious interest. "Catches me doing what?" Esmie asked.

"Don't play your games with me, Esmie Bennett. You're a deep un and no mistake. I'll warrant there's more to you than you'd like knowed."

They stood in the stable yard waiting for the cart to come and carry them into Fowey for the weekend. "I'm sure I don't know what you're talking about," Esmie said, but her stomach turned slowly and her heart missed a beat.

"You was trying to catch the master's attention," Fennel said, her eyes sharp with spite. "Robins'll have your place and send you packing if she finds out. See if she don't."

Esmie raised her chin. "And who's going to tell her?" She hoped she looked braver than she felt. "Not that I was doing any such thing." Bullies like Fennel were everywhere, and they thrived on frightening anyone they considered weak. Esmie had had plenty of experience with bullies.

"I'm going to find out about you," Fennel said, looking down on Esmie from her superior height. "Where you come from and why you don't 'ave much to say. And then us'll see how high and mighty you are, Miss Esmie Bennett, with your fancy talk and your fancy manners. Above yourself, you are."

An apprehensive chill climbed Esmie's spine. Fennel must not discover anything of what Esmie's life had been. Surely there could be no way for people here to learn the truth. If certain events were to come to the attention of her new employer, she had no doubt dismissal would be instant. And then where would she go? Already she'd been forced to set a trap for herself, a trap she could only hope would never be sprung.

"Thinkin' about it, I sees," Fennel said with a satisfied sniff. "I 'spect you think you're lucky with me being the only other servant what lives in Fowey. But I've lived there a long time and I can find things out. You'll be on your way from here afore Christmas, you see if I'm not right."

Esmie turned away. Ever since she'd secured her position at Tregonitha, Fennel had been unfriendly. Her pale blue eyes held something Esmie had seen before, in other eyes: jealousy. Why Fennel should be jealous of her, Esmie had no idea. The other girl was blond and pretty, tall and blessed with the sort of figure men admired. And, according to Fennel, the pleasant-faced young man who met her in Fowey each weekend had already spoken for her.

"Sir William is a handsome one, though," Fennel said. "As long as you don't look at what 'appened to the one side of 'is face. Fearsome, *that* is."

Esmie held her tongue. The wide white scar that slashed Sir William's face from temple to jaw caused her no fear. Rather she wondered what had caused the wicked-looking injury. Esmie wished she might touch it . . . touch and stroke it and stroke his strong jaw, and the dimpled grooves his rare smiles caused beneath each high cheekbone . . . and rest her fingers on his wide, firm mouth with its uptilted corners. And how exquisite would be the opportunity to look as long as she pleased into his dark blue eyes . . . She dared another glance at the tall man with light, sun-streaked hair who stood on the far side of the stable yard. For two days he'd failed to be present at nursery tea. Esmie gathered her cloak more closely about her. On that last afternoon he'd at first seemed friendly and kind. But then, just before he turned away, he'd looked angry, and she had no idea why.

"All that passion bottled up inside," Fennel said in a low voice. "Fair scares a girl, don't it? If I was you I'd as soon not catch that one's eye."

Startled, Esmie stared at Sir William's broad shoulders, shown to advantage since he'd discarded his coat and rolled up his sleeves to groom the horse he'd just ridden. She frowned. "Passion? Bottled-up passion?" He certainly worked over the horse's coat with almost violent energy. She had never known another gentleman of his rank to perform such menial duties for his own cattle. "What can you be talking about, Fennel?"

The maid giggled. "You're a sly one. Don't pretend you don't know why he sends all us females home on the weekends. Don't trust hisself longer than a few days at a time. Got to put temptation out of reach till he's got his lusts under control again." She shuddered and sighed at the same time.

"Lusts?" Esmie said weakly.

The arrival of the cart was a relief. Esmie climbed in behind Fennel and sat on a rough seat along one side. Two runs were made every Friday afternoon to take Tregonitha's servants home, the first, with a full load, to the village of Polrithen. Esmie didn't mind that she had to wait and get back to Fowey so much later. If it were possible, she'd rather remain at Tregonitha permanently.

"Ooh!" Fennel elbowed Esmie. "He's coming this way. I think 'is limp makes him ever so mysterious."

Esmie thought so, too, but she would not speak to Fennel about Sir William.

He came, turning down the full sleeves of his white linen shirt. His waistcoat was of fine but plain black cloth, the coat he carried the best of dark blue kerseymeres.

"Good afternoon, Fennel," he said solemnly, and the girl mumbled an appropriate response.

"Good afternoon, Esmie." Turning the full force of his deep blue eyes on her, he planted his dusty top boots apart. "The days are grown very cold. Is that cloak warm enough?"

Esmie blushed to the roots of her hair and knew any attempt to hide the fact would be useless. "Quite warm enough, thank you, Sir William." She fixed her eyes on buff-colored trousers that showed the man needed no padding anywhere—and promptly blushed even more furiously.

"Hurry along, Sam," Sir William called to the old man who drove the cart. "It's getting late. Be certain you're timely on Monday morning."

Barely hearing the driver's answer, Esmie kept her face bowed while the carthorse clomped away, dragging the rocking conveyance over the cobbled yard.

"The days are grown cold," Fennel said in an artificial voice once they were well away from the house. "Is that cloak warm enough?"

Esmie clenched her hands into the folds of her skirt and said nothing.

"I don't hold with fast ways. Neither does Mrs. Robins. It's girls like you that make men think they can have their way with us good, God-fearing ones."

The less she said the better, Esmie thought, and settled in to watch the landscape they passed. Rough stone walls and scraggly lines of ice-etched, bare hedgerow crisscrossed gentle hills mantled in frost. Here and there were sheep, their legs ridiculously spindly beneath the swollen mass of their yellowing, full woolen coats. The animals huddled in clusters, drawing from their collective heat to thwart a bitter wind driving off the nearby English Channel.

"I'll be going to Daniel's on Christmas day," Fennel said dreamily. She'd tied a bright blue kerchief around her head and the color suited her eyes. "By next year I'll be 'is bride. Me Mum and Dad'll let us live with them until a cottage comes vacant.

Daniel's doing well. 'E hopes to 'ave his own boat afore too long. Then I'll help with the saltin' and look after 'im. I won't be at no one's beck and call no more."

Everyone wanted the respect of being his or her own master, Esmie thought, softening to Fennel somewhat. "Tell me about Tregonitha at Christmas," she said, trying to sound friendly. "You were there last year, weren't you?"

"I've been there four year," Fennel said with pride. "Not that any of us—except old Nanny Thomas—gets to be part of the celebrations. We help with the preparations, and that's that. Sir William packs us off. Not that 'e ain't generous. Always sends a nice basket of food 'ome with each of us."

Which was no more than Esmie would expect. Sir William was a good man; she knew it. Somehow she'd managed to anger him the other day and she wished she knew how, but worrying the issue wouldn't help.

"Some of us think as how the master's a strange one, the way 'e seems to want the 'ouse to hisself so much." Fennel appeared to have taken Esmie's silence as encouragement to continue. "O'course, Cook stays over. Only she don't 'ave anything to say about anything 'cept what we don't do right. Once out of the kitchen she keeps to 'er room and 'er Bible."

"Have you met Sir William's sister?"

"Lady Hawkesly? O'course. Fair beautiful she is. And generous as the day is long. Doesn't take no lip from her brother, I'll tell you. Starts orderin' him about the moment she arrives."

"Did you? . . ." The next question must be carefully worded. "What of Lady Granville? Did you know her?"

Fennel shook her head. "Dead afore I come to Tregonitha. Died after the little'un was born, so they say. A fisherman's daughter from over Salters Cove. Maria Pollack. His—Sir William's family didn't approve of 'er and they never knowed about the marriage until after Maria died. There's a lot of wickedness went on in that family, I can tell you. But it's not my place to say how Sir William's stepbrother tried to 'ave Sir William murdered at sea. That was so the stepbrother could get 'is 'ands on the estate. It's little wonder Sir William's so moody, what with all 'e's been through. Wounded at sea—by his best friend, no less—and left for dead. Taken prisoner by the Frenchies. Escaped and cared for by some Frenchy family for nigh on two year, and then getting back to England just in time to stop the stepbrother from killing Lord and Lady Hawkesly. O'course, they wasn't lord and lady then, 'cause they wasn't married yet."

Esmie digested this complicated information. "Poor Sir William," she said at last. "His best friend betrayed him?"

"Yes. And what's more, his best friend was Antun Pollack, Maria Pollack's brother. Fair brokenhearted, Sir William was. Came back and found he 'ad a two-year-old son and a dead wife. And Antun Pollack died, too."

"He lost his wife and his best friend," Esmie murmured.

"Yes. And after his stepbrother and his friend did him mischief like that, well, that's why he makes sure all the staff knows he won't put up with no dishonesty. Dismissed on the spot anyone is what lies or takes the smallest thing. Ask, he says, and he'll give what's needed, but don't cheat him—or you're gone."

Dishonesty. Esmie averted her face. Her whole life had become a lie and there was nothing she could do about it, certainly not throw herself on her employer's mercy and tell him the truth, a truth that might cause her . . . No, she would not think of what vile things could happen to her if certain people found her.

"You said as you live with an old aunt?"

Esmie kept her face turned away. "Yes. Very old."

"Where did you say you live?"

She hadn't said. "Near the quay. Do they decorate Tregonitha for the holidays?"

"Yes." Fennel sounded cross at Esmie's attempted diversion.

"With evergreen boughs and crystal balls?"

"Yes. Not that it's anything to you."

Nothing indeed, except that she remembered other Christmases, too long ago, when she'd been part of warm, safe, evergreen-scented festivities. If only Papa had not wasted everything his fine mind had gained for his small family . . .

"There's holly in the woods," Esmie said absently. "And I saw mistletoe. How pretty the green salon must look with holly and a bough on the mantel."

"I suppose. I hear as how the Reverend Winslow goes to the house to 'elp celebrate on Christmas morning, with Sarah. That's his daughter, what's always been Lady Hawkesly's friend. And with 'er husband Mr. Julian Lloyd-Prescott. I saw 'im once. Fair 'andsome 'e is, too. Not like Lord Hawkesly or Sir William, but a sight for any girl's eyes just the same."

The only man's face that interested Esmie was Sir William's, and any longings in that direction were addlepated nonsense.

The stone buildings of Fowey came into view with Place, the Trefy family's impressive, castle-like home at its center. Esmie might have relaxed if she didn't dread what awaited her in the dismal house where she lodged.

As usual, Fennel's Daniel stood at the curb near The Ship Inn in Lostwithiel Street where Sam always made his stop.

Esmie alighted quickly and made to rush away, but Fennel's hand closed on her arm. "Meet my intended," she said. "Daniel, this is Esmie Bennett, the maid what I told you about."

Daniel doffed his shapeless wool cap and smiled. "Afternoon to you, Esmie." His glance lingered on her, making Esmie acutely uncomfortable.

"Esmie lives by the quay," Fennel said coldly, eyeing her with deep dislike. "With an old aunt. Ain't that right?"

"Yes." Esmie didn't overestimate her appeal to members of the opposite sex, but she could tell that Daniel's undue interest had annoyed Fennel. "I trust the weekend will be pleasant for you both. Good day."

"We're in no hurry," Fennel said with a sly peek at Esmie. "Why not let us walk with you to your lodgins?"

"Thank you, but no. I'm accustomed to making my own way."

"But we'd like to meet your old aunt, wouldn't we, Daniel?" Fennel persisted. "Old folks enjoy a bit of company."

"My aunt doesn't," Esmie said hastily. "She's sick and very cantankerous. The only person she cares to see is me. But again, thank you."

"Our pleasure," Fennel said sweetly. Then she moved close to speak to Esmie without Daniel hearing. "I'm on to you. You're hiding something, and I'm going to find out what it is. Then we'll see what happens." Threading her arm possessively through Daniel's, she urged him away.

Esmie stood watching for a moment. At her back, the half-timbered, whitewashed walls of The Ship Inn leaned oppressively toward the narrow street. With evening already arrived, the people abroad were mostly fishermen on their way to or from their boats and sailors come ashore from a British merchantman anchored off the entrance to the River Fowey. All the men—and what few loud and painted women accompanied them—appeared to have drunk a fair share of ale in the town's taverns. Esmie set out, keeping close to the buildings in an attempt not to draw attention to herself.

Fowey had taken its name from the river that ran past its heart. The house where Esmie lived overlooked the water and belonged to a Mr. Buller, a florid, fleshy man of middle years with yellowed teeth and foul breath. Buller was the reason Esmie dreaded her weekends away from Tregonitha, but no cheaper lodgings were to be had, and even so, she could scarce meet her expenses.

Dodging a band of raucous sailors who called for her company, Esmie gained Buller's house and let herself quietly into a narrow hallway that smelled of vegetables boiled a long time ago.

"Ah, there you be, little Miss Bennett."

She had not been quiet enough. "Good evening, Mr. Buller. I trust you are well."

Her dash for the stairs was in vain. Buller had positioned himself where a single step blocked her way. "I'm a great deal better for seeing you, sweets."

Esmie's skin crawled. Please, please let her save enough money to move to other quarters. "A pleasant evening," she said, pressing the edges of her cloak together. When she'd first found herself stranded in Fowey, her aim had been to leave the town as soon as possible. Now she wished only for a new place to live on the two days between her times at Tregonitha. The reason for her change of heart was one she knew but refused to think about too clearly.

Buller didn't move. "I've been waiting for you." His voice, distorted by pendulous jowls, took on a plaintive note. "Lonely it gets for a man on his own."

A man too lazy to find work. A man who chose instead to scrape by on what rent he could extort for the pitiful little rooms in his house.

"Yes, well, if you'll excuse me." She made to go around him.

Buller leaned his bulk against the wall, cutting off her upward escape. "I thought as how you might like to join me in a pasty. Good they are. Bought 'em this afternoon special."

"Thank you, but no. I've already eaten."

"At that fancy 'ouse, no doubt." The yellow teeth were on display. "Too bad they don't pay you enough so's you could buy something a bit more than them few rags of clothes you got in them drawers."

Esmie narrowed her eyes. He'd been in her room? Gone through her clothes?

"Now, I might see my way to buying you a fancy piece of frippery now and again—*if* you was to be really nice. There's some fine bits of stuff brought ashore—particular from the Frenchies. I might get my hands on a suitable piece or two." He ran his eyes all the way to her feet and back. "I can just see you in some of that fine Frenchy lace. Appetizing picture it is, too."

"You've been in my room?" Esmie made fists.

"Don't get high and mighty with me. Poor girl like you can't afford to pass up a good thing—and I can be that for you."

"*Excuse* me." She approached him with purpose.

Buller straightened. "Come and 'ave that pasty, there's a good girl. And afterwards— Ouch!"

Esmie had sent a fist into the man's soft belly with enough force to drive out his wind.

He lunged for her and she dodged—not quite in time. "Gotcha, y' hell cat." His pudgy hand came down on her shoulder with enough force to make her sag.

"I said, get out of my way!" And, with every ounce of strength she possessed, Esmie stamped one booted heel into his slippered instep and leaped away. Buller howled and stumbled forward onto his knees.

Flying past and up the stairs, Esmie didn't stop until she was locked inside her mean room.

Immediately, she commenced dragging the dresser against the door. This she followed with the washstand and finally, her bed. The last she was able to lodge lengthwise to touch the opposite wall just as the sound of hammering fists thundered from the door.

"Open up," Buller shouted. "Wait till I gets my 'ands on you!"

Esmie threw herself face down on the bed and covered her ears. He'd tire and go away, as he had on the previous occasion when he'd tried to get into her room. Somehow, she would exist until Monday morning and the cart ride back to Tregonitha . . . and Sir William, God help her silly, dreaming heart.

She could not return here again.

"Let me in, I tell you!"

Christmas was coming. With her face in the pillow, Esmie sang inside her head to close out Buller's voice: "I saw three ships go sailing by/On Christmas morn/On Christmas morn . . ." Her father had sung those words to her when she was a small girl.

If only these golden childhood days could have lasted.

If only she were not trying to outrun a nightmare.

If only she could be something other than a lowly servant to Sir William Granville . . .

3

Sir William strode up the front steps of Tregonitha, swinging off his cloak as he went. At the door, he turned to survey the sky. Dark gray cloud, slung so low it blended into the hilltops, already loosed flutterings of fine snow.

Maria had loved snow . . . and Christmas. On a day such as this, she would have been childlike in her gleeful anticipation.

He pressed his lips together. Her face was barely a memory now, except when their son looked at him from a particular angle and smiled. No, he no longer mourned Maria for herself, but for what she had been in his life and for their lost hopes. Passionate he might be. Lonely he might also be. But neither emotion could be allowed to become strong enough to cause the risk of another gentle woman's life.

Esmie Bennett was gentle . . .

William entered the house and went immediately to his library. Less than a week and Lindsay would arrive with Edward and their brood. The thought brought William bittersweet pleasure. He could scarcely wait to see his little sister, but he was merely human, and the sight of a contented family together at such a time could not fail to make him aware of what John lacked—of what he, himself lacked.

Then there was the matter of Point Cottage, the family's guest retreat on a nearby hill. Edward and Lindsay held fond memories of the place and would, as they did on each visit, expect to go there—which meant William needed to make certain it was in readiness. He'd never had the heart to remind Lindsay that he and Maria had once made the cottage their refuge, and that he could scarce bear to walk inside.

Enough of this.

He hadn't taken nursery tea for a week, not since that day when he'd learned a little more about Esmie Bennett—and discovered there was probably much that no one at Tregonitha knew about her.

Today John should join him for tea here in the library. The boy would enjoy that.

William pulled the bell and waited, watching the steady blending together of sky and land beyond the French windows. He'd been honest when he told John it rarely snowed heavily in this part of Cornwall, but they might be about to experience such a rarity. Already the white flakes were larger and closer together.

"You called, Sir William?"

Her voice was unmistakable. William faced Esmie. "Good afternoon."

She curtsied. "Good afternoon, Sir William."

He regarded her steadily. "Come closer, please." Surely she appeared thinner. And were there not dark marks beneath her eyes? "Don't be shy," he added when she hesitated.

Esmie came slowly forward until she stood only feet from him. "Yes, Sir William?"

"Are you well?"

Her eyes slid away. "Yes, thank you, Sir William."

Why did she have to add bloody "Sir William" to every sentence? "You do not appear so. I shall speak to Mrs. Robins."

"Oh, please, no, Sir William."

He gritted his teeth. "Is there insufficient food available to you here?"

"No, Sir William."

"Is your bed not comfortable enough to allow you to sleep?"

"Y-yes, Sir William."

Yes, sir. No, sir. "But your chamber is too cold?"

"Absolutely not, Sir William. I am completely content here. I could not be more so anywhere else in the world and . . ." Her words faded away, leaving her lips slightly parted. To William's consternation, Esmie's green eyes filled with tears. "Very content," she muttered, winding her apron through her fingers.

He didn't believe her. "Very well." The surliness of his own tone annoyed him. "Kindly bring Master John to me. Tell him he's to take tea here in the library with me."

"Yes, Sir William." She dropped another shallow curtsey, spun away and all but ran from the room.

Damn and blast all women. He'd never understand them. Dash it all, he no longer understood himself. He thought of the girl all the time. Her face could be summoned to mind at any moment.

What could be wrong with at least seeking small amounts of her company? Was he mistaken in thinking she did not find his scars repellent?

He limped close to the windows. Snow dusted the terrace now and delicately lined the dark, slender branches of bordering hawthorne trees.

Nothing could be *right* about seeking her out. And she was concealing something. Once Christmas was past, her background must be investigated. He'd check her references personally.

She *was* thinner and she *did* appear tired.

"Papa, Papa!" John cannoned into the room. "I'm come to tea! Oh, Papa, it's snowing."

Behind his son, in the doorway, stood Esmie, her hands slack at her sides.

"It is indeed snowing," William agreed, looking directly at the maid.

"Aunt Lindsay and Uncle Edward may not be able to get here for Christmas."

"They may not. But they'll come as soon as they can. Don't upset yourself."

"And you will send the servants home to their families soon," John persisted. "Nanny says you will because you won't risk them having to stay here for the holidays."

William glanced at John. "That is very true. They deserve to be with their families at such a time. We must watch carefully. It may be necessary to send them very soon."

He looked to Esmie once more—in time to see her grimace as with pain before slipping from sight.

"Look smart, now," Mrs. Robins said. "Sir William's anxious for us to be on our way."

With the other servants, and with all of them dressed for the outdoors, Esmie stood in a line at the foot of the stairs. They were being packed off home before the snow became so deep they couldn't leave.

Home? She had no home.

"Here 'e comes," Fennel whispered into Esmie's ear.

Sir William, in a black coat, his neckcloth startlingly white and simply tied, descended the stairs with a stack of envelopes in his hands. Light caught his blond hair and deepened the shadows on his lean face.

" 'E always remembers us," Fennel said. "But I don't know why Robins told you to come to the boxing line. E's not likely to give gifts to someone what's hardly been 'ere."

"Happy Christmas to you all," Sir William said, advancing along the line, putting an envelope into each pair of hands and smiling. "Your baskets are in the pantry."

"Happy Christmas to you, Esmie."

He pressed an envelope upon her, too. And his fingers touched hers . . . and lingered, didn't they? "Happy Christmas, Sir William," she said softly.

She dared to look at him. He looked back. Troubled? Why should he appear troubled? As quickly as she thought she'd seen it, the shadow left his eyes and he smiled down at her before passing to the next servant, and the next.

"Not right," Fennel muttered. "You've bewitched him, that's what you've done. And maybe a whole lot more. I'd thought to put off a certain conversation I'm going to 'ave. Now I won't wait. I'm going to get my pa to ask Mr. Buller about you and your old auntie. There's plenty to tell, I'll wager."

Esmie tried to take a breath, but there seemed no air in the hallway. She heard Mrs. Robins and Cook hurrying them along to catch the cart. Sam would leave immediately with the Polrithen people—Mrs. Robins included—and be back as quickly as possible to take Fennel and Esmie to Fowey.

Fennel knew she lived at Mr. Buller's. That gentleman would be only too pleased to inform Fennel's father that Miss Bennett had no aunt. He'd probably be happy to make up all manner of lies in addition.

Esmie trailed through the kitchens behind the rest and waited while the villagers went into the passageway leading past the scullery and pantry to the back door.

Buller would give her away. Fennel would tell Mrs. Robins. Mrs. Robins would tell Sir William, and Esmie would be dismissed.

She would not return to Fowey.

"Oh, my!" Holding Sir William's envelope to her chest, Esmie rushed past Fennel. "What can I be thinking of? I quite forgot!"

"Forgot what?" Fennel's voice rose to a confused squeak. "Where are you going?"

"To Polrithen, of course! Didn't I tell you? My aunt and I are spending Christmas there. With . . . an old pupil."

"A pupil of what?" Fennel shouted after Esmie. "Whose pupil?"

"My aunt's. She was a pianoforte teacher. Most unusual for a woman of her generation. Very talented." She grabbed a Christmas basket from the pantry and reached the back door before calling, "A prodigy!" and letting herself out into the snowy kitchen garden.

Keeping close to the house, she slipped rapidly along beneath the windows and into a concealed corner.

Within minutes, the sounds of the servants' voices and the dulled clopping of hoofs faded from the stable yard.

She could not return to Fowey. And she could not go back into the house. Esmie sank down to huddle against the wall. She also could not remain here unless she wished to freeze to death.

After more than a year of running from place to place, hiding, and searching, and finding nothing but deeper poverty, was this to be the end?

The snow became heavier. It began to cover her cloak and flakes settled on her cold face and her eyelashes.

Cramped, Esmie drew herself upright and fumbled to open the lumpy envelope Sir William had given her. From inside she took several gold coins and a beautiful, gilt-edged text. Peering, she made out the words: "Faith, hope and love/And the greatest of these is love." Below was a colored illustration depicting the holy Infant in His manger.

No doubt the texts were Cook's contribution and all the servants had received the same, yet Esmie's throat constricted with gratitude.

There had seemed no place for the infant Jesus, yet after a difficult journey one had been found.

Esmie looked at the basket by her feet. There was a stable here, but she'd surely be discovered. And even if she could get as far as their cottages, the estate tenants would promptly turn to Sir William for an explanation of her predicament.

Nowhere . . . except . . . She looked off in the direction of Point Cottage. Could she make it that far in such conditions? Cramming down her doubts, Esmie picked up the basket and set out.

Faith, hope and love—with these, and with enough courage, she might yet gain a safe haven.

Shadows fingered the night's new white robe. A high moon sought gaps in streamers of indigo cloud to cast its glittering eye upon mounded shrubs and terrace balusters, and statuary, and endless other mysterious forms.

Snow had stopped falling an hour since and, with midnight approaching, William ventured forth into the silent, crystal air.

He closed the French doors to the library and made his way down to the lawn, his boots scrunching with each step. The still beauty of the scene drew him on around Tregonitha, until he stood at the front of the house with its view past the woods to the distant pale blur of rising fields.

The clouds began to cluster over the hills. There would be more snow yet. Despite his lack of a cloak, William scarce felt the cold, but he'd best get inside.

To the south, over Tregonitha's most seaward headland, a single wisp of cloud spiraled. Watching the odd formation, William turned to retrace his steps. Paler than the other clouds, it gradually dissipated, to be replaced by another almost the same.

He paused. Point Cottage was on that headland—and if he didn't know better, he'd say the cloud might, in fact, be smoke from the chimney. It couldn't be.

At the corner of the house, he stopped and narrowed his gaze on the dark outline of that hill. He saw the smoke again, a thin stream that wafted skyward, then faded.

Could there be some soul stranded there? Surely not. Any of his tenants likely to be abroad would be able to return to his own home.

Imaginative, he might be. Fanciful, he refused to become! Time for some good brandy before a fire that did exist.

William dismissed his imaginings and returned to the library.

4

A SUDDEN RATTLING ROUSED WILLIAM.

Damn. He'd dropped the book he'd been trying to read and dozed. Aching muscles in his back attested to the foolhardiness of allowing himself to fall asleep in a chair in the library.

The fire had burned low. Dealing with his own

comforts was one of William's pleasures. When they'd breakfasted tomorrow, he would take John and lay in a goodly supply of wood.

Rattling sounded again—the French windows shaken by the wind. He looked to the small, gilt and enamel clock that had been his mother's. Three in the morning. Recollection of what had kept him from his bed flooded back: smoke. Point Cottage. In recent years the cottage had been all but abandoned. Even basic supplies had been neglected. If he had seen smoke earlier it would be little wonder that it came and went in puny wisps, since any wood was bound to be wet.

He got up, easing stiffness in his leg, and left the room.

If some scoundrel were ensconced in the cottage—well, good luck to him. He could be dealt with soon enough. But should someone be there who was in need of help . . .

Dash it all.

William took a cloak, pulled on gloves, and strode out into driving snow. A conscience could be a wretched handicap.

He saddled Hades and led the willing stallion from the stables.

A lifetime of following the same trail, together with the help of what dark twigs showed from buried hedgerows, guided William over the hills toward Point Cottage. The final climb was the worst. Hades's breath formed billows of vapor about his tossing head, and he strained against the incline.

Finally they crested the rise and fell into an uneasy trot.

Trees clustered atop the hill. The cottage lay at the center of these. William urged his mount on, guiding him through dense trunks to a clearing.

His own breath rasping, William reined in and shielded his eyes from wind and snow.

Not fancy. Not imaginings.

The horse pranced and wheeled. And William stared at a meager light through a window. He realized, too late, that he had not thought to bring a weapon.

Swiftly, he dismounted. "Quiet," he whispered to Hades. "Gently, gently," he added soothingly and moved rapidly away from the animal. Bending low, he gained the cover of the cottage wall and slipped along to flatten himself beside the window. Whoever was in residence had thoughtfully failed to close the curtains.

With great caution, William edged closer until he could see inside. The fire that sputtered at the hearth was pitiful.

The figure that crouched before the mean blaze was also pitiful. William let out the breath he'd held. A child? Swathed in a blanket, the body was small and curled almost into a ball.

His temptation was to rush in and gather the creature up. Such an action would no doubt scare the child out of its wits and do more harm than good. Best knock and give notice of his arrival.

William gained the door and rapped with a knuckle. A muffled crash sounded from inside the cottage. He attempted to brush back his tangled hair, the better to present a less fearsome impression.

The door did not open. And it still did not open

when he knocked again . . . and again.

The child *had* taken fright. There was nothing for it but to go in.

He entered slowly, sliding open the door until he could call out, "Don't be afraid. I am come to help you." And then he thought he heard an indistinct cry. A chair lay amid a tangle of wet clothing that must have been drying before the fire. Of the child there was no sign.

"Come out," William said, as gently as he could. "You have nothing to fear. I shall not hurt you."

Gradually, from behind the old couch, a blanketed head came into view. From beneath that blanket a mass of curly black hair tumbled over a white face.

William took a step forward and halted. "Good God," he murmured.

"I'm sorry, Sir William. Very sorry."

There could be no greener eyes than the worried ones that stared at him now. "Esmie?"

Bundled in several blankets Sir William had collected and with the additional cover of his cloak, Esmie sat rigidly before him on his horse.

"I can scarcely believe you managed to walk to the cottage from the stable yard," he shouted, bending over to shelter her from the storm. He had lodged her sideways in the grip of one powerful arm.

"The snow was not as deep then," Esmie said loudly.

"After the thaw I shall speak to Sam. He should have ensured you were present before leaving."

Esmie swallowed. "It was my fault. There was

much confusion. Please don't blame Sam." Her burden of deceit grew by the minute.

The horse was big and strong, but he labored against the slippery downhill path.

Sir William settled Esmie even more firmly against him. "You should have come back to the house." His warm breath fanned her temple. "The moment you discovered you'd been left behind by the cart, you should have come to me."

More lies. More reasons for him to turn her away forever. She could expect nothing more. "I'm sorry," she whispered, closing her eyes. Where his breath met her skin she tingled, and a curious heat spread inside her body, defying even the bone-freezing cold that made her hands and feet numb.

"Undoubtedly you will sicken, and in this weather there will be no hope of bringing the doctor."

"I shall *not* sicken," Esmie announced, finding her voice again together with a surge of annoyance. "I am *very* strong." And she did not like to be considered otherwise.

"It is a pity your wits do not match your vision of your strength—or your impudence."

She pursed her lips and kept silent. At least she had put off the inevitable for the duration of the bad weather.

At last they reached Tregonitha and the stables. Sir William settled Esmie on a bale of hay, removed his cloak, and swathed it about her whilst attending to the stallion's needs with speedy efficiency.

"Now we shall see to getting you warm and dry and into bed," he said, after tossing a blanket over the great animal's back.

Although the storm had lost much of its fury,

approaching dawn turned the still-falling snow to a blinding white blur. Quiet anger hovered in Sir William's dark blue eyes, and Esmie dared make no protest when he swept her up into his arms and carried her through the kitchen gardens and into the house.

A blast of heat met them in the kitchen. "There you are!" Nanny Thomas stood over a copper pot on the range, her thin face red from the rising steam. "What can you be thinking of, Master William? Rushing off in a storm without a word! Cook found out you'd gone and went off into one of her fits of the vapors. I've had to put her to bed. Now I'll be left with everything to do. What *were* you thinking of, that's what I'd like to know."

"Yes, yes, Nanny," Sir William said without apparent rancor at the old lady's disrespect. "There'll be time enough for explanations later. This foolish girl has all but managed to cause her own death."

Esmie roused herself and retorted, "No such thing!"

Sir William's withering glare silenced her. "I left her clothes and shoes at Point Cottage. She can use the chamber next to mine. It'll be the warmest."

Effectively silenced, Nanny Thomas followed Sir William as he bore Esmie upstairs and along a corridor leading to the wing where the family slept. In the room next to his own, he deposited Esmie in a pretty armchair covered with daffodil-yellow brocade.

He bent to light a fire. "There must be some of Lindsay's things ready to hand, Nanny."

Esmie dared not remind him that a few of her

own clothes were in the servants' quarters. In fact, the ominous expression on his face made any comment at all seem ill-advised.

"You'll get warm and dry," he announced with a fierce frown as Nanny Thomas scurried away. "Then food will be brought to you. After you've eaten, you will sleep."

"Yes, Sir William," Esmie said meekly.

He got to his feet and stood over her, an impressively tall, well-built man. "When the rest of the servants return, there will be more said about this dangerous incident. Thanks to someone else's carelessness—and your own foolish actions—you might well have died in that cottage."

Esmie began to shake her head, but changed her mind. "Yes, Sir William. I'm very sorry, Sir William."

"Don't—" He brought his lips together and color shot along his high cheekbones. "Even if Sam is not to blame for this—and he must bear some of the responsibility—even so, the other maid who rides with you should have spoken up."

With every moment she sank more deeply into a horrid quicksand of her own making, yet she could not possibly explain the truth of it all and expect understanding. Misery washed over Esmie and she closed her eyes.

"Yes," Sir William said in an odd voice that did not sound like his own. "Of course you've fallen asleep. You're tired." Several silent seconds passed before he spoke once more, very softly. "Sleep, gentle little one. Nothing shall harm you with me. I'll discover the truth about this event soon enough."

The truth. Esmie kept her eyes tight shut and listened while footsteps left the room and receded.

She pulled her feet beneath her on the chair. Even now Fennel was probably persuading her father to go to Mr. Buller's. And there the truth—as much of it as was known—would be revealed and would prove adequate to damn Esmie.

In her mind, Esmie heard Sir William's voice softly saying, "Nothing shall harm you with me," and she prayed that the snow might fall forever.

5

"ARE YOU AWAKE?"

Esmie's mind focused slowly on the voice.

"You are, aren't you? I can feel you thinking."

Feel her thinking? She opened her eyes the merest fraction and saw John Granville's serious young face close to her own.

"You *are* awake. I can see your eyes." Small, cool fingers touched her cheek. "This is so exciting."

Esmie's eyes flew wide open. "Exciting?"

John stood level with her shoulders, looking down at her with an expression of pure delight. "Oh, yes. But I'm not supposed to say anything.

Uncle Edward explained . . . Yes, anyway, I know this is not something I'm to do anything about. So I'll just wait until it all happens." He grinned, showing front teeth that were not quite grown in. "But it *is* exciting. And in time for Christmas, too."

Esmie blinked and refocused. The child spoke nonsense, but she hadn't the heart to question him further. "I should get up." She rose to her elbows and found that even that movement caused pain in every muscle. Yesterday's events poured into her mind and she fell back. She would pay for her efforts—and a great deal more.

"Papa's bedchamber is there," John said, pointing to her right.

"Yes."

He drew his shoulders up to his ears. " 'Course you knew that."

Esmie watched him. John watched Esmie and puffed air upward from a jutting bottom lip.

"You can sew things, can't you?"

She nodded.

John sighed hugely. "That's good, then."

Esmie smiled at his happy face. He seemed content simply to stand and look at her. The events of the previous evening returned in a rush and she looked down at the white lawn nightrail she wore. Delicate bands of embroidery threaded with the narrowest of pink satin ribbon edged the low neck and long sleeves. There had been a time, when she was small, when she'd owned such fine things. That had been before Papa died and seemed very long ago.

"Nanny said Papa found you at Point Cottage and brought you back. But I'm not supposed to talk about that." He waited, scrutinizing her narrowly. "So, anyway, I won't talk about it. I expect it was all part of what's supposed to happen."

Esmie chewed her bottom lip.

"Papa says you're to use Aunt Lindsay's things because your clothes were all wet. Nanny's thrown away something called a shift because it's ruined."

Early that morning, Nanny had been matter-of-fact in helping Esmie to wash and put on the nightrail. "Nanny Thomas is very kind."

"Yes," John agreed. "This really is topping. Wait till Uncle Edward comes . . . and my cousin, James. He has a baby brother, you know. His name is Simon."

There was a code to be broken here, but Esmie did not feel at all up to the task. "How many days are there before Christmas?"

"You *know.*" John looked scandalized before he laughed and wrinkled his nose. "You jest, Esmie. It is only five days—including today. So we shall have to . . . well, you *know.*"

She felt uncomfortably adrift. There was one possible subject to which John might be referring. "Five days. Not very long. Did the *papier-mâché* birds dry completely?"

"Oh, yes. Completely. Are you still sure Papa will like the one I made up?"

"Absolutely." Several weeks earlier she had encountered John wandering through the hallways. He'd confided that he wanted to make a special gift for his father for Christmas and couldn't think of anything suitable. The birds had been Esmie's idea, and had immediately pleased John. "The robin will be wonderful," she continued, "and Sir William will appreciate your attention to accurate detail, but the bird of your imagination will intrigue him."

"You *are* sure?"

"Indeed I am." Sir William had a great interest in nature and particularly in birds. "Perhaps you should give the imaginary bird a name."

"Blue Jonathan," John said promptly. "Do you think?—"

"I certainly do," Esmie said, laughing. "Of course, the name is so obvious I shouldn't have had to ask you about it. We shall have to find a way to do the painting in secret." Once she returned to her room in the servants' quarters there would be no difficulty in helping the boy complete his gift unobserved.

Esmie looked toward the window, but the bright yellow draperies were closed. "Is it still snowing?"

"No."

She smoothed the fine bed linen. Was it possible that she might actually be able to stay through Christmas? And, when she did have to leave, where could she hide next? Certain was the fact that she must depart before Fennel could get back to Tregonitha. Facing Sir William, seeing his disgust at the story he would be told, would be more than Esmie could endure.

"There's lots of snow," John said, an anxious note in his voice. "It won't be gone for a long time."

Esmie's eyes flew to the boy's face. Then she relaxed. "Good. I do enjoy snow." Of course he was not able to read her mind. She'd always been told that her moods showed clearly on her face.

"We don't get a great deal of snow here," John said, sounding even more concerned. "Will that matter?"

"Matter?"

"No, of course it won't. It's just that this is all so much better than I hoped it would be, and I don't want you to change your mind."

Whatever John was referring to was of deep importance to him. Esmie smiled reassuringly at him. "What is it you think I might change my mind about?"

His frown gradually faded. "Oh, I'm sorry. I forgot what Uncle Edward said. I'll try not to talk about it anymore."

The child thought they both knew what he was talking about. "What exactly did your Uncle Edward say?"

"You *know*."

Sir William approached the bedchamber with caution, only to discover that the door stood wide open, giving a clear view of the bed.

In the darkened corridor, he must be invisible to Esmie and to John, who stood beside her. William couldn't hear what they were saying.

He watched, aware of his reaction to the girl in the bed. Last night at the cottage, when he'd seen glimpses of pale skin and known that she wore little beneath the blanket, her effect on him had been like a rushing tide of heat that left him momentarily weak. Carrying her, holding her against his body, had driven him to the brink of loosing control.

Hungry longing overtook him. Six years ago he'd left England a husband, only to return two years later as a widower. John and Tregonitha had come into his care together. The chamber where Esmie lay should have been his wife's, yet no woman had ever lain there waiting to draw him into her bed . . . into her body . . .

Arousal came swiftly. William took a deep, calming breath and stepped into the light that spilled from the room.

He tapped the open door. "Good afternoon, Esmie. Do you have everything you need?" Surely his comments didn't sound as banal to the girl as they did to him.

"Papa! Come and talk to Esmie."

William cleared his throat. "I doubt if Miss Bennett is anxious for company, in fact, you—"

"Yes she is. Aren't you, Esmie?"

After a moment's hesitation, the girl said, "Yes. John is—er—entertaining me very well."

She hadn't exactly asked him to enter, yet he would choose to interpret her words as an invitation. "Didn't Nanny send you up to speak to Miss Bennett about food, John?" He went into the room, but stood at a considerable distance from the bed.

"I am not hungry, thank you."

He walked across the room and put wood on the fire. "It is near afternoon. You haven't eaten in a day."

"Everything is going very well, Papa."

William turned to look at John. "I'm pleased." About what, he wasn't certain.

"You promised we would collect boughs and some holly and decorate. Of course, Esmie will come now. And a snow fight will be much better with three, will it not? And we'll get out the crystal decorations Aunt Lindsay brought last year. Esmie will like setting them in the boughs."

"John—"

"I know, Papa. We must not take Esmie away from the sewing she'll soon wish to begin."

William met Esmie's eyes. Without spectacles they were even more remarkable. "Sewing?" he said.

She shrugged, and the nightrail slipped to reveal one slender shoulder.

Against his will, he averted his face. "Please go and tell Nanny to make Miss Bennett something light to eat."

"Yes, Papa," John said meekly. He passed William and paused. "Uncle Edward didn't say exactly when the sewing should begin. I wonder how we'll know." John wandered out, his brow puckered in concentration.

William glanced at Esmie. Her hair tumbled loosely about her face and shoulders in dark contrast to the pure white of the bed linens and her skin—skin so pale and soft, yet faintly flushed in the glow from the fire.

His being here—alone—with an innocent girl was improper, yet he couldn't bring himself to walk away. "John has been too much alone," he said when the silence became oppressive.

"He is a happy child," Esmie said. "And he obviously loves his father a great deal."

William shifted from foot to foot and then strolled over to draw back a drape. The afternoon was dark, and little light pierced the window. "It will be well for you to stay quiet until you are recovered from the shock and the elements."

"I am not suffering from shock."

Again, there was that defiant determination he'd heard in her whilst they'd ridden home. "People suffering shock often do not know as much."

"I would know," she announced. "It is time I at least went to help Nanny Thomas. Is Cook recovered?"

"It pleases Cook to keep much to herself when the rest of the servants are not in residence. Nanny does well enough with our small needs. You will remain in bed." He turned toward her slowly.

She'd sat up. The color in her cheeks might be the result of annoyance, but it suited her. "I have my room in the servants' quarters," she informed him. "And there is a dress there that I can wear."

He did not want her to go to the servants' quarters. "That part of the house has been locked up until it's time for the staff to return. The area will be cold, damp even. No, no, better that you remain here." Where, *damn the drive of his hunger,* he could hope to catch more glimpses of her in dishabille.

"I shall have to go and get my dress." She sounded obstinate now.

"No, you shall not. Again, the garments are probably damp."

"They can be aired."

"More trouble than the effort would be worth."

"I need my clothes, Sir William."

Snarling at her would gain him nothing. "You will use some of my sister's clothes," he said carefully. What exactly did he hope to gain from Esmie Bennett? "After all, you would quickly tire of one dress, particularly in the festive season." He wanted to see her in pretty, feminine clothes that would enhance rather than conceal her charming curves . . . and perhaps he wanted a great deal more.

"Very well," she said at last. "If you would be so kind as to tell me which of Lady Hawkesly's clothes I may borrow, I'll fetch them now."

"Nanny will help you—tomorrow."

"I wish to get up and be useful."

"Tomorrow. You are not strong and must rest, at least for today."

"Of course I'm strong." Her lips parted and her eyes grew wide and fierce in a way that sent a surge of excitement through William. "I'm getting up—*now,*" she added forcefully.

"You will remain in bed." The smile that threatened wasn't easy to quell.

"Ooh, men can be so lofty!" With a flurry of tossed sheets, a pair of slender ankles and feet—and calves—appeared to dangle over the side of the bed. Esmie marched to stand before him. "I am extremely grateful that you rescued me. But I did not ask you to do so."

This time William didn't attempt to stop a small smile. The chit was showing fire that promised other passions. "Perhaps we should not forget that the cottage is *mine,* and that this house is also mine."

She plunked her hands on her hips, apparently oblivious to the effect on the garment she wore. "That is all very true. And I am indebted to you for your kindness, but I am perfectly well and rested, and I wish to be *useful.*"

Unable to do other than be a man, William surveyed soft, white shoulders revealed when the nightrail—somewhat too large—had slid down. The fire's soft light shone through thin cotton fabric to outline a lovely woman's body in achingly stimulating detail. Esmie's waist was tiny, her small hips flared, and her legs long and shapely. Her breasts were engagingly full for one so diminutive and pressed insistently against bands of embroidery, so that he could not fail to see the darker points of her nipples.

Her breasts rose and fell with each angry breath. "I demand to be of service, Sir William."

Ah, but of what service she could be to him. "You *demand?*" If she were experienced enough to read what must show in his face, her fiery gaze would instantly go elsewhere and find proof of her effect upon him.

She made to walk past him.

"I think not," William said and caught her arms. "You will take a chill in such scant clothing."

"Chill?" Haughty determination dissolved. "I don't think so, Sir William."

Sir William, Sir William. If he tossed her on the white bed now, tore the wisp of a nightrail away and drove into her soft body, what would she call him then? In the wild, marvelous moments of burning pleasure he knew she would bring him, in the throes of abandoned womanly satisfaction he felt shimmering beneath her innocence—waiting for release—what would she call him then?

"I'm sorry, Sir William."

William, she would cry, *William!* And he would silence her with kisses that would leave her mouth swollen even as she reached for more.

His hands rested near her shoulders, where the nightrail met smooth skin. "You have no need to be sorry." A slight adjustment and he could hold her breasts—he could, with the merest tug, send the gown falling about her waist. Her white flesh would fill his hands, and he would test that delicious, soft weight with his fingers, bring her nipples to begging peaks with his thumbs . . . and then take them into his mouth. "You have no need at all to be sorry, Esmie." His voice had an odd edge he hardly recognized.

"I have made you angry." She wrapped her arms tightly around her ribs and the gown fell farther of its own volition. Her breasts had become the barrier that stopped the flimsy garment from falling and leaving her half-naked. "You deserve my gratitude. What can I do that would please you?"

He made himself look at her eyes, only to glance lower once more—at her moist mouth. "You owe me nothing." A force pulled him closer and he felt his own lips part in readiness to meet hers. Summoning restraint he almost wished he lacked, William squared his shoulders and eased the nightrail into place.

Esmie looked at herself and gasped. She tried to cover her breasts.

William stepped back and said, "I think you would be warmer in bed, don't you?"

With a small, distressed cry, she whirled around and fled in the direction he suggested—not without providing him with more aspects guaranteed to make blood pound in regions now completely beyond *any* restraint.

He left her then and made his way quietly from her room and into his own bedchamber, where he poured a large brandy and sat beside his own fire. Clearly the girl was not disgusted by either the scars on his face or his limp. But those were not the only marks of violence he bore. How would she react to the rest? There was a simple way to find out.

She had assured him he deserved her gratitude. "What can you do to please me?" he whispered. Only his dressing room separated them. Two doors that could be opened whenever he chose. "What indeed? It would give me the greatest pleasure to show you."

6

RHEUMATISM, INDEED! NANNY THOMAS CROSSED swiftly to the library windows and peered out. That rascal William. The moment he'd made an excuse of her "rheumatism" to delay Esmie Bennett from leaving nursery tea, she'd known he was more than a mite interested in the girl. Violet Mae Thomas, spinster and hard worker through every one of her seventy-six years, had never had a twinge of a rheumatism pain. Good living, honesty, and godliness kept a body healthy. No wicked, conniving thoughts ever crossed Nanny Thomas's mind, and she had the proof of it in every answered prayer the Lord rewarded her with.

She laced her fingers together and prayed aloud, "Please, Lord, let Master William stop wasting valuable time and bed Esmie Bennett. Let him bed her and wed her and get her with child so he and young John can have a proper family." For an instant she thought, then squeezed her eyes shut. "I know that they should properly be wed before bed, but these are special circumstances. You sent the snow to keep them together because you knew he wasn't about to do anything with his feelings for the girl if you didn't help out. He can't wed her without calling the banns and all. That means they can't marry till after the thaw. But if he doesn't bed her and the thaw comes, he'll likely convince himself out of the whole thing. I know him, Lord. He blames himself for Maria's death because she died from giving birth to his son. And he won't listen to me when I try to tell him otherwise. So You just take the whole thing out of his hands and put the two of them where they need to be. He'll not walk away from her after that." She opened her eyes. "There. That's *that* done."

Nanny leaned near a pane to see in one direction, then shifted to look the other way. There they were, only yards away, just below the stone terrace railings. John and William rolled a ball of snow around, increasing its size with each swipe. Dressed in Lindsay's green velvet cloak with the swansdown trim, Esmie Bennett stood watching the man and his son. Lovely, Esmie looked in that cloak, too. Matched her eyes and made her look like an angel with white skin and curly black hair. And she was a lady. Nanny and Robins had put their heads together over that. Esmie Bennett was a lady come down in the world, but even if she weren't, she'd still be perfect for Master William.

Esmie and Nanny's William would make beautiful children. The girls would be lovely, feminine little things like their mother and the boys, like John, would have Master William's fine, manly figure and his strength.

She sighed. "Lord, you might want to do something with Esmie, too. I can see she's sweet on Master William but she's an innocent, and overwhelmed by him. Not that I blame her, mind you. Scars or no scars, he's a handsome one and no mistake. And he's worldly. But they're meant for each other." Meant for each other or not, as long as the silly baggage behaved like a skittish foal, William's finer feelings would make him keep his distance.

"Sometimes, Nanny," she murmured to herself. "Sometimes the Lord works through humans."

Icy air smote her face as she opened the door. "John! John!"

He turned a ruddy face in her direction and waved.

Nanny gestured to him to come in and, slowly at first, he headed toward her. As usual, he'd discarded his cap and his red hair made a nice match for cold-whipped cheeks.

"Come in," she said when he drew close. "Cook's said we can make some suggestions for dinner. I'd like you to help me decide."

With a puzzled pucker between his brows, John entered the library, and Nanny closed the door behind him. She stood back out of sight and peeked outside again. William looked toward the house, then at Esmie, and Nanny held her breath. *Do something, William.*

He held out a hand, and slowly, Esmie put her fingers in his. He guided her through the snow to stand beside him and pointed to the ball that now reached almost as high as the girl's shoulder. Nanny saw William laugh, and Esmie cover her mouth, and then the two of them set to work making another ball of snow.

"Ah, that's better," Nanny said, before remembering John's presence.

"It's working," he said, with obvious glee. "Just the way Uncle Edward said it would."

Nanny regarded him thoughtfully. "That's several times as you've mentioned something your Uncle Edward's been telling you. Why don't you tell me what sort of foolishness he's been filling your head with?"

"You *know*." John began unbuttoning his coat, a smug grin stretching his mouth.

"And you've said that a few times lately, too. Only I don't *know*."

"Yes, you do. You know about the mama room and the sewing."

It was Nanny's turn to frown. "Maybe I do and maybe I don't."

"You saw what happened when Uncle Edward found Aunt Lindsay, didn't you?"

She wasn't about to explain that she hadn't been present at the precise moment. "Maybe I did. Anyways, I'd enjoy hearing it all in your Uncle Edward's own words." Lord Hawkesly was a devilishly handsome man with a wicked sense of humor, and he and Lindsay loved one another to distraction. But viscount or no viscount, Nanny would not put up with his confusing John.

John removed his coat. "I asked Uncle Edward how gentlemen get ladies to want to be mamas."

Nanny's hand went to her throat. "What did he say?"

"He waved his arms. And he looked different. His face went quite red, but he told me that first a gentleman sees a lady he thinks would make a good mama. Then he finds a way to get her to spend time with him. After that, the lady moves into the bedchamber next to the gentleman's and that's that. After a while everything works."

"Everything works?" She should have been keeping a closer watch on the boy's development. Some grew up faster than others.

"You don't know, do you?" The shake of John's head was pitying. "Very soon, the lady starts sewing clothes for her baby, and then the baby is born. Sometimes it takes quite a long time, but we have to be patient."

When he didn't continue, Nanny asked, "Is that all your uncle said?"

"Yes. But I asked and he said it doesn't always take very long at all. It would be perfect to have a baby in time for Christmas. There's four days yet. A boy, like James's Simon, would be nice. But a girl would be all right, too."

A holly leaf pricked Esmie's ankle, and she squealed.

"What's the matter?" Sir William asked, and dropped the evergreen bough he'd just dragged into the entrance hall.

"Nothing," Esmie said breathlessly. It seemed that Sir William had only to say a word, or send a glance in her direction and her breath instantly decided to rush away. "It's nothing at all. A holly leaf inside my boot."

"Stand still," Sir William commanded, striding toward her with that slight hesitation in his step that intrigued her so. "If you move you'll only make it worse."

"I can manage," she told him when she realized his intent. Yesterday, when he'd come into the bedchamber . . . No, she would not think of that again. This morning, when they'd made a big ball of snow to finish John's snowman, their hands had touched—and even through gloves, Sir William had had the power to singe her flesh.

He shut the front doors and advanced on Esmie. "Here we go." With obvious ease, he swept her up into his arms and took her into the green drawing room. He used a foot to close the door and carried her to a chaise.

"Really, I can do this," Esmie said, reaching for the boot.

Settling her hands in her lap, Sir William sat near her feet and lifted the appropriate ankle onto his thigh. "It will be easier for me," he told her and slid up the hem of the moss green morning gown she wore. With particular care, he held her leg and took off the fur-lined, green leather boot. A holly leaf's sharp spines clung to the sheer silk hose she wore.

"Thank you," she said, hastily trying to withdraw.

Sir William held her firmly. "You may thank me when it is done," he said.

Cold air had whipped color into his face. His thick, fair hair fell over his forehead. Surely, Esmie thought, he is the most handsome man in the world, and the most desirable. A flush stole over her body—born not of guilt but awareness.

"These . . . things"—he passed his fingertips over embroidered bowknots on her hose—"are the deuce. A man might swear they have teeth." His brows drew together whilst he took pains to extricate the tenacious holly leaf.

At last he held it aloft. "There. Free. Now let us see if the skin is broken."

She could do nothing to stop him from running a hand beneath her leg and turning it for his inspection.

"I'm sure it's quite all right." Esmie tried to pull herself more upright and farther from Sir William's disturbingly solid body.

"I do believe it is," he said, but he didn't release her. "You are finely made, Esmie." His hands were warm and strong where he slowly stroked from her toes, to her ankle and, even more slowly, on to her knee.

Where he touched her, she tingled, and the tingling spread to become an ache in that deep place for which she did not even know a name.

"Every part of you is so perfect, so desirable."

There were no appropriate words of response. She found she could not breathe quite properly.

Sir William looked at her face, and an upward curl of his lips drove the dimples into his cheeks. "That cloak is perfect on you. You were born to wear green velvet hoods trimmed with swansdown—and finer things."

"I'm grateful to have borrowed them," Esmie said, her mouth dry.

"They are yours. Lindsay would want it so."

"Oh, no!" Horrified, she leaned toward him. "I could not, *would* not accept such things."

"Yes, you could. And you will." Still smiling, he took a hand from her leg and gently removed her spectacles. "At first I thought your eyes reminded me of a particularly intelligent house cat. Now I know I was mistaken. They would bring pride to a panther—a small and very feminine panther."

Esmie only shook her head.

Sir William set the spectacles on a japanned teapoy and returned his attention to her silk-clad limb. "I have tried not to notice how beautiful you are." Crooking her knee, he set her foot on the chaise and raised the filmy skirt until it slipped to rest about her hips.

"I don't think—"

"*Don't* think," Sir William said. "Trust me, Esmie. I will not hurt you, only bring us both some measure of pleasure."

"But this should not be." Her heart beat too rapidly.

He studied what he had revealed and his face grew tense. "I think this should most definitely be," he murmured. With a single fingertip, he outlined the place where the stocking rested against bare skin. The finger moved on, flattened, traced smooth skin upward until Esmie let out a small cry. "Ah, yes," Sir William said. "This should be, but not too much, too soon."

Leaning over Esmie, he slid the hood from her head and pressed her back against the chaise. Then, as he seemed about to kiss her, his night-blue eyes flew to hers and she saw the darkness she'd seen there before.

"Do you find . . . Does the scar on my face frighten you?"

At first she thought she had misheard him. "The scar?" Wonderingly, releasing a soft breath, she raised a hand and lightly brushed the backs of her fingers down the jagged white arc on the side of his face. "No. Oh, no. It is part of you and I . . . And it pleases me greatly." What she had almost said she would not consider.

His eyelids lowered and he caught her hand, pressed his lips to the palm almost violently. The next instant, his mouth sought hers with the same demanding force. Sir William parted her lips with his own, and she gasped at the surprising sensation of his probing tongue. But the sensation was pleasant—so pleasant. Esmie closed her eyes tightly and tried to imitate each move of his mouth until he groaned. And all the while, he rubbed the sensitive underside of her leg, moving higher and higher and, finally passing beneath her clothes to knead a hip, to trail across to that place . . .

Esmie jerked her head away. "No!" She struggled, and immediately he withdrew. As quickly as her immodest position allowed, she scrambled to stand. "I'm sorry."

"There's nothing to be sorry about." Sir William was at once beside her. "Esmie, you are passionate—and I want to release that passion for both of us."

She shook her head. "I've never had these feelings before."

"Good." He did not sound angry. "Please don't turn away from me," he said, guiding her to stand before him.

Her face flamed.

"Ah, Esmie, Esmie. I tried not to do this, but I'm only a man." As he spoke, he unfastened the cloak and tossed it aside. "I shall not press you, sweet one. In time you may be ready for me."

Esmie kept her eyes on his white shirt.

"You *are* an innocent." He bent to place a kiss at the corner of her mouth then said quietly, "I want to look at you."

She did as he asked, lifting her chin until she met his gaze directly. "What is it that you want to see?" she dared to ask.

"More than you are ready for me to see," he said. "I shall content myself with the slightest sampling—if you will allow it?"

There seemed no question of denying the request. Esmie nodded.

"Yes," he said on an expelled breath. "Oh, yes, sweet girl."

The back of his forefinger came to rest beneath her jaw and slowly, so slowly, passed downward over her neck.

Esmie swallowed. "Sir William?"

A muscle in his cheek flexed. "William. Call me William." Onward his finger moved, to the dip above her collarbone. "Say it."

"Sir . . . William."

Past the bone and slower and slower, more and more lightly—his touch barely met her skin. "William, Esmie. Say *William*."

The dress she wore, of the softest muslin and a

little large, was far too low at the neck. She stood very straight, the better to ensure that no more than the inevitable was revealed.

"Come, my sweet. *William*. Say it."

"William." Esmie sighed and, of their own volition, her eyes drifted shut and her head arched back. "William."

That morning, she had tried not to look at the indecent amount of breast the low-cut dress revealed, choosing instead to rapidly hide herself in the cloak. Now the cloak was gone, and William's finger had reached the swelling curve she should have found a way to drape.

"Open your eyes, Esmie. I want to see your pleasure."

Now he spoke riddles, but she did as he asked.

"Watch my hand," he instructed and, when she did, he pursued his exploration at the same leisurely pace to the narrow lace that edged the dress's neck. His hand was tanned against her pale skin.

Her knees weakened and she reached to clutch his waistcoat for support.

"Yes," he whispered. "These are the feelings you are meant to enjoy. You are a woman intended for moments like this."

The bodice already hid little, and it did not serve to keep William from his goal. Dipping inside, he spread his fingers to cover and lift her breast.

A gasp escaped Esmie. Somehow, her sleeves slipped from her shoulders and William bent until she could no longer see how he stroked her nakedness, how his thumbs passed back and forth over her suddenly hard and throbbing nipples.

"Oh! Oh, William!" He had . . . He had taken a

nipple into his mouth to suckle, and to pull with his teeth. And the sensation . . . burning, pulsing sensation from that spot all the way deep inside her until she could scarcely stand.

William raised his head and she looked into eyes that glittered. Again his thumbs rubbed.

"No! No, this is wrong. I cannot."

His mouth turned down, and his eyes narrowed. "We cannot? Perhaps, my sweeting. Yes, perhaps you are right." With apparent resignation, he straightened the gown. "Thank you for reminding me of something I forgot for a short while."

"What did you forget?"

A slight but bitter smile made Esmie feel cold. "Why, that John and Nanny Thomas will be finished with whatever they're so secretly about in the nursery."

Painting John's Christmas present for his father. "Yes, they're bound to be down soon." Every inch of Esmie's body seemed to beg for more of William's touches.

"John charged us to produce his decorations for the house. We must not disappoint him by failing to have enough holly and evergreen boughs, must we?" His gaze slipped over her rapidly. "I'll finish alone. You would do well to rest until dinner. Too much exertion is not a good thing in one so fragile."

At the door, William hesitated and seemed about to speak.

Esmie took several steps toward him. "I've displeased you. I'm sorry. I am not experienced in these things. I—"

"Stop!" He raised wide an arm, then let it drop.

"You are perfect. And that is why we shall both forget my lapse. Do you understand?"

"No, I—"

"Forget, Esmie. As I already have."

He left and she stood in the middle of the room, looking at the open door. But of course, her innocence had made him change his mind. And he thought that because of her innocence the responsibility for holding at bay what he termed her "passion" was his.

A tremulous, tight little smile curved Esmie's mouth. He could do what he pleased with his *responsibility*. What she chose to do with her *passion* was her own affair. Sir William Granville was not to remain sole master in these matters.

7

"SWEETMEAT TARTS," JOHN SAID, HIS EYES CLOSED and his nose lifted to smell the fragrant scents of the kitchen. "I shall eat ten of them for tea."

"And you'll be giving in to temptation, Master John," Cook said, her round, perspiring face folded into its customary gloomy mold. "The flesh is the devil's tool. Its hunger is what Satan—"

"Too many tarts, my boy"—Nanny interrupted without looking up from a giant bowl of shell paste—"will make you sick."

William laughed and shook his head, as relaxed and at home seated on a bench by the range as in his wingback library chair. Nutmeg and cloves boiled among bobbing slivers of orange in a nearby pot. He leaned to push a wooden spoon through the syrupy brew.

"Five tarts, then," John said, squinting one eye and holding a finger and thumb over the tart tins as if measuring the potential size of each confection.

Clucking disapprovingly, Cook hefted a plate bearing a shivering red jelly shaped like a small castle and tromped in the direction of the dairy scullery, where the jelly would stiffen atop a cold slate slab.

"*Five* tarts," John persisted when the sound of Cook's footsteps faded.

"If Nanny agrees," William said, "then you may have *one* tart at tea. Christmas day is not until tomorrow. *Then* we may allow you to fill your greedy stomach to bursting and put you to bed. You'll moan and cry, and we shall be too engrossed in our celebrations to pay you notice."

Esmie watched William and his son and Nanny Thomas with sad, sweet yearning. They were comfortable together, and secure in presuming what this day would bring, and the next, and the next.

"Could you fetch me more eggs, Esmie?" Nanny asked, her bony arms coated with flour to the elbows. "In the basket by the sinks."

The foundation for the kitchens had been built partly underground. Esmie went to the deep sinks before a window almost on a level with the ground outside and picked up the basket of eggs.

"It hasn't snowed since the night before last," William commented. "If there's any warming, the thaw will soon free this valley."

Esmie looked out at the earth's white covering. Already there had been enough melting to form a crystalline coating pocked with holes made by drips from dissolving icicles in the eaves.

"You're quiet today, Esmie," Nanny Thomas said. "I expect you're worried about your family missing you."

"There's no one . . ." Esmie gripped the edge of a sink and closed her eyes. There was nothing to gain by ruining Christmas Eve with her parade of wretched falsehoods. Soon enough for the frightful revelation when Fennel arrived. "No one will be concerned for me. It will be assumed, correctly, that I am here."

"That's well enough, then," Nanny said. "That blush color suits you. The pearl lace sets it off perfectly, don't you think, Master William?"

In the silence that followed, Esmie felt herself blush a much darker shade than the pale pink dress.

"The dress is charming," William said at last, and Esmie released a soft sigh.

"I can hardly wait for tomorrow," John said and added anxiously, "We shall have plum pudding, too? And lemon cakes and preserved ginger?"

"And a vegetable or two, I shouldn't wonder," Nanny said, but indulgently.

Drips from the eaves fell faster. There was no certain knowledge as to the depth of snow throughout the hills. Even now someone might be on their way to Tregonitha from Polrithen . . . or Fowey.

Perhaps she should find a means to slip away now.

"I'll take the eggs then, Esmie."

She started and carried the basket to Nanny before retreating to the window once more.

"Are you sure your family won't be concerned for you?" William asked, his deep voice as formal as it had been since the disastrous—and disturbingly wonderful—episode of the day before yesterday.

"I'm quite sure," she said, praying he would not press the subject further. "Your jam roll will soon be cool, John."

"Yes, yes. I'm going to taste it." The boy's stool scraped the flagstones. "James is not yet old enough to bake jam rolls, is he, Papa?"

"Possibly not."

Yesterday, and this morning, William—*Sir* William had maintained a stiffly polite countenance in Esmie's presence. In fact, he had all but avoided even glancing in her direction.

"This roll is good," John mumbled around a mouthful of food.

"You behave yourself, young master," Nanny said promptly.

Esmie heard William chuckle. "He has been too long away from his lessons. It's well the snow is melting. Soon the servants will return, and your instructor with them, no doubt."

And Fennel.

Esmie's eyes stung. "Excuse me," she said abruptly. "There are things I must attend to in my . . . upstairs."

"Sewing, I expect," John said. "Wait till Uncle Edward gets here. And James. How surprised they'll be."

Without another word, Esmie hurried from the kitchen and through the cool corridors below stairs. The big house felt quiet and still—almost as if it waited for something.

Esmie mounted the stairs and paused. The door to the green drawing room stood open, and she could smell the scent of the evergreen boughs draped along the mantel. Crystal ornaments sparkled among the branches and painted china angels hung from ribbons of gold gauze.

Tomorrow a fire would blaze in the fireplace, and William and John would laugh together over gifts. Later they would play in the snow again—such snow as might be left. At least Esmie's own journey would be made easier. Somehow she must go to the servants' quarters to collect what few possessions she had there. When she set out for her next unknown destination, it would be without those things she'd left at Mr. Buller's.

Esmie continued up the stairs with heavy steps. Regretting the loss of borrowed finery was childish, but Lady Hawkesly's gowns and delicate slippers did please her—as did the fine hose William had so admired. Her blood heated again. He had admired far more than the hose she'd worn that day.

The tall case clock at the top of the stairs ticked loudly. Everywhere she turned there were reminders of how time moved on unaided and took her closer to leaving behind what she wanted more than she'd ever wanted anything: Sir William Granville.

Lighter footsteps thudded rapidly behind her and John caught up as she opened her chamber door. "I decided it would be best if I helped."

"Helped?" She walked into the pretty room with its airy, primrose yellow draperies and upholstery.

"Yes. To get started. I brought some things from the nursery earlier and put them in here. Sit beside the fire and I will bring them to you."

Again John seemed transported into some make-believe of his own invention. He guided Esmie to the chair and added wood to the fire.

"Did your papa teach you to build fires?" Esmie asked.

"Mm. He thinks all people should be able to look after themselves as he can."

Sir William Granville wore his strength and capability like invisible armor. "You will grow to be as strong as your father—and as gentle and kind." Yes, he also wore gentleness and kindness as easily as his broad shoulders carried a cloak.

She studied the boy's profile and saw his father. No matter where her travels led, she would never feel a soft salt breeze upon her cheek and *not* see William's lean face turned up toward the sky, his thick hair whipping and glinting. And on that breeze she would hear his deep laugh. After these weeks at Tregonitha, her world would forever carry an emptiness where William's powerful compassion had all too briefly dwelled.

John carried a small workbox to her side and set it on a chest inlaid with mother-of-pearl. "This is Aunt Lindsay's, but she never uses it." He hurried away and returned with his hands full of the softest white lawn and lace. "And these will do very well. They've been in the nursery, and I know you'll agree that they're better put to use than left lying in an old box."

On her knee, Esmie straightened the garments John gave her. A tiny pleated gown with a matching cap that tied beneath the chin with satin ribbons. "These are beautiful." More clothing proved to be just as beguiling, particularly a long robe trimmed with yards of delicate lace and having an underlay of several embroidered cotton slips. "A christening gown," Esmie remarked. "Very lovely."

John's head was insinuated between Esmie's face and the clothes. "If you look closely, you will see there is mending to be done. Some of the threads are coming undone and there are holes. Little holes, but they make the clothes unsuitable for a new baby, don't they?" He glanced up for affirmation.

"Oh—yes, yes. Undoubtedly." Suddenly she guessed what all this was about. John wished to give gifts to his new baby nephew and wanted to be certain they were perfect. Esmie nodded and opened the workbox. "Let me see if I can find appropriate thread here."

"Good!" John said, lacing his fingers together. "Capital. How long will this take you?"

"Um—"

"Roughly. Just so I can know what to plan for. It would be so nice if it could happen by Christmas." He looked at her earnestly. "That's tomorrow."

"I know." If she promised, she would have to honor that promise. And that might mean staying longer than she intended. "Well, it's possible I can finish before tomorrow." If she worked hard, she could complete the minor repairs by tonight and leave in the dark hours of early morning.

"It'll be done by then?" John asked, his eyes wide.

"I shall do my best," Esmie assured him.

"Capital! In that case I must leave you alone. Uncle Edward warned me that men do not belong at times like this."

After John had slipped away, Esmie selected a long white coat made entirely of lace and threaded a needle. She began putting tiny stitches into the fallen hem.

The coat and several other garments had been mended, when a rap on the door startled Esmie. "Come in." Even before William's face appeared, she knew who she would see. "Good afternoon," she said, for the day was beginning to wane.

He stepped inside. "Are you well?"

"Yes, thank you, Sir William."

"Good." He frowned. "I had asked you to call me William."

He had indeed, but she'd doubted he still held kind thoughts toward her. "William," she said clearly.

"I spoke with Nanny about the sewing." He was abrupt. "I gather John has found you a particular project."

She held aloft the smallest of infant shifts. "Indeed. He has not given me the child's name, but I assume he has a particular infant in mind for this."

The smudges of color that flared across his cheekbones surprised Esmie. "Do not allow John to make you uncomfortable," he said.

"He hasn't—doesn't."

"I think you are being kind in humoring the boy." William approached until he stood only inches away, looking down upon her. "We haven't spoken of what passed between us the other afternoon. My fault, I fear."

Slow heat began burning within Esmie. "There is nothing to say, except that I regret not being able to please you."

His hand, stroking her hair, stilled her. Her fingers curled into her palms.

"You are able to please me," he told her. "It is the consequence of such pleasure that cannot be endured."

He puzzled her but she dared not ask his meaning. "As you say."

"John has come to love you. He wants to keep you here." The rhythmic stroking across her crown lulled Esmie. "Would you consider moving into the house permanently? Would that be a great inconvenience to your family—to lose your company?"

Esmie's heart seemed to stop beating entirely. She could not fathom what he meant—unless he was suggesting one of those infamous liaisons she'd heard hinted at in connection with certain arrangements between men and women. She dropped the needle and pressed her hands to her heated cheeks. A *ladybird!* He thought that since she'd succumbed so easily to his advances, she'd willingly become a kept woman!

"No, Sir William," she managed to say at last. "That would not be possible. Absolutely not. And now I think I would prefer to be alone." Alone with her shame and the certain knowledge that she must depart Tregonitha with all haste.

He left her without speaking again.

Esmie sat silently. The skin on her face felt stretched and her eyes prickled with unshed tears. Whatever happened, she would not regret the time she had spent here with William. Somehow she would find an answer to her problems and make a life for herself, but there could never be anyone who would erase the memory of the way this man made her feel.

From the next room—his room—came muffled sounds.

He'd asked her to remain in the only capacity a man of his rank *could* offer a woman of the station to which Esmie had sunk. She should not blame him for that. And he'd lost much, suffered much. He deserved some comfort.

With shaking hands, she set aside the infant clothes.

What could it hurt for her to offer him comfort, at least in the last few hours before she left this house forever?

Esmie stood up and smoothed the pink muslin with its stripes of pearly silk threads. An embrace, shared warmth . . . a kiss . . . She could give him these if they pleased him.

Too few steps took her into the corridor and to his bedchamber. Here she almost lost her nerve, but she knocked. The door opened immediately and Esmie almost cried out. Naked to the waist, a glass of some liquor in one hand, William stared at her with the thunderous concentration of an angry stranger.

"I'm sorry." She made to turn away.

William's free hand closed on her arm and she was drawn into his room. "Do *not* say again that you are sorry." He steered her before the fire where she stood, her gaze firmly fixed on the floor.

"Why are you here?"

Pulsing in her throat threatened to choke her. "I don't want you to be angry with me."

"I'm not. Why have you come?" His glass clicked as he set it down.

She could not simply blurt out the reason. "John means a great deal to me. I would like to make him happy if I could."

William made an impatient noise. "That's gracious of you. You have fine feelings for children."

And for this child's father, she wanted to shout.

"Look up," William demanded.

Hesitantly, she did so. Heavy russet drapes closed out the waning light of a gray late afternoon. Behind William stood a heavy mahogany four-poster. It was at the bed that Esmie looked, and she easily imagined him stretched out there, his fine body relaxed, the sharply carved lines of his face vulnerable in sleep.

More images to carry with her.

"Look at me, Esmie."

This she also did. He was half turned from her and the fire formed a nimbus about his blond hair and the outline of his muscular torso and massive arms. Clothes had not done the man's physical power justice.

"You like what you see?" There was a suggestion of mocking amusement in his voice. "How much, I wonder, could you like all of me?"

Esmie was helpless to resist the arm that swept

her against his chest—even had she wished to do so. She lowered her lashes, spread her fingers on warm skin covered with soft, gilded hair and braced for William's fiercely possessive kiss.

"This, I know, pleases you," he said. His breath fanned her brow. "There is so much I could teach you; so much I long to show you."

Then teach me, show me, her heart begged him, but she said nothing aloud.

Shyly, she stroked his wide chest, felt the pattern of muscles made hard by the physical work he enjoyed.

William held her head and rested his cheek atop her hair. "Your touch is like sunlight on skin too long hidden," he told her. "The warmth brings intense pleasure. So gentle, Esmie. You are so gentle."

Rising to her toes, she rested her hands on his shoulders and pressed her lips to his neck—and felt him stiffen. Where this daring had come from she knew not, neither did she care.

His fingers worked in her hair, removing and dropping pins until the weight of her black curls slid down her back. William enfolded her, held her close in arms that trembled even as they made any escape impossible.

"Sweet one." With one hand he tilted up her chin until he could look down into her eyes. His own were a blue so dark as to be almost black. "Dear God, tell me what to do." He sounded agonized.

Esmie frowned and sighed afresh as he rested his mouth on her brow. Again and again he kissed her there, all the while gently running his fingers through her curls. In turn, she combed the hair on his chest with her fingertips. Never before had she seen a man without a shirt. After William she would never care to do so again.

His lips made a path down the side of her face and, finally, to her mouth. With lips closed, he gently, so gently kissed her, rocked her head from side to side with sweetly searing passion, then raised his face to study her once more. He smiled, a small, unbearably sad smile. "This is the night for making wishes," he told her.

"Christmas Eve," Esmie whispered. "Yes. Wishes."

He linked his hands loosely about her neck and tipped his head to one side. His eyes fell shut the instant before the kiss began again. Back and forth, grazing sensitive skin with exquisite control, he played her mouth until the tip of his tongue delicately parted her lips and slipped inside. Esmie's breath grew short and she stood on tiptoe again to increase the pressure and depth between them.

When they were both gasping, William crossed his arms around her shoulders and gazed down into her face. "Stay, Esmie," he said. "Grant me my Christmas wish. Remain with me."

The happiness she felt might be foolhardy, but it was irresistible. To whom would it matter in what capacity she continued in this house? To Fennel? To the other servants? To Nanny Thomas? The last thought turned Esmie's stomach, but she was fond of the old lady and believed her feelings were returned. There might be hope for understanding there. As for the others, they would learn to accept, or at least to be silent.

With hope and joy slowly unfurling in her breast,

she stared back at William. "Perhaps." Her gaze fell to his chest. Wonderingly, she stroked it again and drew lines downward with her forefingers. "What will your sister say? And her husband?"

"They will accept my decision in this, as in all things."

"But—" She paused, frowning afresh, and involuntarily took a step away. Her right hand had met something knotted. Esmie dropped her arms and surveyed what her touch had encountered. On William's left side, the side that had been turned from her, and disappearing beneath the waist of his breeches, were a terrible scattering of vicious scars. Twisted white lumps overlapped the widened evidence of a great sickle-shaped wound. Across his abdomen more poorly-healed lacerations stretched like the claw marks of some huge cat.

"Esmie?"

She moved farther away from him. "Such cruelty." Her eyes sought his again, and she saw deep pain there. So this was the reason for his moody withdrawals from her. This was why he would no longer allow himself to completely trust another human being. Once he had given such trust, and it had almost caused his death.

William Granville had nothing more to give another than the fleeting attachment his still-wounded spirit would allow.

The pain in his eyes . . .

Esmie parted her lips to breathe but discovered she could not. She loved him! She would always love William. If she could, she would gladly hold and keep him forever and soothe away the pain from his soul, and the loss.

"Esmie?" He moved toward her, but she retreated. "Can you not accept me as I am?"

As he was? A man wounded not by the weapon that almost killed his body, but by the scars that remained in places she could not see. She loved him more than her life, but to stay with him would surely cost her that life. All he wanted was to possess her for the moment. Already her heart ached with her need for him. Not for one more second could she endure looking upon him and knowing he would, all too soon, turn her aside.

"Esmie? Can you?"

"No! No, I cannot." Shaking her head, she turned and fled.

8

WHAT MAID WOULD NOT HAVE LOOKED UPON HIS wrecked body with disgust?

William prowled about his room. He'd discarded strong liquor as a panacea hours ago. It didn't touch the darkness in his soul, or the rage that had swept in again—after years of absence—against Antun Pollack. His *friend* Antun Pollack had sold William in the name of greed—and Maria with him. And now, when there might have been hope for renewed joy, Pollack's work had robbed William yet again.

No sound came from Esmie's room.

"Esmie, Esmie." Even the sound of her name, whispered in the darkened room, whipped his desire for the girl.

He'd given her no warning. And he'd shocked her.

William braced his hands flat on the wall and let his head fall forward. The case clock at the end of the hall struck. One, two, three, and on and on to eleven. In an hour it would be Christmas Day.

William wanted to spend Christmas Day with Esmie. He wanted to spend this night with her wrapped in his arms . . . in his bed.

Two doors—and he could be beside her.

He hesitated only a few seconds more before quietly easing open the door to his dressing room and passing inside. Closing himself in to cut off light, he felt his way to the other side and let himself slowly into Esmie's bedchamber.

The room was empty.

William cast about, looking this way and that, but no—she was not there. On the bed lay a folded sheet of paper and he snatched it up.

"My dearest William," she had written. *"Thank you. These few days spent with you will be treasured for the rest of my life. Tonight I felt what you could never have told me; some evil touched you and stole away any peace you might have had. I am not strong enough or clever enough to help you forget what is past. I am also far beneath your station and could not become the helpmate you need, a woman to be proud of in any circles.*

"There are certain other things I have wanted to tell you—about myself. I never found the courage and now they no longer matter.

"So I go, William. I could not stay even one hour more knowing I am helpless to ease your pain, but I pray that at this holy time of year, the Lord will bless you with a new beginning, with someone who can be what you want and need her to be.

"Forget me, loved one, for I am not what I appear and—although injustice has been my lot—the apparent truth would surely turn you from me forever.

"Yes, William, I do love you. Esmie."

William stared at the paper until the words blurred.

I do love you.

He must find her. Immediately. Where could she be? The probable answer chilled William to the bone. She would leave Tregonitha and attempt to go, God knew where, through the ice cold night. Calculating wildly, he tried to fathom how long ago she might have left. Minutes or hours, he had no way of knowing. Casting back over the time since she'd quit his bedchamber, he tried to recall when the sounds of her moving in her room had ceased.

Not so long ago, surely?

The sooner his search began, the sooner he might find her. William still wore top boots, and left the upper floor without stopping for a coat. In the entrance hall, he donned a heavy cloak and let himself out into air so cold it seared his throat.

Running, he made a circle to the back of the house and returned again to the front. A high white moon cast shadows upon the crusted snow.

Where to start? Where would a slip of a woman go beneath the moon and stars of a frozen night that was the herald of Christmas Day?

He would saddle Hades and search until he found her. Without Esmie, there could never again be peace for William.

Retracing his steps, this time he struck out for the stables. As he entered the low stone building, a ragged chorus of whinnies met him, together with the restless scuffling of hoofs.

In the tack room, he hefted a saddle over his arm and snagged Hades's bridle.

Something moved.

William swung on his heel in time to see a flash of green disappearing through the stable doors.

"Esmie!" He dropped the tack and ran after what could only have been the hem of Lindsay's cloak, worn by the only woman likely to do so this night. "Esmie! Stop! Stop—*now,* I tell you!"

In the brittle light of the moon, the small figure in swirling green showed clearly. Esmie—he knew it was she—sped over the crunching snow, heading for gates that led to the driveway.

William paused for the moment he knew he could afford. Relief and gratitude filled his heart to bursting. "Yes, William," he murmured. "I *do* love you." And she would not escape him, not tonight or ever.

He followed her then, followed until he heard her poor, rasping breath sobbing vaporous clouds into the darkness.

"Stop," he said, drawing close enough to shoot an arm around her.

Rather than obey, she tried to spin away. "Let

me go!" Pushing at him, gasping, she scrambled and began to fall.

William grappled with her flailing hands. "Little fool," he said through clenched teeth. "Esmie, *cease.*"

Too late. Esmie's foot connected with his knee. Still holding her in one arm, William pitched forward to sprawl atop her on the snow's blessed cushion.

The impact jarred his injured leg and he ground his teeth more tightly together.

"I could not get into the servants' quarters."

He stared down into her eyes. Somewhere in the struggle her spectacles had been lost. "And what"—he took in a deep breath—"what, pray, would you have done there? Hidden for the rest of your life?"

Green velvet and swansdown made a beguiling frame for her loose hair and lovely but frightened face. "I would have taken my own things, but I could not get them. Of course, my own cloak is at Point Cottage. But I would have sent Lady Hawkesly's things back as soon as I could."

"Esmie—"

"I was not trying to steal them. I have never stolen anything in my life."

"Of course you haven't. Were you going to ride a horse to get away?"

"No! Oh, no. I would never take anything from you, William. But I saw you leave the house and sought to hide until you went back inside again. Since you left by the front doors I did not consider that you might go to the stables."

Somewhere in the moments since they'd fallen

together, her hands had stolen over his shoulders. She clung to his neck.

"Aren't you cold, Esmie?"

Her great eyes showed no comprehension.

"I am. I think we should go where we can be warm, don't you?"

She nodded yes, and William got to his feet. Once upright, he promptly lifted her into his arms and walked slowly toward the house. "I found your note."

"Oh." Esmie turned her face into his chest.

"It embarrasses you that I read what you wrote?"

"I did not expect to see you again—not ever."

He chose to enter Tregonitha by the front door. Once inside, he took Esmie to the library, where the embers of a fire still glowed. Without fear that she'd flee again, he set his light burden down and added wood until flames blazed afresh.

He took longer than necessary over the task, stealing time to make up his mind about what he wanted to do and what it was that he believed good and honorable. Maria's death after childbirth had been the result of a fever in unsuitable circumstances. Nanny Thomas had begged him to believe this and put aside the blame. Tonight, for the first time, he wanted nothing more or less than to accept what he'd been told.

"Esmie"—he faced her—"I should like to lie here before the fire with you. I should like to make your body my own and offer myself to you . . . unless you find my scars offensive."

"No!" She raised a hand to his face. "You are beautiful, William. Tall and strong and straight. And the evidence of those wounds humbles me and makes me want to heal. Not heal what I see, but what I cannot see. That's why I left you, because I thought I couldn't help you. Do you understand?"

He understood. "You were wrong." Smiling a little, he caught her wrist and kissed the fragile skin there. "Our cloaks will make an adequate bed, Esmie. If you agree."

"John? And Nanny Thomas?"

"The door is locked."

He felt her tremble, and a shock of possessive desire traveled his veins. Despite his need for her, she was an innocent, and this must be accomplished gently.

William swung off his cloak and spread it atop the skin rug before the hearth. Before he could straighten, green velvet joined heavy black wool. Her boots were swiftly dispensed with.

He began to unbutton his shirt, but Esmie covered his hands and lowered them. She fumbled over the task, but he made no attempt to help her remove the shirt. His pulse quickened to thunder at his temples. This girl's sweet ministrations, her determination to please despite her inexperience, softened his heart as he'd thought would never again be possible.

"Should I do the same?" she asked, her voice a husky whisper.

"Yes," he told her, sinking to his knees, reaching for her waist.

"No." Very firmly, she stopped him. "If looking at me brings pleasure, then I shall give you that pleasure as my gift."

He smiled up at her. "Your Christmas gift to me, perhaps?"

"Just so, William." Raising her arms, she loosed the tapes that closed her bodice. In seconds the gown fell like a pool of pink ice about her feet. "Whatever I am is all I have to give you."

"And it is more than I dreamed of possessing," he told her, scarcely able to breathe at all now.

Clad only in a diaphanous shift, Esmie stood before him, bracing her slight weight on his shoulders. "This is very strange," she told him. Slowly crossing her arms, she pulled the shift from her shoulders, and just as slowly, her lush breasts, tipped by thrusting nipples, were revealed.

The shift fell. Esmie closed her eyes and stood very still, firelight sending dancing shadows over her body. William devoured her with his gaze, but forced himself to wait, to watch. Her hipbones shaded a smooth, flat belly, and the dark triangle below was as black as the hair that cascaded around her shoulders. Her only garments were the silk hose still tied above the knees.

Muscles in William's thighs jolted. His restraint thinned.

When he grasped her hips, Esmie jumped. He kissed her belly, slipped his hands to span her waist and on, upward, to take and test the firm weight of her breasts, to carefully pinch her rigid nipples.

"*William*," Esmie moaned.

Every nerve in his body demanded release. "Yes, my love. Cry out! Let go and *feel*."

"I . . . I . . ." Her breath sobbed, and she jutted her hips in mindless response.

William smiled. "I think this is what you seek, Esmie." Gripping her waist once more, he dipped his face and slipped his tongue into that place sheltered by silken darkness.

Esmie cried out again and her short nails raked his shoulders. He revelled in the pain, even as he flicked the small nubbin that swelled to his tongue's touch.

"William!" Esmie writhed, and he felt her flesh leap and shudder in wave after wave whilst her legs weakened.

He supported her, took her slight weight and lowered her to their tumbled bed of cloaks.

"I do not know how to—"

"Hush," William said and silenced her with a long, searching kiss. With his knees astride her thighs, he stroked her breasts, and his own need pulsed in screaming swords along his veins. Through gritted teeth he said, "Take what I give you. This is what your body has waited for." And he slid his face down until he could fill his mouth with first one breast and then the other.

And she cried out, sobbed out the exquisitely quickened awareness that must wrack her body, a body fashioned for his.

Suckling, slanting his face to feel the soft, heavy pressure of her flesh against his cheek, William worked loose his breeches. He kissed her lips, rolled aside to remove the rest of his clothes, knelt again and drew her up to meet him.

Thigh to thigh, breast to breast, they strained to give, and to take. "Esmie, sweet, may I make you mine?"

Against his lips she murmured, "I am yours."

His manhood sprang ever harder and hotter—

even more ready. William fought for control whilst his fingers tested her readiness. She gasped. Her passage was small and tight. He must not rush her. Gently probing and withdrawing, he drew forth her sweet moisture until Esmie panted and clamped his hand against her, and he could bear no more.

Gasping, fighting for the last shreds of control, William rested his brow on hers and willed his heart to be calm.

Between them, he felt Esmie's hand slide down. She touched him and he cried out. Her fingers closed around him and she drew in a sharp breath. "I did not know," she said. "So . . . much?"

"Hush, sweet one." Shuddering from the effort of restraint, he stretched her out once more on their soft bed of velvet and wool.

"William?"

"My love. This will not be exactly as I would wish. But next time you shall know the fullness of what we will share."

He took her slender wrists above her head and held them there. Carefully, supporting his weight on his elbows, he parted her thighs with a knee. When he entered her, he heard her name jar past his lips, heard her cry, "William! William, I love you."

There was the slim barrier that still kept him from her, and then it was breached. The drive of his manhood could no longer be contained. He thrust, and thrust, and the woman in his arms took, and gave—and sobbed with him into the hot, dark place where minds are laced together without seams.

In the distance, the case clock chimed—one, two, three, four, and onward to midnight.

"Happy Christmas, Esmie," he said softly and rolled until they lay side by side, her head on his shoulder.

Yes, it was good and honorable to . . . to love this woman.

Esmie awoke to find herself alone in William's big bed. He had carried her there some hours earlier. Alarmed, she turned her head and immediately relaxed. He stood by the window, looking out at the approaching dawn.

"William?" She bit her lip. Now she must tell her story. "William, it's time."

He looked at her over his shoulder but she couldn't see his face. "Time?"

"I shall tell you quickly and you must not try to stop me. What you believe you believe. *I* shall not try to change your mind." And afterward she might well quit this house, and William, forever.

"I forged my letters of recommendation," she said in a rush. "I have never been a housemaid before."

After a short pause he said, "You are not one now."

"You were not to stop me, remember," she reminded him. "Because of my father's gambling debts and his subsequent death at the hands of an enraged creditor, my mother and I were left with nothing but a house in London and no means with which to make our living.

"I will not bore you with all the ins and outs of my sordid story. Mama gave our house to a couple in exchange for keeping a roof over our heads. In time, after Mama died, I was permitted to remain as long as I served as a tutor to the young ladies who came to what was then an academy."

"Esmie, my poor dear one." William came to sit beside her.

She would not let him take her hands. "Please, let me finish before you decide you want to touch me again. In time a gentleman, an acquaintance of the woman who took over our house, showed an interest in me and asked for my hand."

William's stillness was not of her imagination. "This angered the woman's daughter, who wanted the man for herself. She managed to *mislay* a valuable brooch. Then the brooch appeared in my room and I was accused of theft. I fled before the constable arrived."

When William didn't respond, she covered her eyes. "We never had any relatives that I knew, but I remembered Papa talking about a cousin in Cornwall, and that's why I came in this direction. That was a year ago. What little money I had ran out and then I was forced to find a place. I had arrived in Fowey when I heard of a vacant position at Tregonitha."

"And what of the aunt with whom you live?"

"I . . . I have no aunt. So, you see that I am a liar and you only have my word that I am not also a thief."

After a silence that seemed endless, William stood and said, "Yes, only your word. I shall go and tend the fires. Soon John will be up and demanding his gift."

The door opened and closed and Esmie was left alone.

9

"ESMIE! AT LAST!" JOHN, SCAMPERING IN THE DIRECTion of the drawing room, had spied her hovering on the stairs. "Happy Christmas! Papa said you were probably tired and I might not awaken you."

"That was considerate." *Tired?* An inadequate description for the mixture of wonder and confusion that had kept her pacing the bedchamber until she found enough courage to come down.

"Papa *guessed* my fantastical bird's name was Blue Jonathan all on his own!"

"Your father is a perceptive man." But he had not perceived Esmie's masquerade, and the discovery had, rightfully, disappointed and turned him from her.

John approached. "Papa gave me a telescope. He said it is for now and for the man I will become—a grown-up telescope."

"Do not grow up too fast," Esmie said, a tight feeling about her heart. "Your papa is a fine man, a fine father—and you will be just like him, but I'm very fond of the boy you are now, too."

"So am I."

Esmie's hand went to her breast. William's voice had the power to stun her, and she knew she would always be able to close her eyes and remember its timbre, even when she was far away from Tregonitha in both time and distance.

"How are you, Esmie?"

Was he also thinking of last night? She did not look directly at him, but bobbed a brief curtsey and said, "I am well, thank you. It is a beautiful Christmas morning, is it not?"

"Indeed. If the sun continues to shine so, we shall soon be set free."

Set free? No doubt he meant that he would soon be free of her. Esmie wished the thaw need never come.

"Come and see my telescope." John marched ahead into the drawing room.

"Yes, Esmie," William said. "Do see John's gift."

Wearing no coat, and with his fists on his lean hips, he stood in the hallway, looking up at her. A full-sleeved white shirt and neckcloth contrasted startlingly with his black waistcoat. Esmie's gaze dropped to his wide chest, his flat waist, and on . . . to braced legs she had no difficulty remembering without his skin-hugging breeches.

Would she forever continue to burn at the mere thought of this man's gentle force?

"Come," he said, extending a hand. "John is excited. It's important to him that you share his pleasure."

And what of you? she silently asked. *Do you not long, just a little, to share again your pleasure with me?* Hesitantly, she descended the remaining stairs and placed her hand into his warm, strong fingers.

"The dress becomes you," he said quietly. "Only a woman of your vibrant coloring could wear silk the color of flame."

"If you like it, you should compliment Nanny on her taste." Stopping her wretched blush was impossible. "She set it out for me. And the slippers, and the rope of pearls and silk roses for my hair." She need not mention that Nanny had left these things in William's room whilst Esmie slept in his bed.

"I take it you approve?"

"Beautiful. All so beautiful." And all borrowed.

The sun he'd spoken of shone through the amber-colored fanlight above the front door to burnish his hair. Esmie drew in a breath and held it. In this light his eyes were black and unfathomable—and daunting. She looked to his mouth and felt her own lips part.

He smiled slightly before leading her into the drawing room. "I understand I have you to thank for the wonderful birds."

She stood beside him. "John made them himself," she told him. "I merely told him how they could be constructed." Her head barely reached William's shoulder, and his superior strength seemed to surround her.

A fine brass telescope was positioned near a window, but rather than hover over the instrument, John waited in the center of the room and studied Esmie closely.

"So," she said. "This is your gift. Truly a man's telescope."

The boy frowned. "You did not complete the sewing, then?"

"Now, John—"

"John and I had an agreement," Esmie said, interrupting William. "And I intend to keep the bargain I made. The mending shall be done just as soon as possible."

"But—" John paused, his head cocked. "Listen. Horses!"

There was no time to listen, and certainly not enough to allow for looking out the windows, before a great commotion commenced at the front doors.

"Master William!" Nanny's excited voice sounded from that region. "Oh, Master William, *do* come!"

William promptly strode from the room with John at his heel. Esmie remained behind and sank to sit on the edge of a couch. The dress settled around delicate red satin slippers like a pool of silken fire—or, as William had said, flame.

"They're here!" John barrelled back into the drawing room, his dark eyes shining. "Uncle Edward and Aunt Lindsay. It is too bad James is too *little* to have accompanied them on horseback, but Uncle Edward will tell him our news and that will be almost as good."

Esmie wished fervently that she might disappear. The thought of facing a viscount and the undoubtedly perfect lady who was his wife made her feel quite faint.

"Take me to her *at once.*" An extraordinarily husky female voice preceded the appearance of a small, very blond woman who seemed on the brink of bursting from excitement. "Aha! Just as I thought. A beauty, but with character. Such eyes and hair!"

Walking ahead of William, a very tall, very dark-haired man followed in the woman's wake. One glance at his face and Esmie did indeed feel almost faint. No man could equal William Granville's male beauty, but if a female were more attracted to dark than to fair-haired men, this one would render her paralyzed by longing. Even Nanny Thomas, who hovered near the woman, seemed awed by this new male presence.

"Lindsay, love," he said, pulling the woman against him where he could keep a possessive arm around her waist. "Do go a little slower. Give the girl a chance."

Lovely blue eyes smiled upon the man before they were returned to a scrutiny of Esmie. "I'm very precipitous. Everybody says so, don't they, Edward? William?"

"Mm," the men intoned in unison.

Edward, Viscount Hawkesly, and his lady would command complete attention in any company.

Esmie plucked uncomfortably at her skirts. "Lady Hawkesly, I do hope you'll forgive me for using your clothes, but—"

"Don't mention it." That lady flapped a hand in dismissal. "Clothes are to be worn and you needed them. That looks far better on you than it ever did on me. It's yours."

Trying to refuse would be rude. "Thank you, my lady." Esmie ached with embarrassment.

"And now it's my turn to speak," William said, moving to her side. "This is Miss Esmie Bennett."

"I *knew* it." Lady Hawkesly pivoted to allow her husband to remove the hooded fur cloak she wore over a riding habit the same shade of blue as her eyes. "Ever since we heard that perfectly terrible story in Fowey I *knew* she would be here. I felt in my heart that providence had somehow kept her here in William's care." Shiny black feathers swept beguilingly from a small velvet bonnet to frame one ear.

Despite gathering alarm, Esmie could not help but smile. William's animated sister demanded good humor.

"You were right to keep her here, William," Lord Hawkesly said gravely. "That ruffian's a monster. To think of a poor slip of a girl unknowingly falling into such hands. Turns the stomach."

Silence followed. Lady Hawkesly's smile wavered.

"I take it you speak of Mr. Buller," Esmie said. This discomfort was of her making, and she would end it with all speed. "Sir William knows nothing of that person."

"Why?" Lady Hawkesly asked. "I don't understand. The tale is all over Fowey. That—that, *person*—very much in his cups, I might mention—anyway, he bragged in some inn of how he'd caused a foolish maid to run away, leaving behind her few wretched possessions at his boarding establishment. These he had sold for drinking money. His *due*, he said, since she left without paying her rent and after turning aside his *generous* offer of companionship. Hah! One can well imagine the nature of *that* offer."

"What is this to do with Esmie?" William asked quietly.

"*She* is the poor maid, of course," Lady Hawkesly said. "Although she certainly doesn't resemble any servant I ever encountered before. The father of a girl named Fennel—also an employee of yours, William—anyway, he went to Reverend Winslow and told every word exactly as Mr. Buller told it to him. We've been staying with Reverend Winslow, by the way. Julian and dear Sarah are there, too. Anyway, Reverend Winslow said he was certain the girl had told you her predicament and that you were taking care of her."

"I told another lie," Esmie said miserably. "I did not miss the cart to Fowey by accident."

William's arm, surrounding her shoulders, sent Esmie's breath rushing from her body. He looked down into her face. "My poor darling girl. You did not dare to go back to Fowey. That is the story, isn't it?"

She nodded.

"So brave," he murmured. "We shall talk more of this."

"Uncle Edward," John said, suddenly and loudly. "It is all going *very well.*"

All eyes centered on the boy. The viscount inclined his head questioningly. "Is it indeed?"

"Oh, yes. Papa found Esmie—who is very happy to spend time with him." He drew himself up. "She is moved into the room next to his, just as you said was necessary. And she can sew!"

"Can she, by Jove?" Edward said, a smile beginning to spread and reveal very white teeth.

Lady Hawkesly smiled, too—rather like a beautiful blond doll who had received her most fervent desire.

"John, this can wait," William said and his grip on Esmie tightened. "More importantly, I have to tell your uncle and aunt that Esmie and I are betrothed."

Uncomprehending, Esmie stared up at him.

"Since the hills are now passable, I shall be riding to see Reverend Winslow shortly to make the necessary arrangements."

The chuckle Esmie heard was Nanny Thomas's. The old lady folded her arms and nodded smugly.

"You are even more clever than I thought you were, William," Lady Hawkesly announced. "I knew we had only to give you time to find the perfect wife."

"And mama," John said stoutly. "She had hoped to finish the clothes by today, Uncle Edward, but they won't take much longer, will they, Esmie?"

She shook her head.

"There!" John radiated triumph. "May I go with you to tell James that—"

"We'll decide later," William said, releasing Esmie just long enough to usher his son to the door. "Take him in the kitchen, Nanny. Give him those ten sweetmeat tarts. And lots of preserved ginger. And lemon cake. Give him *anything.*"

In mid-afternoon, promising to pave the way for a wedding, Edward and Lindsay departed for Reverend Winslow's rectory taking John with them. Nanny Thomas, yawning behind a gnarled hand, reminded William that she was "too old for such excitement" and excused herself.

William prowled the drawing room, pausing from time to time to regard Esmie. "Are you tired?" he said at last. She had sat, unmoving, since Lindsay and Edward left.

"No."

He moved on again, past four elegant windows draped with green damask, in front of the white plastered fireplace he'd always admired, and behind the couch where Esmie sat—or rather, perched.

"You feel uncomfortable with me?"

"No."

"You're angry?"

"No."

From his spot behind her, he looked down on a fragile white neck and shoulders charmingly teased by black curls that spilled from a loose concoction at her crown. Through these were threaded a rope of fine pearls and sprays of tiny, red silk roses. He drove his fingers into the back of the couch. He wanted to touch those curls, and her shoulders.

"Esmie, will you kindly tell me why I have this feeling that you are vexed?"

She turned sideways but kept her eyes downcast. "You feel it because I *am* vexed."

The dress, square cut at the neck and extremely abbreviated of bodice, showed off her splendid breasts—which he would also like to touch.

They were alone, dammit, and *betrothed*. And he wished to enjoy every moment of these wonderful developments. "I asked you to explain why"—he frowned—"Did you say you *are* vexed?"

"Yes."

Women! They could be so damnably difficult, yet so very endearing . . . and so very desirable . . .

"Would you care to tell me why you are not happy?"

"I didn't say I wasn't happy. I said I was vexed—with you." Her chin came up and she aimed a ferocious glare at him. "*You* selected these beautiful clothes for me, not Nanny Thomas. She told me."

"And that vexes you?"

"Not nearly as much as the fact that you never asked me to marry you."

William bowed his head to hide a smile. "Ah, so that's it. I was supposed to do things correctly. Down on the knee and all that."

"You were supposed to at least consult me before taking me for granted and announcing to the world that we were to be married." She took off her spectacles and rubbed them fiercely with a fold of her skirt. "And what, pray, possessed you to be so impetuous in so important a matter?"

William went to the front of the couch and stopped her as she would have replaced her spectacles. Instead, he took them from her and set them aside. "Can we really call my announcement impetuous?"

"I do not understand you."

Now he grinned. "You are most charming when you're overset. Should I find some hartshorn, or merely carry you off to bed?" Ah yes, what an excellent idea.

"You are laughing at me."

"No, no." He shook his head emphatically. "I assure you that I am not laughing at you, Esmie."

"You chose to say we were betrothed without so much as a word to me."

"Indeed, I did. That is *exactly* what I did."

"And . . . You do not even attempt to deny it?"

"Absolutely not." He found her pert nose intriguing, and her soft lips, and . . . "We shall be married just as soon as the formalities can be dispensed with."

"Oh!" Esmie's lips remained parted. "You are so *arrogant*. So sure of yourself."

"True."

"*True?* Just like that?"

"You told me you loved me."

"When?"

Grinning wickedly, he dropped to one knee before her and raised one of her hands to his mouth. "You wrote it to me in a letter. And—although, of course, a gentleman does not usually remind a lady of such things—but there were several moments last night when you referred to love, weren't there?"

She turned a delightful shade of pink. "That does not explain your behavior with the Hawkeslys."

"Perhaps not. However, since they assume we are already expecting a happy addition to our family, it seemed . . . politic?"

"I beg your pardon?"

"Surely you noted Edward's concern for your health."

She frowned and said slowly, "Yes."

"Yes, well, you may or may not be with child, but John has clearly indicated that the event is only a matter of time, so . . ."

Her shocked expression amused him. His thumb, pressed to her lips, stopped the threatened outburst. "It is all a matter of your ability to sew," he told her, and followed with a brief explanation of John's understanding about the finer points of human reproduction.

At first Esmie's eyes widened with stunned disbelief, only to soften to twinkling mirth. "And I trotted merrily into such a pickle," she declared. "One day I shall have words to say to Lord Hawkesly."

"In good time," William said, sobering. "For now, I should like it very much if all your attention were for me. Can you forgive me for not inspiring trust in you?"

She laced her fingers with his. "I do trust you, William."

"You didn't trust me enough to tell me how cruel life had been to you. You suffered trying to hide your past, when you should have been able to confide in me. That causes me pain."

"Is that why you left me this morning?"

He felt again the self-disgust he'd suffered then. "Yes. I needed to be alone. But, if you'll agree to be my wife I'll never want to be alone again."

"Yes."

"I know what I did with Edward and Lindsay amounts to shameless manipulation, but I promise we'll have a good life." From a drawer in a nearby satinwood chest he removed a long black leather box. "This belonged to my mother. It is my gift to you—for Christmas if not for—"

Esmie cut off his words with her lips. She kissed him softly, sensuously, slipping the tip of her tongue along his bottom lip. "William," she said, lifting her face to look at him. "I said yes. *Yes!* I want to be your wife. And John's mama."

Nothing had prepared him for the swelling emotion that smote him. "You will?"

"I will."

His. She would be his. Framing her face, he kissed her soundly until she beat on his shoulders and pushed away, gasping for breath.

William opened the black case and presented it to Esmie, and laughed aloud at the shocked "Oh," she uttered. "Rubies, my sweet. For a woman who should often wear the richness of fire and flame."

She seemed overwhelmed and almost cringed when he took the collar of gems and draped it about her neck. Gently, he eased her forward until he could fasten the piece. "Thank you for agreeing to be my wife. Not that you could possibly have cried off."

As Esmie fingered the stones, her eyes gradually regained focus. Her lips became pursed and her green eyes sparked. "And why, pray, could I not cry off?"

"Because your reputation would be ruined." Getting to his feet, he lifted her slight weight into his arms. "And our child would be a bastard."

"Child?" she sputtered. "Edward's little joke with John is just that. A joke. We are *not* expecting a child."

"How do you know?" He marched from the room and mounted the stairs. At the top, he paused to kiss her again before whispering, "And how will you be sure tomorrow morning?"

For once Esmie seemed speechless.

"This is the most beautiful Christmas Day I remember," he told her. "Thank you."

Her arms went around his neck. "Thank you, William. And thank you for my marvelous gift. I never thought to own something so wondrous. I wish I had something to give to you."

A pulse beat at his temple and echoed through his body, building until he could no longer wait to lie with Esmie. In his bedchamber, he set her carefully on the edge of his bed and knelt before her once more.

Again it was Esmie who kissed William, and Esmie who began, with great concentration, to remove his clothing.

"Sweet"—he caught her wrists—"You have given me the greatest of gifts this Christmas."

"What is that, dearest?"

"Love. And I give my love to you—forever."

SEASON'S GREETINGS
from . . .
STELLA CAMERON

I've seen Father Christmas. No, I'm not kidding, and I don't mean I imagined the big man who came so stealthily to stand beside my bed. He wore a hooded cloak (I couldn't see his face) and the air seemed to pop and shiver—correction, the air *did* pop and shiver where he stood.

He'd come to deliver my doll house. I was four years old.

Christmases past . . . a strand of memories like special ornaments on the family tree, each one captured and treasured and brought out again and again in a sweet or soft or funny or poignant moment to make us say, "Ah, yes. I remember."

I remember Christmas as a five-year-old when dolls were more of a luxury than my family could afford. That was the year my older sister planned a *new* doll for me regardless. She painted a white doll black. The paint never dried.

Ah, yes.

At ten, whilst my mother slept, I got up hours before dawn and opened all my presents and goaded my much-younger brother into following my example. I remember my mother's face when she found us, and I remember wishing I'd stayed in bed.

And then I was grown and gone from that strand of memories, gone to make a new one with my husband. I remember a first Christmas in the United States and being poor and walking through deep snow past brilliantly decorated houses to midnight mass—and laughing and loving and being so happy I was afraid to blink for fear I really was imagining this time.

But that was all real too, as real as the turkey we cooked on Christmas day, a six pound turkey (oh, yes, *six* pounds) that resembled a magician's rubber chicken.

And then there were children of our own, one, two, and three, and more memories to make.

God is good. He gives us gem times to outshine the rocky ones and I'm never more aware of his loving gifts than at Christmas.

May God bless all of my readers. As we say in England, "Happy Christmas," and may you gather many more memories to treasure.

Falling Stars

Loretta Chase

1

Wiltshire, England,
11 December 1818

IF A MAN COULD SLEEP THROUGH THE RACKET OF early morning London, Marcus Greyson told himself, he could certainly sleep through the noise of lively children. He pulled the pillow over his head, but he could hear it all the same: shrill voices and the thumping of little feet up and down the corridors. Even in the intervals of silence, he was waiting, braced for the next outburst of shrieks and thumps.

With an oath, he flung the pillow aside and dragged himself out of bed. He had slept only three hours. That, evidently, was all the sleep he was going to get. A glance at the window told him morning was well advanced—a winter morn so crisply bright it made his eyes ache.

Despite his grogginess, Marcus washed and dressed quickly, while his mind ran over a dozen possible excuses he could give his elder brother and sister-in-law for turning up in the dead of night.

Julius and Penelope probably still weren't aware he was here.

They had all been asleep when he'd come. He had simply let himself in with his own key, and gone up to the room they always kept ready for him. While they'd be delighted Marcus had changed his mind about spending Christmas at Greymarch, they were sure to wonder about his bizarre traveling schedule.

He gave his thick mane of tawny hair the usual slapdash brushing, and pulled on his coat. Since he didn't have a reasonable explanation, he might as well give an unreasonable one, so ludicrous they'd be too busy laughing to ask any more.

He opened the door and stepped into the hall just as a matched pair of fair-haired little girls came barreling round the corner. One neatly dodged and shot past. The other tripped over his foot.

Marcus caught her before she hit the floor and briskly set her back on her feet. As he met her dazed blue stare, he inhaled sharply. He knew those eyes . . . no, it was impossible.

"Delia! Livy!" came a feminine voice from the stairway.

His head swung toward the sound.

"Yes, Mama," the little girl called out. "We're just going to the schoolroom." Flashing Marcus a grin, she darted down the hall.

"Not before we have a discussion, young ladies."

Even while his mind denied, disbelieved, his senses recognized, and stirred.

The voice's owner came round the corner, then stopped dead.

All else stopped, too—his heart and breath—as

though they'd collided physically. The impact sent him reeling into the past.

He had met her in summer, but hers was winter's beauty. Her hair was pale sunlight framing the snowy purity of her skin, and there was winter, too, in her eyes, clear, ice-blue. Christina.

He regained his breath and managed a bow. "Mrs. Travers."

"Mr. . . . Greyson." The fingers of her left hand curled and uncurled against the grey woolen gown. No wedding ring. When had Arthur Travers died? Some two or three years ago?

"I was not . . ." Her full mouth formed a tight smile. "I was unaware you were here. Penelope said—that is, no one mentioned your arrival."

That low voice with its trace of huskiness . . . so like a caress . . . He pulled his wandering mind back.

"They couldn't have known," he said. "I arrived late last night. A spur-of-the-moment decision." His heart was beating too fast—because he was taken aback, Marcus told himself. He knew she and Penny still corresponded, but from all he'd heard, Christina hadn't left Cumbria since she was married. He hadn't been told she'd be here, and couldn't possibly have expected it.

He backed away a step. She did, too.

"How . . . pleased Julius will be," she said. "And Penelope. And of course, the boys. They've boasted of their uncle to the twins."

"The little girls," he said tautly. "Yours, obviously."

She nodded. "Delia and Livy." Her ice blue gaze melted a fraction. "Seven years old last month. And dreadful hoydens, as you've probably noticed. I hope their noise didn't wake you."

Seven years old. That seemed impossible. But it had been ten years since he'd last seen her, and she'd married soon thereafter—a mere three months thereafter, he recalled, with a sting of bitterness that startled him. He retreated another pace.

"The children didn't disturb me at all," he lied. "I was just going down to breakfast."

"Then I mustn't keep you."

She moved past him, a breath of scent teasing in her wake. Lavender.

He'd known many other women who wore lavender. The scent should have conjured up recent memories. Instead, as he stood in the hall listening to her light step fade, the scene opening up in his mind rose from a decade ago.

It had been late May, a fortnight before Julius's wedding, and the first group of houseguests had arrived. Julius was taking them on a tour of Greymarch, and he'd nagged Marcus into going along.

Though acutely aware of Penny's beautiful friend, Marcus had kept his distance. He detested prim and proper Society, and above all loathed its featherbrained misses, with their virginal white gowns and twittering voices and mincing, mannered ways. The males weren't much better: a lot of complacent hypocrites among whom not a single original thought could be found.

While the guests explored the old gatehouse—the Greysons' Picturesque Ruin, Julius called it—Marcus had gritted his teeth and kept his mouth shut, resolved for Julius's sake to endure boredom and frustration in silence. Marcus had been leaning against a fir tree, softly whistling the melody of a bawdy song, when Penny's friend had shyly approached.

"What is the song?" Christina had asked in that foggy, beckoning voice.

He had carefully avoided looking at her, because he'd seen what happened to other men who did. In less than twenty-four hours, this eighteen-year-old girl with her platinum hair and silver-blue eyes had effortlessly turned every unattached male at Greymarch into a dithering imbecile.

Marcus had looked at the gatehouse, the rocks, the trees, and the blue, cloudless sky—anywhere but at her—while he answered acidly that the melody was beneath the notice of good little girls because its composer wasn't anyone *genteel* like Haydn or even Rossini.

"Oh," she'd said. Only that, and she was just backing away—as he'd believed he wanted—when the spring breeze carried the lavender scent to his nostrils. It had swirled into his brain—and, dizzy, he'd looked down and watched her face slowly turning to profile, her eyes downcast so that the long lashes almost brushed her cheek. He'd watched her soft mouth turn downward ever so slightly, then saw his hand reaching to touch her muslin sleeve, while he heard his voice gentling as he said, "Shall I whistle Rossini instead?"

She had turned back, lifting doubtful blue eyes to his. Then, in the space from one heartbeat to the next, the moment of her silver-blue gaze sweeping up to meet his, he'd tumbled headlong into love . . . and two weeks later, into heartbreak.

Marcus recoiled from the memory as though it had been a physical blow. The present swung back sharply into focus.

Christina Travers was nothing to him, he told himself as he headed for the stairs. He'd scarcely thought of her in years. Young men fell in love every day, and had their hearts broken, or else they got their hearts' desire and wed. Some lived happily ever after—as Julius had—but more often they existed with their wives in a state of stultifying boredom or endless quarrel.

Christina had wed wealth and comfort—as she'd been reared to do, Marcus was well aware. According to gossip, she'd lived in virtual seclusion in the Lake District ever since, while he'd spent seven of the last ten years abroad. Had he encountered her in the interim, today's meeting wouldn't have disconcerted him. His strong physical reaction and his mind's reversion to the past were confused responses to the unexpected . . . and to her beauty, of course. He wouldn't have imagined she could grow more lovely.

Naturally he wouldn't. The last time he'd seen her, he had been a callow youth of four-and-twenty who believed Christina was the most beautiful girl in all the world. He'd believed a great many foolish things, once.

Having seen the children settled in the schoolroom under Miss Finch's competent tutelage, a shaken Christina went to the sitting room to write a letter to her great-aunt Georgiana. She took up a sheet of paper, dipped her pen into the inkwell, then had to wipe the pen and put it down because she couldn't keep her hands—or her thoughts—steady. She studied her uncooperative hands in dismay, as though they belonged to a stranger. A short while ago, in the hall, she had felt like a stranger to herself. She had behaved like a tongue-tied schoolgirl—like the weak-minded young miss she'd been a decade before—frantically babbling small talk while she turned hot and cold by turns under Marcus Greyson's intent, gold-glinting stare. Worst of all, she had snatched at the first excuse to run away.

Rising from the desk, Christina moved to the window. Below her, Greymarch's formal gardens lay tranquil, their winter barrenness softened by the deep emerald of evergreen shrubs. To her right, the branches of leafless oaks etched dark webs against the vibrant blue of the sky. To her left, well beyond the winding stream, ancient fir trees blocked her view of the old gatehouse.

She didn't need to see it to remember, though.

It had been two weeks before Penny's wedding. Christina hadn't seen Penny in several months, but they'd corresponded. Julius Greyson turned out to be just as Penny had described in her letters: tall, dark, handsome, gracious, witty, and obviously in love with his bride-to-be. That much Christina managed to digest before she was introduced to his brother.

She saw a bronze god: thick, tawny hair streaked with gold, a sculpted, sun-burnished countenance, and intent, amber-flecked green eyes that lit to gold when he glanced down at her and muttered some barely polite greeting. Marcus Greyson was the most beautiful man she'd ever seen. He was also, at first, the least amiable. Bored, his impatience palpable, he couldn't be bothered to say another word to her during the subsequent tour of Greymarch.

As far as he was concerned, she didn't exist. As far as she was concerned, no one existed but him. To approach a gentleman she didn't know—who evidently preferred to know nobody—was unthinkable. To keep away was impossible. And so, when the group paused at the gatehouse, she'd walked—shaking in her half-boots—across the clearing and up to him, and said the first inane thing that came into her head.

He'd snapped at her quite rudely, which no one had ever done in all her eighteen years, and which should have sent her scurrying back to the safety of her well-mannered acquaintances. But he'd leaned against a fir tree, and there was the cool tang of evergreens about her, and some other scent—tansy and cloves, she'd guessed—emanating from him. There was something else as well—strange and different and dark—and this had slowed her retreat. When he'd touched her sleeve, she'd looked up into his eyes. He'd smiled, and she had too, helplessly, because she'd found the welcome she wanted.

His eyes had not been welcoming this morning. His handsome countenance had hardened to stone the moment he saw her, and the only emotion she'd discerned in those changeable eyes was annoyance.

Well, the surprise hadn't been altogether agreeable for her, either.

Turning from the window and a view that stirred unwanted ghosts from the past, she tried to consider the situation rationally and fairly. His annoyance very likely had nothing to do with her—or, more precisely, with the Christina of the past. He'd surely forgotten most, if not all, of what had happened. After all, she had been merely one in an endless stream of infatuated females.

If he was vexed to find her here, that could easily be because he'd expected to spend a quiet Christmas with his family. Now there were twice as many children as he'd expected—which meant twenty times the racket—and a widowed friend of Penny's he'd have to make polite conversation with.

She wasn't exactly delighted about making polite conversation with him, either, Christina thought defensively. But that was ridiculous, she chided herself in the next instant. She was far too mature to hold a grudge for ten long years.

All the same, she couldn't help remembering. She saw clearly in her mind's eye his letter with its black, lashing script, each word sharp as the sting of a whip. At the time she had believed her shattered heart would never recover.

So the young generally feel when they first experience betrayal, the mature Christina told herself. The fact was, he'd done her a favor in destroying her illusions. She bore no grudge. She simply hadn't forgotten the painful lesson he had taught her. She had nothing to fear from him. He couldn't hurt her again. She was no longer a naive eighteen-year-old girl.

As soon as they were released from the schoolroom, Kit and Robin hunted their uncle down, and formally introduced him to their new playmates. Within a very few minutes, Marcus discovered that Livy was quiet and reflective, while Delia was bolder and restless. It was Livy who ran to seek their mama's permission to play out of doors with Mr. Greyson, while Delia was already racing for her coat and mittens. She was first at the door, shoving a ridiculously frilly bonnet onto her head, and heedlessly pulling her mittens on backward.

Marcus crouched down before her. "May I help?" he asked politely.

At her nod, he straightened the mittens, then proceeded to tie the bonnet ribbons.

"Your eyes are two colors," she told him. "There is green and little gold speckles. Did fairies do that?"

"They might have done."

"It is very pretty. I wish I had fairy gold in my eyes."

He stood up and pulled on his gloves. "You have fairy silver," he said. "Like a blue sky with silver dust. It is much, much prettier."

"A blue sky with silver dust." She considered. "And Livy, too, then. And Mama."

"Yes."

"Yes," she repeated with a satisfied nod. She took his hand, and looked up at him, and smiled.

This was merely a child's smile of trusting innocence, and a child's tiny, mittened hand clasping his own. There was nothing in it to disturb or surprise him. He was disturbed nevertheless, because he felt the small gesture too deeply, as though it pricked some sensitive place in his heart, some old wound.

He looked away from the girl's innocent, upturned face and the too-familiar silver-blue eyes, and the troubling sensation passed. Marcus told himself his mind was addled, that was all, and he was oversensitive from lack of sleep.

Christina was in the sitting room, embroidering a handkerchief while she listened to Penelope fret over arrangements for the following night's Yuletide ball.

"I can't think what's to be done." Pushing back from her cluttered writing desk, Penny folded her hands over her just-noticeably swollen belly. "I can hardly tell Miss Nichols to keep away. And it's no use hoping she'll break an ankle. When she learns Marcus is here, she'll come, even if she must be carried on a litter."

"I take it Miss Nichols has set her cap at Mr. Greyson." Christina jammed the needle through the fabric with rather more force than necessary.

"She'd set her hounds on him if she could. Since she can't, she'll plague him to death."

"She's a near neighbor," Christina said. "You could hardly *not* invite her, even if you'd known he was coming. Besides, he may not object to her interest." She felt a tweak of something nastily like jealousy. She glared at the knot she'd just made. "I expect she's grown quite lovely. She was a beautiful child when I first—when I last saw her, at your wedding."

Penelope turned a bit in her chair. "We weren't much more than children ourselves. Was that the last time you saw Marcus?"

Christina nodded stiffly.

"Then you find him much changed, I daresay."

"I should hope so," came a masculine voice from the doorway. "I should hate to appear a callow youth when I'm teetering on the brink of senility."

At the sound of his voice, Christina's heart gave a quick, foolish leap, just as it used to do whenever he came near. She set her jaw and resolutely turned her head toward the door.

Marcus leaned against the frame, his eyes dark and unreadable in the shadow of the doorway. He had changed little physically. He had been tall, lean-muscled, and strong ten years ago. Maturity had added a fraction more breadth to his shoulders, to his hard chest . . . but she'd noticed all that earlier, she chided herself. She didn't have to take *measurements*, for heaven's sake. She dragged her gaze away.

He had made his own way in the world—alone, she reflected, while she listened to Penny tease him for eavesdropping. People had mistrusted him once, because Marcus Greyson made his own rules, respected no authority, no boundaries set by others. But in the time since she'd known him, he'd dared and risked and won, stunning the world with the magnitude of his success. He now possessed both wealth and power, and it showed.

That didn't altogether explain why, as he eased his six-foot frame away from the doorway, he seemed to fill the room, or why her senses should bristle and quicken at his slightest motion.

She felt his knowing green-gold eyes upon her, a swiftly assessing glance, come and gone in seconds. Yet her flesh prickled and heated under it, as though under his hands, and she felt she'd been unclothed . . . and teased . . . and abandoned.

She yanked her needle through the linen.

He stopped a moment to look over Penny's shoulder at the untidy heap of paper, and teased her about preparing for a party as Wellington might a war campaign. Penny laughed and made some joking answer.

Then he moved toward Christina. She felt a frantic fluttering within, and a memory rose that sent a mortifying heat rushing up her neck.

The day after she'd first spoken to him, Marcus had found her alone in this sitting room. She'd been daydreaming out a window.

She'd heard him come up behind her, but hadn't moved. She'd felt the same inner flutter then, and a confusing warmth, and the same mingled anxiety and anticipation. He'd stood behind her, not uttering a word. She'd held her breath, waiting, wondering what would happen next, all the while terrified someone would come—and hoping someone would. Then she'd felt his breath, a whisper against her neck that sent a warm tingle down her spine, all the way to her toes. "I just want to be near you," he'd said, his voice so low it was a wonder she'd heard it past the frantic beating of her heart.

Her idiotic heart was growing frantic now, as he paused mere inches from her chair. What she felt was a perfectly sensible anxiety, she told herself. If he was still annoyed about finding her here, he could make her stay uncomfortable. And she must stay. Her house let for the next twelvemonth, Great-Aunt Georgiana gone to Scotland, Christina was trapped at Greymarch until the New Year.

At the moment she felt trapped in her chair by the tall masculine body looming over her.

"I've come to ask if you'd paint with us, Mrs. Travers."

His rich baritone came from directly above her bowed head. She was staring at his gleaming boots, a handsbreadth from her grey kid shoes. She didn't want to look up until she had collected her rapidly disintegrating composure. He had already made her blush once, and she would rather hang than do it again—like the awkward schoolgirl she'd been all those years ago.

"I beg your pardon?" There was an infuriatingly childish wobble in her voice. She stabbed her needle into the handkerchief.

"We've decided to paint dragons. Delia and Livy said you're an expert dragon painter."

"Oh. I . . . well, that is very kind, but . . ." Oh, wonderful—stammering, too, like a tongue-tied adolescent.

"Also, Delia will not wear her smock, which Livy says she must do," he went on. "Which places me in an awkward predicament."

Christina raised her head quickly, but not quickly enough to avoid the lean, muscled length of male between the boots and the glint of gold in his eyes. Was that amusement she saw—or mockery?

"Good heavens, Marcus," Penny exclaimed, "could you not leave it to a nursery maid?"

"Not before I'd ascertained the facts," he answered. "For all I knew, the child might have a terror of smocks. Children do take unaccountable aversions, I'm told. Since she's been otherwise perfectly agreeable, I concluded I had stumbled upon a strongly-rooted aversion."

Christina found her voice. "It *is* an aversion," she said. "But not to smocks in general—only Livy's in particular, which are starched."

"There, I knew it must be significant," Marcus triumphantly told his sister-in-law. He turned back to Christina. "Starch, is it? She only said it was horrid, and she wouldn't wear it."

"Nor will she." Christina rose. "I never thought to explain it to the maid. I'll go find one of Delia's smocks—unstarched—and—"

"And one for yourself," he prompted. "You don't want to spoil your gown with dragon paint."

Yes, one for herself, of course. He'd come only because he wanted her to take the children off his hands. Firmly crushing a twinge of disappointment, she hurried out to find the dratted smocks.

Marcus had meant to leave the children in Christina's care, and get away where he could put his thoughts back into order—for the angelic-looking twins had disordered them to an alarming degree.

He'd discovered that looking after little girls was nothing like minding rough-and-tumble little boys. Christina had called her daughters hoydens, but they seemed to Marcus the most fragile of china dolls. Out of doors, he found himself worrying that they weren't dressed warmly enough, then that they were overwarm, and would take a chill in consequence. Every game seemed too rough; all the places he'd taken for granted as perfectly safe for children abruptly became fraught with perils.

Aware his anxieties were absurd, he'd refrained from acting upon them and, as one would expect, no tragedy had occurred, not even a scraped knee. He'd spent the whole time on the edge of panic, all the same.

When they were safely indoors at last, he'd hardly begun to relax before Delia threw the fit about the smock, setting off all the ridiculous alarms again.

He'd given up and gone for their mama—and stumbled into other, worse difficulties.

He was thrown off-balance in the sitting room because Christina had blushed when he'd spoken to her, and the blush had drawn him too near. The scent of lavender wafted about her, and while he watched the faint pink steal slowly up her neck, the ghost of a long-banished memory had stolen upon him.

Once, in that same room, he'd wanted to touch his mouth to her flushed neck, but hadn't dared, only stood and let her scent steal into his blood and make him desperate.

Despite all efforts to banish it, the recollection still hung in his mind. The blush was long gone, and she seemed cool enough at present, her attention on her painting. Marcus sat the length of the playroom table away, his nephews diligently working on either side, but he couldn't concentrate.

The room was cozy and warm. From time to time the lavender scent stole toward him, then vanished. If it would only make up its mind and do one or the other, linger or go, he might make up his mind, too, and settle to his work or depart. But her scent continued to beckon and withdraw, leaving him uncertain and restless.

As he looked up for the hundredth time, he found Delia studying him, so gravely that he couldn't help but smile. She answered with an impish grin. Then she slid down from her chair and scampered to his side, where she stood on tiptoe, balancing herself with one hand on his arm while she tried to peer over the table at his painting.

Marcus picked her up and sat her on his lap. It never occurred to him to ask if that was where she wished to be. The action was reflexive. It must have been correct, for Delia settled there, perfectly at home, and offered to help. Even to a seven-year-old it was obvious he wasn't making satisfactory progress.

"I shall rinse the brush for you," she said, "and help you pick the colors."

Livy took umbrage at this. "You don't know the right colors. Your dragon is pink and blue."

"Perhaps Mr. Greyson *likes* pink and blue dragons," Christina said. "If he doesn't, he is perfectly capable of telling your sister so. Mind what you're doing, Livy. Your dragon's tail is about to go off the paper and onto the table."

Livy frowned. "I've spoiled it." Ignoring her mother's reassuring murmur, the child scrambled down from her chair, snatched up the painting, and trotted to Marcus.

"It's spoiled," she told him, her countenance dejected as she held up the painting. "Delia made me spoil it."

"I did not," said Delia.

"It's not spoiled," Christina said, "and you are not to plague Mr. Greyson."

"It's just broken," said six-year-old Robin.

"Uncle Marcus will fix it," his brother consoled, patting Livy on the head with all the condescending superiority of his eight years.

"You have to fix it yourself," said Delia. "I'm helping him with his dragon."

Marcus heard a faint, choked sound, suspiciously like laughter, from the other end of the table. But when he glanced that way, Christina's countenance was sober.

"You made me spoil it," Livy accused her sister. "You were whispering secrets to Mr. Greyson and telling wrong colors."

Another smothered chuckle. This time, he discerned a twitch at the corner of Christina's mouth. That was all. No reproach for the girls, no assistance to him in parlaying a truce.

Marcus took the painting from Livy and studied it. "It isn't spoiled at all, but different and interesting. It looks to me as though your dragon has a strange and mysterious kink in his tail."

Livy edged closer and, putting her hand on his, lowered the painting to her eye level for scrutiny. "What is a kink?" she asked. "Is it pretty?"

The little hand on his told Marcus what the matter was: if Delia sat on his lap, Livy must, too. "Come, I'll show you," he said. He shifted Delia onto one knee, and took Livy up on the other. Hostilities ceased.

Taking up his brush, he finished the dragon's tail, making it curl up and around in the space Livy had left for the sky.

Delia grew restive. "Now her dragon is more beautiful than mine," she complained.

"No, it can't be," he said. "I'm sure your dragon is quite handsome."

Delia shook her head. "It isn't. Mine is horrid."

"Since you have promoted Mr. Greyson to chief artist, we shall let him judge." There was an edge to the mama's voice and a flush on her countenance as she held up Delia's painting for Marcus's perusal. He wondered whether she was vexed, and with whom.

"It is very fine," said Marcus, his gaze moving from the painting to the mama. He remembered that delicate tint: a whisper of pink upon alabaster. The first time he'd dared to take her hand in his, she'd colored like this, but she hadn't pulled away. He'd held her small, gloved hand as carefully as though it had been the most fragile of eggshells, and died of happiness during that too-brief moment. Then they'd heard the others coming, and he'd had to break away and pretend he'd only just that instant accidently encountered Christina in the garden.

She wore no gloves now. Her hands were slim and elegant, smooth and white and soft.

He wrenched his mind elsewhere, to Delia, who tugged at his coat sleeve, asking him to make a kink for her.

"Perhaps Mama would be so kind as to pass Delia's painting this way," he said tightly.

She rose instead, and brought it to him, then lingered to watch while he gave Delia's dragon strange and mysterious pink and blue claws in lieu of a kinky tail.

He wanted to get away.

He found the little girls adorable and their fondness for him touching. He didn't mind their negligible weight or the tiny kid shoes absently kicking at his shins. It wasn't on their account he wanted to bolt, or even entirely on account of their mother, standing a few inches from his shoulder.

Marcus wanted to get away from himself, to disengage from the flesh-and-blood Marcus, because that flesh and blood was responding quite on its own, as though his body belonged to someone else.

He was painfully aware of Christina's nearness and of her too-familiar scent and warmth, and of long-buried longings stirring to life.

When he added a whirl of smoke above Delia's dragon's head, Christina's voice with its trace of huskiness came from above his shoulder: "Now you must give Livy smoke, too, Mr. Greyson. Then I would advise you to add no more adornments. Otherwise the rivalry will go on endlessly, I promise you."

It was a mama's voice, wise in the ways of her offspring. Yet Marcus could hear its distant echo from long ago: *I promise you, I'll be there. I promise.*

He had waited all those long, miserable hours . . . and she never came.

He set his jaw, and painted smoke for Livy's dragon, and promised himself that ghosts or no ghosts, no woman, however beautiful, would make such a fool of him again. That, beyond doubt, had ended a long time ago.

At tea, Julius and Marcus argued about Greece, so hotly that Christina was sure they'd come to blows. Her tension must have been evident, because Penny edged closer on the sofa and patted her hand. "They won't kill each other," she said. "It's simply that Marcus doesn't believe it's a proper discussion unless everyone loses his temper. In that, you see, he hasn't changed at all."

She had to raise her voice to be heard above the men. Even so, the brothers had been so furiously involved in their debate that Christina was startled when Marcus abruptly turned toward the two women.

"I don't believe it's a proper discussion," he said, "when one's opponent is incapable of comprehending the simplest facts. I'm obliged to raise my voice in hopes of getting some small piece of information into my brother's thick skull."

"You won't persuade me it's in our government's interest to support the cause of anarchists," said Julius. "Only look what came of revolution in France."

"Only look at the American colonies," Marcus retorted. "Which is ridiculous to ask of you, since you've never ventured farther west than Falmouth."

"It's ridiculous to insist that a man can't make reasonable judgments about any circumstance he hasn't personally witnessed. Even our foreign ministers—"

"Perceive the world as someone else has told them they must. They believe whatever their teachers told them, or whichever ignorant blockhead has designated himself an authority."

No, Marcus hadn't changed in this, Christina thought. It was partly his radical views, but more his tactless, often insulting way of expressing them, that a decade ago had made him unwelcome at most social gatherings and alienated virtually all his peers.

"You're frowning, Mrs. Travers," Marcus said. "You take exception to my opinion."

His expression was mocking. She wondered if he thought a mere female was incapable of possessing an opinion, let alone disagreeing with that of a male. "I certainly don't agree that the two revolutions arose from the same circumstances, or had the same result," she said.

"Both chose to overthrow what they perceived as tyranny."

"That appears to be the only parallel," she said. "The French beheaded their monarch and most of their aristocracy. The Americans merely severed a *relationship*. It was England that made a war of it."

His dark eyebrows lifted. "Indeed. England, in your view, was rather like a lover the Americans had tired of."

"If I pursue that curious analogy," she said evenly, "I might say that the Americans found their lover's demands *unreasonable*."

She discerned what might be a flicker of surprise in the gold-glinting eyes, and then, more clearly, a flash of anger. She felt a small, fierce stab of satisfaction. He had started it. If he'd thought he could hurt her with the oblique reference to the past, if he thought she would shrink away and blush, he had another think coming.

"And I might say the mistress was *capricious*," he returned.

She met his challenging stare straight on. "You might, but you don't believe that. Your sympathies are with the Americans. You're merely playing devil's advocate, Mr. Greyson. You baited Julius, and now you're baiting me."

"Certainly. He baits everyone," said Julius, moving to the tea table. "There is nothing he likes better than a great, noisy row. Come, Marcus, stop up your mouth with a sandwich, and stop staring at

Christina as though she's sprouted another head."

Marcus opened his mouth, then shut it, and Christina felt a prickle of annoyance with Julius. The argument had hardly begun, and he had smoothly squelched it. No doubt Julius thought she couldn't defend herself. He, too, had another think coming.

Marcus silently approached the tea table, but made no move to take anything. He looked at the tea tray, then at her. *Look,* however, was too passive a word to convey what he did. He had a way of taking possession with a glance and fastening all one's consciousness on him.

Christina tried to think of something to say to Penny, some excuse to divert her attention elsewhere. But her brain refused to consider anything but the man opposite.

Marcus did not sit up properly in his chair with his feet neatly planted upon the carpet, but leaned back, his long legs bridging the space between them, one boot crossed comfortably over the other just a few inches from her feet. Christina was rivetingly aware of the dark wool stretched taut over his muscular limbs and of the smoke from the fire clinging to his garments. There was also the scent, faint as an elusive memory, of tansy and cloves.

She darted a sharp glance at his politely blank countenance. His eyes, she found, were neither blank nor polite. They were intent, assessing. In this way, she reflected, he must have countless times sized up business rivals, not to mention women. The scrutiny was disquieting—as he meant it to be, she thought crossly. It was as deliberate as the way he manipulated the physical awareness. He enjoyed putting others off-balance. He was obnoxiously good at it, even better than he'd been ten years ago. Practice makes perfect, she thought. She wanted to strike him. He had no business playing this stupid, silent game with her.

"I think you've grown . . . taller since the last time I saw you," he said reflectively. "That was—when was it?—years ago, anyhow. What were you then—sixteen, seventeen?"

"Eighteen," she said. "A year younger than Penny." She turned to Penny for confirmation, and was startled to find that her friend had left the sofa and was on the other side of the room, talking to Julius. Christina calmly turned back to Marcus. He was wearing a faint, amused smile.

"But you are quite right regarding my height," she said. "I did grow another half-inch. How keenly observant you are."

Twin sparks lit his eyes. "I did not mean a mere half-inch. I must have confused you with some other girl. There were a great many of them, as I recall."

"Ah, well, you mustn't mind the error," Christina answered in tones laden with compassion. "Failure of memory is common with advancing age—it cannot be helped."

His expression remained cool, but for the muscle that jumped in his jaw, before he answered, "That's one frailty you obviously don't suffer. Your memory is keen indeed. You recall not only how old you were, but your exact height."

She wanted very much to fling the teapot at his smug face. Instead she smiled. "Not long after Penny's wedding, I was measured for my own bridal gown. I can't imagine any woman forgetting what size and age she was when she was wed."

She felt his withdrawal an instant before his long legs pulled back and his posture straightened. "Yes, of course," he said tightly. "I had altogether forgotten."

Christina had started it, Marcus told himself as he jammed the diamond stickpin into his neckcloth. She had sat upon the sofa looking cool and detached and superior, listening to Penny speak of him as though he were an ill-mannered child. But Christina had also finished it, he admitted as he turned from the looking glass.

He had only wanted to fluster her, make her blush, obtain some hint that she remembered something, anything. Instead, she had found and pierced a tender spot that shouldn't have existed: a mere three months after tossing him aside, she'd wed; it had taken Marcus three times as many months to recover. The reminder had hurt. It shouldn't have, but it had.

A great deal was happening that shouldn't.

He had spent more than an hour dressing for dinner, when it should have taken a quarter of that time. He'd just spent a full twenty minutes choosing the stickpin—as though she cared a straw what he wore, as though he gave a damn whether or not he met her standards of elegance.

Giving his cuffs an unnecessary tug, he headed for the door, then paused, his fingers inches from the handle, when he heard Christina's and Penny's voices in the hall outside.

He didn't emerge from his room until the voices

faded. Then he headed for his nephews' room, and spent a quarter hour there telling riddles and jokes, instead of offering his customary "good night" from the threshold.

He owed them the attention, he told himself as he left the room. He'd focused too much on the twins all day, and children were sensitive to such unintentional slights—as the girls' behavior in the playroom had demonstrated.

He was positive he'd done nothing—certainly not deliberately—to win the girls' affection, let alone lure them to him in the playroom. They'd simply come . . . as their mama had done once, long ago.

Then, he had believed that she, too, felt the current between them, and the sense of inevitability as their gazes locked. Gad, what a moonstruck young fool he'd been. Obviously all that had drawn her was curiosity or vanity. He had kept away, when other men couldn't; naturally, this had intrigued her.

What her children saw in him was even less significant. Children took likings and aversions for reasons adults could rarely fathom. Delia liked him as she liked pink and blue dragons; Livy, as she liked starch in her smocks. This sensible adult reflection brought a twinge of sadness.

Marcus paused at the head of the stairs. He really should bid the girls good night as well. One must be even-handed, after all, though they were the children of a stranger.

He was heading toward the guest wing even as he thought it. Halfway down the hall, he felt misgivings, and his steps slowed. But soft light streamed into the hall from their open door, beckoning his reluctant feet on.

He reached the door and looked in. Though a candle was lit, they were buried under the bedclothes.

He felt the stab of sadness again, and quarreled with it, for the two little girls were simply asleep, as they should be. He spoke anyway, his voice just a whisper: "Good night, my dears."

Two flaxen heads popped up from the bedclothes.

"Oh, you *have* come," Delia exclaimed. "I *told* you," she chided her sister.

"You did not," said Livy. "You said *maybe*. I said *maybe*, too."

He shouldn't feel so very gratified, but he did, and all the adult common sense in the world couldn't keep Marcus from entering the room and savoring their quarrelsome welcome.

"I hope you didn't stay awake on my account," he said, though he rather hoped they had.

Their blonde heads bobbed up and down.

"Oh, dear," he said. "That will never do. Next time, I shall have to dress more quickly. It took me much longer than it should have, I'm afraid."

"Mama takes hours," Delia said. "There's all the things for underneath, and then the things on top of them."

"Yes," said Livy. "There's the chemise, and the corset, and the stockings and the petticoat and—"

"Ladies' garments can be very complicated," Marcus hastily interjected while he tried to banish the seductive vision Livy had evoked. "Though a gentleman's are much simpler, he must contend with his neckcloth, which is not very easy to tie properly."

Livy gravely considered the neckcloth. "You have a star," she said. "I like stars."

She meant the diamond stickpin. It was too gaudy, he decided, too demanding of attention. Someone might think he was trying to impress . . . someone.

"It's not a star," Delia told her sister. "It's a diamond."

"A *star,*" said Livy.

"A *diamond.*" Delia drove her elbow into Livy's arm.

"Do you know what I think?" Marcus put in before the disagreement could escalate into violence. "Maybe stars are diamonds with which angels adorn the heavens. Maybe sometimes they drop them, and they fall all the way to the earth."

Twin blue gazes swung abruptly back to him.

"Oh, yes," said Delia. "The ones in the sky do fall sometimes. We saw it, didn't we?" she asked her sister. "Last night we saw one fall."

"You *promised* not to tell," Livy reproached.

"He won't tell Mama."

They lifted pleading countenances to him.

"You won't tell, will you?" Delia asked. "It was very late, and we went to the window."

"When you were supposed to be sleeping?" he whispered conspiratorially.

They nodded guiltily.

Marcus crossed the room to the window and looked out. "It's very pretty, isn't it? Dark and quiet and magical. When I was a little boy, sometimes I woke very late in the night, and couldn't fall asleep again right away. I would climb onto the window seat and look at the stars, and imagine things. If I tell on you, I suppose I must tell on me, too. Otherwise, it wouldn't be fair, would it?"

The blonde heads shook back and forth.

"Well, I can't possibly bear to tell on myself. It's a special secret."

The sisters looked at each other.

"It was very, very late," Delia said.

"I counted twelve chimes," said Livy.

"Then we saw the star fall, over there." Delia's small finger pointed eastward.

Marcus felt a tingle at the back of his neck.

That was the direction he'd come last night. At the stroke of midnight, he had left the comforts of Marlborough's Castle Inn and climbed back onto his carriage, to continue the remaining thirty-odd miles to Greymarch. He couldn't explain that sudden decision any more than he could the one that had driven him from London in the first place. There seemed to be a great deal lately that he couldn't explain. A long, long time ago, he would have believed the falling star explained everything.

As a child, he had truly believed angels looked after the stars, and after him as well; and when they dropped a star, it was to send him a special message. Even as a young man—for he'd been a dreamer, as idealists generally are—he'd half-believed still.

During the fortnight preceding Julius's wedding, the clear night skies had been filled with star showers. On one such night, a week after Christina's arrival, she had slipped out to the garden to meet him. She was warm, flushed with dancing, and one cornsilk tendril had slipped from its pin to dangle at her ear. He'd brushed it back with his thumb, and she'd shivered. Then, out of the corner of his eye, he'd caught the flash of a star, torn from its moorings, taking fire as it plummeted to earth. The fiery journey would consume it, he knew—as love would consume him.

If it was a warning, it came too late. He was already bending close to brush his mouth against her ear, and trembling at his own daring. She trembled, too, but that was all. She didn't push him away as he'd feared. And so he took courage and wrapped his arms about her and, whispering love, touched his lips to her silken cheek. Then he breathed her name, and brought his mouth to hers . . . and died of happiness and lived of it, in that first sweet, stolen kiss.

The chime of the hall clock yanked him back to the present, and to the pair of fair-haired angels gazing innocently at him. "I'd better say good night," he said, "or I shall be very late for dinner."

Christina wore the diamond pendant Arthur had given her on their first anniversary, and wished she hadn't. The cold stone burnt her flesh. There were moments when she could almost believe this was because it had caught fire from the one flashing opposite in Marcus's neckcloth. There were other moments when she suspected the heat came from elsewhere: the smoldering gaze that slid from time to time to the pendant dangling between her breasts, and seemed to brand her deeper each time.

It was the gown, she told herself. It was too *risqué.* Yet it wasn't, either, for countless other gowns were cut as low or lower, and thoroughly respectable women wore them. Fashionable gowns were part of her new-won freedom, part of the pact she'd made with herself during the last months of mourning. She'd kept that pact and assumed control of her life, extricating her children, her home, her activities, and her wardrobe from the suffocating grasp of her sisters-in-law.

The struggle had been long and painful. She was entitled to enjoy her victory and her freedom.

She wished she'd worn a shawl.

She wished she were not so conscious of the man opposite. Every time he looked her way—as he must, when they conversed—the vast dining room grew correspondingly smaller and hotter, while her throat constricted and her muscles tensed another degree. By the time dessert was served, she was taut as an overwound watch spring, ticking off the seconds until she and Penny could withdraw and leave the men to their port.

When Penny finally did signal that it was time to leave, Christina sprang up from her chair like a jack-in-the-box.

She had just stepped over the threshold and was drawing a breath of relief when she heard Marcus's voice behind her: "You are *not* going to make me sit and swill that awful stuff, Julius. I never could abide port, any more than I could the tiresome rite of exchanging the same bawdy stories our ancestors told each other six centuries ago."

"What you could never abide," said Julius, "was keeping away from the ladies."

"Which is only logical," came the light answer, very close behind Christina now. "They're infinitely more aesthetic than a room full of drunken men."

He'd moved quietly, and far more quickly than she, Christina discovered, because he was at her side even as he uttered the last words.

"What enigmatic name, I wonder, have the *modistes* given the color of your gown?" he asked, dropping his voice. "I should call it russet, but that isn't fanciful enough. *Terre d'Inde*, perhaps."

"I believe she called it brick red," Christina said.

"I remember you always in white," he said. "White muslin. Silk makes . . . a different sound." His voice dropped lower still. "Another sort of . . . whisper."

As slowly and reluctantly as he uttered the words, her gaze moved up to his. Their eyes caught and held a heartbeat too long, while the corridor grew darker and hazier, thick with shades of the past.

They broke free in the same instant, turning from each other and instinctively quickening their pace. As if they both sensed that some dangerous abyss had opened in the hallway, they hastened for the safety of the drawing room.

Two cornsilk braids formed a thick coronet about Christina's head, the severe style softened by a few wavy tendrils framing her pale countenance. No plumes or lace, ribbons, or jewels adorned the simple coiffure, only the shimmering threads of goldfire where the candlelight played. It lit the silver dust in her eyes as well.

The rest was fire and ice: the graceful arch of her neck, the snowy smoothness of slender shoulders, and the swelling curves, blindingly white against the vivid russet of her silk gown. A diamond pendant shot fire sparks, as though the flesh it touched set it aflame. Marcus dragged his gaze away for what must be the thousandth time this night, and tried to attend to the story Christina was reading aloud. Of all books, she'd chosen *Frankenstein*, as though this day had not been gothic enough.

Whenever Marcus came near her, the memories rose like ghosts, palpable as her scent. When she moved, the whispering silk beckoned him nearer, and he was mortified to find that it was as hard to keep away now as it had been ten years ago.

Then, he'd almost envied the men he generally despised, because they, unlike the black sheep of the Greyson family, might woo her openly. He, on the other hand, hardly dared look at her, because to look was to long for, and he hadn't yet developed the skill of disguising his feelings. If anyone guessed those feelings, they would snatch her up and take her away, far from his corrupting influence.

Ten years ago, he'd been hemmed in by others' disapproval of his character. At present, he had to hem himself in, because he didn't approve of what he felt. He shouldn't be so obsessed with her.

He was too tired to cope with this, Marcus decided. He should just go to bed. Now. Christina was turning the page, and he was just opening his mouth to excuse himself when a servant entered and, with an apologetic bow to the company, hastened to Penny.

The footman said something in a low voice. Penny put down her knitting and rose.

"Well, this is not convenient," she said, "but tomorrow would be less so, and one must be grateful for that, at least. Julius, you must order the carriage brought round. Sally Turnbull's first has decided to make his debut this night," she explained, "and the midwife cannot be found."

Her husband frowned. "For heaven's sake, Penny, there are scores of women in the village—"

"She is young and frightened, and she's asked for me."

"You can't go in your condition, especially on such a cold night—"

"My condition, indeed. Your mother was eight months gone with Marcus when she helped a neighbor in a similar case." Penny moved to the door. "I'll fetch what I need, and I'll expect to find the carriage waiting when I'm ready to leave."

Christina put down the book. "I'd better come with you," she said as she stood up.

"Certainly not," Penny said. "What if one of the children wakes with a nightmare? You won't wish to leave Marcus alone to tend to a frightened child. He became distraught over a smock, recollect."

She left, and a grumbling Julius after her.

Christina sank back onto the sofa.

The room grew oppressively still. Marcus took up a poker and stirred up the fire.

"I wonder who—or what—has made off with the midwife," he said into the taut silence. "Frankenstein's monster, undoubtedly. Poor, confused fellow. He probably mistook old Mrs. Hobbes for his mama."

"I didn't realize you knew the story," she said. "You should have said so, Mr. Greyson. I could have read something else. How bored you must have been."

"I wasn't bored." He turned to her. "You have a most expressive reading voice. Because I was familiar with the tale, even the most harmless passages became fraught with foreboding, and gave me gooseflesh."

"Delia and Livy have ghoulish tastes, I'm afraid. They like nothing better than stories that frighten them out of their wits. And Mama must tell the tale in a creepy, bloodcurdling voice, of course."

"Ghosts and goblins?" Marcus's eyes widened. "I can't believe it of those delicate little girls."

"I believe it is a rebellion of sorts," she said. "Their activities were strictly circumscribed by others. There was a great deal not permitted. These last two years we seem to be making up for it."

She looked up then. "At present, the twins' manners aren't all they should be, as you saw in the playroom. On the other hand, two years ago they were so timid they wouldn't have dared speak to you. I did not want to undo their progress. I had rather they be a bit overbold than . . . stifled."

"Certainly," he said, stifling his own surprise. "Children aren't adults in miniature. As to manners—ah, well, I'm no judge, for mine were always dreadful, deliberately so, and still are, though I've polished the roughest edges. I saw nothing objectionable in your daughters' behavior." He managed a smile. "On the contrary, it swelled my vanity to be fought over."

She picked up the book again, and straightened the marker. "I assumed you were capable of expressing your disapproval—or simply leaving—if they annoyed you. I thought they must deal with the consequences of their behavior, for

Mama will not always be there to make everything as they wish it."

"A life lesson," he said.

"Perhaps." The corners of her soft mouth turned up a very little bit. "Although their aunts would be appalled at what would appear to be a lesson in vying for a gentleman's attention."

"Oh, yes. Aunts." He moved a step closer. "Travers had four unwed elder sisters, I recollect. I suppose you were a great comfort to one another after . . . after your loss. I was sorry to hear of Travers's passing," he said dutifully. "It must have been a great shock to you. You'd known each other from childhood, hadn't you?"

She nodded, laying the book aside. "He had never been strong. His sisters had reared him, and they were accustomed to pampering him. They coddled me, too, and the children. I'm sure the ladies meant well, but they were—oh, I can't think how to say it without sounding horribly ungrateful—but they were narrow. Their world was small, their views—It wasn't what—" She shook her head. "Once Arthur was gone, I found I couldn't live that way any longer," she went on hurriedly. "He left me well-fixed, as all the world knows. I bought another house, and simply left. The aunts descended upon that house and tried to convince me that grief had disordered my wits. And so I've fled again. After the New Year, the girls and I depart with my great-aunt Georgiana for the Continent."

He wasn't sure what he had expected to hear. He knew only that this wasn't it: hearing her complain of a *narrow,* conventional life, hearing her speak of rebellion. There was no female in England less likely to rebel against *anything* than Christina. Or so he'd thought. But then, she'd surprised him earlier, too.

"You've changed," he said, moving another step nearer, "a great deal."

"Most people change after ten years."

"Have I?" he asked. "Do you agree with Penny that I'm much changed?"

She nodded. "You're more confident. You always were outwardly, but now you are inwardly as well. As you should be," she quickly added. "You've accomplished a great deal, I understand."

He dropped into the chair opposite. "Oh, yes, of course. I got enormously rich. That makes a great difference. Those who shut their doors to me years ago can't open them fast enough now. This last year and a half in London has been an education."

"You didn't *get* rich," she corrected. "From what I've heard, you worked hard for every farthing, and took tremendous risks. Those shipping ventures in Greece, for instance—"

"It would seem you've followed my progress very closely," he said.

Despite what he was discovering about her, he still half-expected her to blush. She didn't. There was a quick flash in her eyes before they chilled to cool blue blanks.

"Penny's letters are devoted to the doings of the Greyson family," she said. "You, however, seem to be her favorite topic, which isn't surprising, for you seem to be a never-ending source of sensational stories. She's devoted whole pages to your financial enterprises, and even more ink to your amorous ones. You'll find me, therefore, well-versed in the

Greek ventures, as well as in the height, coloring, wardrobe, and disposition of your last mistress."

He sat bolt upright. "How the devil can Penny pretend to know of any such thing, when she only comes to London for two months out of the twelve?"

"You can't expect to be so much in the public eye and not have your activities noticed," she said. "The gossips, naturally, pass their observations on to your sister-in-law."

"And she passes them on to you." He felt terribly exposed, which was ridiculous. He'd done nothing to be ashamed of. Nevertheless, Marcus felt like a boy called to account for some misdeed.

"Evidently she believes you an *interested* party," he said. "Which would seem altogether odd—unless, of course, she'd somehow learned of what passed between us long ago."

Her chin went up. "You hadn't used to be so roundabout. Are you implying that I told her?"

"It's nothing to me if you did," he said. "Girls generally boast of their conquests, just as men do."

"Then perhaps you'll allow me to wonder whether *you* boasted to Julius. That would also account for their believing me an *interested* party."

"I never told a soul," he snapped. "Men don't usually boast of being played for fools."

"I *never* played you for a fool, Marcus Greyson." Her eyes were flashing now, blue fire. "And I can't believe a grown man of four-and-thirty could believe such a stupid thing."

"Stupid?" He clenched his fists.

"I was eighteen years old. It was the first time I'd been out of my little village, my first time in anything like Society. What in heaven's name could I have known of such games? Where could I have learned them?"

"Women are *born* knowing that game."

"Then I must have been born wrong, because I didn't."

"Then what were you about?" he demanded. "You were as good as engaged to Travers—practically since birth, I was told—yet you let me—"

"Indeed—and what were *you* about?"

He couldn't find the answer. He knew he had one, because he always did. Argument was as natural to him as breathing. But the retort he needed was stuck somewhere, and while he tried desperately to locate it, his eyes were busy too. They were taking in the blue sparks in her eyes and the flush of anger in her smooth cheeks—and its faint sister flush below, where her bosom rose and fell with her quickened breathing . . . where the diamond quivered, flashing fire.

Her slim white hand moved to shield her breasts from his stare. Ineffectually.

"I don't remember." His voice was foggy, dazed. Tearing his gaze away, Marcus shook his head. "I can't believe we're arguing about that episode after all these years. I can't believe *you* are arguing. I can't believe you're wearing that gown. How can you possibly expect me to argue intelligently? Gad, how is a man to think at all?" He got up and poked at the fire again, then stood and glared at it.

"According to report," came her low, taut voice, "your last mistress wore considerably more revealing attire. I don't see why you must take issue with mine—or blame your illogic on it."

Marcus swung round. "I don't see why you must keep plaguing me about my mistress. Or why you must continue this wrangling."

She folded her hands in her lap. "I see. I'm to hold my tongue and let you say whatever you like. That isn't in the least fair."

"It's not fair of you to pick a quarrel when you're wearing a provocative red silk gown."

"Don't make it sound as though I wore it deliberately to provoke you!"

"You wore it to provoke *somebody*—and Julius is already taken!" He stormed back to the sofa. "And you've got that great, gaudy diamond stuck between your breasts, winking at me."

"It's no gaudier than yours," she said. "And yours winks, too."

"You're not obliged to look."

"Neither are you."

They looked, nevertheless, not at diamonds, but at each other. Blue fire clashed with gold, making the space between them crackle. He could almost hear it. He certainly could feel it, crackling inside him, the current he remembered, the inexorable pull . . . to disaster.

He stepped back a pace, his heart racing. "We sound like a pair of children. The instant the grownups depart, we break out in a row."

"We could hardly have this particular row before others," she said.

"We shouldn't have had it at all." He raked his fingers through his hair. "I really am beginning to feel—" He bit back the "haunted" in the nick of time. "I don't feel quite myself," he carefully amended. "I'm tired and out of sorts. And it's absurd to blame my ill-temper on gowns or diamonds or . . . Well, you do look very beautiful, but that's hardly your fault. I just seem to have difficulty . . . digesting—that is, one can't expect you to wear modest white muslin frocks forever, and this is far more . . . aesthetic."

"Thank you," she said.

"I should also have realized that you would grow out of your timidity and learn to speak your mind," he went on, feeling as though he were picking his way through a field of nettles. "It is . . . refreshing . . . quite . . . stimulating."

"I daresay *you* find it so," she said. "However, I feel as though I've been battling a tempest. You give no quarter, do you? You say whatever comes into your head, and all the common rules of politeness, of what one may and may not say—" She made a sweeping gesture. "Gone."

"It's more interesting that way," he said. "*You* are vastly more interesting when you're vexed than when you're cool and proper and polite. For instance, I'd no idea you could be so obstinate. Or that you were so fascinated with the *demimonde*. The first time you mentioned my mistress, I nearly dropped into a faint. I'm shocked at you, Christina."

She did not appear to notice the use of her Christian name. "Until now, I've succeeded in shocking only four very unworldly middle-aged women," she said. "Perhaps I'm better prepared for Paris than I thought."

He glimpsed an escape route from this uncomfortable exchange and hastily took it. "No Englishman or woman can possibly be prepared for Paris," he said. "The Parisians are not French, but a breed apart. They are—" He shrugged. "I needn't tell you. You'll see for yourself."

"Not the Paris *you've* seen," she said. "I wish you would tell me about it."

When Julius and Penny returned, Marcus and Christina were still in the drawing room, talking. After an hour or more of Paris, they'd returned to discussing the plight of the Greeks. They were debating the pros and cons of various diplomatic strategies the British government might pursue when their hosts entered with the news that Sally, after some initial difficulty, had given birth to a healthy, noisy, little boy.

"You shouldn't have waited up, all the same," Julius reproved his brother. "It's past three o'clock, and in a few hours the house will erupt into chaos. You may be able to sleep through the racket, but Christina will be awakened at dawn's crack by overexcited children. By nightfall she'll be too tired to dance at the Yuletide ball. In consequence of which, several gentlemen are sure to blow their brains out. Really, you're most inconsiderate."

"It isn't his fault," Christina said before Marcus could retort on his brother. "I nagged him to tell me about Paris, then Greece, until he's hoarse from talking. Moreover, the twins will never think of waking me. They'll be too busy interfering with the party preparations and being tripped over by servants."

"And I shall ask the gentlemen to step outside to shoot themselves or hang themselves or whatever their disappointment moves them to do," said

Marcus. "We can easily collect the corpses next morning."

"There, it's all settled." Penny patted her husband's cheek. "What a fuss you make over nothing, Julius. Come to bed."

Marcus kept by Christina as they trailed upstairs after the other couple, but he didn't say a word. He continued on with her, walking to the guest wing, although his room was in the wing opposite. She should have pointed this out to him, and meant to, but she couldn't find the right words. Every imagined sentence seemed to attach too much significance to what was surely no more than absent-mindedness. Marcus had said before that he was weary, and he did appear lost in thought at present.

When they reached her door, she paused. "Thank you for giving me your company." Her voice was carefully polite. "You were generous to indulge my curiosity, and very patient with my ignorance."

"One could hardly expect you to know what most of your government doesn't. You at least ask intelligent questions. And your mind is open to new ideas."

The servants had left two candles lit in the hall. In the flickering light it was hard to read his face. The troubled expression she discerned might simply be shadows.

"I like to learn," she said. "I told you my life had been narrow."

"Yes, you did. I'd thought . . ." He looked away. "But you mean to make up for that, I see. It'll be good for you to go abroad, and good for your little girls. I'm . . . I'm glad your great-aunt goes with you. She is Julius's godmother, you may recall."

"Yes, I remember." If her parents, rather than her great-aunt, had chaperoned her ten years ago, there would have been no stolen moments with Marcus Greyson in sitting rooms or gardens or woodland paths.

"She'll be an excellent traveling companion," Marcus said. "She's highly knowledgeable and far more liberal minded than most of her generation. Equally important, she'll see that no one takes advantage of you. Innkeepers and shopkeepers, I mean. And guides. The Continent is a net of perils for the unwary."

He shook his head. "But I'm keeping you from your rest." He moved to open the door for her.

His coat sleeve brushed her arm, a breath of a touch, soft wool against her skin. For one pulsing moment they stood frozen, and the air between them warmed and thickened. Christina felt the way she had earlier when their gazes had locked: as though they were teetering on the brink of a precipice. She was afraid that if he gave the smallest tug, she would fall . . . and he was bending toward her. But he drew back quickly, almost in the same breath.

He clasped his hands behind his back. "Good night," he said.

"Good night," she said.

Then he turned and swiftly walked away.

The following day, while the two women dealt with the last minute frenzy of preparation for the ball, Marcus and Julius gathered greenery outdoors, with the dubious assistance of four rambunctious children. The girls were supposed to supervise only, according to Marcus's stern orders. They couldn't seem to do so, however, without inspecting every evergreen branch and pricking their fingers on holly. Then they must tumble about in the cart with the boys and crush their fancy bonnets and lose their mittens—and generally turn themselves into dirty little frights, as Marcus unchivalrously told them.

"What will your mama say?" he asked as he was wrestling Delia's hideously fussy bonnet back into place for the hundredth time.

"Off with those dirty things and into the bath!" she shrieked.

Livy giggled, which made Delia giggle, too, and the boys mocked them, squealing like pigs. Delia instantly dashed off in pursuit of Kit, while Livy went after his brother. The bonnets tumbled askew again, and mittens dropped into the dirt. By the time they returned to the house, all four children looked as though they'd spent the last month mucking out the stables.

Leaving Julius and the boys to carry the greenery to the ballroom, Marcus planted Livy on the antique porter's chair by the door and began tugging off her boots. Delia, as might be expected, couldn't wait for assistance. She was sitting on the cold floor wrestling with her muddy footwear when Christina entered the vestibule.

"Good heavens, where did these little ragamuffins come from?" she asked, her voice laced with amusement.

"A gypsy," Marcus answered. "He gave me these disorderly creatures in trade for Delia and Livy."

"No, no! It's *us*, Mama," Delia cried. "He didn't give us away."

"I'm sure he wishes he did." She shook her head. "I suppose you've been driving Mr. Greyson out of his wits."

"Oh, no, we were *helping* him," said Livy. She fixed an earnest blue gaze upon Marcus. "We *did* help, didn't we?"

"Certainly," he said. "I never could have found such lovely boughs without you." After carefully setting the right boot down next to its mate, he rose and turned to Christina. "I'm afraid we've lost a red mitten. I'm told a squirrel made off with it. Also, our bonnets are . . ." He gestured helplessly at the soiled, mangled bonnets. "I believe the only solution is to burn them. I *am* sorry. I should have—"

"Nonsense," Christina said briskly. "We've plenty more. Heaps of them, just waiting to be destroyed." She stepped nearer to add in a low voice, "The aunts, you know. Unfortunate tastes in millinery, yet they will keep sending the silly things."

"I did wonder," he said, reflexively lowering his own voice to the same conspiratorial pitch. "You're not at all fussy in your own attire, yet the hats were awash in ribbons and ruffles."

Her blue eyes sparkled. "They are ghastly, aren't they? I dread the arrival of those packages, because the instant the girls don their finery, I want to break out in whoops. One of these days I'm sure to strangle, trying *not* to."

"Mama, you're telling secrets," Delia reproached. She bolted upright and grabbed her mother's hand. "Tell *me*."

"Me, too," said Livy, scrambling down from the

chair. She tugged at Marcus's cuff. "Tell me what she said, Mr. Greyson."

He scooped Livy up on one arm, then held out his other for Delia. With a grin, she released her mother, and let herself be taken up as well.

"Really, Marcus, you mustn't," Christina protested. "They're too big to be carried."

He headed down the hall, obliging her to follow. "I can hardly let them run about the cold floor in their stocking feet."

"They're not nearly as delicate as they appear, I assure you."

Ignoring her, he proceeded up the stairs.

"Tell us the secret," said Delia.

He shook his head.

"*Please,*" her sister coaxed. "We won't tell anybody."

"Neither will I," he said. "I'm a very good secret keeper. I shan't tell your mama's, just as I shan't tell *yours.*"

Christina, mounting the stairs beside him, looked up sharply. "Oh, they've been telling secrets, have they?"

"Just one," he said. "But my lips are sealed."

"Very well," she said. "We shall simply have to pry one of your own out of you, to make it even."

The twins looked at Marcus, then at each other, and giggled.

"I see," said their mama. "He's already told you one, has he? Then I shall have to extract a secret all by myself. *A deep, dark one,*" she added in the same hollow tones she'd used when she read *Frankenstein.*

Marcus knew the ominous voice was for the

twins' benefit. His flesh prickled all the same. The girls loved it, of course and, snuggling closer, expressed their hopes that his secret would be quite ghastly and horrible.

He tried to convince himself he had no dark secrets to be extracted, thus no reason to feel anxious. His life, as Christina had remarked the night before, was open to public view, mistresses and commercial endeavors alike.

Until the last two days, the outward life comfortably represented the inner man. Now there was friction. He felt it when the twins talked to him or pulled at his coat sleeves or merely looked at him. He felt an inward tug of affection—natural enough, for they *were* darlings. He didn't mind that at all. What he minded were the other feelings. Old dreams and hopes rose like sad ghosts: the girl he'd wanted to marry ten years ago, the children he'd imagined, the family of his own to care for, and for whom he'd wanted to conquer the world . . . until he'd come to his senses and realized that empire building left no room for domesticity. Until now, he'd experienced no regrets. Now, he held another man's children and ached with a sense of loss.

They might have been yours, the ghosts mourned.

And that, Marcus supposed, was one horrible secret.

Christina frowned at her reflection in the mirror. "I must have ordered this gown with Paris in mind," she told Penny. "It doesn't seem altogether suitable for a country house fete."

"It's perfectly suitable," said Penny. "Your figure is excellent. I can't think of any reason to hide it."

"I can. I don't wish to be viewed as a dashing young widow. People are too quick to believe that when we put aside our mourning, we leave our morals behind as well."

Provocative, Marcus had said last night. The remark still stung, though Christina knew it was unjust and had argued accordingly. She tugged at the low-cut bodice.

"Do leave it be," her friend said. "If I believed it immodest, I'd say so. It's no more revealing than what you wore last night, and even Julius—who can be a trifle pompous at times—approved. He said it was about time you stopped dressing like a vicar's wife." Penny studied the open jewelry box. "You must wear diamonds, of course. That simple pendant you wore last night was—"

"Objected to," Christina said.

Penny looked up, her eyebrows raised. "Was it, indeed? I can only conclude it was Marcus who raised the objection. On what grounds, I wonder?"

"He said it was . . . distracting. And my gown was *provocative,*" Christina answered crossly.

Penny laughed. "Marcus does have a disconcerting habit of saying whatever is on his mind."

"I shouldn't have told you." Christina moved away from the mirror. "But the matter has been plaguing me. Which is ridiculous. He was only goading me, picking a quarrel, which you say he always does, with everybody. But he never used to—"

She turned her attention to selecting earrings. "It was a sore spot, that's all. Arthur's sisters didn't approve of the wardrobe I selected after I left off my mourning clothes. They tried to make me feel like a tart."

"Don't tell me about the aunts, Christina. I know all about the tiresome creatures." Penny stepped closer. "I'd much rather hear what else you and Marcus quarreled about . . . as you never *used* to do."

"That isn't what I said—meant." She snatched up the pendant. "I hardly knew—*know* him." She fumbled with the clasp.

"Let me." Penny took the necklace from her. "You're trembling."

"I'm chilled. I should have worn a warmer gown."

"You'll feel warmer shortly," Penny said as she deftly fastened the necklace. "The gentlemen will swarm about you and strive their utmost to raise your temperature. Marcus will have to fight his way through the throng if he wishes to take exception to your attire. And your other beaux, naturally, will leap to your defense. The evening promises to be most exciting."

"I don't want any beaux," Christina said, pulling on her gloves. "But everyone will think I'm . . . I'm looking out for a man—because of this dratted gown."

"You're just nervous, because you haven't been in company—frivolous company, that is—in eons. But we'll stop and visit the boys, and let them admire us, then get more of the same from the girls. After the children are done telling us how pretty we are, we shall be prepared to face the rest of the world with sublime assurance."

When Marcus stopped to bid his nephews good night, the two women were leaving.

"A topaz," said Penny, studying his stickpin with what Marcus felt was a far too knowing expression. "It matches your eyes."

"It was supposed to match my waistcoat," he said stiffly. "It was also supposed to be subtle. According to Beau Brummel, a gentleman's attire shouldn't call attention to itself."

"I didn't know you were a devotee of Brummel's," said Penny. "I thought you employed a valet to worry about your clothes, since you couldn't be bothered."

"Since my valet is still in London, I'm obliged to be bothered."

At the moment, Marcus was a great deal more than bothered. Christina was wearing a sapphire silk gown. The style was severely simple, bare of ruffles and furbelows, shorn of anything that might distract one from the sensuous curves it enfolded. She might as well be naked, he thought. It was all the same to him—or rather, to the mindless flesh and blood Marcus, whose muscles tightened painfully, whose fingers curled helplessly into his palms.

The other Marcus—the rational, civilized one—coolly answered several more teasing comments from Penny and dutifully complimented the ladies. He promised to join them downstairs very soon, certainly before the guests began arriving, and kept his face utterly expressionless as he watched them walk away.

Then he entered the boys' bedchamber and tried to calm down.

That took more than twenty minutes, which he filled with a story about Aegean pirates. And now he would be late for the party, because he still needed to say good night to the twins, as he'd promised earlier.

He hurried down the hall, round the corner, then stopped short. Two blonde heads poked out of the doorway. Two little faces were looking expectantly his way and lighting up with smiles. Something inside him lit up, too, and made him feel enormously pleased with himself as he continued toward them. He endeavored, however, to appear stern.

"Shouldn't you be in bed?" he asked, with a reproachful glance at the naked toes peeping out from under their flannel nightdresses.

They both nodded.

"Why aren't you, then?"

"We were waiting for you," said Delia, taking his hand.

"To say good night," said Livy, taking the other.

"Indeed. Without your robes, without your slippers, standing in a draughty doorway. If your mama finds out—"

"We won't tell," said Delia. "Will you?"

"You are little minxes," he said. He snatched them up and carried them to their bed. Then he simply let go and dropped them, which they found hilarious and delightful. So much so that they demanded he do it again.

"No. It's not playtime. It's time to sleep," he said. "Under the bedclothes with you."

After they had crawled into their respective places, he pulled the blankets up over them.

"Will you tell us a story?" Livy asked.

"A ghastly, horrible one?" her sister amplified. "Mama told one, but it wasn't horrible at all."

"It was too short," Livy said. "Mama had to hurry."

"As I ought to," he said. "The grownups are having a party, remember. It would be very impolite of me to be late—which I shall be, if I stay to tell you a story."

They thought this over. "You mustn't be late," Livy said at last.

"Will you dance with Mama?" her twin asked.

"Yes, of course. I shall dance with all the ladies who let me."

"Mama will let you," said Delia.

"She likes to dance," said Livy.

"I'm glad to hear it." Marcus neatly tucked them in.

Livy elbowed Delia, who elbowed back harder. Before Marcus could remonstrate, the latter said, "Livy wants to kiss you good night."

He told himself the request wasn't significant. They were affectionate children who liked him, that was all. He bent and politely presented his cheek to Livy. Her lips touched it, light as an angel's wing.

"Me, too," said Delia. She gave him a hug, along with a noisy smack.

He felt the tug again as well as the sadness, stronger than before.

They weren't his. He wished they were. Wished it fiercely.

He straightened, and forced a smile. "Good night and happy dreams, my little angels."

To Christina the ballroom seemed thick with ghosts. The men swarmed about her just as Penny had predicted, and just as they'd done ten years ago. The compliments now were warmer, the flirtations bolder. Otherwise it was all the same because, like the young girl of the past, she scarcely heard a word, only answered automatically, while all her consciousness fixed on the one man who kept away.

That also was just as he'd done all those years ago, even though the barriers of the old days no longer existed. Christina was no longer a green girl, and he was no longer a social outcast.

She answered her dance partner's compliments and witticisms while she wondered why Marcus was avoiding her. They had managed to get along so well last night—after that short, nerve-wracking row—and today, too. But not altogether well, she silently amended. The past remained like some galvanic current, pulsing under the surface of everything they said and did. There was tension, and she couldn't believe she was the only one who felt it.

The dance ended. The next, she knew, would be a waltz. She looked toward the windows where Marcus stood gazing into the darkness. He was not very far away. She could see the gold glints the candlelight made in his tawny hair. On a summer day long ago, a timidly conventional girl had crossed a distance like this.

She collected her courage and moved quickly, before she could think twice, and didn't pause until she stood three feet from his black-clad back.

"Marcus," she said.

Stiffening, he turned to her.

"Won't you dance with me?" she asked.

* * *

Marcus looked at her—all of her: the shatteringly beautiful face with its pale gold halo, the gown, vividly blue against the snowy purity of her skin, and the sinuous curves it clung to and caressed. He thought, *What's the use?*

He also thought, *No, not again.*

He said, his voice strained, "I don't think that would be wise."

"Oh," she said. Her lashes lowered, her mouth turned down a fraction, and she was turning away.

His heart ached, his fool heart, and his fool hand wanted to touch her, bring her back. He kept his hands by his sides. "I mean yes," he said hoarsely. "Of course I mean yes."

Of course, he thought, as her blue gaze swept up to his. Of course he wanted her. How could he help it? How could he let her turn away?

The music started up. Last night, he had scarcely touched her, yet he'd felt the jolt and the current pulsing between them. But last night he'd been tired and vulnerable, he told himself.

He brought his hand to her waist . . . and the shock of contact darted through his nerve endings. She gave a tiny gasp, and stiffened . . . shocked, too.

"Too late now," he said under his breath. One overwarm gloved hand firmly clasping her waist, the other tingling against her gloved palm, he whirled her into the dance.

It seemed as though every eye in the ballroom was fixed on them. And why not? This was the first waltz of the evening, and he of all men had won the privilege of partnering her. How shocked they'd all be if they knew Christina Travers had broken the rules and asked *him.*

"Why did you ask me?" he said.

"Because you forgot to ask *me.*"

"I see. Every other man in the place has fallen victim to your snares. Now your conquest is complete."

He spun her into a turn that brought her thigh against his and made the silk gown ripple about his legs. He thought of soft thighs pressing against his and of the rustle of sheets. His breath quickened and his grip of her waist tightened.

"Marcus," she gasped.

He looked down. Her face was pink. "What is it?"

"You are driving the whalebone into my back."

"Whalebone?"

"My *stays,*" she hissed, flushing more deeply.

Of all things, she had to remind him of her undergarments. Reluctantly he eased his hold. "What the devil do you want with a corset? You scarcely even dressed."

He gazed down at the creamy expanse of bosom offered to his view—and that of every other male in the ballroom. "By my calculations, you took three hours, only to come out half-naked."

Her head went up. "I am not half-naked. And I did not take three hours. Only two. And a half. Stop looking at me that way. You'll make everyone stare."

"If you didn't want people to stare, you should have put on the rest of your gown."

"Oh, very well," she said. "Look if you must."

"Of course I must. There is that great diamond,

like a tavern sign, demanding my attention."

"Yes, Marcus," she said patiently. "I wore it on purpose to vex you."

He was vexed—not by the diamond but by the circumstances. Waltzing was very much like making love to music, but not enough like.

He wished her low voice didn't beckon so irresistibly. He wished he didn't find her combative retorts so adorable. Above all he wished that he hadn't found the woman of twenty-eight so very much more exciting and desirable than the girl of eighteen.

He drew her closer.

"I thought we were supposed to keep twelve inches apart," she said breathlessly.

"I'm too old and set in my ways to start following such stupid rules now," he said, also painfully short of breath. But then, waltzing wasn't the mildest of exercises.

She, too, was growing overheated. Her face was flushed, and there were traces of moisture at her temples. A strand of silky hair was coming loose near her left ear. It was making him desperate.

He drew her into another turn, steering her to a doorway, then through it, to the dimly lit hall that led to the backstairs.

"I think we'd better talk," he said. He let go of her waist and, taking her by the hand, led her into the shadows. He was aware of her body tensing in resistance, though she didn't try to break away.

"I suppose, because I asked you to dance, you've leapt to certain conclusions," she said, a shade of belligerence in her voice.

"Yes," he said.

"I suppose as well that you think my gown constitutes a deliberate provocation."

"Oh, yes."

"I don't see why I must dress like a dowd or obey every persnickety rule of behavior to please you," she said.

He bit back a smile. "But you aren't trying to please me," he said.

"Certainly not."

"You're trying to drive me distracted."

"I'm not trying to do anything."

"And you've succeeded." He brushed the wayward strand of hair back with his thumb. She trembled.

"I suppose you think I'm going to kiss you now," he said. "I suppose you think you're irresistible."

"I suppose you think *you* are," she said.

"I must be. You couldn't keep away."

"I did not drag you into a dark hallway."

"I didn't *drag* you."

"You said you wanted to *talk*."

"Must you always have the last word?" he asked impatiently. "Will you not give one inch?"

After a moment's consideration, she let out a sigh. "Very well," she said. "Kiss me if you must. You might as well get it out of your system."

"Very well," he said. "If you *insist*."

Still holding her hand, he bent toward her. Her head tilted back ever so slightly, ever so reluctantly. Her fingers tightened on his and that small pressure vibrated through him . . . a pulsing current, irresistible.

He bent closer. A breath away from her lips he paused, his heart hammering. He remembered vividly the aching loss, the grief and rage . . . weeks, months of it. But he also remembered the sweetness and tender yielding of the kisses he had stolen long ago.

His lips touched hers and there was a shock, sharp and sweet at once, and softness, too, so familiar . . . and the piercing ache of yearning. It was the yearning that made his arms slip round her to gather her close, and kiss her long and deeply . . . as he'd never dared to do all those years ago.

But it was different now. Christina was no longer a naive young girl, easily frightened by desire. Her mouth parted to his coaxing tongue and she melted against him, answering his erotic summons with a woman's tender passion.

She was as warm in his arms as homecoming, warm as love and belonging. Yet this was no safe hearth, either, he speedily discovered, for her warmth fueled his need, and the fire built swiftly.

Her firm breasts pressed against the wool of his coat, but it wasn't enough. His hands moved over her back, pressing her nearer, but still not close enough, for this was gloves on silk, and he wanted flesh on flesh. His hands moved to the base of her spine, to the sweet curve of her hips. She was near enough to be aware of his aching arousal. He wanted her closer still, wanted to crush her to him, but that would only make matters worse. He was already losing control.

He released her mouth. He meant to release her altogether, but the instant she began to pull away, his hands fastened on her waist.

"You can't go back now," he said thickly.

"You're all . . . mussed." Delectably mussed. Her neat coiffure was tumbling undone, her gown was tantalizingly rumpled, and her breath was coming in quick gasps. He thought about how much more tousled and heated he might make her, and his own breathing grew more labored. He tugged her closer. She stiffened, resisting.

"Don't tease, Christina," he said. "I only want another kiss."

"No," she said. "I gave you the inch you wanted, and you took ten *miles*. Then you have the audacity to tell me I'm mussed—as though I did it myself—on purpose to vex you, I suppose."

"I plead guilty to the charge of mussing," he said. "But you did cooperate."

"You seem to have a certain skill in eliciting cooperation," she said. "But then, you had it ten years ago. Evidently, my powers of resistance remain some years behind your powers of persuasion."

"You never even tried to resist, then or now," he said, bridling. "On the contrary, you deliberately sought me out, both times, and led me on."

"Very well, I led you on," she said. "You're a helpless victim of my irresistible wiles once again, though you're a successful, powerful man of four-and-thirty. And because I don't care to be seduced on your brother's back stairs—just as I didn't care to run off with you and be ruined—I'm a heartless tease." She glanced down at his hands. "Perhaps it's time I released you from my wicked clutches."

For one furious instant, he wanted to hurl her aside, out of his sight, out of his thoughts, out of existence.

He caught his breath and looked down at his rigid hands . . . then at her. As he searched her hurt, angry eyes, his own rage washed away, leaving him chilled.

"Dear God, is that what you thought?" he asked. "That I only wanted to seduce you?"

He took his hands away. She didn't move.

"I wanted to *marry* you, Christina," he said. "I told you so, again and again."

"You told me a great many things," she said tightly. "All lies."

He felt a surge of anger, instantly swamped by a flood of grief. Old grief. He drew a shaky breath. "You're wrong," he said softly. "I think we need to talk, but not here." He held out his hand.

He wouldn't have blamed her if she hadn't taken it, but she did—and that was a start, he thought, a proper beginning. He wasn't sure he could make a proper finish, but something, obviously, must be done. They must lay the ghosts to rest, regardless how painful the process might be. Otherwise, the past would taint everything he and she felt for and wanted from each other.

He led her down the back stairs, down another hall, and into a small, quiet parlor at the rear of the house.

He closed the door, firmly shutting out the rest of the world. She slid her hand from his and moved to the window.

"It's started to snow," she said.

He joined her, and looked out into the darkness at the fat snowflakes lazily drifting down. "I did love you," he said. "I did want to marry you. Did you believe *nothing* I told you?"

"I believed everything you told me," she said. "Every word you said to make me fall in love with you, then, every word you wrote later, showing me what a fool I'd been. You wrote that I needn't worry that you'd trouble me again. You thanked me for making an otherwise dull fortnight tolerably amusing." Bitterness edged her voice. "You said I mustn't mind my lack of sophistication, because I was pretty, and the world requires no more in a female. According to you, my future husband would be content merely to look at me. My heart untouched by any base human emotion, I should provide him the same tranquil pleasure a lovely painting or statue offers. There was more, all put very cleverly. You described everything that was wrong with me in words I might take for flattery—if I were the empty-headed miss you thought I was."

His face burned with shame. "It was a childish letter. I was . . . very angry."

"You had spent two whole weeks weakening my mind and morals. But in the end, I wouldn't run away with you and be ruined. Certainly you were angry. You had gone to so much trouble for nothing."

"You've got it all wrong," he said. "That may be what everyone else would believe, but not you. You understood me, trusted me, I thought."

"I loved you," she said. She spoke quietly, not trying to convince, merely stating a simple fact. He believed her.

"In other words," he said, "I had your love—then killed it with my letter."

She nodded.

He had been a fool. A proud, hotheaded fool.

"The letter was all lies," he said. "It was—" He searched his heart for the truth. "I was unacceptable," he said. "I knew that. All the world knew it. You saw how the chaperons watched me. You, like the rest of the young misses, must have been warned to keep away from me."

"Yes, I was warned," she said.

"I was warned as well. Before you came, Julius told me about your strict parents and about Arthur Travers and his spotless reputation and his forty thousand a year. Julius asked me not to flirt with you, because if your parents heard of it, they'd have you sent home, and Penny would be heartbroken. I promised both Julius and myself that I'd have nothing to do with you. Then I spent two weeks pretending, sneaking about, snatching stolen moments—and hating myself and all the world because I couldn't court you openly."

"My conscience wasn't easy, either," she said softly.

"And all the while, time was ticking away," he went on. "I knew your parents would arrive the day of the wedding—and that would be the end, because they'd take you away and I'd never be allowed within twenty miles of you. I knew—perhaps you did, too—that I hadn't a prayer of winning their approval. Ever."

"I . . . knew."

"I was terrified of losing you, Christina. That's why I plagued you to elope with me. That night before Julius's wedding was our last and only chance. I was so sure you'd meet me, as you promised, at the gatehouse. Everything was ready.

The carriage was packed, waiting. I waited, hours, and you didn't come. And when at last I gave up and returned to the house, I found your note in my room, and I . . . I just wrote out all my rage and hurt in a letter I should have burnt, not sent."

She turned to him. "I couldn't do it, Marcus. I couldn't break my parents' hearts. I couldn't subject Arthur to public humiliation."

"I know," he said. And he did, at last. He understood now what he'd been too heartsick to recognize then. "If you had, you would have been the flighty, unfeeling creature I claimed you were in that letter." He turned his gaze back to the night. "The whole situation was hopeless, wasn't it? I should have faced it and accepted it, like a man. Instead I lashed out at you, like a spiteful child. That was . . . unforgivable."

She shook her head. "I think now that it was better you wrote as you did. Otherwise, I might have grieved for what might have been for—well, a long time. Instead, I was able to pick up the pieces of my broken heart, telling myself I'd had a lucky escape, and go back to Arthur, and be a good wife to him."

Arthur's wife, when she should have been his, Marcus thought bleakly. Arthur's children, when they should have been his. She had gone back to Arthur, while Marcus had gone on, heartsick, for . . . oh, months only, though it had felt like years. But he'd picked up his broken bits of heart, too, and gone on to build his empire. He'd been too busy to be lonely. And there had been other women. He had fallen in and out of love half a dozen times at least.

But never so deeply. Never again had he loved, body and soul, as he had loved one eighteen-year-old girl. He had taken many risks since then, but never fully, with all his heart. Never had he been tempted to do so. Until now.

His gaze slid back to her. He hadn't even wanted to like her again, but he couldn't help it. She'd grown not only more beautiful and desirable but cleverer, bolder, infinitely more . . . exciting. If he let himself fall in love again, he had no doubt he'd fall harder. And then . . .

How would it end—if he let it begin—this time?

"It sounds as though we forgive each other," he said cautiously.

Smiling, she moved away from the window. "Yes. How mature we've managed to be, despite an unpromising beginning. Perhaps we might even manage to stop bickering."

"I don't mind bickering with you. It's—"

"Stimulating." She pushed a lock of hair away from her face. "However, I'd rather not return to the company looking quite so *stimulated*. I had better go to my room and put myself to rights." She headed toward the door. "If you're in a mood to be chivalrous, perhaps you'll explain to Julius and Penny that you accidentally stepped on the hem of my gown and tore it. That may, just barely, explain my overlong disappearance."

She hurried through the door before he could answer.

She would have to leave Greymarch, Christina told herself several hours later while she lay awake, staring at the ceiling. She had finally put her life together as she wanted it and was at last becoming the woman she wanted to be. She couldn't let Marcus Greyson turn everything upside down again. She'd spent only two days under the same roof with him, and already the world was tilting dangerously askew.

He had played havoc with her morals ten years ago. He said tonight that his intentions had been honorable, and she believed him. *Then,* however, wasn't *now.* This night, the instant he'd taken her into his arms, her morals had disintegrated completely.

He hadn't taken any outrageous liberties. His hands hadn't wandered where they shouldn't. He hadn't unfastened a single fastening. Nonetheless, in a few simmering minutes, without so much as taking off his gloves, Marcus Greyson had done to her what her adoring husband had never come close to doing in seven years of conjugal intimacy.

She was all too hotly aware of what Marcus might do to her if he took off his gloves.

She had thought the tension between them was because of the past, and even the physical attraction must somehow be part of it, because it was too feverishly intense. He was an attractive man, admittedly. All the same, he shouldn't make her feel so . . . desperate.

Yet even after they'd laid the past to rest and forgiven each other, the desperate feelings remained. She had fled the room to keep from hurling herself right back into his arms.

She closed her eyes. Heaven help her. Two days in his company and she had turned into a besotted schoolgirl . . . if not something worse.

* * *

Despite a restless night, Christina rose in time to go with Penny and the children to church. The men were still abed when they returned, and only Julius came down to luncheon. After that, Christina took the children outdoors. It had snowed throughout the night, leaving a thick blanket, the perfect consistency for sledding.

Aware that Kit could be trusted to take his brother down the small hill safely, Christina could give most of her attention to her own and her daughters' entertainment, which she did with gusto. She had two years' practice to give her confidence and two thrill-seeking seven-year-olds to encourage daring. They raced the boys, beat them twice, and were beaten twice.

It was during the fifth race that her skirt caught on a runner. The sled went out of control, veering toward a tree. She was aware of shouts above, then of flying through the air, Delia clasped in her arms, before she landed hard, a few feet from the tree.

Delia rolled free, shrieking with laughter, while Christina lay stunned and breathless, blinking at the vivid blue sky. In the next instant, she was staring into the very white, rigid countenance of Marcus Greyson.

Before she could utter a syllable, he caught her in his arms and pulled her tight against him. His chest heaved as though he'd been running for his life. She could have told him she was quite uninjured, and the only damage she was like to suffer was if he crushed her ribs. But she held her tongue. She wasn't in any hurry to be released.

"Me, too," Delia demanded.

Marcus's ferocious grip relaxed. He gave Delia a hug, then helped Christina to her feet. "That was well done," he said in a muffled voice. "I was . . . congratulating your mama on her fine handling of the sled."

He briskly brushed snow from the back of Christina's coat. "Why don't you go to the house and change into something dry?" he said. His voice was not altogether steady. "I'll look after the children."

"I'm all right," she said. "A little snow won't hurt me."

"You're soaked to the skin," he whispered fiercely. "You nearly broke your neck. In another moment, I shall shake you until your teeth rattle. *Go away*, Christina."

She turned away, her eyes widening in astonishment. He was very agitated, more than she'd guessed. Very likely he *would* shake her.

She straightened her bonnet and walked back to the house, her heart thrumming with hope.

Marcus was well aware that he'd just made a complete fool of himself. He had rushed down the slope in blind panic—doubtless alarming the children—and clutched Christina to him in a perfectly demented manner. He had all but wept with relief to find she was still breathing. Then, to cap the performance, he'd threatened to shake her.

After a half hour of brisk exercise with the children, he still hadn't recovered.

He had behaved like an idiot, but he wasn't one. He knew perfectly well what the trouble was. What he'd felt in that chilling moment when he'd thought he'd lost her told him all he needed to know. Somehow, in less than three days, he had stumbled out of his senses and fallen in love with her.

He looked down at the little girls trotting alongside him, confidently holding his hands. He loved them, too. That, too, in only three days. And in less than three weeks they'd be gone. Unless he could manage a miracle.

Christina didn't see Marcus again until shortly before dinner. She had just settled down to tell the twins a bedtime story when he appeared in the doorway.

"I just wanted to say good night to the young ladies," he said. He made a courtly bow. "Good night, Miss Delia, Miss Livy. Happy dreams."

Two childish countenances fell.

"What has happened to your manners?" Christina asked them. "Say good night to Mr. Greyson."

Delia's lower lip jutted out. "He's too far away. Livy can't kiss him."

Livy kicked her twin under the bedclothes. "You can't, either."

Christina looked at Marcus, her eyebrows raised.

He hesitated briefly, then entered and advanced to the bed. "I beg your pardon," he told the twins. "My mind was addled. I forgot the rules." He bent and politely accepted a kiss and a hug from each girl. The pouts vanished and he was bid smiling good nights.

Without another word, he left.

Christina turned back to her children.

"Mr. Greyson is very nice, isn't he, Mama?" Delia whispered.

"Yes. Very nice."

"He likes us, doesn't he?" Livy asked, gazing hopefully at her mother.

"I believe he does."

The girls glanced at each other.

"Do you like him, Mama?" Delia asked.

Christina bit back a smile. "Certainly. Didn't I just agree that he was very nice?"

"He has gold speckles in his eyes," Delia told her. "He said the fairies did it."

"Us, too," said Livy. "He told Delia she had silver fairy dust, and me, too, and you, too, Mama."

"And he said the angels dropped the stars and they turned into diamonds," Delia said.

Christina remembered nights long ago when the heavens were alight with shooting stars. "They're diamonds," he'd whispered as they watched. "We'll travel the world, and I'll find them for you. I'll shower you with diamonds. I can do it, love. Believe in me and I will. I'll give you the world."

"Is it true, Mama?" Livy asked.

Christina came back to the present. "It very well may be," she said.

That night, Marcus remained in the drawing room after the others went up to bed. He touched the book Christina had held and thought of her gloved hands curled about his neck when he'd kissed her. He thought about her low, foggy voice. He thought about her soft, welcoming mouth and her sweet curves melting against him. He thought about tumbled coiffures and rumpled sheets and silken skin.

He thought he had better stop thinking about it and do something.

At breakfast the next day, he tried to start an argument with her about the Corn Laws. She couldn't debate that topic, she said defensively, because she knew little about political economy. Immediately after breakfast, he drove to Bath and found a copy of Adam Smith's *The Wealth of Nations,* which he gave her that afternoon. Then he offered to show her a more challenging hill for sledding.

He took her and the children sledding that day and skating the next. The next day he took them on a tour of Bath, which he conducted in French, so that the girls could practice for their trip abroad. The following night they attended a ball. Though he danced with her only twice—for propriety's sake—he didn't keep entirely away the rest of the time. He had a campaign to conduct.

And so he wandered back to her side from time to time to share an amusing observation or a bit of gossip or a joke. He couldn't keep the other men away—not without committing violence—but he could make sure she didn't forget he was there. She would have to get used to having him about, after all, and learn that this wouldn't be a bad thing.

With this goal in mind, Marcus exerted himself in the following days to display all his good points. Rather like a horse offered at auction, he thought wryly.

At a concert in Bath, he made up his own ludicrous lyrics to the music, which he sang softly off-key in her ear during the interval until she was breathless with laughter. He taught the three Travers ladies Italian folk songs. He bribed his brother's cook, and spent an afternoon in the kitchen teaching Christina how to make Greek pastries while the fascinated twins looked on. He argued with her about education, religion, and art, and spent hours with her, poring over maps while they debated international politics.

Not once during this time did he make anything that might be construed as an improper advance. It wasn't easy. Nothing he'd done in the last ten years, in fact, had been so difficult. Never in that decade, however, had so very much been at stake. If he succeeded, Marcus reminded himself, he would have a lifetime for lovemaking. He could certainly endure another week or so. Besides, all the signs were promising. After ten days' steady campaigning, he felt sure he was making progress.

She was no longer uncomfortable with him. She shared her own observations and gossip and jokes, and her face lit up with glee when they launched into an argument. Twice when she'd been busy at some task and the twins had repeatedly interrupted with their squabbles, Christina had distractedly waved them away and told them to go bother Mr. Greyson.

Most encouraging of all was a minor episode the night before Christmas Eve, when they were preparing to leave for a musicale at the Nichol's. The clasp of her pearl necklace came undone as Marcus was helping her with her wrap. Though Penny stood only a few feet away, Christina turned to Marcus to refasten the pearls.

She was beginning to take him for granted, he reflected happily the next morning when he came down to breakfast. She wasn't simply getting used to his being there; she was beginning to count on it.

His pleased grin faded when he discovered only Julius at the breakfast table.

"Where is—where are the ladies?" Marcus asked.

"Where do you think? It's Christmas Eve day. They're locked in the sitting room amid a heap of silver tissue and ribbons. They're wrapping gifts this morning because there won't be time this afternoon," Julius elucidated. "We're taking the children to play with another thousand little beasts at Alistair House."

"No one mentioned Alistair House to me," said Marcus, moving to the sideboard.

"They'll probably spring it on you at the last minute. But you needn't come. It's meant mainly for the children, and very exciting it is, too: a fir tree in the hall, lit with candles, with a lot of gaudy trinkets and ribbons hanging in the boughs. I suppose we'll have to do it next year. The Duchess of York's German customs appear to have taken permanent hold. I wonder how many houses will burn down before we adopt a less hazardous foreign custom."

"I think it's an excellent custom," said Marcus. Next Christmas he would have a tree lit with candles, he decided. There would be a silver star at the top, and a lot of shiny geegaws hanging from the boughs. And angels. Three golden-haired angels in the tree. He had seen some in a shop in Paris. They had tiny golden halos and gossamer silk wings and gold threads in their snow white robes.

He brought his plate to the table and sat down. "I'll have to be excused from Alistair House," he said. "I've something to do in Bath."

"Something," Julius repeated expressionlessly. "You are too confiding, Marcus. You must try for more self-restraint. Though I am your brother, you really needn't tell me everything."

"I beg your pardon, Julius. I shall try to contain myself in future." Grinning, Marcus took up his knife and fork.

By eleven o'clock that night, they gave up waiting for Marcus and prepared to go to church.

The twins were beside themselves. They had been looking for him and asking for him since they'd returned from Alistair House. They had refused to nap because he hadn't come to wish them happy dreams—which meant, according to Delia, that they would have horrid ones. Because they hadn't napped, they were contrary and petulant.

After a lengthy struggle, Christina got them into their coats, mittens, and bonnets.

"But we can't go now, Mama," Delia wailed as Christina led them to the door.

Livy tugged at her mother's coat. "Can't we wait a little more? Can't I wait for him?"

"No, I'll wait," said Delia. "You go to church with Mama and I'll come later with Mr. Greyson."

"No one will wait," said Christina. "Mr. Greyson is perfectly capable of getting to midnight services by himself, if he wishes to. Come along. The others are already in the carriage, and Kit and Robin's papa is waiting in the cold."

"It isn't fair, Mama."

"Mr. Greyson will be all by himself. Maybe he won't know where we are."

"He'll be sad, Mama."

"He might be lost. Maybe we should look for him."

Christina knew it was no use trying to reason with them. If she was going to get them to midnight services, she must be an utterly heartless mama. She hustled them to the carriage and ordered them in. As they sulkily obeyed, she turned to apologize to Julius for keeping him waiting.

"I was happy to wait," he said gallantly. "It gave me an opportunity to gaze at the heavens and be properly awed."

Christina looked up. It had snowed off and on during the day, but the sky was rapidly clearing, the last wispy clouds chased by a brisk wind. It was an awe-inspiring sight, as Julius said. The heavens stretched out like a robe of blue-black velvet set with countless winking diamonds.

"The angels are putting the stars back," she murmured. "How busy they must be, and yet so careful. There is Orion, precisely as he always is, with three stars in his belt, and there—"

She caught her breath as a star shot past the astral hunter and down, to disappear behind the fir trees.

"A falling star," she said softly. "Isn't that—"

"There's another," Julius said.

There was another and another, a shower of falling stars, all dropping behind the fir trees that surrounded the old gatehouse. But of course they hadn't. It only looked that way.

All the same, her flesh prickled. She thought of angels dropping stars that turned into diamonds. She took a step away from the carriage, then another. She looked at Julius.

"I can't go to church," she said. "I have something to do."

"Something," he repeated. "Yes, of course. Some of us have something to do and some of us haven't. I beg you will not tell me what it is. I had much rather die of suspense." He made an elegant bow. "Good night, my dear. I shall see you . . . eventually, I trust."

"You're very understanding, Julius."

"I'm one of the two most understanding fellows in England." He smiled and climbed into the carriage.

Blushing, Christina hurried back to the house.

Marcus reached the house not long after the others had left. He had scoured Bath without finding the angels he wanted. As a result, he had spent a great deal of money and waited a great many hours while a dollmaker transformed a trio of tiny china dolls according to Marcus's specifications. He would have reached Greymarch in time for dinner if he hadn't come across a carriage accident and decided to be a good Samaritan.

Still, he did have the angels, and if he made a push, he could join the others before the midnight service ended. He gave the packages to the footman with orders to put them in his bedchamber.

Marcus was moving to the front door when his glance lit upon a side table. A hymnal lay upon it.

"Mrs. Travers forgot her hymnal," he said.

"Oh, Mrs. Travers didn't go to church, sir," the footman said. "She said she had a headache. She went out a few minutes ago to take a turn about the garden. She said a short walk in the cold air often helps."

Marcus changed direction and headed for the ballroom, whose French doors opened onto the terrace. From the terrace, he surveyed the formal gardens. There was no sign of her.

Out of the corner of his eyes he caught a flash of something, but when he looked that way it was gone. The wind rustled the leaves of the rhododendrons.

"Christina?"

Where in blazes was she? Where could she have gone in the dead of night, in the dead of winter?

Tonight, Christina. It must be tonight.

He shook his head, but the recollection wouldn't be shaken off. Then it began again: the past crowding into his mind and tangling with the present as it had done two weeks ago, before they laid the ghosts to rest.

Run away with me, Christina.

"No, I'm going to do it right this time," he muttered. "Courting and a church wedding and—"

Meet me at the gatehouse at midnight. Promise.

Yes, I'll be there. I promise.

His gaze moved to the fir forest where the old gatehouse lay hidden from view . . . where the flash had come from.

She couldn't be there. He was losing his mind—which was hardly surprising. These last ten days of keeping his hands to himself were taking their toll. He was probably going mad with frustration.

All the same, he couldn't keep himself from hurrying through the garden and down the path to the stream, then across the narrow bridge. He broke into a run when he reached the path leading to the gatehouse. It was nearly midnight. He couldn't be late, he thought wildly. He didn't know why. All he knew was that he mustn't, couldn't be late.

He reached the clearing just as the village church tolled the first stroke of midnight. A lantern stood on the stone ledge of the gatehouse window.

A figure stood in the shadow of the doorway.

He raced across the clearing and swept her into his arms.

If she had taken leave of her senses, Christina reflected a while later, at least she wasn't the only one.

They should have simply returned to the main house. But she had shown him the gatehouse key she'd stolen from Julius's desk, and Marcus had unlocked the door and taken her inside. Then, because she was shivering, he had built a fire. She wasn't at all surprised that the place was well stocked with coal, and not at all amazed to see the stack of blankets and cushions heaped near the hearth, just as though she and Marcus had been expected. This night, she could believe anything.

It also seemed the most natural thing in the world to be snuggled cozily with him in front of the fire. It was right that she should be in his arms, her head resting on his chest while she tried to explain how she had come to be there.

She didn't even try to make up a face-saving excuse. She couldn't think why she needed to save face.

"There were stars falling," she told him. "It was a shower of stars . . . and I just had to come . . . to find diamonds, perhaps . . . or maybe it was myself I came to find."

"Yourself?"

"From long ago. I did what was best then, I know, because it was hopeless for us. And my life hasn't been empty or miserable. I haven't been pining for you all this time. I was a good wife, and fond of Arthur, and content, and I had two children to love frantically. And yet tonight it seemed . . . it was as though I left some part of myself behind that night ten years ago. And I think it was the girl who loved you and wanted to follow you to the ends of the earth."

"And did you find her?" he asked softly.

"Yes."

"Will she follow me to the ends of the earth?"

"Yes."

He gave her a quick, fierce hug. "It may be enough if she marries me. Will she?"

"Oh, yes. She's been waiting for you to ask." She looked up at him. "I was beginning to think you'd *never* ask."

"It's only been—" He frowned. "Gad, Christina, it's been two weeks. Just like the last time."

"Yes. You work very quickly."

"I was trying to proceed slowly, to work my way into your affections by degrees, until you found it impossible to live without me. I wanted you to have no doubt that we're ideally suited, that I'm the perfect mate for you and shall make a superior papa for Delia and Livy."

"You did that very well." She smiled up at him. "You've made me fully aware of all your many assets."

"Not all of them." His eyes burned into hers. "But that can wait until after we're wed. I love you very much. I can wait."

"So can I," she said.

He nuzzled her head affectionately. She pressed a bit closer. His lips touched her forehead. Her hand slipped under his coat to his waistcoat. His hands slid down her back to the base of her spine. And tightened. She tipped her head back. His mouth brushed hers. Her fingers strayed under the waistcoat to the soft linen of his shirt. His mouth brushed hers again, then lingered. Warmth trickled through her, but it tingled, and she shivered. His arms tightened around her and the kiss deepened.

Then his hands were moving over her, stirring muscles and flesh to aching awareness. The world dissolved to haze, and the trickling warmth built to a torrent of heat. It raced through her veins and whirled in her head.

The haze darkened and fiery stars danced in it.

Things came undone . . . buttons, hooks . . . his, hers. His coat fell away, her gown. A neckcloth slid to the carpet, a shirt, a chemise . . . shoes, trousers, stockings. Her hands moved restlessly over rock-hard muscle while her body strained and yearned under his simmering caresses, and her flesh sizzled under the hot touch of his lips and tongue.

She felt the worn carpet, soft as velvet against her back, as his powerful body bore her down. She heard his voice ragged with tenderness, coaxing, reassuring. She tried to answer.

"Marcus . . . oh, dear God . . ."

"I love you."

His hands moved insistently, willing her farther, on to the brink and beyond. Then, in the instant that rapture claimed her, the thrust came, and there was raw power surging inside her, driving her farther still. She cried his name and her love, and they blazed together at last, and became but one shooting star.

When Livy woke on Christmas morning, she found an angel on her pillow. It had golden hair and a tiny gold halo and silk wings and gold threads in its white silk robe. There was one just like it on Delia's pillow.

They gasped and exclaimed and laughed and hugged the angels. At last they noticed the two adults standing by the bed.

Then they noticed Mr. Greyson's hand, which was tightly clasping their mama's.

Twin blue gazes lifted questioningly to their mother. She quickly erased her smile.

"As you can see, I found him," she said.

"Oh, yes. Thank you, Mama," Delia said.

"Yes, thank you, Mama," Livy echoed.

Their voices were breathless.

"I thought I had better hold on, so he doesn't get lost again," Christina explained.

"Yes."

"Oh, yes."

"But I can't hold his hand forever," she went on. "And so I was thinking I might marry him."

Two eager nods.

"But then he would be your papa," she said dubiously, "and that might be rather a bother, you know. We should have to go live with him in his house, and give him kisses every single night—maybe sometimes even in the daytime. And sometimes I would have to let him tell the bedtime stories, and I am quite sure that now and then when we were naughty he would scold us."

Their gazes swung to Marcus.

"Well, I might," he said.

They looked at each other.

Christina heaved a sigh. "Perhaps we'd better not marry him," she said. "It will be a great deal of work."

They considered.

After a moment, Delia said, "I'll help you, Mama."

"Me, too," said Livy.

Marcus released Christina's hand to sit down upon the bed. "Are you quite sure?" he asked. "I would try my best not to be a terrible bother, but—"

"Oh, you won't be." Delia hastily crawled out from under the bedclothes to pat his arm reassuringly.

Livy quickly followed. "I'll help you be good," she said.

Marcus looked up at Christina. "Well, Mama?"

"He's very nice," Delia said, patting his head as though he were a puppy.

"He can teach us to cook," Livy pointed out. "And he sings funny songs."

"And he speaks French."

"And he can make the sled go very fast."

"And he has gold speckles in his eyes."

"And he came on the star."

Christina blinked. "He *what?"*

"On the star?" Marcus said, equally startled.

"You remember," Delia said as she crept onto his lap. "The clock chimed twelve times and the star fell. And you came."

"And I came," he said wonderingly.

Livy elbowed her sister onto one knee, and claimed the other. "The angels sent you on the star to be our papa," she explained.

His eyes met Christina's.

"I see," she said. "Angels. That explains everything. Well, he shall have to marry us, I suppose. I wouldn't dream of disappointing the angels."

At this the twins went into transports. They hugged him and kissed him and jumped up and down. Then they flung themselves off the bed to hug and kiss their mama and promise to help her take care of him. Then they grabbed their angels and rushed out to shriek the news to the household.

Christina called out a rebuke, which was completely ignored. She shrugged and turned back to him. "You came on a star," she said.

"The angels sent me."

"To be their papa."

He grinned. "And all this time I thought it was you playing tricks on my mind and luring me with provocative gowns and diamonds."

"Certainly it was me," she said, lifting her chin. "The instant I saw you in the hall I said to myself, 'Here's an eligible man. I think I shall catch him.' "

He laughed.

"But I didn't make you come to Greymarch," she said. "What made you come?"

What had it been? Boredom? Restlessness? No, worse.

"I believe I was lonely," he said rather sheepishly. "I wanted to be with my family, among those who loved me."

"And so you came and found an eligible family, and decided to trap us," she said. "You see how simple it is? It wasn't angel magic. The angels take care of the stars. The rest is up to us. If we want magic, we must make it ourselves. And so we did."

"And so we did," Marcus repeated, his gaze traveling possessively from her tidy slippers to the top of her slightly touseled head. A wash of pink tinged her cheekbones.

He rose from the bed. "I'd much rather believe it was our own doing. I'd rather not be dependent upon angels all the rest of my life." He gathered her into his arms. "I'd rather count on you," he said softly.

"I'll be there," she whispered as his mouth lowered to hers. "I promise."

MERRY CHRISTMAS
from . . .
LORETTA CHASE

I live in Worcester, Massachusetts, in a seventy-year-old house with my remarkably supportive husband and too many books. It's long been obvious to him that I am a fount of obscure and useless knowledge. (He wonders, for instance, why I can trace on a map six different mail coach routes from London to Brighton, but can't find fifth gear on my VW.) Having decided early on that I would be less dangerous to society and myself if I became a full-time writer, he's employed all his masculine wiles to that end. Even before my first book was finished, he persuaded me to quit my day job and Just Write. The result has been seven novels in eight years, dozens of video scripts, and several awards, including an RWA Rita for *The Sandalwood Princess*. Avon, which has produced the paperback versions of most of my Regencies, recently published my first historical romance, *The Lion's Daughter*. "Falling Stars" is my first Christmas story. It was inspired by a photograph I saw some time ago of an elaborately fanciful gatehouse—all that remained of a centuries-old estate.

The Scent of Snow

Linda Lael Miller

1

Cornucopia, Washington
December, 1892

DELICATE, SILVERY FANS AND CURLICUES OF frost decorated the windows of the farmhouse that morning when Rebecca lit the bedside lantern, arose, and hastily donned a wrapper and slippers. Since the room was far too cold for washing, she took the light and the calico dress she meant to wear that day and hurried down the steep, narrow stairway to the first floor.

Reaching the large kitchen, with its many shelves and cupboards, she set the lantern in the middle of the scarred oak table, draped the dress over the back of a chair, and took a handful of kindling from the woodbox beside the stove. When the banked embers of the fire flared around the dry, pitchy pieces of pine, Rebecca smiled and lifted the lid on the reservoir at one side of the massive black Kitchen Queen. The water inside was tepid, perfect for quick morning ablutions.

After washing, Rebecca fed more wood into the stove, then quickly exchanged her nightgown and wrapper for the calico, one of the three dresses she owned. She warmed her bare toes in front of the stove while unplaiting her waist-length, chestnut brown hair, brushing it thoroughly, and then winding it deftly back into its customary thick braid. Once that was done, Rebecca put on her stockings and practical shoes, went out onto the back step, and tossed the contents of the washbasin into the snowy yard.

She carried her nightclothes back upstairs to her room while water for cornmeal mush heated on the stove. She made her bed—at least, she'd certainly come to *think* of it as her own—and tapped at the twins' door as she passed along the hallway.

"Annabelle, Susan," she called, as she did every morning. "It's a new day."

Her ten-year-old half sisters groaned so loudly that she heard them from the hall—and that, too, was part of the routine. A smile touched Rebecca's mouth as she made her way to the stairs. Annabelle and Susan were very young, so it was easy to forgive them for a lack of perspective. It would be years before they fully realized how fortunate they were to be living in that solid farmhouse, with plenty to eat, warm clothes to wear, and the opportunity for an education.

Rebecca's smile faded as she reached the kitchen and began preparing breakfast. As dawn spread across the sky, turning the frost patterns on the windows to glorious shades of pink and apricot, a sense of uneasiness troubled her. Over the past two years, she'd made a place for herself and the twins, there on that patch of land just outside the small town of Cornucopia, in the wheat country of Washington state. They were an accepted part of the community, a family, the three of them, and by sewing and taking in the occasional roomer, Rebecca managed to make an honest living.

She put three broad slices of bread into the oven to toast and then cracked a trio of brown eggs into a pot of boiling water. Annabelle clattered into the kitchen, hopping on one foot while she tried to pull on the opposite shoe. Her bright, honey-gold hair was tousled from sleep, and her woolen dress was misbuttoned. Susan, the more graceful of the pair, glided into the room fully and correctly clad, her hair already brushed and neatly tied with a ribbon.

She gave Rebecca a pained look and started to set the table, while Annabelle struggled, muttering, into her coat.

"Such a big fuss over a little task like feeding a few chickens," Susan remarked.

Annabelle glowered at her sister. "We'll see who makes a fuss tomorrow, Miss Priss, when it's *your* turn to see to those cranky birds."

"Wash up and have your own breakfast first, Annabelle," Rebecca interceded gently. "I don't want you to be late for school."

Minutes later, the three of them sat down to eat. The dawn was still struggling against the darkness, and the light of kerosene lanterns flickered cozily in the warm kitchen.

"Mary Alice Holton is getting a doll for Christmas," Susan announced. "Her brother sent it all the way from San Francisco. He works on the docks."

Rebecca felt a pang. She'd managed to give her half sisters food and shelter and a great deal of love since her ne'er-do-well father had dropped them off at her door back in Chicago nearly three years before, when she herself had been but nineteen. Luxuries like store-bought dolls, however, were out of her reach.

Annabelle, the less fanciful of the two, made a face. "Mary Alice Holton is a crybaby. Her brother probably sent that doll just so she'd quit her sniveling and give her mama and papa some peace."

Although she smiled at this observation, a lump thickened in Rebecca's throat. Whatever Annabelle might say to the contrary, and despite the fact that she was an avowed tomboy most of the time, Rebecca knew she wanted a pretty doll every bit as badly as Susan did.

"It cost two whole dollars," Susan went on, ignoring her sister's comment. "It has glass eyes and a china head and real hair. Mary Alice named it Jeanette."

Annabelle gave a long-suffering sigh. "If this doll is supposed to be a Christmas present, how come Mary Alice knows what it looks like? It's only the first week in December!"

"She peeked, of course," Susan replied loftily.

"Hurry, now," Rebecca said in a brisk tone, rising from her chair and reaching for her empty bowl, her silverware, and the plate that had held her toast and poached egg. "You'll be late for school. And don't you dare forget to feed those chickens, Annabelle Morgan."

Annabelle and Susan looked at each other—although they often squabbled, the twins had an uncanny way of communicating without words when they so desired—then followed Rebecca's lead and carried their dishes to the cast iron sink. Soon they were bundled up in coats and boots, hats and scarves, school books and lunch tins in hand.

Rebecca watched from the back step as they trudged through the deep snow, sunlight pooling around them, to the chicken pen. Susan dutifully held Annabelle's things while her sister attended to the chore of feeding the squawking birds.

The schoolhouse was just down the road and around the bend—the smoke from the building's wood-burning furnace curled gray against the dove-gray winter sky—but Rebecca kept an eye on the children until they had disappeared from sight.

A strange sense of apprehension dogged her as she went about the morning tasks of tidying the kitchen and chopping more wood for the fire. For some inexplicable reason, her gaze kept straying toward the quiet, snow-shrouded road.

She had work to do, she told herself, and tried to shake off her troubled state of mind as she spread the lush red velvet for Miss Ginny Dylan's Christmas dress on the table. She'd made the pattern pieces herself, devoting a full afternoon and part of an evening to the task, using a page torn from a fashion book as a guide. Even though she'd checked the paper panels carefully against Ginny's measurements, Rebecca inspected each one again before pinning them into place. The velvet was costly, and she could not afford to make a mistake.

The sunlight grew brighter as the morning passed, and the frost portraits melted from the window panes. Despite her concentration on the task at hand, Rebecca still felt nervous and fitful. Once she even wrapped her shabby woolen cloak around herself and walked down the path to the very edge of the road to look long and hard in both directions.

She was glad, as she returned to the house and her sewing, that there was no one around to see her odd behavior and ask for an accounting.

Lucas Kiley had bought his wagon and team in Spokane, within an hour of stepping down off the westbound train, but he'd waited to purchase the other supplies he needed. Since Cornucopia was going to be his home from now on, he thought it was only right that he do as much commerce with the local merchants as possible.

He was chilled to the bone when he finally reached the small town he'd thought about so often—during the long years in that factory in Chicago and then, afterwards, while he was recovering from the accident—but a sense of celebration lifted his heart.

Lucas took a long look around him, taking in every detail of the small town that would be his home from now on. God knew, the place wasn't much—just a general store, a bank, a church, a livery stable, and a couple of saloons, huddled together on the prairie. A few sturdy little houses flanked the main street buildings, but because of the cold, there was no one out and about except for one skinny yellow dog.

He reined in the two big sorrel draft horses and set the brake lever with one foot, sparing a second glance toward the Green Grizzly Beer and Pool Parlor. It was late afternoon, surely a proper hour for a glass of whiskey to melt the icy splinters in his blood. But he was going to need every penny of the money he'd saved to stock his farm and woodshed and see himself through the winter.

Lucas entered the general store instead, and felt strengthened by the blast of warmth from the large potbellied stove that stood in the center of things. Two old men sat with their feet toasting on the chrome rail, and a pretty dark-haired woman with a gracious manner swept out from behind the counter. She was in her forties, Lucas guessed.

"You're a stranger here," the lady observed kindly, her wise eyes full of friendliness and humor. She held out one hand, just as readily as a man would have done, and Lucas liked her instantly. "My name is Mary Daniels, and I run this store."

He shook her hand. "Glad to meet you, Mrs. Daniels. I'm Lucas Kiley and—"

"Lucas Kiley!" the storemistress interrupted, beaming. The minor impoliteness seemed almost elegant, coming from her. "Well, it is *about time* you showed your face in Cornucopia! That delightful little family of yours has been carrying on without you quite long enough!"

The wind seemed to rush from Lucas's lungs, just the way it had once in Chicago, when he'd gotten into a fight and taken a hard punch in the gut. *What delighful little family?* he wondered stupidly. For a moment, he almost believed he'd married at some point and then forgotten both the woman and the ceremony, but then he overcame his shock enough to begin, "But I don't—"

"She's a trooper, that Rebecca," Mrs. Daniels butted in again. She stood with her hands on her narrow waist, looking up at Lucas with bright eyes. "Why, she's taken that run-down old place and made it into something, all on her own. You ought to be proud of her, Mr. Kiley."

Lucas swallowed any further protests. He was tired, hungry, and confused, and ever since he'd lived at Mrs. Ella Readman's Boardinghouse in Chicago, several years before, the name "Rebecca" had had a stunning effect on him whenever it came up in conversation.

Obviously, this wife business was a misunderstanding. Lucas was a methodical man, not given to tangents or impulse. He would sort the matter out soon enough.

He bought a wagon load of groceries—mostly staples like sugar and flour and beans and coffee—and set out through the snapping cold of that pristine winter afternoon for the farm he'd purchased, sight unseen but completely furnished, just a few months before the factory accident that had set him back for so long. He didn't need to look at a map; Lucas knew the road by heart, having traveled over it a thousand times in his imagination. The landmarks were like old friends.

There was the abandoned Halley place, just as the last owner had described it, and there was the single oak tree jutting up in the middle of the field—two hundred years old if it was a day. Beyond that was the schoolhouse, a one-room structure.

Lucas smiled as he passed. Class was just letting out for the day, and children were bursting through the doorway like gravel from a shotgun, shouting and laughing and pelting each other with snowballs. Lucas's tired heart rose another notch, and he turned his light green eyes toward the next bend in the road.

Although the homestead itself wasn't quite visible, he saw smoke twisting slowly against the sky, and considered Mrs. Daniels' mention of a wife. He frowned and urged the horses into a trot, even though the snow was fairly deep and the going was hard.

The storemistress's warning and the spiral of wood smoke notwithstanding, Lucas was surprised when his house and barn came into view and he saw a woman wrapped in a cloak standing on the step, one hand shielding her eyes from the sun as she watched his approach.

Curious as he was for a look at the place itself, it took some doing to tear his gaze from the figure of the woman. He gazed with approval on the solid-looking barn and whitewashed two-story house. There was a wellhouse, too, and a fenced pasture, and the fields looked smooth under their mantle of snow.

He turned his attention almost resentfully to the woman.

There was something familiar about her tall, slender figure and that rich fall of red-brown hair, and Lucas rubbed his beard-stubbled chin thoughtfully as he drove closer. It was almost as though she'd been expecting him, this trespasser standing so brazenly on *his* back porch.

As he pulled the wagon to a stop in the dooryard, she lifted her skirts a little and stepped gracefully down the stairs. Her cheeks were bright crimson—and not from the cold, Lucas reckoned—as she made her way toward him.

Recognition crackled between them as he looked down at her from the wagon box and she gazed up at him from the ground. For an instant, it seemed they were back in Chicago, at the boardinghouse, sitting across the dinner table from each other.

"Hello, Rebecca," he managed, his voice raspy. "I understand you and I have tied the knot, though I confess I don't recall the first thing about the ceremony."

The blush on her beautifully-shaped cheekbones intensified, but her maple-brown eyes, glowing as if lanterns burned behind them, regarded him steadily. "Come inside before you catch your death," she said, with resignation.

2

EVEN THOUGH REBECCA HAD HAD A PREMONITION that something disturbing was about to happen, and even though she kept her back straight as a poker walking ahead of her "husband" into the farmhouse, she was in a state of inner turmoil. She would have been less surprised if a plague of locusts had descended on the snowy landscape than she was by the arrival of Mr. Lucas Kiley.

After all, she'd had every reason to believe he was dead.

Lucas paused on the narrow porch to shake out his hat and stomp the snow from his boots. Rebecca bustled to the stove, unable to meet his gaze, at a distinct loss for a proper explanation for her presence.

"I suppose you're hungry," she said, using all her considerable willpower to keep the words light and steady.

"As a bear," Lucas agreed. His voice was deep, just the way she remembered it.

She poured coffee from the small blue enamel pot at the back of the stove—like everything else in that solidly built farmhouse, she'd come to think of it as hers. And she'd been fooling herself the whole while, because the homestead belonged to Mr. Kiley—lock, stock, and barrel.

"Please sit down," she said, blushing when she realized she'd just invited the man to take a seat at his own table. He accepted the mug with one hand, and out of the corner of her eye Rebecca saw that he was looking at the bright scraps of red velvet littering the table.

"You've come up in the world since I saw you last," he observed. There was no rancor in his tone, no sign of an accusation, and yet Rebecca felt defensive.

"I don't wear velvet, Mr. Kiley," she said crisply,

turning away to go to the pie safe for the leftovers from last night's supper. "I sew for those who can afford such things, to make a living."

Lucas gave the cold meat and vegetable pie she set before him an appreciative glance, then pulled off his muffler and shrugged out of his heavy sheepskin coat. The brief, slanted smile he offered Rebecca caused a warm, spilling sensation inside her. "I'm waiting for an explanation," he said, taking up the fork she gave him and tucking into his dinner without further ado.

Rebecca might have told Lucas exactly what had brought her to Cornucopia and that modest farm, if the door hadn't burst open just then. Annabelle and Susan hurried in, cheeks red from the cold, eyes bright with curiosity as they sought and found Lucas.

"That your team and wagon, Mister?" Annabelle inquired, bouncing from one foot to the other while she separated herself from her boots. At the same time she used her teeth to pull off her mittens.

"Yes." Lucas's green eyes twinkled with quiet amusement as he regarded the child. He wasn't a handsome man, Rebecca reflected, but there was something solid and appealing about him all the same.

Susan, who had managed to shed her winter garb with easy grace, kept her distance. "Are you a boarder?" she asked. "If you are, you got here too late, because Mr. Pontious always takes the room in the barn on Friday evenings, on his way back to Spokane for more supplies. Once he stayed a whole week."

Lucas arched one eyebrow at Rebecca—who

promptly went as red as the scraps of velvet she was scooping up from the tabletop—then answered Susan's question. "I don't reckon I'm exactly a boarder," he said moderately, pausing to take a sip from his coffee. "In other words, if anyone around here sleeps in the barn, it isn't going to be me."

Rebecca put a hand on each of the twins' backs and shooed them toward the parlor. "Go on, now, and do your lessons for tomorrow. There's a nice fire going."

Annabelle and Susan obeyed the command, but they weren't tractable about it. They dragged their feet and kept looking back at Lucas in curiosity and concern.

Once they were settled by the hearth, in the shadow of the big potted palm Mr. Pontious had once given Rebecca in lieu of rent on the room in the barn, she returned to the kitchen.

Lucas had finished his pie and coffee and carried the dirty dishes to the sink. He stood with his strong, workworn hands braced against it, gazing out the steamy window into the gathering twilight.

Rebecca paused in the doorway, taking advantage of this opportunity to study him unobserved. He wasn't an especially tall man, but his shoulders were broad and powerful, and his light brown hair curled over his collar. There was an air about him of dignity and quiet strength, the qualities Rebecca had first noticed when they'd met three years before in Chicago.

"Looks like more snow," he said, without turning around.

Rebecca thought she'd been silent, entering the room. "Not surprising, since it's December," she replied. There was a cheery, optimistic note in her voice, but it rang false.

Lucas turned, folded his arms, and leaned back against the sink, regarding Rebecca with an unreadable expression for a long moment before he spoke. "What are you doing, living in my house and telling folks you're my wife?" he asked.

She sighed, crossed the room, took her cloak down from a peg on the wall. His coat hung next to it, smelling of fresh air and snow. "I have to see to the chickens," she hedged, taking a colander full of potato peelings from the work table and proceeding outside. "If you would care to join me, Mr. Kiley—?"

Lucas snatched down his coat and followed her out. In the middle of the yard, where his team and wagon still stood, he gripped her arm and stopped her.

A muscle clamped briefly in his jaw, and she saw frustration in his eyes. Huge snowflakes began drifting down, catching in his rumpled hair. "Damn it, Rebecca," he breathed, "I am at the end of my patience! What's going on here?"

Rebecca swallowed hard, and unwanted tears stung her eyes. She and the girls would be destitute after this, but she would always be grateful for the warmth, comfort, and safety they'd enjoyed up until Lucas's return.

"One day while you and I were both living at Mrs. Readman's boardinghouse," she began gravely, "my drunken, no-account father turned up with Annabelle and Susan." She paused, sniffled. "His second wife, their mother, had died, and he was going to abandon them if I didn't take them in. They were near-starved and scared to death. Mrs. Readman fed them a good meal, but she made it clear she wanted no children in her establishment, so we left. I found a shack near the factory where I worked and—and—" She had to stop again, remembering those days, reliving the hopelessness, the chronic cold and hunger, the bone-deep weariness. "I went back to the boardinghouse to fetch some things I'd left with Mrs. Readman, and she told me you'd been hurt in an accident, and that you'd very likely died. She gave me some papers that belonged to you and asked me if I'd drop them off at the hospital, to be forwarded to any kin."

Lucas just stood there, silent and stern, still holding Rebecca's arm fast in his fingers. "Go on."

"I went to the hospital nearest the mill where you'd said you were working, and they had no record of you. Then I called on your employer, and a clerk in the office said you were dead, that you'd been crushed when some crates fell from a platform, and that as far as they knew, you didn't have any family."

The memory of the accident was visible in his face for an instant, then it faded. "Obviously," he said, "I'm not dead."

"Obviously," Rebecca retorted. The word came out sounding a little tart; she was cornered, the game was up, and the resultant fear made her testy. She drew a deep breath, tried vainly to pull free of his grasp, and went on. "I finally went through your papers, hoping to find the address of a friend.

Instead, I came across the deed to this farm."

Lucas's tone was deceptively soft. "And you just decided to come out here, take over my land and my house, and tell everybody you and I were married? How did you explain my absence, *Mrs. Kiley?*"

Rebecca looked away for a moment, unable to bear the accusation in his eyes. The snow was falling thicker and faster, and the wind was bitter. She wondered where she and Annabelle and Susan would sleep that night if Lucas ran them off his property—something he had every right to do.

"I told them you were working back east," she replied miserably. Rebecca had made plenty of fresh starts in her life, but in those moments things looked impossible to her, and she felt as if she'd aged a century since morning. "I said we wanted to buy more land—the Halley place—and that you'd be joining us as soon as you'd saved enough of your wages. I . . . I said you planned to adopt my sisters once we got settled in."

Suddenly, he released her and, to Rebecca's great surprise, she nearly fell. She'd thought he was holding her prisoner, but now it seemed he'd been keeping her upright instead.

"What did you tell those children in there?" He cocked a thumb toward the house. "Or did you get them to lie, too?"

Rebecca lowered her head, but Lucas cupped her chin in his hand and make her look at him. "They think I have a husband in the east, same as the townspeople," she managed.

Lucas turned away—in frustration or disgust or perhaps both—and muttered a curse. Then he stomped over to the wagon and began unloading the supplies.

Afraid to speak at all, let alone ask Lucas what he meant to do about her trespassing, Rebecca hurried off to toss the potato parings into the chicken pen. Then she went inside to see about supper.

Lucas didn't say a word to her all the while he was carrying in bags and crates and stacking them in the pantry, nor did he join Rebecca and the twins when they sat down for the evening meal.

"That's him, isn't it?" Annabelle asked, wide-eyed, as the sounds of Lucas driving the team toward the barn seeped through the walls of the kitchen. "The man you married to get us this place?"

Susan dropped her fork to the table with a clatter, and the color drained from her cheeks. "You said he'd never come out here and bother us!" she breathed.

Rebecca broke one of her own rules then, set her elbows on the table, and dropped her forehead to her palms. "Well," she answered, on the verge of weeping, "I was mistaken."

On orders from Rebecca, Annabelle and Susan went to bed early that night—Rebecca was hoping Mr. Kiley wouldn't be hard-hearted enough to throw sleeping children out into the snow—and then went upstairs for her wrapper and slippers. Lucas had already said he wasn't going to pass the night in the barn, which meant he'd want his room. Rebecca planned to stretch out on the parlor settee. Heaven knew she wouldn't get a moment's rest, so she'd spend the time trying to think of a solution to her obvious problem.

She had just turned away from the tall bureau—like the other furnishings, it had come with the place—folded nightdress in hand, when the door opened and Lucas quietly entered the bedroom.

Rebecca's heart slammed against her backbone. For the second time that day, she was utterly and thoroughly stunned.

Lucas favored her with a tired, crooked smile and hooked his thumbs under the straps of his suspenders. "I think I'm going to like having a wife," he said, running his gaze over her person just as if he had the right not only to look, but to touch in the bargain. "I've been alone a long time."

A hot feeling surged through Rebecca's body, and her strong legs suddenly felt weak. She even wondered what it would be like to be kissed by that impudent mouth, and that fact troubled her more than anything.

Resolutely, she moved toward the door, chin high, but when she went to pass Lucas, he stopped her.

"Get into bed, Mrs. Kiley," he said, reaching out and clutching her.

"I'll scream." She whispered the threat, struggling—even though she didn't really want to get free—but he held her fast.

"Who will rescue you?" he asked reasonably. His eyes danced with an enticing wickedness that caused her heart to beat still faster. "Those two little girls across the hall?"

Rebecca's temper was flaring, and she was scared, but there was an even worse emotion to deal with. She was as attracted to this man as she had been when they'd lived in the same boardinghouse, and the idea of sharing his bed, innocent as she was, made her light-headed with wanting.

Still, her pride would not let her give in. "You wouldn't dare force yourself on a decent woman!" she hissed.

He leaned close, his nose a fraction of an inch from hers. "I wouldn't force *any* woman, decent or otherwise. But I worked for years to buy this place, lady, and the thought of it was all that kept me going after the accident, when I was laid up in the storeroom of a two-bit tavern on the waterfront. In the meantime, you've been right here, living off the fat of *my* land, wearing my name just as if you were entitled to it. I think, Mrs. Kiley, that if I want the softness and warmth of a woman lying next to me in my bed—and I sure as hell do—you owe me that comfort."

Rebecca opened her mouth, closed it again.

Lucas gave her a little push toward the bed and, to her own amazement, she didn't balk. He blew out the single lantern, plunging the room into total darkness, and she listened with her heart in her throat as he undressed.

"Do you promise not to take advantage?" she asked shakily, unable to believe she'd been reduced to such a situation.

"Yes," he answered, and the bedsprings creaked as he stretched out. "I presume I can expect the same promise from *you?*" And he smiled in the darkness.

3

NIGHTDRESS BUTTONED TO HER CHIN, REBECCA LAY stiffly on her side of the bed, so near the edge that any sudden movement would almost certainly send her toppling to the floor. She was only too aware of the heat and scent and substance of Lucas's unclothed body next to her; his weight tilted the mattress.

"I thought you were dead," Rebecca said.

"That's obvious," Lucas replied, with a sigh.

"What happened?"

He spent some time settling in. "There was an accident in the factory where I worked. I spent more than a year recovering, and used up a lot of my stake. Once I was up and around, I had to earn some more money."

Rebecca absorbed his words thoughtfully. "All things considered," she allowed, after a pause, "I'm glad you're not dead."

"Thank you," Lucas replied, in a wry tone.

She sighed. Once again, she and the girls were going to have to make a new start in a new place. "The twins and I will leave tomorrow," she said, near tears at the thought. She loved the farm, and Cornucopia, and all its people.

Lucas shifted, stretched, gave a long, decadent, and purely masculine yawn. "Um-hmmm," he said. "There's no need to dangle off the side of the bed like that, Mrs. Kiley. Like I said before, I don't take women who don't want taking."

Until that day, Rebecca hadn't blushed more than two or three times in her life, by her private accounting. Just since Lucas's appearance that afternoon, however, she'd felt her face flood with stinging color at least half a dozen times. It happened again as she assimilated the outrageously frank words he'd just uttered.

She bit her lip in an effort to get a grip on her temper, then said, "You're making me stay here just to torment me."

He chuckled, and the low, rich sound set things to tumbling and melting inside her again. "To 'torment' you? Great Scott, Rebecca, is your passion that intense? I'm shocked."

Rage flooded Rebecca's being; if she hadn't been afraid of the repercussions, she would have clouted him with her pillow. "You flatter yourself," she said evenly, when she could trust herself to speak. "Let me assure you, Mr. Kiley, you most certainly do *not* inspire my—my passion."

Lucas settled deeper into the feather mattress and let out a rather theatrical snore.

Rebecca lay rigid, staring up at the dark ceiling, wondering what to do. After a seeming eternity had passed, and she felt certain that Lucas was truly asleep, she started to rise, intending to follow her original plan and make a bed downstairs on the settee.

Before she could sit up, however, Lucas reached out, spread one hand over her stomach, and pressed her gently but firmly back to the mattress. Although the weight of his palm and the strength of his fingers lingered against her for only a few moments, Lucas's touch sent ripples of alarming sensation flowing from Rebecca's center into every extremity.

"Good night, Mrs. Kiley," he said pointedly.

After that, Rebecca didn't try to get out of bed again, not even when she needed to use the chamberpot. She just lay there, thinking that she had indeed woven a tangled web of her deceptions.

Somewhere near dawn, she drifted off to sleep from pure nervous exhaustion, and when she awakened she was alone in the room and the house felt unusually warm. The light at the window was thin, and small flakes of snow were swirling in a busy wind.

Quickly Rebecca jumped up, dressed, brushed her hair, and hurried downstairs. Since it was Saturday, their only day to sleep late, she didn't awaken the twins.

Lucas was in the kitchen, standing near the stove and sipping from a steaming mug of coffee. He gave Rebecca one of his slanted grins.

" 'Morning, Mrs. Kiley."

It was a glorious luxury, rising to a warm house and finding the coffee already brewed, but Rebecca could not afford to enjoy the pleasure. She and the twins would soon be out in the cold, with nowhere to go and very little money to sustain them.

"I think it's about time you stopped addressing me as 'Mrs. Kiley,'" she said, taking a cup from the shelf and pouring coffee for herself. "The joke is beginning to wear thin."

His eyes danced with amusement as he watched her over the brim of his mug. He was wearing trousers, a plain woolen work shirt, suspenders, and boots, and although his unruly hair had been brushed, he needed a shave.

"May I point out that this whole situation is your doing, and not my own?" he asked.

"I was desperate!" Rebecca whispered angrily. "Can't you see that? I didn't mean any harm. I was just looking for a way to put a roof over my sisters' heads!"

Lucas raised one eyebrow and pondered her thoughtfully before asking, "If you were so destitute, how did you scrape together the money to come out here from Chicago?"

Rebecca turned away quickly, afraid her aversion to that question, not to mention its answer, would show in her face. "I had saved a few dollars," she said, and that was true enough, though it wasn't the whole of the story. "And I borrowed from a friend." That, in contrast to her first statement, was an unadorned lie. Duke Jones certainly hadn't been her friend by any stretch of the imagination, and he had taken part of her soul in return for the small amount of money he'd given her.

Silence pulsed in the cozy, lantern-lit kitchen, while Rebecca struggled to assemble an expression that wouldn't betray her. Finally, after much effort, she was able to face Lucas squarely. "I am truly sorry, Mr. Kiley, for taking advantage of your name and property. My sisters and I will be out of the house before noon." There was only one small problem: she had nowhere to go. But she would worry about that later.

The look of amused puzzlement in Lucas's eyes turned to one of concern. "There's no need for that. As I said yesterday, I sort of like the idea of having a family."

Rebecca set her coffee cup aside with a trembling hand and said coldly, "I've told lies, and I've trespassed, but I am not a whore. I won't pay for our food and shelter by sharing your bed!"

He shoved the splayed fingers of one hand through his hair, mussing it, and uttered an exasperated sigh. "How many times do I have to tell you, Rebecca? I won't so much as kiss you unless I have your permission."

She put her hands on her hips, and blood pounded in her ears. "And yet you insist that I lie beside you at night, just as a wife would do!"

"Keep your voice down," Lucas said sternly. "Do you want the children to hear you talking that way?"

Rebecca made a strangled sound of immense frustration, but at the same time hope was pulsing inside her bosom like a second heartbeat. Maybe she wouldn't have to uproot her sisters after all. At least, not before Christmas.

"Will I or will I not be required to sleep in your room as I did last night?" she hissed.

"Yes," Lucas replied flatly. "You will."

"And you promise not to . . ."

"Make love to you?" he finished, when Rebecca hesitated. "Yes, Becky, I promise. But I'm ready to wager you'll be behaving like a real wife before the month is out."

"What a scandalous thing to say!"

He toasted her with his coffee mug. "Scandalous," he agreed, "but true." He sighed philosophically. "Now I could do with some breakfast, if you don't mind. There's a lot I want to get done today, and a man needs his nourishment."

Rebecca's mind was spinning. Under other circumstances, she probably would have told Mr. Kiley exactly what he could do with breakfast, but it was freezing outside and she had very little money and two little girls to provide for. She couldn't afford to turn down this man's hospitality, much as it nettled her to comply with his wishes.

She got out a kettle and set it on the stove top with a *clank*.

Early that afternoon, after the house had been put to rights and she'd basted the sleeves of the red velvet dress into place, Rebecca changed into her going-to-town dress, pinned her braid up into a coronet, and put on her bonnet.

"I don't understand why we can't stay here with Lucas," Annabelle complained, watching as Rebecca resolutely tied the ribbons of her bonnet under her chin. "It's no fun sitting around the church while the choir practices!"

Rebecca turned from the kitchen mirror and reached for her cloak. "You can't stay here with *Mr. Kiley* because—because he's busy. Now, get your coat on and let's go. Mrs. Fitzgillen will be upset if I'm late."

Susan was already wearing her winter gear. "Couldn't we visit Mrs. Daniels at the store while you're singing with the choir?" she asked sweetly.

Despite her situation, Rebecca had to smile. Susan was the diplomat of the family. "I think that's a very good idea, and I'm in favor as long as you don't make pests of yourselves."

Annabelle scrambled into her coat and boots, anxious to cooperate now that she wouldn't have to sit quietly in a pew for upwards of an hour and a half. "Maybe Mrs. Daniels will let us touch that doll with the blue dress, the one that's in the window."

Rebecca's pleasure over the prospect of an outing was tinged with sadness at the mention of the longed-for doll, but she didn't let her feelings show. "You'll keep your grubby hands to yourself, Annabelle Morgan," she said briskly, "or I'll know the reason why."

A hammering sound echoed from the barn as Rebecca and the twins crossed the yard, headed toward the road leading into town.

"I could run inside and tell Luc—Mr. Kiley that we're going to town," Annabelle volunteered, a bit too eagerly for Rebecca's tastes. It was plain that the child had already come to like her elder sister's alleged husband, and Rebecca couldn't help wondering how that exasperating man had won the canny Annabelle's esteem so quickly.

"There's no need to tell him anything," Rebecca replied, with a sniff.

Susan put in her two cents' worth. "Maybe he'd hitch up the wagon and give us a ride into town if we asked him," she ventured uncertainly.

Rebecca's patience was strained. "We would be imposing," she said, with finality, and led the march toward the road. Annabelle and Susan had little choice except to follow.

The walk into town took a full half hour and, by the time the twins had descended on the general store and Rebecca had made her way to the church, her feet were numb with cold.

Since firewood was at a premium—having to be brought from some distance by wagon or train—the small sanctuary was chilly. Like the other members of the choir, a stalwart group of scant numbers, Rebecca kept her cloak on while she sang.

As always, the music lifted her above the cares and worries of the normal world. While practicing her joyous solo for the special community service scheduled for Christmas night, she was able to forget that she'd gotten herself into a Situation.

When the rehearsal was over, she said goodbye to the other choir members and walked slowly back to the general store. Normally, she looked forward to her chats with Mary, since the older woman always gave her tea with sugar and lemon and made her feel welcome, but that day she dreaded facing her friend.

Like everyone else in Cornucopia, Mary believed that Lucas Kiley was Rebecca's husband. Thus, Rebecca would be expected to behave like a happy wife just reunited with her mate, full of news and blushes and secrets.

As it happened, there were customers lined up along the counter, and Mary was much too busy for idle conversation. She smiled and waved at Rebecca, but went right on with her work.

Rebecca lingered by the stove for a few minutes, to warm herself for the walk home, and looked around for the twins. They were unpacking a crate, setting brightly painted toys on a shelf for Mary to sell.

There was a wooden replica of Noah's Ark, complete with a dozen different kinds of animals, all in pairs, and tiny, painted people, as well as a miniature fire wagon pulled by a metal horse, a storybook with cloth pages, and a lovely fair-haired doll wearing a pink dress.

Briefly, Rebecca considered dipping into her small savings to buy the doll as a Christmas gift for the twins, but she didn't dare give in to the impulse. The pitifully few dollars tucked away in the bank's vault were all that stood between the three of them and a very difficult world.

She turned away, only to find herself unexpectedly face to face with Mary.

The older woman held out a well-worn copy of a Spokane newspaper; she always saved them for Rebecca to read.

Accepting the folded paper, Rebecca allowed herself a moment to sorely regret stepping inside the store. Now Mary would ask about Lucas, and Rebecca would be forced to make up some story about how happy she was to have him home.

Instead, however, Mary whispered, "I'll put the doll back for you, and you can pay for it later, a little at a time."

Pride straightened Rebecca's spine and brought her chin up. She'd never bought on credit before, and she wasn't about to start then. "There's no need," she said, with quiet dignity. "I can manage Christmas presents for my sisters."

Mary sighed with affectionate exasperation. "That good-looking man of yours must not mind having a hard-headed woman for a wife," she observed. "Or have the two of you been apart so long that he remembers you as a sweet and pliant thing?"

"Hush," Rebecca scolded, embarrassed, but Mary only chuckled.

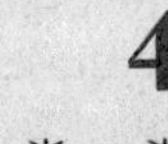

4

LUCAS WAS WAITING IN THE KITCHEN WHEN REBECCA and the twins arrived home again, just before sunset. He sat astraddle a chair, his arms resting against its back, within close range of the stove. There was a pipe clamped in his teeth, and in one hand he held a small book bound in blue cloth. *Everyman's Astronomy*.

He took the pipe out of his mouth and grinned cordially, but he didn't rise from the chair. "The wolves didn't get you after all," he commented.

Rebecca wanted to ask whether he was pleased by this outcome or disappointed, but she did neither. She took off her cloak and bonnet and sniffed the air. "Have you been cooking?"

Lucas nodded and gestured toward the oven door, pipe in hand. "I'm roasting one of the hens," he said. "Hope she wasn't a favorite."

Annabelle and Susan were staring at Lucas, round-eyed. No doubt they were as surprised as Rebecca to encounter a man who would cook when there was a chance of foisting the task off on some hapless female instead.

"Wash your hands and set the table," Rebecca said to the twins, since she couldn't bear the silence and had no idea what to say to Mr. Kiley.

The children hastened to obey, but Rebecca wasn't mollified. She suspected they were out to please Lucas, not their tiresome elder sister.

She watched him in bemusement as he pushed back his chair, set aside his book, lifted one of the stove lids and tapped the contents of his pipe into the flames.

He caught her staring and winked, and Rebecca flinched as though he'd reached out and touched her with one of his calloused hands.

During supper—there were boiled potatoes and canned spinach to complement the roast chicken—the girls chattered about school, Christmas, and the dolls on display in Mary Daniels's store. Rebecca kept her eyes on her plate and contributed next to nothing to the conversation, her thoughts all atangle.

Night was creeping across the land, and soon she would lie beside Lucas again, painfully aware that his body was a natural counterpart to hers. Perhaps, she reflected, his presence was God's way of punishing her for all the times she'd pretended Mr. Kiley was reclining next to her, and imagined herself to be his real wife.

Once the meal was over, Lucas appropriated the newspaper Mary had given Rebecca and retreated to the parlor. Rebecca set the girls to washing dishes while she heated water for their weekly baths.

When the tub was positioned in front of the stove, full of steaming water, Susan balked. "I'm not taking off my clothes with a man in the house," she said.

"Me neither," Annabelle agreed.

Rebecca sighed. She'd hoped to avoid having to speak to Lucas any sooner than necessary, but she clearly had no choice. She went into the parlor, where she found him stretched out on the settee, his stockinged feet dangling over one end. A fire crackled on the hearth, and he was reading the newspaper with an expression of solemn concentration.

"Mr. Kiley."

He looked up, grinned. "Mrs. Kiley?"

Rebecca would not stoop to correct him. "The twins are about to have their baths, and we would appreciate it if you would avoid the kitchen until they're through."

He turned his attention back to the newspaper. "Call me when they're decent," he said distractedly, "and I'll carry out the water for you."

First Lucas had cooked supper, and now he'd volunteered to haul a heavy tubful of water outside. In an odd way, his offhanded kindness nettled Rebecca; she'd been more comfortable when there was a barrier of disagreement between them.

"Thank you," she said stiffly, and returned to the kitchen.

After the twins had been scrubbed and shampooed, and had donned nightgowns and been sent to bed, Rebecca returned to the parlor. This time, Lucas was standing on the stone hearth, gazing thoughtfully into the fire.

"It's safe to go into the kitchen now," she said, and from the way her voice trembled, anyone would have thought she'd made some momentous announcement.

Lucas smiled and started toward her, and Rebecca scrambled to get out of his path. It was herself she was afraid of, however, and not Mr. Kiley.

True to his word, he emptied the tub, and Rebecca wiped it out with a cloth and hung it in its place on the pantry wall. When she came out of that small room, Lucas was waiting for her, his eyes warm with mischief.

"I've got some things I could be doing in the barn, if you wanted to take a bath yourself," he said.

Rebecca imagined herself naked in this man's kitchen, as she had been on many other bath nights, and turned her head to hide another rush of color. "I couldn't," she replied, and went to take her sewing basket from a cupboard in the breakfront.

Hoping Lucas would go on to the barn anyway, she sat down at the table and took out the two dolls she was making for Annabelle and Susan. The small bodies were formed of wooden spools, with painted faces and yellow yarn hair. Using scraps of the red velvet from the Christmas gown she'd been hired to make, she began to fashion simple dresses.

Lucas joined her at the table, watching her work in companionable silence.

Rebecca kept fumbling, but she persisted. She would make other clothes for the spool dolls, from the scraps of other projects, and on Christmas morning Annabelle and Susan would have something in their stockings.

The clock on the breakfront ticked ponderously through minute after minute, until an hour had passed. Then Lucas gave a yawn.

Without a word, unable to face the mirth she knew was twinkling in his eyes, Rebecca carefully put her handwork away, smoothed her skirts, went over to bank the fire in the stove. Once she'd finished, Lucas took the lantern from the table and led the way through the center of the house and up the stairs.

Rebecca checked to make sure the twins were covered and sleeping soundly, and when she entered Lucas's room, he was already in bed. His muscular chest was bare, since the sheet and blankets barely reached to his waist, and his arms were folded behind his head. Rebecca averted her eyes and crossed the room to turn down the lamp.

She ached with strange longings and wild embarrassment, and silently prayed Lucas wouldn't guess that—for all her brave, defiant words—she felt a lewd attraction to him.

Rebecca took off her dress in the darkness, praying Lucas's eyesight wasn't too sharp, and pulled on her nightgown. Beneath it, she wore her camisole, drawers, and, for good measure, a petticoat.

Even through all that muslin and flannel, she could feel Lucas's warmth as she lay carefully in bed, keeping as far to her own side as she could. And for all those precautions, she thought she would surely die if Lucas didn't take her in his arms and kiss her.

She whispered his name, without meaning to.

He rolled easily onto his side, encountered the fullness of the petticoat, and chuckled. "What is it, Becky?" he asked, with gruff gentleness.

"I've never slept with a man before."

His tone was wry. "I'd guessed that, somehow."

"Do you think I could be sent to hell for this?"

A smile lingered in his voice, and his hand came to rest on her middle, fingers splayed. Her nipples pushed against the soft fabric of her camisole in response, even though he hadn't touched them. "No. There's no sin in just lying there, wearing every last stitch you own." He paused, sighed. "And clothes or no clothes, what a temptation you are, Miss Becky Morgan."

He'd remembered her last name. Somehow, the knowledge warmed Rebecca. Not that her temperature wasn't soaring already.

"What if you kissed me and I didn't try to stop you?"

Lucas chuckled, even though she was entirely serious, and traced the outline of her cheek with the tip of his forefinger. "I don't know. Let's find out."

In the next instant, Lucas's mouth was teasing hers, shaping it, persuading her lips to open for him. For Rebecca's part, she was suddenly rocked with alarmingly sweet sensations. She opened herself to Lucas's kiss, and he took full advantage, his groan of desire echoing against her throat.

He moved over Rebecca, letting her feel his hardness and power without crushing her beneath his weight, and still he kissed her. She whimpered softly when he finally left her mouth to nibble at the side of her neck. Although she didn't fully understand what he had to give her, she wanted with all her soul to accept.

Lucas moved downward a little, cupped one flannel-and-muslin-covered breast in his hand, and scraped the hidden nipple lightly with his teeth.

Rebecca bit her lower lip to keep from crying out in startled pleasure, and she yearned to be bared to him, to let him initiate her into all the secrets of her own flesh. "Lucas," she whispered again.

To her surprise, he shoved himself away and gave a great, despondent sigh. "Not yet," he breathed, after a long time, in answer to the question she didn't have the nerve to ask. "I won't have you saying I seduced you."

Rebecca's heart was pounding so hard that she feared Lucas would hear it, and the feminine parts of her either ached or felt like so much melted wax. Lucas's kiss, and the sensation of his weight resting against her, had combined to make matters much worse, instead of easing her discomfort as she'd hoped. Lying next to him, throbbing with the unfulfilled promise he'd awakened in her, was sheer torture.

The next morning, she awakened early, and once again the house was deliciously warm. This time, however, Lucas had returned to the bedroom, bringing coffee for both of them.

Rebecca had never had anyone wait on her that way in her life, and she was completely taken aback. For all her unsettled emotions, however, she didn't miss the fire burning in Lucas's eyes.

It gave her no little satisfaction to know that he wanted her as badly as she had wanted him the night before, and now that the sun was up and there was more space between them, she was struck by a reckless impulse. Perhaps there was a way she could repay him for the sweet suffering he'd subjected her to the night before by poising himself over her and kissing her until she'd thought she'd die of need.

She set her coffee aside on the bedstand, climbed out of bed, and brazenly pulled her nightgown off over her head.

Lucas fell back against the closed door of the bedroom, staring at her in amazement.

The old Rebecca was gone for the moment, replaced by a brazen, mischievous imposter. She stepped out of her petticoats, humming softly under her breath, and then removed her camisole—and drawers, too.

Lucas's Adam's apple moved the length of his neck, and he swallowed hard. His eyes were round as he watched her take out fresh undergarments and put them on, then pull her Sunday dress from its peg on the wall and step into it.

"Would you fasten the buttons, please?" she asked sweetly, approaching Lucas and turning her back to him. That would teach him to make sport of her innocence the way he had the previous night.

She felt his fingers fumble against her spine as he worked the tiny buttons through their loops of fabric. She was not immune to his touch, or to the sense of him standing close behind her, but she didn't let her reactions show.

Not, at least, until Lucas finished with her buttons and bent his head to kiss her lightly on the side of the neck. "I wouldn't tease if I were you," he warned, in a gruff whisper. "The next time you flaunt that delectably lush body of yours, Mrs. Kiley, I may just call your bluff."

The practical Rebecca returned in exactly that instant, bristling with mortification. She whirled, glaring up into Lucas's laughing eyes. "Kindly get out of my way," she said. "I don't want to be late for church."

He gave a grunt of amusement and laid his hands on either side of her waist. "Think about tonight, Becky," he taunted. "Think about how it will be, lying beside me, wanting the kind of loving that will shake your soul. Think about *this*." With that, Lucas hauled Rebecca against him and kissed her hard.

5

REBECCA WAS MOST INATTENTIVE IN CHURCH THAT morning, and the fact that Lucas insisted on accompanying her only made matters worse. She sat up front, with the rest of the choir, and for the whole of the sermon, Mr. Kiley watched her instead of the preacher.

When the pastor publicly welcomed Lucas to Cornucopia and said what a good thing it was that a family had been reunited, Rebecca thought sure the Lord would send a bolt of lightning right through the shingled roof of that little church to strike her dead. Lucas beamed, delighting in her discomfort, and during the social hour following the worship service, he called Rebecca "dear" and made a point of slipping an arm around her waist whenever he got the chance.

He was popular with the townspeople, too. By the time the members of the small but dedicated congregation were ready to return to their homes, Lucas had garnered no less than three invitations for supper. Of course, he was supposed to bring Rebecca and the twins, too.

Graciously, he refused the offers, saying he was still renewing his acquaintance with "Mrs. Kiley's" cooking and promising to be more sociable once the honeymoon was over.

"The honeymoon?" Rebecca protested later, mortified, when she was settled beside Lucas on the seat of his wagon. Annabelle and Susan were riding in back, absorbed in some discussion of their own. "Lucas, how *could* you embarrass me that way?"

He grinned as he bent to release the brake lever, then urged the team into motion with a light slap of the reins. "I was only doing my part to shore up your story, Becky," he said reasonably. "When a man's been away from his wife as long as you claim I have, he naturally feels a need to make up for lost time. Fact is, folks will be looking for you to have a baby in the next year or so."

Rebecca's cheeks flamed, but she held on to her dignity. "Then 'folks' will be disappointed."

Lucas chuckled, and there was no doubt in Rebecca's mind that he was thinking of her scandalous responses to the kisses he'd stolen, not only the night before, but just that morning. "Maybe," he said.

The implication made Rebecca livid. Yes, she'd lied, and trespassed. And there was no denying that she'd behaved like a shameless hussy that morning, deliberately taunting Lucas with her nakedness—dear God, what had possessed her? But she wasn't an immoral person. She was pure, and she'd never stolen in her life, even though she'd often been hungry. She tried to live in a proper and upright fashion, working hard for what little she had, and she was kind to others. Mr. Kiley had no earthly right to imply that she would ever surrender her body to him or any other man.

"You are quite arrogant," she said loftily, and a new snow began to fall, dusting the horses' broad, strong backs and rimming Lucas's hat with fat, fluffy flakes. A blanket of stillness covered the land. "Furthermore, you have vastly overestimated your charms."

Lucas smiled, clearly unruffled by her comment, and pushed his hat back with a practiced motion of one thumb. "You grew up poor in Chicago," he observed, "that's plain. But I can tell you've had schooling by the way you speak. How did you manage to get an education, Becky?"

Rebecca kept her gaze fixed on the pristine landscape. Lucas had pulled her soul close to the surface, and she didn't want him to see the pain that remembering caused her. In fact, showing him her body had been far easier.

"My mother died when I was seven," she said softly. "Pa couldn't manage, so he left me off at his sister's gate. Aunt Martha was an invalid, and I had to take care of her day and night to earn my keep, but she did teach me how to read. I consumed every book I could beg or borrow, and I guess some of what I took in must have stuck." When she could, Rebecca looked at Lucas. "What about you? Did you go to school?"

Lucas adjusted his hat again, glanced at the road, and turned his attention back to Rebecca. "For a while. My mother was a schoolteacher before she married my father, and she taught me what she could. Like you, I just sort of gathered up the rest, from books mostly."

A curiously comfortable silence fell between them. The wagon jostled over the rutted road, the twins chattered and occasionally bickered, and the snow came down harder and faster.

When they reached the farmhouse, Lucas drove the team straight inside the barn. The twins lingered to pester him, and Rebecca went into the house to see to Sunday dinner.

She'd found a ham among the supplies Lucas had brought with him when he arrived, and it filled the kitchen with a mouth-watering aroma as it roasted.

Rebecca exchanged her sateen church dress for a serviceable calico, tied a dish towel around her waist for an apron, lit several lanterns against the thickening glower of the winter afternoon, and set the table. While she waited for the potatoes to boil, she set a blaze in the parlor fireplace and sat down to read the newspaper Mary had given her the day before.

One item in particular, an advertisement on the back page, caught her attention. According to the bold print, the men of Seattle and Alaska were desperate for wives, and transportation would be provided for suitable candidates. Even as she shuddered at the idea of marrying a stranger, she fetched her sewing scissors and clipped the panel out, folding it and tucking it into her dress pocket. Then, frowning, she tossed the remainder of the newspaper into the fire.

When the twins came in from the barn, their cheeks were bright with color and their eyes shone with excitement.

"Lucas is making a workshop in the barn," Susan blurted, with uncharacteristic enthusiasm. "You should see all the tools he has!"

"He's going to make tables and bureaus and bedsteads and sell them to people," Annabelle added, with admiration. "He's a carpenter."

"And whatever we do," Susan put in, "we're not to set foot in that workshop between now and Christmas."

Rebecca smiled, but she felt a certain resentment, too. Lucas was a stranger, after all, and already Annabelle and Susan thought he'd descended straight from Mount Olympus, trailing clouds of glory. "Wash your hands and faces," she instructed her sisters, "and next time you come in from the barn, wipe your feet first."

Susan and Annabelle looked at each other and shrugged, then scampered off to do as they'd been told.

When Lucas came in, he brought with him Mr. Pontious, the peddler who sometimes boarded in the hired man's room out in the barn.

"Look what the wind blew in!" Mr. Pontious cried, grinning and spreading his hands for drama. He was a tall, slender man, bald beneath the bowler hat he invariably wore, and always full of good cheer. For all his bluster, though, there was a troubled expression in his blue eyes.

Rebecca greeted him warmly, wondering if he'd somehow guessed her deception and reasoned out that Lucas Kiley wasn't really her long-lost husband. She put another place at the table and poured coffee for her boarder, and all during the meal he and Lucas talked about farming.

It was generally agreed that wheat was the best crop to grow around Cornucopia, and now that the train came through once a week, marketing wouldn't be a problem. What the town needed, Lucas and the peddler decided, was a flour mill.

Rebecca cleared away the dinner plates, when most of the food had been consumed, and put out a dried apple pie.

"I don't mind saying I'm glad Mrs. Kiley and the children won't be alone out here anymore," Mr. Pontious said, chewing appreciatively even as he spoke. "The way folks are today, what with all the crime and everything, it just isn't safe."

Lucas tossed Rebecca a mischievous glance. "Don't worry," he said. "I'll look after my wife."

Maybe so, Rebecca agreed silently, but who was going to protect her from her so-called husband? Although he'd promised not to seduce her, Lucas was doing a pretty good job of making her want him all the same, and without any apparent effort.

That night, by the light of the kerosene lanterns, Mr. Pontious and Lucas played cards until late. The twins were sound asleep, and Rebecca had long since consigned herself to Lucas's bed, when her "husband" finally entered the room.

Rebecca pretended to be asleep and, to her combined relief and disappointment, Lucas didn't touch her. He just undressed, crawled under the covers, and let out a yawn loud enough for a bear getting ready to hibernate.

It irritated her no end that he only had to lie there to make her scandalously conscious of his strong arms, his hard chest and muscular stomach, his powerful legs . . .

Morning caught Rebecca by surprise, since she had expected to suffer instead of sleep. Lucas was already up and hammering away in the barn, and the twins had gotten ready for school on their own.

"Lucas made pancakes," Annabelle explained, when Rebecca said she'd fix toast and fried eggs for their breakfast.

"Mr. Pontious said he'd never eaten better flapjacks," Susan remarked. Then she squinted at her elder sister in concern. "Are you feeling all right, Rebecca? You look sort of peaky."

"I'm fine," Rebecca replied, and if the words came out sounding a little snappish—well, she couldn't help it. Taking care of Annabelle and Susan was her responsibility, not Lucas's, and she didn't appreciate his interference. "Don't forget to put on your boots and button your coats before you start for home this afternoon. And whose turn is it to feed the chickens?"

"Lucas did that," Annabelle said, and then the two were gone, racing through the snowy morning.

Mr. Pontious came in just as Rebecca was washing the last of the breakfast dishes. "That's a fine man you've got there," he said, but the look in his road-weary eyes was a somber one.

Rebecca offered no comment on Lucas's character. She poured a cup of coffee for her favorite boarder, and he sat down at the table.

"Something's been troubling you ever since you got here," she said gently. "What is it?"

Mr. Pontious cleared his throat and wrapped his long fingers around his cup to warm them. "Maybe you'd best sit down, Mrs. Kiley."

Before, Rebecca had only felt curiosity, but now there was a flash of alarm. She joined the peddler at the table, and he glanced nervously toward the door, as if expecting Lucas to appear.

After a long interval, he finally spoke again, at the same time taking a small leather folder from the inside pocket of his tattered woolen vest. "As you know," he said hoarsely, "I get up to Spokane fairly regular, so's I can pick up new merchandise to bring out here to the farm country. Last week, I met a feller there, and he sold me this."

Even before Rebecca reached for the object Mr. Pontious so reluctantly pushed toward her, she knew what she would see when she raised the cover of that folder. Still, her heart all but stopped when she saw the photograph inside. It was one of the images Duke Jones had taken, during those desperate days just before Rebecca and the twins had left Chicago, and her own eyes stared back at her from the tintype.

That wasn't the worst part, though. She'd posed in just a thin camisole and a pair of scanty drawers, and her hair tumbled loose down her back, like a harlot's. Her face had obviously been painted, and she'd assumed a seductive expression, at Mr. Jones's insistence.

Rebecca rubbed her nape, where a headache was stirring. She knew little enough about Lucas Kiley, but she was well aware that he held shameless women in very low esteem. Once, back in Chicago, she'd heard him speak contemptuously of an actress who had stayed at the boardinghouse for a short time. When that same woman had flirted openly with Lucas at the dinner table, he'd cut her dead with a cold stare.

Now, in the warmth and decency of Lucas Kiley's kitchen, Rebecca felt more like a trespasser than ever. She covered her mouth with one hand and uttered an involuntary groan.

Mr. Pontious looked at her pityingly. "I guess you must have had a good reason for what you did," he said. "Still, I don't suppose folks around here would take kindly to a likeness such as this one."

Rebecca closed the folder and kept it covered with one trembling hand, as if she could guard her secret that way. "The man who sold you this," she whispered brokenly. "What was his name?"

"Jones, if I remember correct-like," Mr. Pontious said. "He was fixing to set up a studio in Spokane. I ran into him in the—er—the Rusty Spur Saloon one night, and that's when he showed me your picture. I bought it for ten cents."

Rebecca knew without looking in a mirror that she'd gone pale as the snow mantling the land for miles around. Shaking, she went to the breakfront, took a dime from the tin box she kept in the top drawer, and offered it to Mr. Pontious.

He refused the payment with a shake of his head and pushed the photograph toward her.

Stricken, Rebecca studied the image once more, then carried it resolutely to the stove, dropped it inside, and watched in grim silence as it curled into ash.

AFTER MR. PONTIOUS HAD GONE OUT TO THE BARN to bed down in the spare room, Rebecca went to the pantry, moving like a woman in a trance, to get the washtub. Her mind was filled with the image of herself posing for Duke Jones's scurrilous photographs; she didn't see the kitchen around her, the kettles she filled with water and set on the stove to heat, the tub itself.

She was startled out of her reverie, at least briefly, when the back door opened and Lucas came in, along with a rush of cold air.

He looked at the bathtub and the kettles and raised an eyebrow. "I thought you'd decided your virtue would be in peril if you bathed while I was around," he said. He took off his coat and hat, and hung them on the pegs next to the door.

Rebecca was still in shock, and seeing that awful picture had left her feeling dirty. Even though she knew she couldn't wash away what had happened back in Chicago, in Jones's studio, she was sure she would go mad if she didn't strip, step into a tubful of hot water, and scrub herself from head to toe with strong soap.

"Becky?" Lucas prompted, when she didn't say anything in reply. He came to her, took her chin in a hand fragrant with the scent of new lumber, and made her look at him. "What is it?"

She wanted to tell him, she truly did—but in that moment, she came to the cataclysmic realization that she loved Lucas Kiley. That was the reason she'd tried to find him after hearing about his accident in the factory in Chicago, and why she'd come to live in his house, posing as his wife. He was enjoying the game of pretending to be married now, and he had been kind and generous.

Once he learned that Rebecca had sold herself the way she had, however, he would hate her. It wouldn't matter that no man had ever made love to her, that she'd only posed for the pictures to get the money to start new lives for herself and the girls. Lucas wouldn't see past the fact that she'd sat for a photograph in just her dainties—no good, decent man would.

It was just too much to ask.

"I'm—I'm all right," she finally said, twisting free of Lucas's gentle hold on her face. "A little bit tired, that's all. If you'd just agree to let me have my privacy—"

Lucas nodded and stepped back, but his eyes were full of questions. Clearly, he knew Rebecca was a whole lot less than "all right." He put on his hat and coat again, lit the lantern he'd been carrying when he came in, and went back out into the cold.

Rebecca went upstairs for a nightgown and wrapper, and then sat in the dark kitchen, staring numbly out the window, while she waited for the water to finish heating. When it was hot enough, she filled the tub, took off her clothes, and sank gratefully into her bath.

She scoured every inch of herself, scrubbing until her skin stung. But as she'd expected, the feeling of being filthy would not be washed away. Finally she reached for a towel and dried off, then put on her nightclothes.

Lucas knocked politely at the back door, after some time had passed, and Rebecca's voice was hoarse when she called, "Come in."

He set the glowing lantern on the table, gave Rebecca one unreadable look, and hoisted the heavy tub. While he was carrying the water out of the house, Rebecca fled upstairs to the master bedroom and plunged under the covers. She was still wearing her wrapper.

Lucas appeared presently, carrying the lamp. "Stop pretending to be asleep," he ordered, in a kind but firm tone. "I know you're not."

Rebecca felt as though all her nerves were outside her skin, exposed and vulnerable. She wasn't naive enough to think she'd solved her problem by burning that one tintype; there were surely other pictures circulating in and around Spokane. Frantically, vainly, she searched her mind for a solution.

"Thank you for going to the barn while I bathed," she said woodenly. God in heaven, why did she have to love this man? When and how had his opinion of her become a matter of life and death?

The mattress gave as Lucas sat down on its edge and began pulling off his boots. "Think nothing of it," he replied cordially. He undressed completely, as casually as if he and Rebecca had shared a bed for half a century, and got under the covers before reaching over to turn down the wick in the lantern. "I'm getting pretty tired of washing in a basin myself. Maybe tomorrow I'll have a nice hot bath. Feel free to stay right there in the kitchen and wash my back, Mrs. Kiley."

He was only teasing, and Rebecca knew that, but something in his words or the gentle, humorous tone of his voice broke down the flimsy barriers she'd been hiding behind all evening. Without warning, without so much as a sniffle to foretell the onslaught, Rebecca began to sob.

Lucas was taken aback for a few moments—she could sense that—but then he reached out and pulled her close to him. "There now, Becky," he said, somewhat helplessly. "There now, don't take on so; you might hurt yourself."

Rebecca would have laughed if she hadn't been so full of despair. As it happened, all she could do was let out a low, miserable little wail. She was a strong woman, and she'd endured more than most, but she'd finally reached her limit.

He kissed the top of her head, entangling his fingers in her hair, and held her very tightly. "Whatever it is," he assured her, "I want to help."

She wailed again, muffling the sound by clutching the edge of the quilt and bunching it against her face. Her spirit was in terrible turmoil—and at one and the same time, her body was betraying her. Lucas felt so strong, so hard, pressed close to her like that. He was a brick wall that could protect her from any danger.

Rebecca put her arms around his neck, laid her cheek against his chest, felt his heartbeat, steady and fast. Soon the photographs would turn up in Cornucopia—maybe they already had—and when Lucas saw them, her world would end. Her time with him was limited, and it was precious.

"Make love to me," she whispered.

He pressed her onto her back and leaned over her, his face no more than a shadow in the darkness of the bedroom. "What did you say?"

"I—I want you, Lucas. You said I would ask for—for intimate relations, and you were right. I'm asking."

Disbelief echoed in his voice. "Are you sure?"

Rebecca nodded. And she *was* sure. When she had to leave Lucas and the farm and Cornucopia forever, in disgrace, she would at least have one special memory to look back on. "Yes," she managed to say.

His mouth fell to hers; he kissed her long and hard, and they were both breathless when he finally broke away. "It's your first time?"

Tears burned in Rebecca's eyes, and she was glad he couldn't see them. Physically, she was untouched, but a deeper part of her had been conquered long ago. "Yes, Lucas," she told him. "You're the first."

He muttered something, then gently raised her nightgown over her head and tossed it away. She flushed when he lit the lamp, and tried to cover herself, but Lucas wouldn't allow that.

He straddled her thighs and looked at her face and her breasts, her belly and her most private place, as though she were a glorious painting, or a never-to-be-forgotten sunset. "Ever since I first saw you, way back when we both lived in the boardinghouse, I've wanted to see you like this, to touch you."

Rebecca felt shy, and attempted to hide her breasts under her hands, but Lucas gripped her wrists and held them easily against the mattress. "Will it—will it hurt?" she asked.

Lucas reached out to touch one of her nipples, and it hardened obediently beneath his fingertip. "Just this once," he replied. "I promise I'll make it all worthwhile, though, if you'll just trust me."

She closed her eyes, arched her back slightly, and moaned as he continued to caress her breast. "I trust you," she said.

He lowered his head, took a well-prepared nipple into his mouth, and began to suck softly. At the same time, he pressed the heel of his palm to the moist delta between Rebecca's thighs and made a slow, circular motion.

The more he suckled and teased, the more she pitched beneath him, wild as a mare with her stallion. When he trailed a path of kisses down over her belly and then burrowed through and took her femininity just as he'd taken her nipple, she pushed her knuckles between her teeth to keep from crying out in stunned pleasure.

When he eased a finger deep inside her, Rebecca's body buckled in a delicious spasm. Lucas reached up and covered her mouth with his free hand, and he was just in time, for her shouts of surrender vibrated against his palm.

The response seemed to go on and on, and Rebecca was damp with perspiration when the wild, sweet convulsions finally ebbed away. She lay snuggled against Lucas, unable to speak, dazed by the glory of all he'd made her feel.

He held her for a long time, until his own need became too great. He parted her legs and mounted her.

"This is your last chance," he whispered. "If you're going to refuse me, for God's sake, do it now."

Instead, Rebecca spread her hands over the taut muscles of his back and urged him closer.

Lucas sighed and then, very, very slowly, he glided inside her. She felt a stretching sensation, and then a brief, sharp stab of pain. He held his body still while she adjusted to him, kissing her eyelids, whispering raspy words of comfort.

The first twinge of pleasure surprised Rebecca so much that her eyes flew open. She gasped and arched her neck, and Lucas kissed the underside of her chin.

"Shall I stop?" His voice was like distant thunder.

"No," Rebecca whimpered. "No—*please*—don't draw away—"

He chuckled and began to move upon her. Her womb contracted in the first sudden and startling throes of renewed passion.

"Lucas," she murmured, as her body began to flex beneath his, meeting every lunge and parry of his hips. "Lucas—is it supposed to be like this?"

Lucas laughed and nipped at her earlobe, sending another storm of sensation raging through her system. "Yes, Becky," he answered. "It's supposed to be *just* like this. And I always figured it would be, if you and I ever found ourselves under the same blanket."

Rebecca was breathless, fevered. She twisted and writhed in obedient rebellion, and her fingers delved deep into his shoulders. "It's—oh, Lucas, I can't bear it—it's too much—"

He tasted her lower lip, captured her mouth with his, lined the underside of her jaw with soft kisses. "Let it happen," he told her, and when she curved her back and stiffened, he kissed her again, swallowed her cries of satisfaction.

The pleasure was so intense that Rebecca was only half conscious when Lucas finally reached his own pinnacle. He plunged deep and moaned, and she felt his warmth spilling inside her. In some ways, that was even better than the flurry of frantic delight he'd caused her minutes before.

She held him, comforted him, when he collapsed beside her, recovering from the force of his release.

"Now I'll go to hell for sure," she said forlornly, when a long time had passed and her breathing had settled back down to its normal rate.

Lucas chuckled. "Not likely," he replied. "They wouldn't have the first idea what to do with you down there."

Rebecca wasn't sure whether she'd just been complimented or insulted. "I'd probably have exactly the same problem in heaven," she said sadly. "Wherever I go, it seems like I turn out to be the onion growing in the petunia patch."

He kissed her lightly and caressed her cheek, then pushed her hair back to trace the shape of her ear with a fingertip. "Oh, Becky, believe me, you're not an onion. You're a wild rose, beautiful and fragrant and so thick with thorns that it takes all a man's courage to touch you."

A tiny muscle tightened in Rebecca's throat. "You talk in poetry sometimes, even though the words don't rhyme. Has anybody ever told you that?"

Lucas cupped her breast in one hand, bent his head to idly brush its tip with his lips, touched it with his tongue when it hardened for him. "No," he answered. "But it doesn't necessarily take words to make a poem. When you move under me the way you did a little while ago, trying to take me deeper and deeper inside you, that's poetry too."

She plunged her fingers into his hair and held his head to her breast while he suckled, and even though she was silent for a long time to come, her body gave an eloquent recitation of its own.

7

ALL REBECCA'S DOUBTS AND FEARS RETURNED WITH the morning, and she wondered at this duplicity in herself that allowed her to fluctuate so wildly between bluestocking modesty and a distinct inclination to behave brazenly. She supposed there was some flaw in her nature that kept her from being like other women; no doubt it was a legacy from her unscrupulous father.

Mr. Pontious joined the household for breakfast, and there was a certain awkwardness between him and Rebecca. He hastily left, after settling up with Lucas for the cost of a night's lodging. Lucas headed for his workshop in the barn, and the children crunched happily through the deep, crusted snow, schoolbooks and tablets in hand.

Rebecca had finished the red velvet dress, except for final alterations and putting up the hem. At noon, Ginny Dylan arrived for the last fitting. She was a lovely young girl, with dark hair and bright green eyes, and in that splendid gown, she was a vision.

Just as Rebecca was putting the last pin in Ginny's hem, around noon, the back door opened and Lucas entered the kitchen, along with a wintry breeze. Rebecca felt an absurd fear that he would look at the beautiful Ginny and forget all that had happened in the night.

He greeted the visitor with a cordial nod, hung up his coat and hat, went to the stove for coffee, and then wandered into the parlor. Rebecca was embarrassed by the depth of her relief; it appeared that Lucas had barely noticed Cornucopia's most celebrated beauty.

Ginny was used to charming men of all ages, and she sulked a little as she sipped her tea and waited for Rebecca to finish hemming the dress. When the task was completed, and deemed acceptable, Ginny paid Rebecca the sum agreed upon and left, driving herself back to town in a small, fancy surrey with spindly wheels.

Rebecca might have mourned the lovely gown for an hour or two, if her mind hadn't been so full of the damning photograph Mr. Pontious had showed her the night before. She stared down at the money Ginny had given her—she *had* been planning to add it to her modest savings—and knew she must use it instead for stagecoach fare to Spokane. Her only chance of finding peace of mind and true happiness lay in locating Duke Jones and persuading him to destroy the photographic plates that held her image. She wouldn't be able to track down all the copies he had made from the plates and she could only hope there weren't many, but once the plates were destroyed, the chance of a photo turning up in Cornucopia would be much less.

Her heart rushed into her throat when she turned and saw Lucas leaning against the woodwork of the parlor doorway, arms folded. His expression was speculative, somewhat worried, and his words came as a total surprise.

"You should be wearing velvet dresses yourself, instead of sewing them for other women."

Rebecca found Lucas's kindness nearly intolerable, given the fact that she was keeping a secret from him. She managed a faltering smile and tucked the money into her apron pocket before turning away to begin assembling the midday meal. "I'd look silly in such a gown," she said. "Silly and pretentious."

Lucas caught Rebecca off guard by stepping up behind her, laying his hands gently on her shoulders, and turning her to face him. "No," he said, his voice gruff. "You must have looked into a mirror a thousand times, Becky. How could you have failed to notice that you're beautiful?"

Sweet anguish filled Rebecca; she tried to pull away from Lucas, but he held her fast. "Please, Lucas—" she murmured. She knew what he was going to tell her, and with the entirety of her soul she longed to hear the words, but at the same time, she dreaded them.

"It's time we made things right between us," he insisted. "We ought to be married. For real."

Tears brimmed in Rebecca's eyes, but she blinked them back. Lucas had not offered her a flowery, poetic declaration of devotion, and yet she knew he cared for her in his way. If he hadn't been at least a little smitten, he would have thrown her and the twins out of his house the first day after his return.

"You don't understand," she faltered. "I'm not—I have a past."

Lucas's smile was crooked and painfully endearing. "We all do," he replied. "What did you do, Becky? Set a brushfire? Hold up a stagecoach?"

Life had made Rebecca practical. Much as she would have liked to indulge in the delusion that Lucas might see the fact that she'd posed for a stranger's camera—practically in the altogether—as a mere lapse of judgment, she knew better. Men were proprietary creatures.

"It was nothing you need to know about, Lucas Kiley," she said stiffly. "Now, if you don't mind, I'd like to get the midday meal on the table before it's time to start supper."

Still puzzled, Lucas released her, but it was clear that he wasn't willing to let the subject drop so easily as that.

"I know you don't have a husband or a lover tucked away somewhere; I was definitely the first man to have you." He must have seen the blush glowing in her nape, though he said nothing about it. "Tell me, Becky—are you running from the law?"

"No," she said, stirring the pot of beans she'd put on earlier, then moving on to slice the accompanying cornbread. "I've committed no crime."

She heard the legs of one of the kitchen chairs scrape against the floor as he slid it back to sit, and he sighed.

"Your father's in prison," he guessed, sounding weary and not a little frustrated. "Or maybe one of those places where they put crazy people."

Rebecca bit her lower lip for a long moment, fighting the urge to say yes, it was one of those things. She'd done enough lying since coming to Cornucopia, though, and another false claim would have caught in her throat. "My father might have wound up in either place, if he hadn't drunk himself to death first."

She spooned beans into a bowl, stacked several slices of cornbread on a plate, carried the light meal to the table. She was careful not to look into Lucas's eyes, fearing that if she did, her soul would go tumbling through them, never to be her own again.

"I need to go to Spokane," she said, in a businesslike voice. "Annabelle and Susan will stay with Mary, at the store."

Lucas caught hold of her wrist, but while she probably could not have escaped his grasp, the gesture was in no way threatening. "It's almost Christmas," he said. "How can you go away now?"

Misery filled Rebecca. While other women were making last minute preparations for the holiday, roasting geese and keeping wonderful secrets, she would be jostling along on the hard seat of a stagecoach. She would be searching for Duke Jones, begging him to destroy the pictures that might well ruin her life.

"I have to," she told Lucas simply.

"Then I'll go with you."

"No!" she cried out, startling herself as well as Lucas. "No, this is something I have to do for myself."

"Will you come back?"

Rebecca wouldn't meet his gaze. "Yes," she answered, failing to add that, if she was unsuccessful in dealing with Jones, a prospect that seemed likely, she would return to Cornucopia only long enough to collect her sisters from Mary Daniels.

That afternoon she packed. When the girls came home from school, she immediately presented them with a large satchel, containing everything they'd need for several days. They looked at her in heart-wrenching bewilderment, probably remembering the uncertainty of their days with their father, and how he'd finally abandoned them in someone else's care. Still, they asked no questions.

Lucas drove the three of them to town in his wagon, grimly silent throughout the trip, and Rebecca sat rigidly on the seat beside him, keeping her eyes on the road. Reaching the general store, he unloaded their baggage onto the wooden sidewalk and then left, a brief touch to the brim of his hat his only farewell.

"Where are we going?" Annabelle asked, in desperation.

"You're staying right here in Cornucopia, for the time being," Rebecca answered. "I have business in Spokane."

"But it'll be Christmas soon!" Susan wailed. "What if you miss it?"

Rebecca sighed as she pushed open the door of the shop. A cheery little bell tinkled overhead. "It wouldn't be the first time," she answered, a bit irritably. In truth, Rebecca had been looking forward to the holiday herself, mainly because of Lucas. Although, as usual, there would have been few presents, she'd planned to cook a special meal and decorate the parlor with paper angels and strings of popcorn.

Mary's bright smile faded when she saw the satchel Rebecca carried. "What is happening here?" she asked, her tone full of polite insistence.

"I'd be obliged if the girls could spend a day or two here with you," Rebecca said, speaking carefully in an effort not to burst into tears. "I promise they'll make themselves useful when they aren't at school."

Annabelle and Susan looked at each other, but neither spoke.

"And where will you be during this time, pray tell?" Mary inquired, rounding the counter to stand facing Rebecca. The purposeful storemistress took hold of her friend's arm and led her back between rows of boots and garden hoes and flour barrels to the main storeroom. "Start talking, Rebecca Kiley."

Rebecca lost her battle with tears and, in a frantic whisper, began to pour out her story. She told Mary how she'd met Lucas in Chicago, when they'd lived in the same boardinghouse, and that she'd been in love with him even then, although she hadn't known it. She confessed that she'd come to Cornucopia believing he was dead, and pretended to be his wife so that she and the twins would finally have a decent life.

Mary smiled when Rebecca got to the part where Lucas returned unexpectedly, to find himself with a wife and family, but she didn't interrupt.

The smile faded to a look of sympathy when Rebecca explained how she'd earned the money to travel west and take over Lucas's farm. "Last night," Rebecca finished, "Mr. Pontious spent the night in the barn room. Mary, he had one of those dreadful pictures, and he said he'd bought it in Spokane, from Duke Jones himself."

Mary sighed and embraced her friend briefly before asking, "What do you expect to accomplish by confronting this man, Rebecca? He clearly has no scruples, or he wouldn't engage in such pursuits in the first place."

"I have to try," Rebecca said, standing stiffly in the crowded store room. "I love Lucas, but if he ever sees one of those pictures, he'll despise me."

"Maybe not," Mary replied, with gentle uncertainty. "Wouldn't it be better just to tell him the truth, and hope he understands? You wouldn't be the first person to come out west with a secret or two buried in their past. Why, lots of folks are here to make a new start of one kind or another."

Rebecca only shook her head. Lucas was a good, decent man—and a proud one. He wouldn't be able to bear the knowledge that her charms were on display to any man who could pay a dime to view them.

She and the twins spent the night in Mary's spare room, the girls sleeping deeply, Rebecca sleeping not at all.

Early the next morning, the stagecoach came through town, and when it headed north toward Spokane, Rebecca was aboard it. She was grateful to be the only passenger, since she couldn't have made polite small talk to save her immortal soul.

The ride was long and extremely wearing. Rebecca could see her breath, and her feet were so numb that she couldn't move her toes.

When at last she arrived in Spokane, night had fallen, and the small city seemed very loud and decadent to Rebecca, now that she'd become accustomed to Cornucopia. Resolutely, she straightened her Sunday bonnet, lifted her reticule from the floor of the coach, and climbed out with as much grace as possible.

Being too embarrassed to ask for directions to the saloon Mr. Pontious had mentioned, she simply followed the sounds of badly tuned pianos, gunshots, and revelry until she came upon a row of scurrilous establishments.

As she stood on the sidewalk in front of the Rusty Spur Saloon, peering over the swinging doors, flakes of pristine snow began to fall all around her, white as goosedown. Rebecca took a deep breath, squared her slender shoulders, and proceeded bravely into the smoke-filled den of depravity where she hoped to find Duke Jones.

8

JONES HAD NOT CHANGED MUCH, REALLY. HE WAS still handsome, in a smarmy sort of way, and when he saw Rebecca, he chuckled with delight, folded the hand of cards he'd been playing, and tossed them into the center of the saloon table.

The men seated there with him were too busy staring at Rebecca to grumble over an early end to their game.

Mr. Jones stood, for all the world like a gentleman, and scolded indulgently, "Rebecca, my dear—for shame! This is no place for a lovely lady!"

Rebecca narrowed her eyes at him, remembering how he'd taken advantage of her desperate need in Chicago, how he'd promised that no one west of the Mississippi would ever see those disgraceful pictures he'd taken. And she'd been fool enough to believe him!

She caught herself, just as she would have spit on his sawdust-coated boots, and summoned up a milder expression, a smile being quite beyond her. "I would like to speak to you privately," she said, with cool dignity.

He clamped a cheroot between his teeth, lit it with a wooden match, and then gestured grandly toward the back of the saloon. "As you wish," he told her. "I have an office in the back."

Just the thought of what probably went on in that place made Rebecca's flesh crawl, but she straightened her spine and preceded Jones along a dimly lit hallway. Everything depended on her ability to reach a satisfactory agreement with the man who held her future in his hands.

Jones opened a door, using a large brass key, and went in before Rebecca to light a lamp. She was relieved—to some extent—to find a desk and chair, a bookshelf and some photographic equipment in the room. At least there wasn't a bed.

"Sit down," he said, gesturing graciously toward the chair facing his desk. "What a wonderful surprise it is to see you again, Rebecca."

Rebecca smoothed her skirts as she sat, with as much dignity as if they were silk and not well-worn calico, and willed her hammering heart to settle into a calmer beat. "I can't imagine that you're surprised," she said. "When you sold my photograph to Mr. Pontious and saw his reaction, you must have guessed that he knew me."

Jones tapped his chin with one finger, feigning deep thought. "Pontious . . . Pontious. Oh, yes—the peddler." He paused to smile around the cheroot he'd lit earlier. "You should have seen him, Becky. He went pale as milk when he recognized you."

His inadvertent use of the nickname "Becky," heretofore reserved for Lucas, stung Rebecca's heart and sent hot venom flooding through her veins. Still, though she knew her color was high and she was definitely trembling, she managed somehow to keep her composure.

"I want you to destroy the photographic plates and give me any copies of those pictures you might have in your possession," she said.

Jones laughed and drew on his cheroot for a few moments before countering, "Oh? You may be the subject of the photographs, my dear, but they belong to me. What do you have to offer in payment?"

Rebecca struggled against the currents of fear and fury that would pull her beneath the surface of reason and smother her, along with all her hopes and fragile wishes for the future. "Nothing," she answered. "I'm depending on you to do the honorable thing."

This statement seemed to amuse Jones even more. "Great Zeus!" he boomed, spreading his hands in jovial mockery. "Look around you, Becky. Is this the sort of place an 'honorable' man would frequent?"

She clutched the handle of her reticule tightly in both hands. "What do you want?" The words came out in a whisper.

Jones smiled, opened a drawer in the battered desk, and brought out two photographic plates and a handful of pictures. "Not so much, really," he said. "You compromised yourself once. What do you have to lose by doing it again?"

Rebecca's blood turned to ice. "What are you saying?"

With a shrug, Jones responded, "It's quite clear that you have little or no money. But money is not all a beautiful woman like yourself can offer in trade."

She stood, shaking with rage and humiliation. "I can see I've wasted my time in coming here. Good evening, Mr. Jones."

He rose rapidly from his previously languid position in the other chair just as she turned her back. "One night in my bed. That's all it would take to persuade me to destroy these plates." Jones slithered to her side, silent as a snake, and handed her one of the sepia-tinted photographs.

Rebecca felt light-headed, and she thought for certain she was about to throw up, but somehow she managed to pretend that she still possessed her dignity. "I would sooner pass the night with the devil himself," she said, and then she walked out, taking the damning photograph with her.

Now, she thought forlornly, as she walked through the main part of the saloon, taking little notice of her surroundings, and stepped out onto the sidewalk, there was nothing to do but go back to Cornucopia, show Lucas the photograph, collect the twins, and leave. She still had the advertisement she'd clipped from Mary's newspaper, the one calling for wives for men in Seattle and Alaska.

Rebecca began to walk, heedless of the ever-deepening snow. Perhaps the twins could board at a mission school until they were old enough to be on their own. Their well-being was all that would matter to Rebecca after this; she would get through her own life by rote.

She had walked some distance before she became aware of angelic voices echoing through the cold, snowy night. The familiar words of Christmas carols penetrated her despair, and when she saw the lights of a church ahead, her step quickened.

Rebecca slipped into a back pew, hidden by the shadows, watching and listening in singular misery as a choir practiced Christmas hymns. The words of the songs soothed her like balm, and eventually she stretched out on the bench, lulled into blessed sleep.

When she awakened, chilled to the marrow, it was morning and the small, rustic church was empty. Rebecca sat up, righted her hat and smoothed her rumpled skirts, and hurried out, praying no one would see her and decide she was a derelict.

As she stepped out onto the sidewalk again, and a rush of icy air struck her, she shoved her hands into the pockets of her thin cloak. On the right side, she found the photograph, a brutal reminder of the hopelessness of her circumstances.

She made her way back to the stagecoach depot and purchased a return ticket to Cornucopia. Then, to bolster herself for the difficult journey, she bought an apple and a thick slice of buttered bread from a grocer and dutifully choked them down.

Once again, she was the sole occupant of the coach, and once again, she was thankful for that. Rebecca could not have borne the effort of making conversation just then; she felt like one big bruise, inside and out, a magnet for all the pain of the universe.

The ride was bumpy and frigidly cold, just as Rebecca had known it would be, and when the coach finally came to a stop in front of Mary Daniels's store, darkness had fallen. "A happy Christmas to you, now," the stage driver said, as he helped Rebecca down.

Rebecca's heart constricted; until that moment,

she hadn't realized it was Christmas Eve. She returned the man's kindly wishes and took her reticule. A light snow was drifting down from a black sky, filling the air with a clean scent, a fragrance of hope and purity.

She approached the entrance of the general store, but when she went in, there was no sign of Mary. Instead, Lucas waited beside the stove, warming his hands, coatless and as much in need of a shave as he'd ever been.

"What are you doing here?" Rebecca asked, not in challenge but in honest bewilderment. She'd been so conscious that their love was over—before it had had a chance to start—that she'd assumed Lucas knew it too.

"I was hoping you'd be on the evening stage," he said. "Let's go home, Becky. The girls are waiting for us."

"But—"

He came to her, touched her lips with one finger, effectively silencing her. "Whatever it is, it can wait until Annabelle and Susan have had their Christmas," he said. "Now, let's get ourselves home, Mrs. Kiley."

The team and wagon were just outside—Rebecca had been so distraught that she hadn't seen them before—and Lucas hoisted her into the high seat as easily as if she were a child. Once he'd lit the lanterns that hung on either side of the rig, he climbed up beside her. Then he carefully covered her legs with a wooly blanket.

Rebecca had never known such tenderness before Lucas, and now she sorely wished she hadn't experienced the sweetness of it for even so much as an hour. For the rest of her days, while she toiled beside some man she didn't love, in faraway Seattle or even the frozen north, she would have to remember the magnitude of her loss.

A single tear stung its way down her cheek.

"We'd best wrap your throat as soon as we get home," Lucas said, as matter-of-factly as if there were nothing wrong between them. "I'll make you some hot lemon juice and honey, too. It would be a shame if you couldn't sing your piece tomorrow at the church party."

Rebecca lifted both hands to her mouth, but the small sob escaped anyway. She wouldn't be able to sing the next day or for a long while to come. Her broken heart wouldn't let her.

Lucas put his arm around her shoulders and squeezed lightly, but he didn't say anything more, and Rebecca was wildly grateful. Even the sound of his voice, deep and certain and strong, was a torment to her then.

Soon they arrived at the farm, where the windows were all alight. Lucas drove right up to the back step, climbed down, and lifted Rebecca after him, refusing to let her so much as carry the reticule.

"Go inside and sit by the parlor fire," he ordered. "I'll be in to look after you as soon as I've put the team and wagon away."

Rebecca had no strength, no desire, to argue. She simply nodded and did as Lucas had told her to do.

Annabelle and Susan had been playing checkers in the parlor, and they were beside themselves with delight when Rebecca appeared. She embraced them, wishing she had splurged and bought the pretty dolls they'd admired at the general store. After all, this would very likely be the only real Christmas the three of them would ever spend together.

"Look!" Annabelle crowed, her small frame fairly vibrating with delight. "We have a Christmas tree, just like Prince Albert and Queen Victoria!"

The potted palm was bedecked with strands of popcorn, plus painted paper stars and angels. There wasn't an evergreen growing within twenty miles of Cornucopia, which was why the houseplant had been elected, and Rebecca was secretly glad that no tree had been chopped down for brief glory.

"Theirs is probably a noble pine," Susan said, with a little sniff, but from the gleam in her eyes, Rebecca knew she was as pleased as her twin.

Rebecca wiped away tears with the heel of her palm.

"Here," Annabelle said, taking charge of her wayward sister. "Sit here by the fire. Susan and I will bring you some supper."

Rebecca laughed, though the sound was peculiarly like a sob, and sank into the appointed chair because Annabelle pushed her, not because she'd chosen to sit. "I'm not an invalid, for heaven's sake."

The girls ignored her protests and ran off to the kitchen, returning shortly with a bowl of savory chicken and dumplings and a mug of spiced cider.

"Lucas cooked supper, and he made the cider, too," Annabelle chirped, clearly amazed at the feat.

Rebecca began to eat, realizing only as she picked up her spoon that she was desperately hungry. "I thought you two were going to stay with Mrs. Daniels until I returned from Spokane," she said.

That was when Lucas appeared in the parlor doorway, his presence as warm and elemental as the fire crackling on the hearth. "Children belong at home at Christmas," he said quietly. Then he shifted his attention to the twins. "You'd better finish that round of checkers soon. It's almost time to hang your stockings and go to bed."

Annabelle and Susan returned to their game, chattering with excitement, and Rebecca's heart splintered as she watched them. She supposed it was a mercy that they couldn't know the future, and that they would have this happy time to remember, but for the life of her, she couldn't manage the merest prayer of gratitude.

9

ONCE ANNABELLE AND SUSAN HAD HUNG THEIR patched woolen stockings from the mantel of the parlor fireplace and gone off to bed, Lucas made good on his earlier promise to take care of Rebecca. He wrapped her throat with a warm scarf, brewed a soothing potion of hot lemon juice and water sweetened with honey, and then he knelt on the hearth to remove her shoes.

Rebecca's heart ached with despair. All her life, she'd yearned for one person who would give her tenderness, who would search for her if she was lost and pamper her if she was hurt or ill. Now she'd found that person, only to lose him again.

Lucas set aside her sodden shoes, rolled down her stockings, and rubbed her feet, first one and then the other, gently restoring the circulation. He might have pressed her to explain her strange behavior, and her absence, but he did not.

Instead, he talked quietly about planting crops in the spring, and buying a milk cow, and building good furniture to sell when he wasn't plowing fields. He found the spool dolls and put them into the twins' Christmas stockings, along with oranges he'd evidently purchased for the occasion. Citrus fruit was a rare treat, and expensive, but Mary had gotten in a special shipment for the holiday.

When Rebecca's great weariness finally overwhelmed her, Lucas lifted her into his arms and carried her upstairs.

There, as tenderly as if she were a child, he undressed her, helped her into a nightgown, and tucked her under the covers.

"Sleep," he told her. "Just put everything out of your mind for tonight and get some rest."

Rebecca's eyes filled with tears. "Oh, Lucas," she whispered, unable to stop herself. "I love you."

He bent, kissed her forehead. "And I love you."

With that, Lucas put out the lantern he'd lit and left the room. Despite her exhaustion, Rebecca lay listening as he moved around downstairs, imagining him banking the fire in the kitchen stove, putting out the parlor lamps, perhaps sitting down in the chair Rebecca had occupied to smoke his pipe.

The bumps and thumps continued, but it was a long while before Lucas finally came to bed. When he did, he gathered Rebecca close against him, making no other demands, and held her fast. She finally slept, heartbroken, in the temporary safety of his embrace.

Morning brought shrieks of delight from downstairs, and it was several moments before Rebecca was able to shift her mind from the murky depths of slumber to the reality of a new day. Then she realized that it was Christmas, and a certain bitter joy filled her heart.

She sat up, imagining the girls emptying their stockings. She hadn't expected them to be quite so thrilled with a pair of homemade dolls.

Lucas was standing with his back to the bed, gazing out the window, wearing trousers and his undershirt, his suspenders hanging down over his hips. His strong, wood-carver's hands were braced against the framework surrounding the frosted glass.

"What do you see?" Rebecca asked softly.

"Snow," he answered, without turning around. "Oh, but it's beautiful, Becky, so perfect and clean. Looking at it, I can almost believe that the sins and mistakes of the world have been covered in purity, that we're all being given a new start."

Rebecca let her forehead rest against her updrawn knees for a moment, while she dealt with the pain of all she faced. "There you go," she said brokenly, looking up at him, "talking like a poet again."

At last, he turned to face her. The expression in his eyes reflected her suffering and his own, but he smiled.

"I'll go down and see what all the fuss is about," he said, and then he left the bedroom, pulling up his suspenders as he went.

Numbly, Rebecca rose, hastily dressed, brushed and rebraided her hair, then followed.

Annabelle and Susan crouched in front of an enormous dollhouse with real glass windows and a shingled roof, walking their spool dolls through the spacious rooms. Against the wall, a beautifully simple wooden sled awaited their attention.

Rebecca looked at Lucas, who was leaning against the mantel, watching the children with a smile in his eyes. In that brief, glittering moment, Rebecca's pain doubled and redoubled, because it was so obvious that this man loved her sisters as if they were his own children. Their loss, when the truth came out, would be as great or greater than hers.

Trembling, she took a packet from the branches of the decorated palm and extended it to Lucas. The gift was small, a half dozen handkerchiefs embroidered with his initials, but he looked delighted.

After admiring the handkerchiefs and carefully folding one to tuck into his back pocket, Lucas disappeared into the kitchen, returning a few moments later with a large, varnished wooden box.

"Happy Christmas," he said, setting the object in Rebecca's lap.

She had received small gifts in the past, oranges and peppermint sticks, and once a sweet-smelling sachet, but no one had ever given her anything so splendid.

"I thought you needed a place to keep your sewing tools," Lucas said, sounding shy as a schoolboy offering some personal treasure to a favorite teacher.

Rebecca was too moved to look at him. She lifted the hinged lid of the box and the scent of cedar perfumed the air. "Thank you," she whispered, overcome.

Moving like a woman entranced, she carried the sewing chest with her when she went into the kitchen to get breakfast started. Lucas soon joined her, putting his arms around her waist from behind, bending to kiss her ear.

"How do you feel today, Mrs. Kiley?"

The use of that precious title stabbed Rebecca's heart. "Well enough to sing my solo at the church party tonight," she answered, marveling that her voice could come out sounding so normal when she was dying inside. Suddenly, it was imperative to pretend everything was right with the world, that all her sins had indeed been covered up and absorbed by the snow. "I don't know what we'll have for Christmas dinner," she fretted. "I quite forgot to prepare a chicken."

With obvious reluctance, Lucas released her, and she heard her own brittle merriment echoing in his deep voice. "I've got a goose hanging in the springhouse, ready to roast. I bought it from a farmer yesterday."

"I guess you'd best bring it inside, then," Rebecca said, with fragile good cheer. "If I don't get it into the oven, we'll be up 'til midnight waiting for our supper."

Lucas hesitated for a few moments—Rebecca felt this rather than saw it—and then he put on his coat and hat and went out. She watched him from the window as he moved toward the barn, marking the perfect snow with his passage, and she tucked the image away in her heart as a keepsake.

Later, Rebecca served breakfast, and the kitchen was warm and fragrant with the roasting goose. The moment the dishes had been washed, Annabelle and Susan bundled up and rushed outside, taking their new sled with them. The small knoll west of the house would be perfect for sliding.

"You've spoiled them," Rebecca said, sitting at the kitchen table and making sure not even to glance at Lucas as she carefully arranged her collection of thread in the box he'd made for her.

Lucas was smoking his pipe and reading from his volume on astronomy. "They haven't had enough spoiling," he replied, "and neither have you."

Rebecca bit her lip and looked away, her vision blurred. She'd spent her life fighting for survival—her own and then that of her twin sisters—and she had never been pampered until this man. "You've been so very kind, Lucas," she finally managed to say.

He reached out, covered her hand with his own. She felt the callouses on his palms, the might of his deft fingers. "Let me love you, Becky," he said. "Stop trying to put up fences between us and just let me look after you like a real husband."

Such a tangle of emotion whirled up inside Rebecca at his words that she was shaken by it. She could lie, and hope that Lucas never had occasion to see the photographs Duke Jones had taken . . .

Rebecca dismissed the idea before it had time to take root. A lie would poison her life with Lucas.

"You won't want me, once you know the truth," she said miserably, after a long, torturous interval of silence had passed.

He tightened his grasp on her hand, but the moment conveyed only affection, not anger or impatience. "Tell me your terrible secret," he said.

She had meant to wait until the next day, but now Rebecca realized she wouldn't be able to carry the burden that long. It was already crushing her.

"All right," she agreed, meeting his eyes at last. She reached into the pocket of her skirt, brought out the photograph Jones had given her in Spokane. "Here's the reason."

Lucas picked up the image, stared at it in consternation at first, then with obvious shock. The color drained from his face, and when he looked at Rebecca at last, she saw cold anger in his eyes.

"Why?" he asked. The word was ragged, and it echoed in the warm kitchen like the report of a cannon shot.

Rebecca had expected his condemnation, had tried to steel herself for it, but nothing could have prepared her for the stunned way he was staring at her then. "He paid me," she said, the words a bare whisper. "I needed the money so the twins and I could come west."

Lucas looked at the photograph again, and a series of unsettling emotions moved in his face. "How many of these are there?" he asked, after a long time. "How many men are looking at your body, Becky?"

She leaped from her chair, propelled by pain and shame and helpless rage. "I don't know," she said, when she could speak, careful to keep her back turned to Lucas. "Jones has the plates, so he can make as many as he wants."

The room seemed to tremble with the force of their joined emotions. Then Lucas went to the door, not even troubling with his hat and coat. "That's why you went to Spokane?" he asked, as the kitchen filled with a wintry chill that didn't begin to match the coldness of his fury. "Because Jones is there?"

"I wanted him to destroy the plates," she said.

"I see. That way, you could fool me just the way you've fooled the townspeople all this time—"

Rebecca whirled, wild in her desperation and her anguish. "No, Lucas!" she cried. "I was going to tell you, no matter what. I would never have tried to deceive you that way!"

Lucas's contempt and disbelief were plain in his face; there was no need for him to speak of them. He turned and walked out, slamming the kitchen door behind him.

After a long time had passed, and Rebecca could hear over the frantic pounding of her own heartbeat, she caught the echoing ring of a hammer striking over and over. Lucas had taken refuge in his workshop.

The girls returned after an hour of sledding, chilled and full of Christmas laughter. They drank hot chocolate and ate the sandwiches Rebecca made for them, then went back to the parlor to play with their dollhouse. When Rebecca looked in on them, they were curled up on the hearth rug like a pair of kittens, sound asleep.

She covered them with a blanket from upstairs, then went back to the kitchen. Because she didn't know what else to do, she peeled potatoes for the meal and baked a dried apple pie for dessert. Then she sat by the stove, still as death, holding her cherished cedar sewing box in her lap and staring sightlessly out at the cold perfection of the day.

Late in the afternoon, she served the Christmas goose, along with a tableful of other carefully prepared foods. Lucas returned from his workshop, but he was very quiet throughout the meal and wouldn't meet Rebecca's gaze. Fortunately, Annabelle and Susan were so busy chattering that they didn't notice the hurt and anger of the adults.

When the time came, Lucas hitched up the team and wagon, and the four of them set out for the church building in Cornucopia, looking for all the world like a happy family putting the finishing touches on a truly spectacular Christmas. Rebecca feared she wouldn't be able to sing, but at the same time she hadn't the strength to decline the task and stay home.

Buggies and wagons were crowded around the well-lit church, and the sounds of music and laughter rolled out onto the snow to greet Lucas, Rebecca, and the children as they arrived. The twins raced inside, carrying their spool dolls in mittened hands, but Rebecca stubbornly lingered while Lucas secured the team.

They entered the church together, and even managed to smile and return the greetings of the merry crowd. The humble sanctuary had been decorated with pine boughs, and the festive scent was a stab to Rebecca's heart.

10

LUCAS SAT IN THE LAST ROW OF PEWS, WHILE REBECCA took her place with the choir at the front of the church. After the factory accident in Chicago that crushed his body, he'd thought this was the worst thing that could ever happen to him. It had even been something of a relief to think he'd paid his dues, so to speak.

He was a man of simple integrity, and the thought of other men leering at photographs of Rebecca tore at his spirit like the teeth of an animal. It was as if she'd *sold* some part of herself.

Now Lucas had learned only too well that a soul—as well as bone—could be broken, and this new pain, this searing sense of betrayal, was wild inside him.

The minister got up, led a prayer, and then spoke eloquently of the meaning of Christmas. The words went straight through Lucas, as though he had no more substance than a mirage, and he never once took his eyes from Rebecca.

She was beautiful, though not in the fragile way of some women. No, Becky was a practical beauty, sturdy and strong, full of spirit and courage.

And lies, Lucas reminded himself.

Her turn to sing came and she stepped in front of the choir, her hands trembling slightly under the hymnal she held. There was a flush on her high cheekbones, and the first words of the old song were shaky, but then Rebecca got a grip on her emotions and let out all the music that was inside her.

She sounded like an angel.

The image of her, posed for Jones's camera, filled Lucas's mind, and he wanted to weep with grief. She was so unbearably lovely—and damn it, she was his. The idea of other men looking upon the secret glory of her was pure anguish.

Somehow, Lucas got through the rest of that evening. When the services were over, he talked with other members of the community and even managed to sample some of the baked goods the townswomen had brought.

The sky was clear, and the North Star shone bright against it, when the time came to get into the wagon and drive home. Exhausted by the excitement of the day, Annabelle and Susan slept in back, on beds of hay, covered with warm quilts brought from the house. Rebecca sat rigidly beside Lucas, her hands folded in her lap, keeping her gaze fixed on the starlit road leading back to the farm.

Once there, Lucas awakened the twins, and he

and Rebecca helped them inside. There were so many things he wanted to say to Becky, but as it happened, he couldn't even bring himself to look at her. He was afraid to lose control of his raging emotions for so much as a second.

He was restless, though, and when he returned to the barn, intending to put the team and wagon away for the night, something was released in the deepest, most hidden passages of his heart. He looked back at the house for a long moment, imagining a life with Rebecca, thinking of rich crops of wheat, flocks of children, and all the Christmases to come.

Lucas unhitched the team only long enough to feed and water them. Without a word to Rebecca, with barely a silent word to himself, he took what remained of his savings from a hiding place in his workshop and climbed back into the wagon box.

For a long moment he just sat there, the reins resting in his gloved hands, looking up at the fiery silver star that seemed to fill the sky. Then, with only the merest whisper of hope in his heart, he began to follow it.

Rebecca wiped steam from the kitchen window to watch as Lucas's wagon disappeared into the night. She wanted to run stumbling after him through the deep, crusted snow, beg him to understand and forgive, but she didn't. Even if he gave in to her pleas and stayed, things would never be the same.

Too injured to cry, Rebecca turned away from the window, banked the fire in the cookstove, took up the one lantern burning in the room, and made her way through the house to the stairway. Sleeping in the bed she'd shared with Lucas would be too painful, so she went into the twins' room instead.

Despite a sadness that ran deeper than any she'd ever felt before, Rebecca smiled at the sight of her sisters. Annabelle slept in a sprawl of unconscious abandon, her arms and legs going every which way, while Susan rested in a tidy alignment of limbs, graceful even in slumber.

Rebecca turned down the lantern wick until the flame went out, then undressed to her camisole and drawers and crawled in beside Susan. One by one, she went over the cherished memories of the day, the things that had happened before she'd shown the photograph to Lucas.

For the rest of her life, she would remember the smile in his eyes while he watched the twins enjoying the dollhouse he'd built for them with his own hands. No matter what happened, or where she went in future travels, she would keep the sewing box with her. Whenever she raised the lid, Lucas's image would rise out of it, along with the scent of cedar.

Rebecca awakened early the next morning, to a house chilled with winter and with Lucas's absence. She left the twins sleeping soundly and crossed the hallway to the other room, staying just long enough to fetch fresh clothes. Though she tried not to look left or right, not to remember how it was to be held and cherished, or driven wild with pleasure, the very walls seemed to exude Lucas's scent and personality.

She hurried downstairs, built up the fire, then put on her cloak and went out to feed the chickens.

The sunlight glared off the hardened snow, scattering the landscape with diamonds, and there was a frigid bite in the air.

After breakfast, the twins washed the dishes, then scrambled outside to take turns sliding down the knoll on their new sled. At a loss, Rebecca went into the parlor, cold without the fire and merriment of the day before, and carefully removed the homemade decorations from the potted palm fronds, putting them away in a box.

She didn't think about the future, for it was so bleak she could not bear to face it. She put away the stockings the twins had hung from the mantel and removed all signs of Christmas.

After a midday meal of sandwiches and soup, when the twins had once again succumbed to fresh air and exhaustion and collapsed on their beds for a nap, Mary Daniels arrived, riding her dapple gray mare. She wore a hooded cloak and carried a basket over one arm.

There was only one person on earth Rebecca would have been happier to see, and that was Lucas. She hastily brewed tea while Mary warmed herself by the kitchen stove.

"I came to look at the furniture Lucas has been building," the visitor said. "There are new people settling around here all the time, it seems, and I believe I could sell tables and chairs and the like through my store."

Rebecca spooned tea leaves into the crockery pot, carried it to the table, fetched cups and sugar and milk. "Lucas is a fine craftsman," she said, hoping her voice didn't reveal too much of what she was suffering. "He made a dollhouse for the twins, and a sled as sleek as any you could send away for."

Mary came to stand beside Rebecca, gently grasping her arm. "Did you tell Lucas about the photographs?"

Tears burned in Rebecca's eyes, sudden and blinding. "Yes," she answered hoarsely. "And it was just as I expected. He can't bear the sight of me, Mary. He got in the wagon last night and drove away, and I don't have any idea where's he's gone—"

"There now," Rebecca's friend said quietly. "He'll certainly be back, once he's worked the matter through and realized you only did what you had to do. Why, if you'd stayed in Chicago, the twins would have been working in that factory right alongside you by now."

Rebecca nodded miserably. "I wanted to give them a better life," she whispered. "Now, instead, I'm going to have to give Annabelle and Susan up to some school or orphanage."

"Nonsense," Mary interrupted. "I'd take those children in myself before I'd see that happen. Just what are you planning to do with *yourself*, by the way?"

Sniffling, Rebecca left Mary's side, lifted the lid of the sewing box, and took out the well-worn newspaper advertisement she'd clipped days before. "I'm going to get married," she said, with shaky resolution. *And I'm never going to allow myself to dream again.*

"Dear Lord," breathed Mary, after reading the advertisement. "You can't do such a thing, Rebecca! I won't let you! Why, you could end up at the mercy of some monstrous man—"

"It's decided," Rebecca said briskly, snatching back the bit of paper.

"But you could stay on in Cornucopia—maybe open a little dress and millinery shop."

Rebecca shook her head. "Even if that were possible—and I don't have the money to set up a business—I couldn't bear to stay on here. I wouldn't be able to stand being so close to Lucas, seeing him take a real wife, and bring her here to live."

"You're getting a little ahead of yourself, it seems to me," Mary said, in practical tones. "Any fool can see that Lucas Kiley loves you, and that you love him. Wait a while, Rebecca. Give him time."

Recalling the look in Lucas's eyes after he'd seen the photograph, Rebecca sighed. He might as well have caught her whoring, he'd been so shocked.

There wasn't enough time in all eternity to heal the wound she'd dealt him. "Were you serious about keeping the girls?" she asked, hardly daring to hope. "They're of an age to help out around the store, and I'd send as much as I could toward their board."

Mary hugged Rebecca. "Yes, I was serious, but I still don't think it's going to come to that. You give some thought to what I said, and don't be too quick to give up the fight."

With that, Mary went to the parlor to inspect the dollhouse. Then she put on her cloak. "There's fruitcake in that basket I brought," she said, "along with a special kind of tea I ordered from back east and some little treats for the children."

A moment later, Mary was gone.

Lucas didn't return that night, and when the girls went off to school in the morning, there was still no sign of his team and wagon on the road.

Just after noon, however, Rebecca heard the creaking of harnesses and axles, and rushed to the back step to see Lucas drive in.

He jumped down from the wagon box and came slowly toward her, carrying a small parcel in one hand. As he drew close, Rebecca could see that his lower lip was swollen and cut, though the look in his eyes was quietly triumphant.

"Here," he said, extending the packet.

Rebecca tore away the paper and plain twine, and found two photographic plates inside. She raised her gaze to Lucas's face, hardly daring to believe, to hope.

"It cost me almost half what I had saved for spring planting," Lucas told her, "but I bought back those plates and all the pictures Jones had in his possession."

Rebecca was so moved that most of a minute passed before she could find words. "Wh-what happened to your face?"

Lucas grinned. "After Jones and I had finished the transaction, I couldn't resist knocking him on his—knocking him down. He fought back, but he only landed one punch before I thrashed him proper and left him sitting on the floor of his office."

She looked down at the photographic plates, then back at Lucas's face. "You've forgiven me, then?"

He stepped closer and cupped her wind-chilled face in his strong, carpenter's hands. "It damned near killed me to think of anybody else seeing you in your unmentionables," he said, "but after I thought about it for a while, I realized what a fine woman you really are. Lord, Becky, but you've got more grit than most of the men I know, and I love you so much that it's like a fever burning inside me. Please say you'll marry me right and proper, and stay right here where you belong."

Rebecca gave a hoarse cry of joy and flung the photographic plates against the woodpile, where they shattered with a satisfying tinkle of glass. Then she hurled herself into Lucas's waiting arms and laughed as he lifted her off her feet and swung her around in the glittering snow.

Finally, he set her down again, though she was still crushed against him, and kissed her thoroughly.

She looked up at him with all her soul showing in her eyes. "I love you so much, Lucas," she vowed, "and I swear you'll never know a moment's sorrow for marrying me."

He slid an arm around her waist, propelled her toward the waiting wagon. "The greatest sorrow I could know would be losing you," he told her, hoisting her easily into the box and climbing up beside her to take the reins. He kissed her lightly on the mouth before releasing the brake lever with one foot. "Let's get to the preacher's house and make our promises, Becky. I want to spend tonight making love to my wife."

Rebecca said nothing. She just scooted closer to Lucas, laid a hand on his thigh, and smiled to think of all the miracles that lay ahead.

HAPPY HOLIDAY WISHES
from . . .
LINDA LAEL MILLER

When I was asked to contribute to Avon's *A Christmas Collection,* I was delighted. The Yuletide has always been my favorite time of year—as a child, I drove my family crazy by playing Bing Crosby's Christmas album in July!

Back then, my brother Jerry and I used to hide flashlights in our rooms and make elaborate plans for Christmas Eve reconnaissance missions; we were hoping to get a peek at the presents Santa Claus had left under the tree, since we were certain we couldn't wait until morning. The infamous sliding door, which stood between us and the loot, was invariably our undoing—it squeaked, and Mom and Dad always heard it and made us go back to our beds. Somehow, for all our scheming, we never thought to oil the darn thing.

Here's wishing you all the wonders and magic of the season. May it be joyous, and may that feeling linger in your hearts throughout the year.

God bless.

Footsteps in the Snow

Joan Hohl

Prologue

The Laughing Fox Inn, near Eagle, Pennsylvania, 1991

THE ELECTRIC CANDLE FLICKERED IN THE WINdow, reflecting not only the dancing flame, but also a pale, sad face, framed by a lacy white curtain of sparkling snowflakes.

Faith Shelby breathed a sigh, momentarily clouding the cold, night-darkened pane with her warm breath.

It was Christmas Eve, almost Christmas morning. Where was the sense of inner joy, the quickening excitement, the anticipation she usually felt on this special night?

Gone . . . all gone, Faith mused, unmindful of the single tear trickling down her cheek. She was alone. The Laughing Fox Inn, with the date 1752 chiseled into the keystone above the recessed entrance door, no longer rang with the sounds of happy, chattering patrons. The waiters, waitresses, and bartenders had called holiday greetings to Faith before leaving to hurry home to spend what remained of the evening with their families.

The dining room was shrouded in silence. The tables were stripped of their red, green, and white holiday cloths, the Formica surfaces with their wood grained-look scrubbed clean. The tabletop holiday decorations, plastic sprays of dark green holly spilling out over the top of small white pitchers set in shallow bowls, were packed inside cartons and stacked in a corner.

The only illumination came from the modern lights designed to look like old-fashioned candles placed on the sills of the uncurtained windows, the dying flames in the wide stone fireplace set into the wall opposite the bank of windows, and the tiny twinkle lights woven through the artificial holly garland festooning the mantel and doorframes and decorating the majestic blue spruce set near the wall to one side of the fireplace.

Reaching into the deep pocket of her crisp white apron, Faith withdrew a digital watch and a leather cigarette case. She pressed the button on the side of the watch to illuminate the tiny window. The digits read 11:17. Almost Christmas. Sighing, she flicked open the cigarette case, then immediately closed it again.

No, she thought decisively. She was trying to quit . . . she *would* quit! Emotional upheaval was no excuse to continue with a habit she knew wasn't healthy.

Faith stuffed the watch and case into the pocket, then sat, tired and dejected, smoothing her palm over the soft material.

It was so quiet. The inn was closed, permanently, as of this last, festive night. A big white and red *for sale* sign had been staked into the ground in the front yard by the road. The realtor had made an appointment with Faith for the day after Christmas, to show the property to a prospective buyer.

Faith felt as though an integral part of herself was being torn from her body, her soul. Giving up the Inn, her birthright, was robbing her life of all meaning.

But she had no choice. Orphaned for several years, and the last of her line, Faith had no other family to turn to for help. And she was teetering on the edge of financial disaster. It wasn't that Faith was an inept business woman. She was smart . . . but also soft hearted. There had simply been too many times when dollars that should have gone into the hands of creditors had wound up in the hands of the sick, the needy, the desperate.

Faith couldn't find it within herself to regret the loss of as much as one of those dollars.

Now, the future of The Laughing Fox, whether as a public inn or a private residence, lay in the hands of the person who eventually purchased the historic property.

Faith's future lay in the hands of God.

She was not afraid. She was young, healthy, a good worker. She'd survive. Losing everything would hurt for a long time, but time would pass, and time would heal.

Memories crowding in on her—happy memories, sad memories—Faith turned from the window to glance around her at the familiar room, imagining she could hear the echoes of over two hundred years of her ancestors' voices, whispering to her from the plaster walls, the wooden beams, the natural stone.

Tears stung her eyes and a pang of sadness clutched at her chest. It did hurt to let go, to lose the last remaining link with her family. Her umteenth-great-grandfather, William Shelby, had built The Laughing Fox with his bare hands.

The solid building, the scents, the textures, the events that had taken place within its walls, its very spirit were a part of Faith, the last of the Shelby line.

Blinking against the hot sting of tears in her dark brown eyes, Faith raised her gaze to the two portraits hanging on the wall above the fireplace mantel, upon which resided the carefully preserved pieces of a hand carved wooden creche, a family heirloom handed down to Faith from her mother's great-grandmother.

They were not very good portraits. The oils used had been applied with a heavy, inexpert hand. Very likely the pictures had been given in lieu of payment for a meal and a place to sleep for a night or so. In addition to the inferior quality of the paintings, the smoke from hundreds of years of fires in the hearth had begrimed the surfaces, making the features of the subjects dark and indistinct.

Faith didn't need to see the face of the woman on the canvas. It was her namesake—Faith Shelby, who had lived in the eighteenth century. Faith had never figured out why on earth her mother had chosen to name her after the woman. She wasn't even a blood relative, but a homeless orphan, and from all indications, a slightly demented orphan at that.

The tale handed down through the years was that William Shelby's wife had found the girl wandering around the Inn stable yard, dazed and babbling, and had brought her into the house. Being both generous and good-hearted, the Shelbys had given the girl a home, treating her like one of their own, a sister to their two sons, for whom apparently no portrait was ever commissioned.

A faint, sad smile shadowed Faith's soft mouth as she gazed at the portrait of the woman, and then down the length of her own body. The colonial serving woman's costume she wore in her role of hostess in the Inn was an exact copy of the clothing worn by the girl in the painting, up to and including the white cap perched atop her long, loosely curled auburn hair.

Faith shifted her gaze to the other portrait. She didn't know the man's name. If anyone in the Shelby family had ever known who he was, it had been long since forgotten. It seemed that at some point in the past, some Shelby had hung the painting on the wall, more than likely because it balanced the portrait of Faith, and fit in nicely with the colonial decor.

A sigh of longing and regret whispered past Faith's lips. From as far back as she could recall, she had been strangely drawn to the dark portrait, to the face of the man whose features were so handsome, so aristocratic, that even the inept artist had managed to make him look incredibly appealing.

That strong masculine face, those fine features, those deep, compelling eyes had haunted Faith throughout her growing up years. To her mind, he was the stuff of dreams.

Staring intently at the portrait, yet no longer seeing it, Faith felt tears spill from her eyes.

Sentimental ditz, she chided herself, swinging away. If she wasn't careful, she'd find herself curled in a corner, bawling like a baby, when what she should be doing was taking down and packing up the Christmas decorations.

Faith felt a painful catch in her throat as she stared at the tree. It was so beautiful, the most perfectly shaped tree she had ever had at the inn. It would be a shame to take the tree down before Christmas, or to pack away the garland and the creche—all the bright and shining symbols of the season. Besides, it had been a long day, and she was tired.

She made a quick decision to wait, at least until late in the day on Christmas—or even early in the morning the day after—and dismissed the task from her mind.

Crossing the dining room, Faith headed for the enclosed stairway that led to the second floor living quarters. She came to a sudden stop as her gaze brushed over, then came to rest on, the outdoor clothes hooked over a row of sturdy pegs set into the stairway wall.

Maybe what she needed was a breath of fresh cold air. Before the thought was complete in her mind, Faith was reaching for her fake fur jacket hanging on the central peg. But, instead of the jacket, her hand settled on the dark, thickly woven wool shawl draped over the last peg.

Experiencing a mild sense of surprise, Faith lifted the voluminous square of material. She hadn't a clue as to why she had reached for the shawl. It was a prop, nothing more. Like her costume, and the ones worn by the other waitresses, the shawl was part of the decor, artfully draped over the peg for effect.

Obeying her impulse nevertheless, Faith flipped the large square around her shoulders. The garment was surprisingly heavy and warm. Hugging the warmth to her breast, she walked to a narrow side door and stepped outside into the snow-covered side yard.

It wasn't a large yard, just a small private area bordered on two sides by flower gardens, on the third side by an herb garden, and on the fourth side by a thick stand of stately trees.

The snow was falling harder than before; the wind moaned through the bare tree branches; the cold bit to the very marrow of Faith's bones.

She barely noticed the elements. Lost in memories of happier days, of family Christmas stories told and retold, of laughter and love lived within the solid walls of her beloved inn, Faith walked to the edge of the yard and the scant protection of the trees. Turning, she noted the deep indentations of her footsteps in the snow, then raised her tear-bright eyes to look back at the inn. Viewed through the whirling snow and the mist blurring her vision, the electric lights in the windows looked like real wax candles.

Inside Faith's mind she heard a memory echo of her mother's voice, explaining to a four-year-old Faith her reasons for placing the candles in the window.

"They're for the Magi, to light the way."

The way. Faith sniffed, coughed, and lost her

tenuous grasp on control. Raising her hands, she buried her face in the snow-dampened corners of the shawl.

"Oh, God, dear God, help me. Give me the strength to let go," she pleaded between broken sobs. "I need guidance to light my way . . ."

1

"FAITH, CHILD, WHAT IN THE GOOD LORD'S NAME are you doing wandering around out here?"

"What?" Faith blinked and lifted her face from the folds of the shawl . . . the *dry* shawl! How . . . what . . . ?

Who?

Brushing the ends of the shawl over her eyes, Faith focused her sight on the woman crossing the yard to her. She was a complete stranger to Faith. Middle-aged, rounded, with a gentle, compassionate face, she was attired in a costume only slightly different from the one Faith herself was wearing.

"What?" Faith repeated, feeling disoriented, confused. Offhand, she couldn't recall another inn close by where the employees dressed in period costume.

"I asked what are you doing out here in the stable yard, child?" the woman said. "The wind's rising and it's getting a mite chilly out here."

Chilly? Faith thought. Try cold, pretty damned . . . Faith's thoughts fractured. It wasn't cold! As the woman had pointed out, it was . . . merely chilly!

A sense of something's being very wrong filled her mind as Faith sent a quick glance around the yard, and felt her world tilt on its axis.

The snow was gone! The ground was dry, clear. Swept along by the wind, crackling leaves tumbled over the cobblestone yard.

"Cobblestones!" Faith exclaimed, gaping at the rounded stones beneath her feet. "How did they get here?" she demanded, raising her eyes to the woman. "And what happened to all the snow?"

"Snow, dear?" The woman frowned; her eyes darkened with concern. "What snow?"

Panic sprang to life inside Faith's mind. What was going on here? How could it be possible for all that snow to just disappear in the space of a few seconds? It was . . . more than freaky; it was flat-out scary.

Faith swallowed, but still her voice came out on a dry, croaking spurt. "There was a foot or more of snow here moments ago!" she exclaimed, looking around at the familiar, yet unfamiliar, scene. It was her home, where she'd grown up—and yet it was different. She didn't understand what had happened. The confusion sent her mind into shock.

"But there is no snow, my dear." The woman stepped closer, hand outheld to offer comfort or . . .

Faith stepped back. "There *was* snow!" she cried.

"It started falling early this afternoon!"

"Oh, child," the woman murmured, shaking her head. "There is something dreadfully wrong with you. It was a beautiful afternoon: warm, pleasant, a perfect late September day."

"September!" Faith stared at the kind-faced woman, alarm exploding inside her. The woman was not well, possibly even crazy. She gulped a deep breath. "You . . . you're mistaken," she said in a soothing, calming tone. "It's December, Christmas Eve . . . almost Christmas morning."

"Christmas!" The woman stared at her in obvious astonishment, then an expression of utter sadness and pity filled her face. "Oh, my dear child," she said, reaching out to her again. "How long have you been wandering the countryside alone, on your own?"

Unsure of the woman's mental condition, Faith backed up once more. Maybe she was harmless, but . . .

"You poor thing," the woman was going on. "Let me take you indoors, child, out of the chill night air. It is warm inside, and there is food."

Aha! Faith thought, certain she had solved at least part of this confusing puzzle. Very likely this woman was one of the growing number of homeless souls in the country, living as best they could under appalling conditions. Her period clothing had probably come from a rubbish heap behind a costume store.

Faith's soft heart melted as rapidly as the snow had appeared to do. But the question of the sudden disappearance of the snow would have to wait awhile to be answered. First things first, she decided. The woman was obviously cold and hungry, hoping for a safe place to rest for the night. The inn was safe, sturdy, strong, and Faith knew the freezer, fridge, and pantry were still full. There were hams and turkeys, steaks and prime ribs, along with all the traditional holiday trimmings. Faith had planned to donate the foodstuffs to local charities.

"Yes," she said, extending her hand to grasp the woman's. "Let's go inside."

"There's a good girl," the woman said, her expression changing to one of relieved satisfaction. "Come along, then, my dear." Holding tightly to Faith's hand, she turned and made a determined beeline for the side door to the brightly lighted Inn.

Brightly lighted? Faith's steps faltered. The only lights she'd left on were the electric candles set in the windows and the tiny lights strung on the garland and the tree. Unless . . . Frowning in concentration, Faith tried to remember if she had flipped on the wall switch for the hanging wagon wheel lights before stepping outside. No! She couldn't have, for she distinctly recalled clutching the shawl to her with *both* hands!

"Coming—" the woman began when Faith hesitated, then went on—"Faith, child, I never asked your name."

"Huh?" Faith stared at her, thoroughly confused. Hadn't the woman just said her name? On the spot, Faith suspected that the poor thing was further around the bend than she had originally thought.

"Your name, child. What is it?"

"Faith," she replied, shaking her head, hoping to

rattle her marbles into their proper order; events were zipping right along, and Faith was fighting to catch up.

The woman gave her an odd look, then sighed. "Faith, you say?" A sympathetic smile curved her lips. "I see."

Well, I sure wish *I* did, Faith thought, attempting to decipher the strange look on the woman's face.

"And where are you from, Faith? Do you live somewhere nearby?"

It was Faith's turn to sigh. Telling herself to be patient, she said, "I live here, right here in the Laughing Fox. I always have."

"Indeed!" The woman seemed momentarily taken aback. Her ample bosoms heaved on a deep exhalation, and she muttered, "Poor girl's daft."

At least, that's what Faith thought she heard. But the woman didn't allow her time to decide one way or the other. Tugging on Faith's arm, she pushed the door open with her other hand and literally dragged Faith into her own home.

Or was it her home?

Faith stood just inside the threshold, her mouth agape, her mind awhirl. To be sure, she had entered The Laughing Fox . . . and yet, it was not the Inn she knew.

What was going on here? Faith demanded in silent confusion. She had been outside for at most a few minutes; not long enough, not *months* long enough for anyone to have made so many drastic changes in the place.

Where were the twinkling holly garlands? Where was her beautiful tree? And what had happened to her precious creche pieces!

Stunned, her disbelieving eyes darting about, Faith moved like an automaton, allowing the woman to steer her to a bench set at a window table—a long, rough-hewn, *unfamiliar* table.

"Now you sit there and rest . . . er, Faith. I will bring you something warm to eat."

Faith wasn't hungry; she was . . . *puzzled* was too mild a word. Other words flashed through her spinning brain. Confused. Astonished. Dumbfounded. Amazed. Stupefied. All good words, none of them able to describe her strange and frightening feelings.

What *was* happening to her? Like the plaintive sound of a child's voice keening in the darkness, the cry resounded through Faith.

Why was everything so suddenly changed? *How* had everything changed?

Hanging on to a modicum of her composure for all she was worth, Faith reined in the rapid movement of her shock-widened eyes to look, closely and hard, at the individual differences within the room.

She didn't have to strain at the task. The candles in the windows, which she had earlier thought appeared real viewed through the whirling snow and the tear mist clouding her eyes, *were* real. There was no mistaking the distinctive scent of hot wax, or the liquefied stream of it flowing down the side of the tapers.

From the candles, Faith's sharpened gaze moved to the tabletop, which consisted of thick boards, worn smooth by years of use, and certainly not the reproduction of the deal table Faith had grown up using.

From the table, she shifted her intent gaze to the ceiling. The heavy cross beams were still there, but the smooth white plaster Faith was accustomed to seeing was now a rough, smoke-stained, inexpertly applied mass with the appearance of stucco, dirty and uneven. The hanging wagon wheels of six lamps each were gone. In their stead were three individual candle lamps, with *real* candles inside, hanging by thick ropes from the beams.

Her breaths coming in shallow puffs, Faith dropped her gaze from the ceiling to the walls, as a lump rose from her chest to her throat.

The walls were also no longer smooth white plaster, but were constructed of sturdy round logs, chinked with a substance that looked like the chunky stucco on the ceiling. And there were no portraits hanging above the mantelpiece.

The huge fireplace was the same—or almost so. The difference lay in the andirons, and the large iron cooking pot and assorted period utensils. Steam curled up from the pot—it was actually being used! Faith wrinkled her nose at the aroma of bubbling rabbit stew. She loathed rabbit stew.

"Here you are, dear." The woman appeared at Faith's elbow, nearly startling her out of her already jangled wits. "I have a nice big bowl of hot rabbit stew, bread fresh from the oven, and a mug of warm buttermilk. That should set you to rights."

Faith suppressed a gagging groan as she stared down at the food the woman had set before her. She loathed warm buttermilk even more than rabbit stew.

"Thank you but, I . . . I'm really not very hungry," she said in a choked murmur, leaning back to distance her nose from the awful smell of the stew.

"But you must eat, my dear!" the gentle woman exclaimed, bending down to peer into Faith's face. "You are quite pale, and have a decided peaked look."

Peaked? Faith swallowed a bubble of hysterical laughter. Who in the world said *peaked* anymore? Well, obviously this odd woman did, she chided herself, feeling reality retreat as unreality advanced.

"Uh . . . perhaps just some bread, then," Faith said, breaking a corner from the warm, thick chunk. And some coffee, with a big dash of Black Label, she mentally pleaded, in mute despair.

"Oh, but a bit of bread would . . ."

The woman's objection was drowned by the sound of raised voices coming from the barroom adjacent to the dining room.

"Now, what in heaven's name is all the commotion about?" the woman muttered, turning to frown in the direction of the barroom.

"I tell you he was defeated at the Brandywine Creek," an irate male voice shouted. "Word is that he's not gonna even try to save Philadelphia."

Brandywine? Save Philadelphia? From what? Faith wondered, her attention captured by the loud voice. He? He who?

"And I tell you I do not believe it!" another loud male voice retorted. "The report was that General Washington had amassed about eleven thousand good men."

"Ill-equipped men!" the first man shouted. "Howe split his forces, and with the Hessian von Knyphausen attackin' from the front, the British circled around to hit General Sullivan's boys from the rear. The battle was lost. There were some nine hundred wounded and killed. Even Lafayette was wounded."

Howe? Von Knyphausen? General Sullivan? Faith's senses reeled. Lafayette! What in hell were these men talking about? Were they drunk or merely raving lunatics? And what in hell did they think they were doing, creating a ruckus in *her* inn? Her closed inn!

"Who are those men?" Faith demanded, starting for the barroom with the intention of ejecting the intruders.

"Oh . . . Oh, dear!" the nice, if demented, woman objected, clutching Faith's arm. "You cannot go in there!"

"And why not?" Faith asked archly, attempting, and failing, to pull her arm free.

"It is unseemly for a lady to enter the barroom," the woman replied, in a tone indicating the answer should have been obvious.

"Unseemly?" Faith repeated the out-of-date—*long* out-of-date—term. "But I own the—"

The first man's voice broke through Faith's protest. "Rumors are rife that Howe then had his forces foragin' and burnin' the whole of the Schuylkill River valley, while Washington positioned his troops on the steep ridges at Valley Hill, down near White Horse."

The Schuylkill River valley. Valley Hill. White Horse. The place names were more than familiar; Faith had lived west of the area all her life. But the man's information was out of context, way out of context—unless, Faith mused, smiling slightly, unless she had been time-warped, "Star Trek" fashion, back to the past, her country's past.

Faith rejected the imaginative but unrealistic possibility out of hand—for even to consider it meant that she, and not these other strange folk, was out of her head.

"Well, will you leave off guzzlin' that there ale and continue?" yet another male voice piped in, drawing Faith's unwilling if fascinated attention.

"Yeah, well, I'm not so sure you want to hear the rest," the first man grumbled. "Hear tell 'twas a mess there at Valley Hill. Had a cloudburst and got thick with mist. Some are already callin' it 'The Battle of the Clouds.' "

"But what happened?" the new voice demanded.

"Well, seems like Washington retreated from the hills, too, even though they say ole Mad Anthony begged his commander to allow him to loose his Pennsylvanians on the British."

The Battle of the Clouds? Mad Anthony . . . Wayne? Faith was beginning to feel a crawly sensation when suddenly she was struck by a new, more palatable consideration. Were these men historians, reenacting the events leading up to the terrible winter George Washington and his army endured at Valley Forge?

Faith slanted a quick glance to the woman beside her, standing stiffly alert to the men's conversation.

Of course! Faith expelled a long sigh of relief. That had to be the answer. It was in December that Washington had moved his army into winter quarters at Valley Forge, and Valley Forge was located a short half hour or so drive east from The

Laughing Fox, depending on how heavy a foot was on the gas pedal.

That was it! Faith was forced to contain a burst of self-directed laughter. What a nit she was, getting all bent out of shape because some half-baked historians were reenacting the past. Everyone in the vicinity knew that The Laughing Fox would be closing permanently after serving dinner on Christmas Eve. These people must have seized on the idea of using the inn to play out their recreation of the events prior to Washington's removal of his troops to Valley Forge.

But, historians or not, costumed or not, these people were trespassing on private property, on *her* private property. Faith's sense of relief changed to one of annoyance. Had they been thoughtful enough, polite enough to ask, she'd have been delighted to give her permission for the play. She would even have joined them. Faith enjoyed that kind of play, never missing a costumed reenactment put on at Independence Hall in Philadelphia. All the same, they should have asked for her permission.

Caught up in the conflicting emotions of relief and anger, Faith conveniently forgot for the moment the changes in the interior of the inn, not to mention the sudden and inexplicable disappearance of some twelve or so inches of snow. She turned to the woman to administer a stern lecture on the penalties imposed on persons apprehended in the act of breaking and entering when once again, she was sidetracked by the raised voices issuing from the barroom.

". . . and a passin' scout told a neighbor, and he told me," the first man was explaining. "Also said that there's a story goin' around that that French General du Coudray drowned 'cause he insisted on stayin' on his horse to board a flatboat to cross a river."

There was a loud snort of disbelief from one man, and an equally loud hoot of laughter from another. "Them Frenchies sure are somethin'."

"Yeah," the first man agreed. "But I for one ain't so much worried about them Frenchies as I am the story I heard about how Howe's troops destroyed Colonel Dewees's place yonder at Valley Forge."

"No!" an outraged voice exclaimed. "But Lord sakes, man, where's Washington now?"

There ensued an expectant hush. Faith imagined that however many men there were in the barroom were leaning forward to catch every word. Figuratively if not literally, she was leaning forward herself.

The answer came *sotto voce*. "Hear tell Washington's restin' his troops at Camp Pottsgrove."

"He's going to build up his forces with new units," Faith called to the men, impulsively jumping into the play, uninvited. "Count Pulaski will be bringing in his regiment of four hundred cavalrymen," she added with sudden recall of the chain of historical events.

There ensued a brief, shocked silence. Then four men, wearing like expressions of astonishment, stormed into the dining room.

"Who in tarnation is that?" demanded a tall, well-built man with a shock of auburn hair and a bartender's apron swathed around his hips. "Emily, was that you who spoke?"

Now rigid with shock, the woman standing

beside Faith shook her head vigorously. "No, no, William. I said nothing. 'Twas the young missy here." She indicated Faith with a helpless hand. "The one I told you I found out in the stable yard, shivering and weeping."

"How came you with such information?" a short, squat man quizzed Faith. "Speak up, girl!"

Girl? Faith bristled. She didn't appreciate the man's sharp, interrogative tone. This clown in colonial clothing had a definite attitude problem. After all, this was her home! Who did these people think they were, quizzing her? Getting into the game was one thing, but sexist attacks were something else altogether. Drawing herself up to her full five-foot-seven inches, Faith leveled her strongest drop dead look at the banty rooster.

"Excuse me, but are you addressing me?" she inquired in ice-coated tones.

"Huh?" The man grunted, gawking at her.

"I said . . ."

"Never mind, missy," the aproned man, apparently playing out the role of local innkeeper, interrupted with impatience. "Answer the question. How do you know these things?"

"I know all, I see all," Faith replied in a flip parody of the intriguing voice she'd heard at a Renaissance fair, adopted by an actress playing the role of a mysterious Romany fortune teller.

As one, the men closed in on her. Faith stood her ground, watching them warily.

"What else do you know . . . see?" the bartender asked in a whisper after a prolonged silence.

"Is this a test?" Faith asked brightly, attempting to

lighten the group's sudden dark looks. "Okay." She shrugged. "Washington will advance on Howe's forces camped at Germantown in early October—and will be defeated," she said, certain that had been his next move.

"Saints preserve us!" Emily exclaimed, wringing her hands.

"Be the girl a witch?" the short stocky man asked after a gulp, noticeably paling.

"A witch, you say?" the man belonging to what Faith had been thinking of as the third voice squawked, taking a step back, while making the sign of the cross with his two forefingers.

Oh, brother! Enough already, Faith decided, rolling her eyes in exasperation.

"Watch out!" the fourth member of the group cried. "She's going into a fit!"

"Right!" Faith shouted, at the absolute end of her tether. "I will have a fit if you yo-yos don't stop all this stupid playacting!"

"Playactin'?" The group, along with Emily, spoke simultaneously, like a well-rehearsed Greek chorus.

Faith was on the verge of tears of frustration; she opted for laughter instead. "You characters are really very good, close to Oscar quality," she complimented them when her laughter had subsided to a soft chuckle. "The accents are first-rate and the costumes are great." She indicated the garments with a flick of her wrist. "And the sets are . . ." Her voice faded.

Sets? Scenery? Stage props? Good grief! Faith chided herself for her slow uptake of the situation. She must have been outside a lot longer than she thought, unaware of the passage of time while lost in her misery.

Of course, that still left the little matter of the sudden disappearance of the snow, but Faith didn't have time to delve into that. She was too preoccupied with inching back, away from the determined advance of her uninvited troop of amateur thespians.

"Mrs. Shelby, what have you brought down upon us by bringing this young miss into the house?" the bartender demanded of Emily.

Mrs. Shelby? Faith blinked.

"I . . . I . . ." Emily stuttered, staring in horrified fascination at Faith. "I was only offering a Christian kindness to her, William."

William? Faith sliced a keen look at the apron-clad man.

"Aye, Mr. Shelby," the man who had made the sign of the cross whispered, raising his hands protectively before his face. "What devil's spawn have y' got under your roof?"

His roof? Mr. Shelby? William! Faith stared at the man apparently portraying her umteenth-great-grandfather. She examined his build—and found it familiar. She studied his features—and noted the similarities to her own. She stared into his eyes—and felt she was staring into a mirror.

Where was she?

A silent scream reverberated inside Faith's head. The answer that followed blew a fuse in her mind.

Lost in time.

No. No! she cried in silent disbelief. Weird and inexplicable things like time travel didn't happen except in the creative minds of fiction writers, and the scrambled interiors of the pitifully demented.

"Don't let her escape!"

The shout jarred Faith into an awareness that she was inching backward, toward the door. Escape? Escape to where? Where could she go?

"I want to go home!" Faith cried aloud.

"Where is your home, child?" Emily asked, not unkindly.

Faith turned a stark look on her. "The twentieth century," she said on a sob. "The end of the twentieth century."

"I told you! I told you!" the stocky man shouted. "The girl's a witch!"

"Leave off, Bridigan," William snapped. "Can you not see the girl's daft?"

"Poor lost child," Emily murmured, clicking her tongue as she reached for Faith's hand.

"I am not daft or demented," Faith said between short gasps of breath. "I'm lost in time!" But even as she said it, she didn't really believe it. There *had* to be another explanation.

"A witch, I tell you!"

"Kill her!" the cross-fingered man yelled, backing away. "Burn her!"

"I think . . . not."

The voice was new, different from the others, cultured and refined. On a collective gasp, Faith's tormentors whirled to confront the unexpected intruder. Faith was forced to crane her neck to peer around the solid frame of the man they called William Shelby to get a glimpse at her would-be rescuer.

And he was a sight to behold.

The man had struck a pose in the spacious opening between the barroom and the dining room. The pose bespoke breeding, station, elegance.

His clothes were exquisitely tailored, and in the very latest fashion—for the last quarter of the eighteenth century. His neck cloth and shirt cuffs were ruffled. His dark brown, tailed coat fit smoothly over his broad shoulders. Gold buttons adorned the deep cuffs on the sleeves. His fawn-colored breeches clung to his slim waist, narrow hips, long flanks, and muscular thighs. Light hose defined the curve of his legs from below the knees to where they disappeared inside his buckled shoes. A dark, caped cloak was draped negligently over his shoulders, falling to within mere inches of the floor.

Faith stared at the man in stunned awe. Not because of his sudden appearance. Not because of his clothing. Not even because he was the single most handsome man she had ever laid eyes upon. Simply because he was the living image of the man in the portrait in her own twentieth century inn!

And the man was staring with cool intensity directly into Faith's shock-widened eyes.

2

"TORY."

Snarled like a curse, the muttered word dropped like a stone into the heavy silence of the common room.

"Prescott Carstairs, sir," Pres drawled, ignoring the muttered word, his cloak brushing the floor as he executed an insultingly brief bow to the assembled group. "Your most obedient servant." As he straightened, he swept each male in turn with a stern look. "And there will be no burning or killing here this night."

In truth, they were a rather disreputable-looking bunch, Pres mused, tilting his head to thoroughly examine the varied and mildly amusing expressions on the faces of those gathered in a semicircle. Excepting the innkeeper and his lady wife, he allowed; they were a decent-looking pair. And, oh, yes, the young woman.

The wench was beautiful.

With the arrogance natural to one of his station, Pres ran a slow, comprehensive look over the woman, beginning with her glorious mass of tumbled auburn curls, to the delicate features of her flushed face, and down the length of her enticingly curved figure. Her breasts were neither large nor small, the perfect size to fit a man's hand. Her waist was small, nipped-in, drawing the eye to her rounded hips and all the way down to her well-shaped ankles, peeking out from beneath the hem of her skirt.

Brief as his glance at her ankles was, Pres was struck by a quality of strangeness. There was something not quite right about the unusual sheerness of girl's hose. Odd, that. He felt an urge to touch, to examine—but of course he did not. He was fully aware that such a breach of propriety would likely earn him a smart rap from her for his trouble—and justly so.

Pres returned his gaze to the girl's wide, fear-darkened eyes. It was a shame, but obvious, that the girl's top story was to let.

The young woman's physical attributes, appealing as they were, were not of primary concern, Pres regretfully reminded himself. His interest lay in the remarks he had overheard her make upon entering the inn.

The girl had not only declared that General Washington had increased his forces with new units, including a regiment of some four hundred cavalrymen under the command of Count Pulaski, but she had further stated that the commander-in-chief would fail in a surprise attack against Howe's army at Germantown in early October.

Since they were just entering the waning days of September, Pres pondered upon the note of confidence he had detected in the girl's voice. A fool? An idiot? A madwoman? Or . . .

Being a man of some distinction, and of the world, Pres had heard claims about people who possessed the "sight," as it were. Considering himself a realist, he had dismissed those claims, and the purported "sighted" people, out of hand.

But, he reflected, supposing there was some truth to the claims, that there were some souls who had an ability to see into the future?

A tingle trickled down Pres's spine. He could make excellent use of any and all information concerning the unfolding of future events.

Within an instant Pres came to a firm decision, and immediately acted upon it.

"I vow, my horse is receiving better care than I," he drawled in a tone of studied indifference. Languidly raising one hand, he swept the cloak from his shoulders, and with practiced indolence strolled forward into the common room. "I judge by now the beast has received both food and lodging."

His dryly voiced comment achieved the desired effect. The innkeeper jerked to attention as though prodded by a white hot poker.

"You wish a room for the night, sir?"

"Indeed." Pres raised one naturally arched brow. "It is a darkening night, and the wind is rising. I thought it best to seek shelter."

"Aye, 'tis so," the innkeeper agreed in a sage and somewhat ominous tone.

"What with that shadowy figure skulking about o' late," the stocky customer muttered.

Pres turned a quizzing look on the bandy-legged man. "Shadowy figure?" he asked, shifting his glance back to the innkeeper. "The vicinity has been plagued by a shadowy figure—a sneak thief, perhaps?"

"Umm," the man murmured. "Though I'm bound to admit I have heard of no instances of any house here 'bout bein' broken into."

"But there have been reports of foodstuffs and livestock gone missing," the stocky man volunteered.

"Ah . . ." Pres said, dismissing the threat with a smile. "I detect a *hungry* shadowy figure. I find it easy to sympathize," he went on, giving the innkeeper's attentive wife a pointed look. "I myself may soon feel the need to begin foraging for a meal."

"Oh! Oh, my!" that good lady exclaimed, appearing about to run in circles. "Pray, do forgive me! You are hungry, sir?"

"A light repast would not come amiss," Pres replied, smiling to set the lady's mind at rest.

The woman bobbed a quick curtsey. "Of course, sir, at once! I have a lovely stew bubbling."

Pres slanted a glance at the nearby table and the victuals upon it, which the young woman had appeared to have rejected. He understood why; the rabbit stew looked less than appetizing.

"Umm . . . no, thank you." Once again, he raised one brow. "A roast of beef, perhaps?"

She appeared crestfallen. "No, sir, I am sorry to say. But there is a meat pie keeping warm by the ovens," she added brightly.

"The pie will suffice," Pres said, moving closer to the table, and the young woman who, judging from her expression, was laboring under the task of taking in every word uttered. "You may serve a portion to the . . . er, young lady, as well," he instructed the woman, avoiding a second glance at the congealing mess in the wooden bowl.

"Oh . . . oh, my! I had almost forgotten her!" Mrs. Shelby cried, sending a beseeching look at her husband. "Mr. Shelby, we cannot turn her out on such a dark and blustery night. May she stay, if only for a little while?"

Pres contrived to look bored while the innkeeper fought an inner battle, presumably with his good Christian conscience. Fortunately, the battle was brief.

"She may stay," he decided. "But she must earn her keep," he added, giving the girl a hard stare.

"You're goin' to house a witch?" The outcry came from the nervous-looking man, who continued to stand back, his hands held protectively in front of his ferret-like face.

Turning slowly, Pres leveled his iciest stare on the sniveling excuse of a man. "My dear man," he drawled, "only very small children, and very big nincompoops, believe in witches."

The man was rendered suitably silent.

"And would you desire ale with your meal, sir?" Mr. Shelby put in.

Pres made no effort to suppress a shudder. "Might one hope for a passably decent wine?" he inquired.

Mr. Shelby drew himself up proudly. "I keep an excellent wine cellar, sir."

"Well . . . excellent," Pres praised, bestowing a smile on the now beaming man. "Bring a bottle of your best." He hesitated, then shrugged. "And two glasses, if you please."

As expected, his request drew a shocked gasp from the men, a murmured, "Oh, my!" from Mrs. Shelby, and, unless he had misheard, a muffled giggle of appreciation from the young woman.

" 'Taint right, givin' spirits to a youngun," the stocky man muttered in protest.

Heaving an audible sigh, Pres appealed to his host. "Along with the food and drink, might one also hope for a measure of privacy?"

"At once, sir!" Mr. Shelby agreed, turning on the other three men. "Into the public room, lads," he ordered, sweeping them before him through the connecting doorway. "Mrs. Shelby!" he called back, jarring that good woman out of her state of shock. "Get about seeing to the gentleman's dinner!"

Mrs. Shelby proved swifter of foot than had the poor rabbit who had wound up in the stew.

"Ahh, alone at last," Pres murmured, facetiously, offering the girl a benign smile.

"You're a hoot, you know that?" The wry comment slipped past Faith's guard; she really hadn't meant to remark on his performance, but it had been so darn good.

"I do beg your pardon," he replied, in a startled tone. "A hoot?"

"Oh, come on," she said on a sigh. "Don't you think you have all carried this game far enough?"

If anything, this man who had introduced himself as Prescott Carstairs now appeared more confused than startled. The crawly sensation wriggling inside Faith expanded, causing a sick feeling to invade her stomach. She swallowed against a tightness in her throat. They just *had* to be acting. Otherwise, the only other explanation would be that she was reliving, reenacting the life of the original Faith. And that would mean that she *was* the original Faith! And that would mean . . .

No! Time travel was not possible, she assured herself, crossing her fingers.

Was it?

"All?" Prescott Carstairs' puzzled query broke into her reverie. "I pray you are not associating me with the others here," he said in a stiff, stern tone. "For I assure you, I have never before clapped eyes on the lot of them."

"No?" Faith taunted skeptically, absently smoothing her palms over her apron.

"No."

"Oh." Faith moistened her dry lips with a quick flick of her tongue and felt a thrill zing through her as his sharp gaze monitored her action. "I . . . ah, I think I must sit down," she muttered, sinking onto the end of the hard bench. "If you don't mind?"

"By all means," he murmured, inclining his head, thereby nearly concealing the small smile tugging at the corners of his too-attractive, very masculine mouth. "May I?" He indicated the bench opposite her with a negligent wave of one hand.

"Be my guest," Faith said. Then, as the thought struck her, she added, "You are, you know."

"Are?" Consternation was written boldly across his handsome face. "Are . . . what?"

"My guest." Faith heaved a deeper sigh; this whole business was getting pretty tiresome. "I am your real hostess. I own this place."

"Indeed!" The arch in his dark brows inched upward to the lock of equally dark hair which had fallen forward onto his forehead. He seated himself elegantly across from her and stared directly into her eyes. "And do the others herein know?"

"You don't believe me."

"Well . . ."

"You think I'm an idiot."

"Er . . ."

"Worse, you believe I'm a raving lunatic."

Prescott Carstairs didn't squirm. He didn't even appear uncomfortable. Faith had to give him Brownie points for his cool control under fire.

"My dear Miss . . ." He paused, raising his eyebrows.

"Faith," she responded. "Faith Sh . . . er . . . Faith," she finished lamely.

"Faith Faith, an unusual name," he drawled. "In that event, may I address you simply as . . . Faith?"

"Whatever turns you on," Faith said a little testily; she *was* losing patience . . . or was it her mind she was losing?

An expression of consternation swept over his strong features once more. "I do humbly apologize, but I'm afraid I do not comprehend this 'whatever turns you on' expression. Is it a local colloquialism?"

"Slang," Faith answered without a second thought. "Universal colloquialism, I suppose," she explained when he frowned. "It means—suit yourself."

"I see," he said, giving her a strange look.

To Faith, it was obvious that he didn't see, and that bothered her. Actually, it frightened the hell out of her.

"Here we are," Mrs. Shelby called, bustling into

the room. "Careful now, the pie is piping hot," she cautioned them, sliding two pewter plates onto the table, then whipping the wooden bowl of stew and mug of buttermilk away. "I shall return with utensils," she promised, bustling away again.

The steam rising from the crusty wedge of meat pie tickled Faith's nose, and appetite. "Umm, that's more like it," she murmured, mouth watering as she inhaled the tantalizing aroma.

"Better than the rabbit stew?" he asked in a teasing voice.

"Oh, gag me," Faith groaned. "I detest it. I think I'd rather starve than eat rabbit stew."

"I most seriously doubt that."

There was something in his voice, a wry shading in his tone that caught Faith's attention. She was on the point of questioning him when Mrs. Shelby scurried back into the room, distracting her.

"Now, then," she chirped, placing two snowy white napkins and flatware on the table. "I'll leave you to enjoy your meal, sir." She turned away, then added in afterthought, "Oh, yes, and you also, Faith."

Prescott Carstairs made an odd, strangled sound. Faith shot a glance at him, catching him choking on suppressed laughter. She was tired, and she was feeling more apprehensive with each passing second. But her sense of humor was alive and kicking . . . Here she was actually lost in time, yet to her flustered hostess she was no more than an afterthought.

Staring into Prescott Carstairs' twinkling eyes, Faith burst into laughter. After an instant's hesitation, he joined her.

They were still chuckling, still staring into each other's eyes, when Mr. Shelby strode back into the room, carrying a large wooden bar tray bearing a tall tapered bottle and two delicate stemmed glasses.

"Getting on together, are you?" he said, shifting a puzzled glance from one to the other.

"Amazing, is it not?" Prescott Carstairs drawled, slanting a droll look at her.

Faith was forced to cover her mouth with her hand until Mr. Shelby poured the wine and retreated.

"Ahh . . . alone at last," she mimicked his earlier remark. Wriggling her eyebrows at him, she stabbed her fork—her two-pronged fork—into the pie, snared a good-sized piece, and popped it into her mouth.

In the process of mirroring her actions, Pres glanced up, dropped the fork onto the plate and, tossing back his head, let out another roar of laughter.

Chewing the portion of pie—which was in fact delicious—Faith watched him with interest. She washed the morsel down with a sip of wine, which was likewise delicious: full-bodied and more potent than any she had tasted before. Then she asked, "Having fun?"

He seemed nonplussed for a moment, then smiled. "Another odd expression, but apt. Yes, actually, I am, as you say, having fun."

"Terrific," she mumbled, continuing to consume the pie. "I'm glad one of us is."

"But you were laughing also," he pointed out, digging into his meal.

Faith shrugged. "Well, you know what they say . . . it's either laugh or cry, and I hate a crybaby."

"You feel a need to weep?"

"Oh, boy, *do* I," Faith replied, taking another, larger swallow of the wine.

"Are you so very distraught?" he asked, frowning as he tasted his own wine.

"Wouldn't you be, in my position?" she countered, feeling oppressed as she glanced around her at the familiar—unfamiliar—room.

He lifted his shoulders in a helpless shrug. "My dear, how could I know, since I have no idea exactly what your position might be."

Deciding the time had long since come to cease and desist with this farce, Faith looked him straight in the eye. "Look, Mr.—" She paused, then went on. "May I call you Prescott?"

"My friends call me Pres," he said.

"Okay, then, Pres, will you level with me?"

He frowned. "Level?"

Faith was beginning to feel as though she was teetering on the edge of a very high cliff, and she wasn't all that wild about the view, either. "Be truthful with me," she said patiently.

"But certainly!" he exclaimed, taken aback.

Faith gazed inwardly, into the abyss, then plunged. "What year is this?"

"Year?" Pres repeated, sounding baffled. "You feared I would be untruthful about the date?"

"What is it?" she insisted in a whisper.

"The year of our Lord, seventeen hundred and seventy-seven," he answered, now looking as well as sounding baffled.

"Oh, gee," Faith moaned, propping an elbow on the table and her forehead on her hand. "I was afraid you would say that."

"Afraid?" Pres shook his head. "Of the year? I do not understand."

"He doesn't understand!" she muttered, fighting a rising tide of hysterical laughter. Lifting her head from her hand, she cried, "Pres—please, please, admit that you, all of you here, are historians, playacting at recreating a segment of the Revolution, a war that was fought over two hundred years ago!"

"Over two hundr . . ." Pres's voice faded, then came back on an incredulous note. "But then, that would make this time, here and now, close to the end of the century . . . the twentieth century!"

"You got it."

Taking great care, Pres again placed his fork on his plate. Then, lifting his glass, he gulped down the remainder of the wine. Apparently the liquid fortification rendered him blunt. "Are you claiming to have come here from the twentieth century?"

"I'm not claiming to be anything," she retorted. "I *am* from the twentieth century."

He was quiet for a moment, studying her, then he smiled, very gently. "And pray, how did you travel backward in time to this place . . . did you fly?"

As far as she knew, Faith reflected, smothering a giggle, United didn't fly the friendly skies of colonial Pennsylvania. "No," she answered. "All I did was walk into the yard, into the snow."

"Snow?" He pounced on the word.

"Well, it was Christmas Eve," she cried. "The customers had all gone home. I was tired and a little depressed. I walked outside for some air and . . ."

"And?" he repeated, prompting her.

"And." She made a face, recalling her statement concerning crybabies. "And I buried my face in my hands and cried." She shrugged. "Then I heard someone call my name. I looked up to see Mrs. Shelby crossing the yard to me. But the yard wasn't the same," she rushed on. "There were cobblestones and no snow and . . . and when she brought me back into the inn, it was . . . different." Faith ground to a panting halt. A rush of tears filmed her eyes. "Things are changed." She blinked and gazed across the room. "The garland and my creche are missing." She sniffed. "And my beautiful tree is gone!"

"Tree?" Pres exclaimed, drawing her attention back to his amazed expression. "You had a tree growing here, inside the building?"

Faith made a face at him. "No, of course not, silly. I was talking about my Christmas tree."

"Silly?" he repeated, in a droll tone. "*I* am silly? You are the individual speaking about trees in the house, are you not?"

"I said a . . ." Faith broke off, recollecting that the Christmas tree didn't come into fashion in the States until somewhere around the early or mid-nineteenth century. "Never mind," she went on, dredging up a weak smile. "You're right, I am being silly."

Pres didn't ridicule; he sympathized. "Why were you weeping in the yard?"

Faith's lips trembled. She tried to brave it out, but she lost the battle. "I felt so alone," she admitted. "I'm going to lose the inn, my home."

"But surely you have family?"

Pres had discarded his languid pose. Though Faith had appreciated and enjoyed his performance, she much preferred the man behind the facade. She felt somehow safe confiding in him. "No," she said. "They're all gone. I'm the last of the Shelbys."

"Shelby?" Pres blinked and cast a glance at the doorway into the barroom. "The innkeeper's name is Shelby."

"Yes, I know." Faith managed a faint smile. "If I really have traveled through time, then Mr. Shelby and his wife Emily are my umteenth-great-grandparents."

"Umteenth?"

Faith sighed and nodded. "I'm too tired to figure it out," she said, crushing her napkin with nervous fingers. She jumped when his larger hand covered her fingers, stilling them.

"You genuinely believe all you have told me," he said. "Do you not?"

"Yes." Faith heaved another deep sigh. "Just as I genuinely believed that you, and the others, had taken over my inn to recreate a portion of history."

"We have not." He hesitated, then continued, "At least, I have not. I cannot speak for the others, this being the first time I have stopped at this inn on my way home to Philadelphia."

"Your home's in Philadelphia?" Faith didn't know why she asked the question; it had nothing to do with her predicament. But she was suddenly interested, in his answer . . . and, more than ever, in him.

"Yes." He smiled.

She caught her breath. "And . . . ah, are you a Tory?" she blurted out, shaken by the stunning effect of his smile, and referring to the appellation one of the men had muttered when Pres had made his presence known.

He seemed to withdraw into himself. "My family are known for their support of the crown," he finally replied. "In fact, they felt so strong in their loyalty, they have removed back to England."

"But not you?" she said, grimacing at stating the obvious.

"Not I," he concurred. "I have holdings in Lancaster and Reading to attend to."

"I see," she murmured, noting that he had neither denied nor admitted to being a Tory himself. Faith was on the verge of questioning him further, wanting to hear him tell her he was for the cause of freedom, when she realized the utter ridiculousness of her pursuit.

What in heaven's name did it matter? she asked herself. Unless she was seriously crazy, she was very likely dreaming or hallucinating, and Prescott was nothing more than an illusion, a creation of her tired and overactive imagination—a handsome, sexy illusion, maybe, but an illusion nonetheless.

She slid her hand from beneath his and slipped it into her apron pocket. A feeling of relief swept through her as her fingers curled around the cigarette case. Solid proof of her origins in the twentieth century.

"Where have you gone now?"

"Huh?" Faith started. "What did you say?"

"You seemed so far away," he said. "I merely asked where you were."

"You think I'm completely bonkers, don't you?"

"Bonkers?"

"Mad," she said impatiently. "A raving lunatic, or the witch that nasty man accused me of being."

"No," Pres denied at once. "I think perhaps you are confused or . . ." His voice appeared to fail him.

Faith laughed, but the sound held no humor. "Or what?"

He shrugged. "I am not quite sure."

"Join the club," she muttered. "I'm not quite sure either."

"A tangle, to be certain," he said, reaching for the wine bottle to refill their glasses. "Join the club," he murmured. "Ah, yes, I understand." Replacing the bottle on the table, he tilted his head and smiled at her. "You have very colorful, descriptive expressions."

"Damned straight," Faith rejoined, trying out another one of her colorful expressions on him.

Pres looked astonished for an instant, then he laughed. "I would suggest you not use that particular expression whilst speaking with anyone other than me," he drawled. "Unless, of course, your aim is to shock."

"My aim is to go home," she retorted.

"But, my dear," Pres murmured around the rim of the glass he had raised to his quirked lips, "did you not moments ago tell me that this *is* your home?"

"Yes, but . . ." Faith broke off in frustration, and glanced around the room once more. "I mean, I want to go back . . . forward . . . dammit! I want to go where I belong, in the twentieth century."

"Umm." Pres took another swallow of his wine

and closely observed her while she sipped hers. "As I entered this establishment," he said, very casually, "I could not help overhear the discussion. Please, correct me if I am wrong, but did I not hear you say that Washington will be defeated by Howe at Germantown in early . . ." He broke off as Mr. Shelby strode into the room.

"A chamber has been prepared for you, sir," he said, shifting a frowning glance at Faith. "You, missy, if you have finished your meal, thank the gentleman, then go help Mrs. Shelby in the kitchen."

"Yes, sir," Faith said at once, jumping up.

"Hold a moment," Pres ordered, reaching out to grasp Faith's wrist to keep her from rushing away. "I wanted to inquire if . . ."

"Please," Faith whispered, pulling against his loose but firm grip on her, "I must earn my keep."

"If you will follow me, sir," Mr. Shelby inserted, "I will show you to your room."

"Yes, yes." Pres scowled his impatience, but relented and released her arm, whispering, "I must speak with you again."

Faith started for the kitchen. "Sure," she muttered, tossing a wry smile at him over her shoulder. "Sometime. That is, if I'm still here."

3

THREE WEEKS HAD PASSED, AND FAITH WAS STILL there, at the inn, in the eighteenth century.

Faith sat cross-legged on the narrow bed she had slept in each night of those three weeks, her shawl wrapped around her shoulders to ward off the damp cold seeping into the tiny bedroom at the very back of the second story of the building. Bedroom? She had to smile as she glanced around; the room had been converted into a walk-in closet years before she was born, and was located near the top of the enclosed back staircase in the dining room.

The only warmth afforded to the room was the heat that radiated up from the large cooking fireplace and ovens in the kitchen directly below.

Kitchen! Faith's smile curved into a grimace; there was no resemblance between the kitchen of her own time and the room below. Instead of restaurant-sized stoves complete with grills and griddles, this kitchen contained a huge fireplace and two brick wall ovens. There were no microwave ovens, no food processors, no blenders, no freezers, no double refrigerator, no central island counter . . . no running water! All the room contained was a long table, and room to do a lot of work.

But, although Faith was expected to earn her keep, the Shelbys—she still found it difficult to think of them as her antecedents—were kind to her, treating her more like a daughter of the house than a stranger found weeping in the stable yard.

As to the Shelbys' own offspring, Faith had yet to meet William Jr. and James, who were thirteen and twelve respectively, as their parents had packed them off to Emily's parents' farm near York to keep them from harm's way when Washington marched his army into Pennsylvania from New York.

But three weeks of toiling in the kitchen from dawn until noon, serving in the common room until closing, then dragging her tired body upstairs to sleep in the cold room, had instilled in Faith a yearning for her own twentieth century bedroom, centrally heated and toasty warm. Though the luxury of central heating wasn't at the very top of her wish list.

First and foremost, Faith longed to submerge her body in a tub of scented water, or at the very least, stand beneath a revitalizing shower spray. She pined for her moisturizing bath soap, shampoo, conditioner, a toothbrush, toothpaste, a blow dryer, jeans, a sweatshirt, her brief but comfortable lingerie and, after her repulsive experience last week, modern personal sanitary products.

Of course, Faith reminded herself, she did have the undies she had been wearing beneath her costume on Christmas Eve, the night of her journey into the Twilight Zone of time travel. But since she had no way of figuring how long she would remain in the past, she hesitated to wear the delicate bra, panties, and sheer French-cut black pantyhose for fear of wearing them out.

The pinging sound of a wind-driven rain mixed with sleet striking the pane in the room's one small window drew Faith to a sharp awareness of her surroundings. Hugging the warmth of the wool shawl to her breast, she turned her head to gaze at the old armoire set against the wall inside the door. Her filmy lingerie was secreted underneath her folded costume inside the ornate cupboard, alongside the few articles of clothing Mrs. Shelby had kindly provided to supplement Faith's meager wardrobe.

After three weeks of wearing the sturdy clothes, hand made of heavy, scratchy wool, and the thick, prickly hose, Faith vowed she would never again complain about the quality of American mass-produced merchandise. About the only item she did find comfortable was the long-sleeved, high-necked, soft cotton nightgown Mrs. Shelby had hand sewn for her.

Three weeks. Faith sighed. Even after twenty-odd days, she was still having difficulty acclimating herself to her unreal predicament. When she crawled into bed every night, she shut her eyes tight and prayed that when she opened them again, she would find herself at home in the twentieth century, where she belonged.

There was one tiny problem with her prayer—unstated, but at the edge of her consciousness. Faith wanted to waken to find Prescott Carstairs there, too, in the twentieth century with her.

The thought of his name brought a sad, self-derisive smile to Faith's soft mouth. Of all the idiotic, stupid things to do, she had gone and fallen head over heels in love with Prescott Carstairs.

And it wasn't even as if she had spent much time in his company, either. Faith had seen him only twice since that first night. Despite his whispered urging to speak with her again, over a week had passed before he had returned to The Laughing Fox.

"Pres."

Whispering his name caused a twinge in her heart. Did he feel a similar attraction to her, Faith wondered—not for the first time. She thought, hoped, prayed Pres felt the same, but it was difficult to tell; the man was so darned enigmatic.

And yet . . .

Shivering, more from an inner thrill than the surface chill, Faith recalled the two occasions on which Pres had stopped at the Inn during the intervening three weeks . . .

"Good day, Mistress Faith."

Smothering a shriek of surprise, Faith spun to face the man who had appeared so suddenly and silently in the dining room doorway. "Good grief, Pres!" she exclaimed, giving him a stern stare. "You startled me."

"I do apologize." Pres bowed his lips and raised an eyebrow questioningly as he glanced around the empty room. "You are alone here?"

"Yes." Faith indicated the room with a quick gesture. "Mrs. Shelby is in the kitchen, preparing the evening meal."

"I pray not rabbit stew," he drawled, sauntering across the room to her.

Warmed by the idea of sharing something with him, even something as insignificant as a mutual dislike for rabbit stew, Faith smiled and shook her head. "No, not today."

"Thanks be." Pres grinned as he shrugged off his long cape. "I was anticipating a substantial meal."

"You've been traveling long?" Faith asked, noticing his mud-spattered boots.

He nodded. "Since first light."

"Then you must be starving!" she exclaimed, turning toward the kitchen. "I'll bring you something to—"

"Hold," Pres ordered, reaching for her hand. "I can wait until the meal is ready." Lacing his fingers through hers, he drew her toward the rough-hewn parson's bench placed near the fireplace. "Come, sit and talk with me while I warm myself."

"I really shouldn't," Faith said, glancing at the kitchen doorway. "I should be getting on with my work." She inclined her head to indicate the bucket of steaming water and cleaning cloths she had gathered to scrub the tables and benches.

"That can wait, also," he said, tightening his fingers around hers. "Your duties include serving the customers," he went on, seating himself and urging her onto the bench beside him. "You can serve me with your companionship and conversation."

The warmth of his hand caused a tingling sensation to skitter from Faith's fingers to the nape of her neck. The intensity of his dark eyes, his soft voice, caused a sinking feeling in the pit of her stomach. She wanted to believe that Pres was interested in her as a woman, but . . .

The talk in the inn the night before had revolved around the renewed sightings of the shadowy figure stealing back and forth through the vicinity. And now, here was Pres, appearing suddenly, out of nowhere.

Was he a patriot or a Tory? Faith bit back the question and instead asked, "What do you want to talk about?"

"You."

Faith glanced away from his probing gaze. "What about me?" She stole a quick look at him, then went on before he could answer, "I mean, what do you want to know?"

"Many things." Pres smiled. "Will you take offense if I ask your age?"

"My age?" Faith stared at him in astonishment, then laughed; and she'd been afraid he would grill her about the future! She shook her head. "I don't mind telling my age, Pres. I'm twenty-four."

"Indeed!" Pres gave her a look of disbelief. "I thought you were older."

"Older!" Faith frowned. "Well, thanks a heap."

"Not because of your appearance," Pres hastened to assure her. "But you have a certain maturity, a presence about you." He shrugged. "I cannot quite explain what exactly it is, but you seemed so much more . . ."

"Independent?" Faith finished for him.

"Precisely." Pres gave a sharp nod of his head. "You possess an air of independence far exceeding that of other females of your age."

"Maybe because I'm from a different time, Pres," she reminded him. "The women of the twentieth century are independent and self-sufficient."

"Are they, really?" His voice held a note of wonder. "Tell me about your life there, the things you do, how you live . . . everything."

"Everything!" Faith laughed. "I'm afraid it would take hours for me to do that, because everything is so very different."

Pres glanced around the room, then brought his gaze back to her. "Are *people* from your time so very different, as well? Do they not laugh, cry, love?"

Faith felt herself leaning toward him, wanting to drown in the depths of his dark eyes; she caught herself up short when her mouth was mere inches from his. "Ah . . . yes!" she blurted out, her face hot from embarrassment. "People are much the same. It's the lifestyle that's changed."

"And you, Mistress Faith, do you love?" His voice was a caress, so low she had to strain to hear him.

"Love?" she repeated, confused.

Pres moved closer, so close his breath feathered over her suddenly dry, parted lips. "Yes, love, Mistress Faith. Do you—"

"Faith." Mrs. Shelby's raised voice cut off whatever Pres was going to say. "Have you finished scrubbing the tables?"

Rudely jolted from her bemused state, Faith blinked and frowned, then jumped to her feet. "No, ma'am," she called, casting Pres an imploring look when he continued to maintain his hold on her hand.

"Well, make haste, girl," Mrs. Shelby ordered. "I need your help out here in the kitchen."

A rueful smile curving his lips, Pres allowed her hand to slip free of his. "Later, perhaps?" he murmured on a hopeful note.

"Perhaps," Faith replied on a sigh of regret. Would there be time later? She strongly doubted it, as she suspected she would probably be kept busy serving the customers.

Faith's suspicions proved correct, as the evening business was brisk.

Positioned near the wide doorway between the bar and the dining room, Pres didn't miss a word of the discussion amongst the customers, though he gave the appearance of bored disinterest.

Other than exchanging a few hurried words when Faith served Pres his dinner, they had no other opportunity to engage in a real conversation.

Faith went to bed that night still wondering if Pres was truly interested in her, or only in the information he could garner from her.

She would have believed the latter, if it were not for the tantalizing memory of his eyes. Pres's eyes, dark and intent, had followed her every move, remaining cool so long as she was left undisturbed to go about her work, flaring with an inner flame whenever a male customer evinced the most casual interest in her.

Faith smiled with remembered disbelief tinged with compassion as the memory of another customer came to mind. In truth, the incident stretched credulity.

The man had arrived at the inn a few nights after Faith's own sudden appearance there, and on the same night as Prescott's second visit.

The man was nondescript, average in height, skinny, somewhat delicate in appearance, harried-looking. To the rapt attention of every person in the place, the man recounted his tale of woe.

It seemed the man was a struggling artist who maintained a small gallery and framing shop in Philadelphia. As he was also a known supporter of the cause for independence, he had decided to choose the path of prudence and had fled the Philadelphia area when General Howe took command of the capital city.

Loading what supplies and stock he could pile into a two-wheeled cart, the man set out, heading for safety with relatives in Lancaster. Since it was common knowledge that Howe's army was ravaging the countryside, the man had taken a circuitous route, sleeping wherever he found a modicum of shelter. After a week on the road, the man felt sorely in need of a roof over his head and a bed, if only for a night or two.

It was at this point of the man's story that the kicker came for Faith.

His soulful eyes pleading, the man prevailed upon William Shelby to give him a few nights succor in exchange for portraits of the innkeeper and his wife, since the artist had no hard cash to pay for lodging.

"Portraits, you say?" William Shelby repeated, snorting. "I've little time for such fancy doings."

"Your good wife, then," the sorrowful man said with a note of desperation.

"Nay," William said, shaking his head. "Mrs. Shelby has no time to sit for it either, man."

The artist appeared crestfallen and on the verge

of tears. Shoulders drooping, he turned to leave the Inn when the kindhearted Emily intervened.

"Pray, Mr. Shelby, grant me a boon," she requested in respectful tones. "Allow the man to paint a portrait of the young miss, Faith."

"Me!" Faith exclaimed, though she knew full well the deed was as good as done; the proof of it hung in The Laughing Fox of the twentieth century.

"Shush, child," Emily murmured. "The man needs our charity." Raising her voice, she appealed again to her husband. "What say you, William?"

"Well, now," Mr. Shelby muttered, obviously not predisposed to the idea. "I do not . . ."

"I think the prospect of a new portrait merits consideration," Pres inserted, his lazy tone of voice a clear indication that he had stepped back into the role of languid aristocrat. "I shall sit," he went on, deigning to smile at the newly hopeful artist. Moving with fluid grace, he flicked a hand in Faith's general direction, while addressing Mr. Shelby. "For a pittance, would you not like a portrait, a keepsake if you will, in remembrance of your mysterious young miss?"

The deed was done. The swiftly—and badly—executed portraits had been completed within a week and a half. The artist had started Faith's that very same night, and done Pres's entirely on the occasion of his second visit to the inn. Pres had requested lodging, and had sat long into the night for the painter. In the morning, as on his other stay, he was gone before Faith awakened. There was no sign of the painting, and the Shelbys assumed Pres had taken it with him. Faith knew better; the painting had to be somewhere in the inn, for at some future date, some future Shelby would hang it on the wall next to her own.

That had been over a week ago.

A soft sigh whispered through the quiet room. Would she ever see Pres again? Faith wondered. Only God knew how long she would remain in the past; she could be whisked forward into her own time every bit as quickly as she had been zapped backwards.

September had passed, as had the first full week of October. The weather grew steadily worse, unusual for so early in the autumn. Would the inclement conditions curtail Pres's movements, making it too arduous to travel back and forth between his home in Philadelphia and his holdings in Lancaster and Reading?

A faint, scratching sound at the window startled Faith out of her less than encouraging speculations. Going stiff, she cast an apprehensive look at the window. Rain and sleet pounded against the pane; the wind moaned through the gnarled old tree—long gone in her time—situated outside the kitchen.

Tossed by the wind, the tree branches were brushing against the window pane, Faith concluded, exhaling a deep sigh of relief. For an instant she had been afraid there might be an intruder.

Fanciful, she chided herself. It was late, she was tired; time to shelve fruitless reflections, and call it a night. So thinking, she hopped off the bed, slipped the shawl from her shoulders, and crossed to the armoire.

Musing on the cold floor, and her colder feet, she

emitted a muffled gasp when a strong arm encircled her waist and a broad hand was clamped over her mouth.

"Peace, Faith, I shall not harm you," Pres whispered close to her ear.

Faith shivered, more from the inner tingling sensations caused by the feel of his warm breath against the sensitive skin below her ear than from the initial spurt of panic she had experienced.

"If you will promise not to cry out, I shall remove my hand," he murmured, causing another wild tingle inside her. "Nod if you are in agreement."

Faith bobbed her head, while noting with excitement that he hadn't said anything about removing his arm from her waist.

His hand fell from her face. Then Faith's mind whirled as Pres spun her around and pulled her into a tight embrace. She heard her name being murmured on a low groan, and then his mouth covered, crushed, devoured hers. He was soaking wet; his clothes, his face were chilled. But Faith hardly noticed. In swiftly accelerating stages, she was warmed, heated, set afire by the hungry pressure of his mouth, the tentative probe of his tongue.

Though Faith had not led a cloistered life, other than a brief, dissatisfying affair when she'd been a junior in college, she had not indulged in intimate relationships. By rights, she should have been shocked by Pres's sudden amorous advances; and in some sense she was. Electrified, she curled her arms around his rain-slicked neck and returned his deepening kiss with a matching ardor.

Pres went stone still for an instant, then a groan vibrating his throat, he dropped his hands to her hips and lifted her into the arching thrust of his taut body.

Faith's senses exploded. A hard knot of desire formed in the pit of her stomach and quickly descended to the most feminine part of her. She burned, ached with a need she had never before believed it was possible to feel. She wanted, wanted . . . everything imaginable.

Shaken by the intensity of her response, Faith slid her hands to his chest and wrenched herself back, away from him and her own clamoring senses.

"Pres, stop, please," she panted, turning her head to avoid the allure of his seeking mouth. "You . . . you're going too fast, too . . ." Her voice faded as, muttering a curse, he released her and stepped back.

"I vow, I owe you an apology," he said in a ragged voice. "But damned if I will make it." His chest heaving, Pres stared at her from eyes glittering with the light of passion. "I am not sorry I kissed you, Faith." His lips curved into a regretful smile. "I am sorry you stopped me from going further."

Faith felt she should chastise him, but in all honesty she could not—for along with a renewed chill in her body, she too was feeling sorry she had stopped him. She took a step toward him, then halted, eyes growing wide with surprise as the strange look of him registered on her calming mind.

Even in the meager light of the flickering candle set on a tiny table beside her bed, Faith could see the roughness of his clothing. Gone was the elegantly tailored attire he usually wore. It had been replaced by the more common garb of pants, loose jacket, shirt and boots, all in dark colors.

He looked . . . shadowy!

"Pres?" Faith heard the unspoken question in her voice and knew her suspicions were reflected in the eyes she raised from his clothing to his face.

"Yes." Pres answered her unvoiced question. "I am the shadowy figure the country folk have been twittering about over their ale mugs."

Faith inched back, coming to a stop when her spine made contact with the armoire.

"On my honor, I swear you have no cause to fear me, Faith." Pres didn't pursue her, at least not physically. But his soft, beguiling tone seemed to coil around her heart.

"But . . . why?" she asked in a whispered plea. "Why do you dress like this and go roaming around the countryside, rattling the locals?"

Pres shrugged. "It serves a purpose."

"What purpose could possibly be served by skulking about?" she demanded in disappointed anger.

"The purpose of scavenging whatever information and food I can avail myself of for my commander-in-chief," he replied coldly.

"Washington?" Faith breathed, staring at him in shock and amazement.

"Yes," he said. "General Washington."

"You're a spy?"

"I am a scout," Pres corrected her severely. Then he grinned. "And a spy." His grin fled as quickly as it had flashed, leaving his face drawn and strained. "I should not be here," he muttered. "But I had a longing to see you . . . and a need to know."

"Know?" Faith frowned. "Know what?"

"Some six days ago we . . . the army was turned

back by the British at Germantown, just as you foretold on the night of your arrival here," he said, watching her through narrowed eyes. "It was as if Howe's forces were expecting us. It was a rout. My comrades and I circled around, deflecting the enemy's attention from our commander." A muscle twitched in his taut jaw. "My horse stumbled, thereby saving my life. The man riding before me took the ball aimed at my back."

"Oh, Pres."

His shoulders rippled, as if he was shrugging off her murmur of sympathy. "The outcome was never in question. General Washington has withdrawn to—"

"Whitemarsh." The place name popped into her mind and out of her mouth.

"But how do you know these things?" Pres said urgently.

"I told you before," Faith answered, slumping wearily against the armoire. "These events are all history to me . . . soul-stirring history of my beloved, *free* country."

"Free?" Pres pounced on the word.

"Yes, Pres, free," she said. "You made the right decision when you chose to side with the revolutionaries instead of the crown, as your family did."

Pres straightened to his full height of over six feet. "There was never a question of where my lo- yalties lay," he said sternly. "I love this country, also."

"I'm glad," she said simply. "I was worried about that. Your dress, your manner . . ."

He smiled. "They also serve a purpose."

"I see that now."

"But this matter of travel through time—" Pres shook his head. "I do not comprehend."

"Mind bender, isn't it?" Faith asked, sighing. "I don't understand it either. All I know is that on Christmas Eve, I walked into the yard . . ."

"Into the snow," Pres inserted.

"Yes," she concurred. "I was feeling so alone, so lost. I . . . I appealed to God for guidance. I buried my face in my hands and cried. Then a voice called my name, and when I looked up, Mrs. Shelby was crossing the yard to me, the snow was gone, and I was here."

"Unbelievable," he murmured.

"But I can prove it!" Faith cried. Recalling the watch and cigarette case in her apron pocket, she turned to open the armoire door.

"No, Faith," Pres said, weariness weighing his tone. "Unbelievable as it is, I do believe you. I must. I will examine your proof another time, perhaps. For now, I am tired." He glanced at his clothes and smiled. "I am also very wet, and rather cold."

"Oh!" Faith leaped away from the armoire. "Yes, of course, the rain! Get out of those clothes at once," she ordered, unmindful of her own wet nightgown, dampened from the contact with him. Rushing to the bed, she pulled off the top cover. "You can wrap yourself in this quilt. It's old, but warm."

Moments later, stripped down to his small clothes, Pres stood before Faith beside the narrow bed, the quilt draped toga-style around his lean body and making him look as imperious as a Roman emperor. A smile playing over his mouth, he swept her body with gleaming eyes and arched one dark brow. "Your gown is damp also," he murmured, loosening a corner of the quilt and holding it away from his body in invitation. "You are shivering. Would you care to warm yourself by joining me inside this cocoon?"

Startled by his observation, Faith quickly glanced down and felt her cheeks grow warm at the sight of her nakedness, the curve of her breasts, her chill-hardened nipples, the vee bracketing her feminine mound, outlined and defined by her damp gown.

"Do not be embarrassed or shamed." Though his voice was soft, it held a hint of command. "You are so incredibly beautiful, Faith. Come, my sweet, be with me, warm me, allow me to warm you."

Uncertain, anxious, Faith hesitated for several long moments, studying the tender expression on his face. She didn't know this man; knew nothing at all about him other than what little she had garnered by observing him on his few stops at the inn. And yet she felt she did know him, and trusted him instinctively.

Still, Faith hesitated. It had been so long since she had shared any form of intimacy with a man. She had been too busy running the inn, too distracted and disinterested to be bothered.

Watching Pres watch her, Faith acknowledged that she was still busy; Mrs. Shelby saw to that. And she was still distracted; who wouldn't be in such weird circumstances? But she was interested in Pres—interested and bothered.

She wanted to be with this man. It was as simple as that. As an anticipatory thrill intensified the shivers skipping over her body, Faith stepped forward, into his open arms, and sighed contentedly as he enclosed them within the warm folds of the soft quilt.

"There, is that not better?" he whispered, ruffling her hair with his breath.

"Yes," she admitted. "But my feet feel frozen."

"Mine also." Pres tilted his head back to smile at her. "If I promise to conduct myself like a gentleman, would you consent to lie upon the bed with me?"

"Yes," Faith answered without hesitation, without reservation.

The transition from floor to bed was made with a minimum of awkwardness, and a muffled giggle from Faith. Then, snug and warm all over, wrapped in the quilt and Pres's arms, she threw caution to the wind and brazenly raised her parted lips to his mouth.

4

"VIXEN."

Faith smiled and once again brushed her mouth over his, creating havoc with his senses—and a most sensitive part of his anatomy.

Suppressing a groan of response, of need, Pres

captured her teasing lips, crushing them beneath the hungry weight of his passion-hardened mouth. The ardor Faith revealed by her own response stole his breath away. Never, never before had he become aroused so quickly, so completely. As depleted and tired as his body was, it quickened with a demanding, painful desire to be as one with Faith.

"You would tempt a saint," Pres whispered, bathing her lips with the tip of his tongue.

"Are you a saint?"

"Far from it," he admitted, laughing softly.

Faith frowned and drew back a few inches.

"I am two-and-thirty, Faith," Pres murmured, hauling her close to him again.

"Are you?" Faith asked, surprised. "I thought you were older."

"Indeed?" Asperity tinged his voice; Pres did not appreciate her opinion, or the echo of his own previous remark.

Faith offered him a soft smile and raised her hand to stroke his taut cheek. "I didn't mean you look older, Pres," she hastened to assure him.

"No?" He arched his dark brows. "What, then, did you mean?"

"Oh, I don't know." She lifted her shoulders in a shrug. "You look so much the man of the world, so mature, so in command of yourself."

"Ahh . . . I do like the sound of that," he said on a purr. "Please continue, I am fascinated."

"Oh, cut me some slack," she said in a choked voice, burying her laughter against his chest, and tickling his skin, and his fancy, with her warm breath.

"Cut you some . . ." Pres's voice was lost to his chuckle. "Oh, Faith, you delight me."

"Do I?" Faith's laughter fled. Raising her head, she stared into his eyes. "Truly?"

"Truly," he repeated, lowering his head to hers. "You are the singularly most delightful and intriguing creature I have ever met." His mouth sought hers, but Faith pulled her head back to stare at him in astonishment.

"Intriguing?" she exclaimed. "Me?" She gave a sharp, impatient shake of her head. "I?"

"Yes, of course, you." Pres smiled. "I know of no other who has traveled through time."

"Then, you really do believe me?" Faith asked in wide-eyed expectancy.

Pres felt a tug at his heart; in that moment, she seemed so like a lost child seeking reassurance. What must it be like for her? he mused. How confusing, how frightening to find oneself in an unfamilar place and time, surrounded by strangers.

"Yes, Faith, I really do believe you," he said with utter sincerity. "I do not know nor understand how or why you have come here, but I do believe you."

She heaved a ragged sigh of relief, and snuggled closer to him, safe and secure in his arms.

Pres's feelings of tenderness, gentleness, caring, protectiveness were touched, negating the baser one of carnal lust . . . or was it simply that his body was too tired to maintain the physical demands?

No matter. He was weary, and when he allowed himself to recall the time spent in the saddle, both during the battle at Germantown and in the days following it, he was disheartened. The recent chain of events did not portend well for the cause of freedom.

The single bright spot in his life at present was the woman he held in his arms, who had aroused unexpected feelings in him, and on her claim that, from her future prospective, the freedom they were all fighting so desperately for was an accepted fact.

Absently stroking silky strands of hair from Faith's soft cheek, Pres pondered the question of why he believed her incredible tale of time travel. She could be mad, or merely deluded, or even a base liar.

But he did not think so.

There was something about her, something inherently honest that spoke to something within him. Faith had told him the truth. Pres was prepared to stake his life on it.

She turned her head to press her lips to his fingers. "What are you thinking about?"

"You," he murmured, absently tracing the contour of her downy cheek with the tip of one finger.

"What about me?" she asked in a whisper, making a soft mewing sound, not unlike that of a contented cat being gently stroked.

"Your present circumstances," Pres answered, trying unsuccessfully to suppress a sudden yawn. Weariness lay heavily on him, tugging at his eyelids. "It must be harrowing for you."

"Yes, at least it was at the beginning," Faith replied. "It isn't as bad now. I've adapted somewhat. I don't understand any of it," she went on, sighing. "I don't know that I ever will." Levering herself up onto one elbow, she peered into his face. "How long has it been since you've had any sleep?"

"Please, forgive me," Pres said, covering his mouth to muffle another yawn. "But I assure you, I have heard every word you uttered."

"Oh, Pres, there's nothing to forgive." Faith smiled. "Or are you just trying to avoid my question?"

"I am sorry," he said, returning her smile rather sheepishly. "What was the question?"

"How long has it been since you've had any rest?" she repeated.

"I nodded off in the saddle several times," he answered, with deliberate vagueness.

Faith started. "In the saddle? But I . . . I assumed you were on foot." She cast a quick glance at the window, at the continuing downpour. "Surely you haven't left your horse standing in the yard?"

"No, I have not," Pres hastened to assure her, pleased by her concern for the animal. "I stabled my mount in an abandoned barn not too distant from the inn. I have used the shelter before. He has fodder and protection from the elements." A wry smile shadowed his lips. "I regret to say that, in all probability, my horse is better quartered than our army."

Faith's expression bespoke compassion. "I read, studied about the appalling conditions." She bit her lip, as if unsure whether to continue, then blurted out, "I'm afraid it's going to get worse."

Pres closed his eyes in an attempt to conceal his despair from her. "I suspected as much," he said. "But I prayed I was wrong." Once shut, his eyelids defied his will to pry them apart. "I . . .

I seem incapable of keeping my eyes open," he confessed.

Pres shivered as he felt Faith bend to him, sighed as her tender lips brushed his eyelids.

"Sleep," she whispered. "Rest. You are safe here with me. I will allow no one to disturb you."

Pres heard her voice as if from a great distance, and yet it soothed him, released his mind from its heightened vigilance. His body relaxed. Within moments, he was immune, if briefly, to the horrors of war.

Faith did not sleep. She was kept awake by her thoughts, her emotions, the realization of her fragile grip on her present situation.

In addition to her very real concerns for the future, her own personal future, Faith was likewise distracted from slumber by the even sound of Pres's breathing, the evidence on his face of the relief from tension, the tug at her heart by the vulnerability of his sleeping form.

She was in love with Prescott Carstairs, a man who, in her normal reality, had been dead for over two hundred years. The concept was more than inconceivable for Faith; it was a real mind blower.

How was it possible? she asked herself repeatedly throughout the remainder of the wind and rain tossed night. How could a physical entity be transferred through time from one century to another?

Divine intervention? Faith pondered, recalling her impassioned Christmas Eve plea for guidance. Not for one instant did Faith doubt that her Maker could change the course of her life with the merest flicker of a thought. No, what she did seriously doubt was the idea that her Maker would evince such interest in just one out of the many billions of earthbound entities—namely, Faith Shelby.

On the other hand, if she rejected the concept of interference from a heavenly source—and she did—that left her swinging in the breeze, so to speak, with her original question left unanswered. How was it possible to be transferred through time from one century to another?

Although Faith's searching mind found no answers, her head produced a record-breaking ache. Pushing back the covers, she slid one leg from the bed, bent on going to the bathroom medicine cabinet for aspirin, but yanked it back before her foot touched the floor.

"Nuts," she muttered, remembering that not only did she not have any aspirin, but there was no medicine cabinet—or bathroom, either.

Faith's headache had dissipated by the time dawn tinged the curtainless window with a watery gray light. The pounding rain continued unabated.

Fully aware that, as there had been every morning since Faith's arrival at the inn, there would soon be a tap on her bedroom door, followed by the soft call of her name from Mrs. Shelby, she crept from the bed, careful not to disturb her sleeping guest.

Creeping to the spindly table by the window, Faith poured icy cold water from the flowered pitcher into its matching bowl, and proceeded with her morning ritual of splashing her face and cleaning her teeth with the corner of a cloth dipped first into the water then into a tiny bowl of salt she had filched from the kitchen.

Banishing her longing for a hot shower, she grimaced as she donned the warm but scratchy garments. The expected tap on the door and soft call of her name came as Faith was stepping into the shoes she had been wearing the night of her incredible journey. She gave silent thanks to the shoe company for making them comfortable, as well as authentic to the period.

Faith paused with her hand on the latch to gaze at the man sleeping so soundly in her bed. A sigh whispered through her lips as her gaze lingered on his strong features.

Would she ever see Pres again? Faith wondered, allowing her eyes to adore his sleeping form. Her position here, in this time, was so uncertain and . . . she loved him so very much.

A sharp pang of regret brought a sting of tears to her eyes. Not for loving him, or for having spent the night in his arms. Faith knew she would never regret that. What she did regret was not having made love with Pres, because she didn't know if she would ever again have the opportunity to do so.

Pres moved, muttering in his sleep. A sad smile curving her lips, Faith slipped quietly from the room.

He was gone when she returned several hours later.

During the following weeks Faith came to view Pres as almost two different men. One man was the aloof, rather condescending Prescott Carstairs who stopped at the inn at regular intervals, always during the daylight hours, stating his desire for a repast and brief rest in his travels to and from his holdings in Reading and Lancaster, and his home in Philadelphia.

The other man was the shadowy, elusive Pres, who entered Faith's bedroom through the window, under cover of darkness.

By mid-November, Faith was hopelessly in love with both men. In her admittedly biased opinion, Prescott Carstairs was charming, with his elaborate sophistication and cutting tongue. But it was the shadowy, disreputable-looking Pres who stole her breath with his murmured words and heated kisses.

But, although, on an average of once a week, Pres spent whatever was left of the night with her, he steadfastly refused to break his pledge of honor to her of maintaining conduct befitting a gentleman.

They seldom slept. Some nights they clung to each other, their voices husky from weariness, murmuring sentiments as old and timeless as life itself.

"I love the feel of your hair," Pres whispered, gliding his fingers through the silky strands. "It's so soft against my skin." Lifting his hand, he brought the strands to his face, his lips.

"And I love your eyes," Faith murmured on a sigh. "Your eyes and your mouth." She drew a trembling fingertip along his lips. "It's so beautifully shaped, so strong, and yet so very sensuous."

"And so very hungry," Pres confessed, brushing her mouth with his.

"Oh, Pres. More, please." Clasping his face, Faith captured his tormenting mouth, settling it onto her own lips.

Conversation ceased, giving way to a more sensuous dialogue conducted with searching lips and nibbling teeth and teasing tongues.

Other nights, more awake and alert, they lay together talking, getting to know each other.

Pres told her a little about his life, his world, and in turn, Faith amazed him by relating some of the events which had occurred between his time and hers. During one such discussion, during which she drew a blatantly skeptical expression from him with her account of the advances made by women, she left the warmth of the bed to retrieve the watch, lighter, and cigarette case she had hidden in the folds of her clothing.

"Have you ever smoked a pipe?" she inquired with seeming innocence, returning to perch on the side of the bed.

"Yes, of course." Pres frowned. "But what . . ." he began, only to break off when she held the case aloft.

"This is called a cigarette," she said, removing one from the case. "It is made from tobacco, something like that used in a pipe." She made a face of consternation. "I'm not sure when the cigarette came into use, but in the twentieth century, they are smoked by both men and women."

"You smoke those . . . like a pipe?"

"No, not like a pipe." Faith hesitated a moment, then she sighed. "I quit before coming here"—she shrugged—"but I will demonstrate."

Faith placed the cigarette between her lips, plucked the lighter from the case and, flicking it on, fired the tip of the smoke. She inhaled. Her senses whirled, and she immediately began coughing.

Pres leaped from the bed. "Faith, are you all right?"

"God! That's awful!" she choked out between coughs. "I think I'm finally cured of the habit." Sliding to the floor, she groped beneath the bed.

"What are you doing?"

"Getting rid of this weed," she croaked. Finding the lid to the chamber pot, she cracked it open, disposed of the butt, then slammed the lid shut.

"How fascinating."

"What?" Faith scrambled up from the floor. The sight that met her eyes brought a gentle smile to her lips; Pres's expression was one of sheer wonder. "Having fun with those toys?" she asked teasingly.

"But these things are incredible!" Pres exclaimed, alternately flicking the lighter on and off and staring in fascination as the digits changed on the watch.

"I suppose," Faith agreed. "At least from your point of view. But, believe me, were you able to travel with me to my time, I could show you infinitely more incredible things."

"I do not doubt it," he said. "What things?" he immediately asked with boyish eagerness.

Faith laughed. "Things like jet planes and cordless phones and computers and . . .

"Stop," Pres ordered. "You must explain."

Faith spent the remainder of that and subsequent nights attempting to describe the products of a technology she herself didn't comprehend.

But by mid-November, Faith was on the point of gritting her teeth in sheer frustration. Lying beside Pres, within the protective curve of his arm, talking, learning about him, feeling his warmth, breathing in the intoxicatingly masculine scent of him, while never knowing him in the ultimate, intimate sense, was for Faith unmitigated torture.

Damn the man's honor, anyway! Faith ranted in silent ire on a blustery night in late November. Didn't the man understand that their days were very likely numbered?

The thought brought a chill to Faith's heart, along with the realization that, engaged in dangerous work as Pres was, *his* days could very likely be numbered.

That thought gave Faith new determination. Come hell, high water, or Howe's considerable army, she and Pres would make love on his next nocturnal visit, even if she had to force the issue by playing the wanton.

Her determination was put to the test the very next night.

It was earlier than usual when Pres raised the window sash and slipped inside.

"Damnation, it is cold out there," he whispered, as he shut the window. Turning to her, he executed a brief bow. "Begging your pardon for the profanity, my dear Faith."

Profanity! Faith had to choke back a burst of laughter. "I can't begin to imagine how you'd react to the vernacular of my time," she said, stifling a giggle as she took his coat from him and hung it on a wall peg.

Pres arched his brows. "Surely it is not coarse?"

"Quite often," Faith said. "And quite explicit. People are more open with one another."

"Indeed?"

Faith hardly heard his comment over the echo of

her own voice ringing inside her head, reminding her of her determination.

"In what way are people more open?"

"Let me show you," she said, unaware of the cold floor beneath her bare feet as she went to him. "But first, let's get undressed and into bed." Concealing her sudden attack of uncertainty and nervousness, and moving with what she hoped was enticing slowness, she drew her nightgown up her body and over her head, revealing her nude form for his shocked inspection.

"What are you about, Faith?" Pres's voice was low, ragged, edged with sensual excitement.

"About ready to go out of my mind, if you don't soon make love with me, Pres," she said with forced calm and blunt honesty.

"But . . ." He paused to swallow. "I gave you my pledge as a gentleman."

"And I'm now releasing you from that pledge," Faith said. She reached for his shirt and began tugging it loose from his pants. "I want, need the man of flesh and blood, not the hidebound gentleman."

"Faith, please, reflect upon what you are doing," Pres protested, though he made no move to still her hands, now busy raising the shirt up his torso.

Faith's smile was soft, utterly feminine, as old and mysterious as the Sphinx. "I've been reflecting upon this for over a month," she muttered, intent on easing the garment over his head.

"Then most certainly you must understand that . . . Faith!" he exclaimed when her fingers grasped the crude waistband of his pants. Yet still he made no move to stop her. "You would not dare!"

Faith tilted her head to give him a gleaming, sidelong glance. "Wanna bet?" she challenged, emboldened by the evidence of heightened excitement leaping in his dark eyes.

"But . . . but . . . oh, Lord," Pres groaned, growing still, color mounting his taut cheeks, as she gripped both the rough pants and softer undergarment and slid them down over his slim hips, freeing his manhood.

Where his cautioning protests had had no effect on Faith's determination, the sight of his arousal brought her to an embarrassed halt. Never before in her life had she acted with such boldness, or viewed a naked male so closely. Her one brief affair had been conducted entirely under cover, so to speak, and the unvarnished sight of Pres brought her to an abrupt, breathless halt.

"I . . . I . . . Pres, I . . ." Faith stammered, gazing up at him in helpless appeal.

"I think I shall take control now," Pres murmured, calmly sitting on the edge of the bed to remove his boots and hose. "Unless you wish to beg off?" he continued, when at last he was as unfettered of clothing as Faith.

"Beg off?" With a measure of her equilibrium restored, Faith found a weak smile for him. "No, Pres, I do not wish to beg off."

"I was praying you would say that," he said, returning her smile as he held out a hand to her. "Come, my sweet traveler through time. I promise I shall be gentle with your maidenhood."

Maidenhood! Faith was struck with an overwhelming urge to bawl like a baby. Why, why had she ever allowed herself to experiment with that green college boy? By succumbing to her curiosity, she had denied herself the pleasure of offering the gift of her virginity to her beloved.

"What is troubling you, my sweet?" Pres asked, frowning when she made no move to take his extended hand.

Though she would never have believed she'd live to see the day, Faith actually hung her head in shame. "Oh, Pres, I must tell you, I . . . I . . ." She broke off to catch a quick breath, then blurted out, "I'm not a virgin."

Pres was very still for a long moment, then his chest heaved in a deep sigh. "I see."

"But you don't see, not really. How could you?" Faith cried. "I couldn't expect you to understand the changes in customs and moral standards that took place over two hundred years." She grasped his hand and held tightly to him. "Pres, I'm sorry, truly sorry, but in my time, there was no wrong in my being intimate with a man. I was free, unattached."

"There was only the one man?" His voice, though low, betrayed strain.

"Yes." Without considering his right to question her, Faith replied with a meekness she had never before accorded a man. But then, she had never been in love with any other man.

"Very well," Pres stated in a softening tone of acceptance. "What is done is done. In truth, it changes nothing." He pulled his arm back, drawing her close. "I confess, I want to be with you, Faith, more than I want to continue breathing."

"That's how I feel about you," Faith said, moving with him onto the bed.

"And I have been plagued by the fear of coming to you, only to discover that you have disappeared as mysteriously as you arrived."

Hearing him express her own fear, Faith flung her arms around him in a tight embrace born of desperation. "I know," she sobbed, seeking the comfort of his eager mouth. "The fear torments me, also."

"Then let us be together, as one, here and now." Revealing the depths of urgency she herself was feeling, Pres crushed her mouth beneath his.

Faith possessed no expertise on the sensual arts, but she recognized a master's touch in Pres's lovemaking. With infinite patience, his hands gently caressed her quivering flesh, his tongue stroked her lips, his mouth explored every inch of her body, sensitizing her, enslaving her to his arousing touch.

"Pres . . . Oh, darling, please, please, I can't bear any more!" Faith cried, throwing her head back as she arched her body high, entreating his possession.

"Soon, my love," Pres murmured, gliding his tongue from her arched throat to the very apex of her raised thighs. "I would taste you first."

Faith went stiff with shock. "Pres, no!" She felt the flicking touch of his tongue and the tense spiral inside her shimmered, shooting sparks of pleasure to every leaping pulse in her body. "I . . . I . . . oh, Lord!" Writhing, moaning, she reached for him. Obeying a voracious need, she grasped his hips. "Pres, I need you. Help me!"

"Yes, yes, now, love, now." Surging up and over her, Pres took possession of her body, claiming her, heart and soul, as his own.

5

FAITH WAS DRAWN FROM THE DEEP SLEEP OF PHYSICAL repletion by the shifting of the covers as they were gently tucked around her shoulders. The room was still pitch dark; pre-dawn had not yet cast its ghostly glow over the horizon.

"Pres?" she murmured, reaching for him.

"I am here," he said, from the side of the bed.

"You're dressed." Faith peered through the darkness at his vague outline. "You're leaving?"

"I must."

"But . . ." she began to protest, only to be silenced by the tip of his finger against her lips.

"My love, please understand," Pres whispered, dropping to his knees next to the bed. "Were it possible, I would ask nothing more of my God than to be allowed to spend my life by your side." He took her hand and raised it to his lips. "Being with you, not only the way we were last night, but in all ways, is all I now require of life." He pressed his lips to her palm. "But it is not possible. I cannot, in good conscience, indulge my personal desires. I must do what little I can to further our cause." His hand gripped hers. "Faith, it rends my heart to see the men. My compatriots languish under appalling conditions while our generals argue over various locations to quarter the army over the winter."

"It will be Valley Forge," she said, raising her hand to stroke his hair back from his forehead.

"So you foretold the night of your arrival."

"Yes." Faith sighed, recalling that night, the surprise, the shock. "I wish I could help in some way," she said. "But I own nothing except the clothes I was wearing when I arrived here."

"You help me just by being alive," he murmured, bending to brush his mouth over hers. "I must go."

"I know." Faith felt her throat tighten with the admission. "I know."

"Know also that I love you." He gave her a hard, fast kiss, then before she could respond, he drew away and moved to the window.

"Pres," she called, as he swung one leg over the sill. "I love you too." The first gray streaks of dawn revealed his adored face to her.

Pres smiled. "You honor me with your love. Keep safe, my Faith. I shall return whenever I can." He was outside, his voice wafting to her on the wind. "Pray for me."

Faith had never prayed so often, or so fervently, as she did during the weeks following his plea.

From the talk of the men who frequented the inn, Faith heard that General Washington had marched his ill-equipped, ill-dressed, ill-fed army out of Whitemarsh on about the first of December. With a number of the men shoeless, their feet wrapped in rags for protection, leaving bloody footprints in the early snow, it had taken the ragtag army a full week to march the thirteen miles from Whitemarsh to Valley Forge.

Of course, Faith knew about the terrible situation facing the army, had read in her own time about the deprivations suffered by the men. But knowing about them from a twentieth century perspective did not prepare her for actually living through the events, even from a secure distance.

And so Faith prayed a lot, and worried constantly, for Pres's safety.

Faith could not recall an autumn so unrelentingly harsh as this one was. Snow began falling weeks before the official arrival of winter. And the knowledge that Pres was out there, enduring the cold and wet, playing his dangerous game of aristocratic dandy and shadowy scout, terrified her.

On the few occasions that Pres managed to stop at the inn, attired in his guise of the wealthy man of business, Faith knew he had either been to, or was returning from, the occupied city of Philadelphia. She also knew that, on the nights he silently slipped through the window into her bedroom, he was engaged in scouting the terrain both for supplies and information. She was frighteningly aware that neither endeavor was conducive to his continuing good health. If he were caught, he would be shot.

The realization that each time she saw Pres might well be the last haunted Faith, making her numb to the approach of Thanksgiving. Since the holiday would not begin to be celebrated for over a decade, the special Thursday in November came and went without Faith's giving it much thought.

It wasn't until near the end of the second week of December that Faith remembered Christmas, and then only because Mrs. Shelby broached the subject.

"William and I were just discussing our trip to York, Faith," she said, bustling into the kitchen, where Faith was kneading bread dough.

Faith glanced up from the floured wooden table to frown at the older woman. "York?" she repeated, at a loss to understand what Mrs. Shelby was talking about.

"Surely you must remember, child," Emily chided. "I told you over a month ago that we would be making the journey to York to spend Christmas day with our children."

"Oh, yes, yes, of course," Faith lied, for in truth, she had been so distracted by her concerns for Pres, she had completely forgotten, even with the constant reminder of the woman herself, who'd been busily employed during the previous weeks knitting long scarves and mittens for her sons. "Ah . . ." she continued. "What about your trip to York?"

Mrs. Shelby gave her a strange look, as she often did, but went on to explain. "Because the weather has been so very harsh and unpredictable for this time of year, Mr. Shelby has decided to depart for York a few days earlier than we originally planned. William intends to make an early start on the twenty-first day of December."

"The twenty-first?" Faith repeated, knowing she sounded somewhat dim. In Faith's natural time, the drive from the inn to York could be made in little more than an hour, even with adverse traffic and weather conditions. The idea of Mr. Shelby's allowing himself so much extra time to traverse a distance of some sixty-odd miles was inconceivable to Faith.

"Yes, dear, the twenty-first," Mrs. Shelby said, slowly and distinctly, as if she were speaking to a rather dull-witted child. "And so, I think it would be best if you accompanied us, instead of remaining here at the inn by yourself, as you wished to do."

"I would rather not," Faith demurred, adamant in her determination to be there if and when Pres put in an appearance.

"But, Faith," Mrs. Shelby argued, "we will be gone nigh onto a week. Please reconsider."

"No." Faith shook her head. "I prefer to stay here and . . . er, rest a bit until you return."

Throughout the following week, Faith jumped every time the door opened during the day or her window rattled during the night, praying that when she turned she would see Pres standing there, smiling.

But Pres didn't come, not in either of his two guises. Overcome with mounting fear for his safety, Faith waved the Shelbys on their way on the overcast morning of the twenty-first, then went back inside to pace through the inn, listening to the hollow sound of her own footsteps on the bare floor boards.

The days until Christmas dragged on, one after the other in seemingly endless succession. Faith filled the daylight hours with work, cleaning her bedroom and the rooms on the first floor, in a fruitless effort to hold her increasing concern for Pres at bay.

The nights were the worst, fraught with dreams in which Faith searched in frantic despair for Pres, and always found him lying on his back, his dark eyes staring sightless, his life's blood staining scarlet the pristine snow around him.

On the day before Christmas, Faith was a near basket case, fighting an urgent inner command to ignore the heavy snowfall and make her way to Valley Forge to satisfy herself about his continued existence.

It no longer mattered to her that she and Pres came from different time periods. She loved him with every fiber of her being, and knew she always would. Even if she should suddenly be swept back into her own time, Faith knew she would continue to love Pres, even as she mourned him.

Near midday on Christmas Eve, Faith called a halt to her frenzy of scrubbing and polishing. Exhausted, depressed, yet resisting a need to scream or dissolve into tears, she hung a huge water-filled iron kettle over the fire to heat, then dragged the heavy wooden wash tub onto the kitchen floor. By the time she had heated two kettles of water and poured them into the tub, she was almost too tired to undress and climb in, but the temptation of an allover soak won out over weariness.

It was full dark when the rapidly chilling water drove Faith from the tub, but her body and hair were clean and her spirits somewhat restored. After wrapping her dripping body in a blanket she had placed near the fire to warm, Faith hurried from the kitchen.

A still, tomblike cold permeated her tiny bedroom. Shivering, Faith pulled the scratchy undergarments from the armoire and, with a muttered imprecation, thrust them back and withdrew the filmy lingerie she had been wearing the night of her travel through time.

There was no one there to see her, Faith mused, fastening the front closure on the lacy bra. And even though there were no outward signs of it—like brightly lighted decorations and the spicy scents of holiday foods—it *was* Christmas Eve, she reminded herself as she stepped into the matching panties. Cold or not, she reflected, smoothing the sheer hose up her long legs, she would indulge herself for the occasion.

Faith was so preoccupied with her own thoughts, she didn't hear the window sash glide up. Her first inkling that she was no longer alone came from the low, raspy sound of a sharply indrawn breath and the dull thud of something hitting the floor.

"Pres!" Faith cried, spinning to face him. In one greedy, all-encompassing glance, she noted the snow on his hair and shoulders, the shocked expression on his face, and the bulging leather saddle bags at his booted feet.

Pres stood stock still just inside the window, his eyes raking her nearly nude form. "You are beautiful, Faith," he said in a ragged whisper. "But what in God's name do you call that costume?"

"My underwear," Faith answered, laughing and crying as she ran to him.

"I should have known," he said wryly, clutching her to him with one arm, while closing the window against the wind blown snow with his free hand.

"Where have you been?" she cried, racing her hands over his shoulders, arms, and chest to make sure he was in one piece. "I was so afraid you were lying out there, alone somewhere, wounded or dead."

"My love, my love," Pres murmured, holding her close, stroking her back. "I assure you I am fine. A trifle damp, perhaps, but fine."

"Damp!" Faith struggled free from his tight embrace. "You're wet," she said, shoving his bulky coat off his shoulders. "Get out of those clothes at once."

"Your servant, Mistress Faith," he intoned, bending slightly in a half bow and slanting a roguish grin at her. "Your wish is my command."

"Right," Faith muttered, ignoring the chill on her scantily clad body as she went to work on the laces of his shirt. "If I truly had my wish, I'd command you to stop all this skulking about, especially into Philadelphia."

"Yes, well, as to that, you may have your wish," Pres said absently, reaching with one hand to trail his finger up her thigh, encased in black nylon, "I recollect being intrigued by the peek I had at your hose on the very night you arrived." He gave her an eloquent look. "I never dreamed it went all the way to your waist."

"Hmm umm," Faith murmured, pausing in the process of drawing his shirt from his pants, motionless and breathless from the sharp desire stirring deep in the most feminine part of her. "Ah, what were you saying about your trips to Philadelphia?"

Pres stared at her blankly, then blinked, as if coming out of a trance. "Oh, yes. Yesterday, a friend quietly informed me that my movements are being observed by the British. Thus, it appears your wish that I stop skulking about may be granted within the near future, at least as far as Philadelphia is concerned."

Relief surged through Faith, enhancing the sensations deep inside her. "Thank God," she breathed. "I've been so worried."

"No more so than I, my love," Pres said, drawing his finger up and over her rounded hip to the elastic waistband of her hose. "I live in constant fear of you disappearing as mysteriously as you appeared." A frown knitted his brows as he hooked the finger under the band to test the elastic.

Faith felt a shiver unrelated to the night cold at the flame that leaped in the depths of his dark eyes. She caught her breath and held it when he raised his hand to lightly touch the lacy edge of her bra.

"Exquisite," he murmured, but he wasn't looking at the garment; he was staring into her eyes. "How does one get into it?"

"The same way one gets out of it," Faith said, beginning to tremble from the explosive mixture of relief, excitement, and desire coiling inside her. "I'll show you." Releasing the folds of his shirt clenched in her fingers, she brought her hands to the bra's clasp and flicked it open, freeing her breasts for the intent perusal of his lowered gaze.

"You are cold." His voice was hoarse, his stare riveted to the hard tips of her trembling breasts.

"And hot," Faith confessed, shrugging out of the bra. "I need you, Pres," she whispered on a sob. "I need to feel you, vibrant, alive, and safe inside me."

"And I need you, my Faith," Pres groaned, gathering her into his arms as he lowered his head to hers. "I have been driven nearly mad these past weeks with needing you."

His mouth took hers in a kiss of tender savagery. She returned his kiss with gentle ferocity. Within fevered minutes, his clothing and her panties and hose lay strewn on the bare floor. Then, mindless with passion, they fell onto the bed, lost to the world in their mutual need to be one.

Faith reveled in the force of his hungry mouth, his hard, demanding body. Pres was there, a part of her, as she was a part of him. For the moment, it was enough.

Faith was awakened by a shuffling noise. Smothering a yawn, she turned her head in the direction of the sound. Fully dressed, but in different, clean clothing, Pres was kneeling on the floor beneath the window, folding his discarded clothes and stuffing them into one of the pouches of the saddlebags he'd brought with him.

"Merry Christmas," she greeted him, sitting up and reaching for the lingerie he had thoughtfully placed at the foot of the bed.

Pres smiled. "Good morning, and merry Christmas to you, my love." He withdrew a large leather sack from the other pouch before rising to come to her. "I have something I would ask you to hold in safekeeping for me."

"Okay, but let me clean up and get dressed first," she said, tossing the covers back. "It's freezing in here."

"Of course . . ." Pres began, but broke off to grin

at her before echoing, "Okay." Then he turned away to give her a modicum of privacy.

Shivering, Faith washed, brushed her chattering teeth, and dressed in her own lingerie and the period costume she had been wearing the night she had run crying from the inn. A smile curved her lips as she patted her watch and cigarette case and lighter in the pockets of her apron.

"All done," she announced, drawing the shawl around her shoulders for added warmth. "What is it you'd like me to keep for you?"

"These." Pres undid the drawstring on the leather bag and dumped the contents on the bed.

"Good Lord!" Faith exclaimed, going to the bed for a closer look at the glittering array of jewelry heaped on the covers. There were necklaces, earrings, bracelets, brooches, and rings, all worked in heavy gold and all set with precious stones. Faith knew little about jewelry, but even she recognized the enormous value of the creamy pearls, the sparkling diamonds, the emeralds, rubies, and sapphires. Some of the stones were larger than robin's eggs. "Are they real?" she asked in an awed whisper, reaching out with trembling fingers to lightly touch the gleaming gems.

"Certainly," he retorted.

"Where did you get them?"

"An inheritance from my grandmother," Pres explained. "In light of what my friend told me, I thought it wise to remove them from my home in Philadelphia." He grimaced. "I doubt I will have the opportunity to do so on my next visit to the city."

"Your next visit!" Faith cried. "Pres, you can't go back there. It's too dangerous."

"I must." His tone was adamant. "I have work to do there for my commander."

Fear returned to clutch at Faith's heart. "Isn't it enough that you're scouring the countryside for food and supplies?" she cried. "Must you continue to play the spy as well?"

"I assure you that I have not been playing, Faith." Pres drew himself up, his back ramrod straight. "The cause looks bleak, and my commander needs reliable intelligence almost as much as he needs supplies."

"But if the British already suspect you, there's no question but that you'll be caught!" she cried, growing desperate.

"It is a chance I must take."

"But . . . but, dammit, Pres, what use will you be to your commander if you're dead!" Faith shouted, distraught and ready to use any argument to dissuade him. "I know the outcome, remember? General Washington will win this war, with or without your assistance . . . or your death!"

"Nevertheless," Pres said, calmly picking up the jewelry and sliding it back into the bag, "I cannot neglect my duty."

Faith stared at him in anguish for long moments, and suddenly the accumulation of three months of confusion, tension, and unendurable fear, for herself as well as for him, was more than she could bear.

"All right!" she cried, tears of defeat and despair running down her face. "Go, I don't care! Get yourself captured or wounded or killed." She was sobbing, talking wildly, unable to stop the words pouring out of her. "Go now and don't come back. But I don't want to hear of your death. I don't want to know . . . I can't bear to know."

Wheeling around, Faith ran from the room and down the stairway. She paused on the last step, sobbing and frantic. Then, without conscious thought or direction, she rushed to the side door, fumbled with the lock, and pulling the door open, ran outside.

She ran only as far as the stand of trees, for though the snow had stopped falling, over a foot of it covered the yard, impeding her progress. Feeling an eerie and fatalistic sense of *déjà vu*, Faith raised her hands, buried her face in the ends of the shawl, and cried aloud for help.

"Oh, God, help me, please help me. I love Pres so much, and I can't bear this uncertainty any . . ."

Faith's voice trailed away. What was she saying? She *did* love him, and she had told him to go and not come back.

"No," Faith whispered, lifting her head to look at the back corner of the building. Her bedroom window was located around that corner. Had Pres already left through that window, never to return?

"Pres, no!" The broken sound of Faith's voice shimmered on the still, cold air. "Pres, wait, don't go!" she screamed, plowing through the snow. "I love you!"

Faith stumbled into the inn and came to a dead stop. Warmth enfolded her, warmth put out from central heating. In that instant she knew.

She was back in the twentieth century.

Where was she? Pres stood by the bed, staring at the empty doorway, no longer aware of his fingers gripping the bulging leather bag.

How long had he been standing there, unable to believe Faith had meant what she had said? Ten minutes? Twenty? After the night they had shared, the love they had sworn for each other, Pres had felt certain she would return within moments of her emotional outburst. He could not believe she meant for him to go and never come back to her.

But where was she? And why was the house so quiet?

Unease stirred inside Pres, and he took a step toward the doorway. Even as he moved, a strong sense that something was wrong invaded his being, filling him with cold dread.

"Faith!" Pres called. Silence drowned out the sound of his heart beating in his ears. "Faith, answer me!"

Pres was across the room and through the doorway in a few long strides. Panic clawed at his gut. She must be here somewhere; she could not have gone back. The fearful thought lent speed to his steps.

He descended the stairs three at a time. At the bottom, the first thing he saw was the side door, standing ajar. Barely breathing, Pres ran outside. A line of footprints in the snow marked Faith's passage into the stand of trees opposite the inn.

"No. No!" Pres shouted, plunging into the snow. Apprehension constricted his chest and tore a cry of agony from his tight throat.

"Dear God, I cannot lose her now. I love her more than my own life. I beg of You, do not take her from me!"

Epilogue

"FAITH, WHERE IN GOD'S NAME ARE YOU?"

Standing in the shadows of the enclosed stairway, Faith froze in the act of hanging the shawl over the last peg on the wall.

Was she losing her grip on sanity? Hearing voices? *His* voice?

Her heart racing, needing to look yet almost afraid to do so, Faith slowly turned around.

Pres stood in the doorway, the bulging leather bag clutched in one hand, an expression of baffled wonderment on his handsome face.

Breathless, unable to move, certain he was an illusion created by her bereaved, deranged mind, Faith watched him as he glanced around, examining the room in exactly the same manner she herself had a short time ago.

She saw his sharp-eyed gaze take in the electric candles flickering in the windows, the smooth plaster concealing the chinked log walls. She saw his gaze drop to the creche on the garland draped mantelpiece, and a faint smile touched his lips when he shifted his attention to the tall Christmas tree standing majestically next to the fireplace, decorated with electric lights and glass balls.

"It is just as she described it to me."

His whisper broke the spell holding Faith immobile. Joy burst like a glorious sunrise inside her.

"Pres!" Launching herself from the shadows, Faith flew across the room and into his arms. "Oh, Pres, oh, darling, I can't believe it!" she cried, skimming her fingers over his face, his lips. "You're here. You're really here!"

Pres kissed her fingertips, then lowered his head to crush her mouth with his. "We are in your time period," he said, as he raised his head and glanced around. "This is your Laughing Fox Inn, the one you told me about?"

"Yes," she answered, laughing and crying at the same time. "This is incredible! I thought I had lost you, and now here you are."

"Yes." A shadow flashed over his face.

"Are you sorry?"

Pres frowned at her. "Sorry . . . for what?"

"That you're here." Dreading his reply, she rushed on. "I know how dedicated you are . . . were, to the cause and to Washington. Are you sorry you won't be there?"

"No." The shadows in his eyes were banished by a teasing gleam. "As you pointed out, General Washington won the war without me." He arched his dark brows. "Did he not?"

Faith smiled with tender understanding. "Yes, darling, I promise you he did. But something is bothering you. I saw it in your expression a moment ago. What was it?"

His frown was back. "You told me you were

going to lose this beautiful inn." Pres raised the hand gripping the bag. "I was wondering if, perhaps, these might help you in any way."

"Your grandmother's jewels!" Faith exclaimed. "Pres, they're worth a fortune."

"They are yours."

Faith shook her head. "I can't accept . . ."

"I insist."

"Thank you." Faith gave in gracefully. "They will save the inn for *us*."

"If I am still here," he said, cautioning her.

The joy dimmed inside Faith. "What do you mean, if you're still here?"

"My love, you were whisked back to your time," he reminded her. "How can we be sure that I will not be whisked back to mine?"

Faith bit her lip, and then an idea struck her, an odd but wonderful idea. "Pres, I can't be certain, of course, but I think—I truly *believe*—that we were meant to be together."

The light of hope flared in his dark eyes. "I pray you are right," he murmured fervently. "But . . . why would you believe that to be so?"

Faith was quiet for a moment, collecting her thoughts. "If you recall," she said, "I told you that on the night I was . . . er, transferred, I pleaded with God to guide me. Pres, I . . . I now believe He sent me to get you."

"Yes!" Pres said in a tone of awed belief. "Faith, when you did not return to the bedroom, I also called out to the Lord, begging Him not to take you from me!"

Faith was crying again, in thankfulness for the miracle. "Oh, Pres, I'm certain He sent you here because we belong together." Faith paused, beginning to frown. "But, darling, how did you get here?"

"Oh, my sweet Faith, cut me some slack," Pres said, grinning at her.

"But how did you?" she persisted, laughing.

"I simply followed your footsteps in the snow."

JOYEUX NOËL
from . . .
JOAN HOHL

I am a romance writer—and proud of it. I am also a wife—to Marv, my mate of thirty-nine years; a mother—to Lori and Amy, my beautiful daughters; and a grandmother—to Erica and Cammeron, my adorable and adored grandchildren. I also hold the titles of: housekeeper, laundress, cook, and chief-bottle-washer. I do not do windows . . . well, at least, not often.

I live in Reading, Pennsylvania, a section of the country rich in the history of the American Revolution. Since childhood, I have been steeped in, and fascinated by, the historical events which led to the forming of this great country—The United States of America.

One of my favorite stories is of the harsh winter General George Washington encamped his troops at Valley Forge. I hope I have conveyed the flavor of that winter in my story—"Footsteps In The Snow." Merry Christmas and happy reading.